Praise for the No[...] of Lauren Will[...]

The G[...]

"Willig delights time and again with her [...] thoughtful Pink Carnation series."

"Eloise, of course, is amazing, but it's truly the plot of *The Garden Intrigue* that shines . . . wonderful!" —Romance Junkies

"[An] enchanting, exciting, and clever story." —Romance Reviews Today

"Enlightening and entertaining as always, and full of plenty of romance and intrigue, this is a strong choice for historical fiction readers."
—*Library Journal*

"As fresh and charming as its floral theme . . . a reliable romp through Napoleon's court, filled with romance and yet another adorable and very active heroine." —*Kirkus Reviews*

"Humor, love, espionage—yet again there is absolutely *nothing* that this incredible author leaves out. . . . [These stories] just keep getting better and better every time!" —Once Upon a Romance

The Orchid Affair

"[A] supremely nerve-racking, sit-on-the-edge-of-your-seat, can't-sleep-until-everyone-is-safe read . . . successfully upholds the author's tradition of providing charming three-dimensional characters, lively action, [and] witty dialogue." —*Library Journal*

"Willig's sparkling series continues to elevate the Regency romance genre." —*Kirkus Reviews*

"Willig combines the atmosphere of the tempestuous era with the perfect touches of historical detail to round out the love story." —*Romantic Times*

The Betrayal of the Blood Lily

"Newcomers and loyal fans alike will love brash, flirtatious Penelope's exotic adventure in Hyderabad, India, told [with] Lauren Willig's signature mix of historical richness and whimsical humor."
—*The Newark Star-Ledger*

continued . . .

"Willig hasn't lost her touch; this outing has all the charm of the previous books in the series." —*Publishers Weekly*

"Willig injects a new energy in her already thriving, thrilling series, and presents the best entry to date." —*Booklist*

The Temptation of the Night Jasmine

"Jane Austen for the modern girl . . . sheer fun!"
—*New York Times* bestselling author Christina Dodd

"An engaging historical romance, delightfully funny and sweet . . . a thoroughly charming costume drama. . . . Romance's rosy glow tints even the spy adventure that unfolds . . . fine historical fiction . . . thrilling."
—*The Newark Star-Ledger*

"Another sultry spy tale. . . . The author's conflation of historical fact, quirky observations, and nicely rendered romances results in an elegant and grandly entertaining book." —*Publishers Weekly*

"Honor and romance again take the lead in nineteenth-century England, as yet another flower-named spy continues this high-spirited and thoroughly enjoyable series." —*Kirkus Reviews*

The Seduction of the Crimson Rose

"Willig's series gets better with each addition, and her latest is filled with swashbuckling fun, romance, and intrigue." —*Booklist*

"Handily fulfills its promise of intrigue and romance."—*Publishers Weekly*

"There are few authors capable of matching Lauren Willig's ability to merge historical accuracy, heart-pounding romance, and biting wit."
—*BookPage*

The Deception of the Emerald Ring

"History textbook meets Bridget Jones." —*Marie Claire*

"A fun and zany time warp full of history, digestible violence, and plenty of romance." —*New York Daily News*

"Heaving bodices, embellished history, and witty dialogue: What more could you ask for?" —*Kirkus Reviews*

"Willig's latest is riveting, providing a great diversion and lots of fun."
—*Booklist*

"Smart . . . [a] fast-paced narrative with mistaken identities, double agents, and high-stakes espionage. . . . The historic action is taut and twisting."
—*Publishers Weekly*

The Masque of the Black Tulip

"Clever [and] playful. . . . What's most delicious about Willig's novels is that the damsels of 1803 bravely put it all on the line for love and country."
—*Detroit Free Press*

"Studded with clever literary and historical nuggets, this charming historical/contemporary romance moves back and forth in time." —*USA Today*

"Willig has great fun with the conventions of the genre, throwing obstacles between her lovers at every opportunity . . . a great escape."
—*The Boston Globe*

"Willig picks up where she left readers breathlessly hanging. . . . Many more will delight in this easy-to-read romp and line up for the next installment." —*Publishers Weekly*

The Secret History of the Pink Carnation

"A deftly hilarious, sexy novel."
—Eloisa James, *New York Times* bestselling author of
A Kiss at Midnight

"A merry romp with never a dull moment! A fun read."
—Mary Balogh, *New York Times* bestselling author of
A Secret Affair

"This genre-bending read—a dash of chick lit with a historical twist—has it all: romance, mystery, and adventure. Pure fun!"
—Meg Cabot, *New York Times* bestselling author of *Insatiable*

"A historical novel with a modern twist. I loved the way Willig dips back and forth from Eloise's love affair and her swish parties to the Purple Gentian and of course the lovely, feisty Amy. The unmasking of the Pink Carnation is a real surprise." —Mina Ford, author of *My Fake Wedding*

"Swashbuckling. . . . Willig has an ear for quick wit and an eye for detail. Her fiction debut is chock-full of romance, sexual tension, espionage, adventure, and humor." —*Library Journal*

"Willig's imaginative debut . . . is a decidedly delightful romp." —*Booklist*

"Relentlessly effervescent prose . . . a sexy, smirking, determined-to-charm historical romance debut." —*Kirkus Reviews*

"A delightful debut." —Roundtable Reviews

ALSO BY LAUREN WILLIG

The Garden Intrigue

A PINK CARNATION NOVEL

Lauren Willig

NEW AMERICAN LIBRARY

Published by New American Library, a division of
Penguin Group (USA) Inc., 375 Hudson Street, New York, New York 10014, USA
Penguin Group (Canada), 90 Eglinton Avenue East, Suite 700, Toronto, Ontario M4P 2Y3, Canada (a
division of Pearson Penguin Canada Inc.); Penguin Books Ltd., 80 Strand, London WC2R 0RL, En-
gland; Penguin Ireland, 25 St. Stephen's Green, Dublin 2, Ireland (a division of Penguin Books Ltd.)
Penguin Group (Australia), 250 Camberwell Road, Camberwell, Victoria 3124, Australia (a division of
Pearson Australia Group Pty. Ltd.); Penguin Books India Pvt. Ltd., 11 Community Centre, Panchsheel
Park, New Delhi - 110 017, India; Penguin Group (NZ), 67 Apollo Drive, Rosedale, Auckland 0632,
New Zealand (a division of Pearson New Zealand Ltd.); Penguin Books (South Africa) (Pty.) Ltd., 24
Sturdee Avenue, Rosebank, Johannesburg 2196, South Africa

Penguin Books Ltd., Registered Offices:
80 Strand, London WC2R 0RL, England

Published by New American Library, a division of Penguin Group (USA) Inc.
Previously published in a Dutton edition.

First New American Library Printing, January 2013
3 5 7 9 10 8 6 4 2

Copyright © Lauren Willig, 2011
Readers Guide copyright © Penguin Group (USA) Inc., 2012
All rights reserved. No part of this book may be reproduced, scanned, or distributed in any printed or
electronic form without permission. Please do not participate in or encourage piracy of copyrighted
materials in violation of the author's rights. Purchase only authorized editions.

 REGISTERED TRADEMARK—MARCA REGISTRADA

New American Library Trade Paperback ISBN: 978-0-451-41560-8

THE LIBRARY OF CONGRESS HAS CATALOGED THE HARDCOVER EDITION OF THIS TITLE AS FOLLOWS:

Willig, Lauren.
The garden intrigue/Lauren Willig
p. cm—(Pink carnation series 9)
ISBN: 978-0-525-95254-1
1. Poets, English—Fiction. 2. Widows—Fiction. 3. Americans—France—Paris—Fiction. 4. Paris
(France)—Social life and customs—19th century—Fiction. 5. Undercover operations—Fiction. 6.
Napoleon I, Emperor of the French, 1769–1821—Fiction. I. Title.
PS3623.I575 G37 2012
813'.6—dc22
768777231

Set in Granjon
Designed by Leonard Telesca

Printed in the United States of America

PUBLISHER'S NOTE
This is a work of fiction. Names, characters, places, and incidents either are the product of the author's
imagination or are used fictitiously, and any resemblance to actual persons, living or dead, business
establishments, events, or locales is entirely coincidental.
The publisher does not have any control over and does not assume any responsibility for author or
third-party Web sites or their content.

ALWAYS LEARNING   PEARSON

To Jenny Davis and Liz Mellyn,
for coffee, Cosmos, and Cayman.
We'll always have Charlemagne.

The
Garden Intrigue

Prologue

A little to the left. . . . A little to the . . . No!"
Crash.

Below me, in the gardens of Selwick Hall, someone was trying to maneuver a large black metal contraption down an alleyway of elderly shrubs. From the sound of it, the score was shrubs: 1, cameramen: 0. Like its owner, the grounds of Selwick Hall were putting up a fight against the invasion of an American film crew.

I was one of those barbarian Americans, too, but I fell into a protected category: I was the owner's girlfriend.

It hadn't always been that way. There had been a time when Colin regarded me with nearly as much mistrust as he did the members of the DreamStone film team. As I kicked back in Colin's desk chair, watching the dust motes dance in the May sunshine filtering through the sash window, those grim days of October felt like an entire universe ago, in a galaxy far, far away.

In October, I had been just another bedraggled American grad student in London, desperately combing the archives for the materials I needed to turn my dissertation from a vague outline into a heart-breaking work of staggering scholarship.

We had been told to go forth and find a gap in the historiography, and that's just what I had done, smugly certain that I would put together pieces no one else had been able to connect, patting myself on the back for my cleverness in picking as my field of study a country in which the language was my own. One of my best friends was immured in the basement of an Austrian monastery, puzzling out Carolingian charters in a version of Latin that would make a classics professor cry; another was in Brazil, in an archive where the air-conditioning regularly broke down and all the women on the beach were waxed in improbable ways.

But me? I was going to England. The mother country. Home of scones, clotted cream, and BBC costume dramas. England, where they speak English better than we do. England, where no one waxes anything because everyone is draped in tweed. It would be just like being home in New York, only with cuter accents. I was going to the land of Mr. Darcy (and Mr. Bean, but, hey, every ointment comes with its flies) to research a dissertation topic that thrilled me down to the polish on my toenails.

Aristocratic espionage during the wars with France: 1789–1815.

Does it get any better than that? There could be little more thrilling than men in knee breeches meeting for huddled conferences in the back rooms of inns from Paris to Calais, smuggling aristocrats out of the clutches of the guillotine, while exchanging terse notes ending with the directive "Burn this letter."

It didn't occur to me until later that there might be a slight problem. Historians are dependent on documentary evidence for the reconstruction of the past. When the people involved routinely burn the documents in question, there isn't a lot left to go on. In fact, there was nothing left to go on. I combed through the collections of the British Library, nagged the archivists at the Public Record Office, and tramped through an infinite number of country records offices, all with the same dispiriting result.

All I had were rumors and legend, garbled and inconsistent stories about the exploits of a spy called the Pink Carnation, who, if the London papers and the records of the French Ministry of Police were to be believed, had been a greater thorn in the flesh of the French than anyone with the possible exception of Wellington. And, of the two, the Pink Carnation had been in operation longer. Or so the stories claimed. On the theory that there ain't no smoke without fire, I had confidently set out for material to verify that. And found nothing.

Until I met Colin. His family archives were the academic equivalent of the Holy Grail.

He wasn't so bad himself.

Right now, he wasn't exactly a happy camper. I could hear the snick of rubber-soled shoes on flagstones, and Colin's voice below, raised over the sound of smashing shrubbery. The word "damage" seemed to figure prominently. The scents of spring wafted through the open window, fresh-cut grass and wildflowers and stale tobacco.

Perched safely above the fray, two stories up, I leaned sideways in Colin's desk chair, craning my neck to try to see out the window. From my current vantage point, all I could see was a confusion of tree branches, exuberant in their spring foliage, and, if I tried really hard, something long, black, and metallic that I assumed was part of the scaffolding for lighting. Either that or a missing piece of the Death Star.

I hadn't been in the gardens since the crew had arrived, but with the noises coming from that direction with earsplitting regularity, I feared the worst. The crew had been on location for two days now, setting up equipment and running light tests and doing whatever else it was that film people do. I had resisted the urge to hover and gawk. After all, I was a mature and responsible academic; we weren't supposed to go all wide-eyed at the sight of things like movie cameras, nor wonder whether anyone would notice if we waved at the camera and mouthed "Hi, Mom!"

Besides, given Colin's feelings about the proceedings, showing too much interest smacked of disloyalty. To say Colin hadn't been thrilled about renting out Selwick Hall to American film star Micah Stone for his latest blockbuster would be like saying that Cookie Monster had a slight thing for baked goods. Colin had been presented with the situation as a fait accompli at his mother's birthday party in Paris two months before, in public, with the cameras flashing. It had not been a good time.

Colin had only just started speaking to his mother again. He still wasn't speaking to his sister, Serena, the weak link, the deciding one-third vote that had enabled his stepfather, Jeremy, to get away with inviting DreamStone to film at Selwick Hall. It was Serena's defection that hurt Colin the most, even more than seeing his beloved home, the one he had gone to such trouble to restore and maintain, trampled under the feet of Micah Stone and his merry men.

Both Colin's great-aunt Arabella and I had made tentative gestures towards a reconciliation with Serena, but Colin had shot down all of our attempts. I wasn't pushing it. My own position in his life was too new and too tenuous to risk.

Tenuous and possibly about to end.

Abandoning the window, I turned back reluctantly to the computer screen. The e-mail was still there. It hadn't obligingly zapped itself back into cyberspace in the past five minutes.

Damn.

On the face of it, there was nothing about the e-mail to occasion forebodings of dread and gloom. No threats, no dire warnings, no offers to make my manhood throb more manfully or share a bank account in Rwanda. It was a perfectly pleasant e-mail from the Modern Germany professor offering me two sections and the position of head teaching fellow for his Modern Europe course.

Not entirely my area of expertise, but still better than that semes-

ter I had wound up teaching Charlemagne, unable to tell my Caro-
lingians from my Carolinas. I wasn't exactly thrilled with the twentieth
century, but I had done a field in it, so I could teach it, and the head
TF position came with an extra financial incentive, payback for being the one in the unenviable position of playing middleman between
a busy professor, demanding students, angsty teaching staff, and
the entire administrative panoply involved in booking rooms, sched-
uling sections, printing course packets, and making nice to the A/V
people.

My fellowship, the one that had sent me to England, would run
out in June. Two sections and the head TF post meant my rent would
be paid. It also meant I wouldn't be piecing together teaching jobs in
different courses, a section here, a section there, which meant triple
the effort learning the material and keeping up with the coursework.
All in all, it was an exceedingly handsome offer.

So why did it make me feel like I'd swallowed a bucket of lead?

I rested my head on my balled-up hands, letting my hair swing
around my face. It was growing out, I thought inconsequentially. Yet
another sign of just how long I had been in England. It had been
more than eight months now, September to May. It had seemed like
plenty of time, back in Cambridge. The other Cambridge. Ten months
in England. I would get my material and go back to America to write
it up, proceeding smoothly through the paces like a good little academic in training.

I hadn't factored in the addition of another person. I hadn't
counted on Colin.

Ten months. What was that? Nothing but a whisper in time, over
before it had begun. I hadn't met Colin until I was two months in.
Then there had been this and that and suddenly we were down to a
month and a half and it just wasn't enough. I didn't want to go back.
I didn't want to go back to my studio apartment in Cambridge, with
all its accoutrements for one: one twin bed, one dresser, one desk. It
didn't matter that I liked my apartment, that it had my books, my

pictures, my coffeemaker. It didn't matter that just five months ago I had been yearning for Cambridge with homesick fervor, for the smell of Peet's Coffee and the peculiar slant of late afternoon light across the floor of the history department library, for the cranberry muffins at Broadway Market and the smell of sweat and suntan lotion on the banks of the Charles on a sunny day.

It wasn't that I didn't want to go back ever. My life was there, I knew that. I just wasn't ready yet.

I'd successfully avoided thinking about it or talking about it. I had dodged questions from my parents about summer plans and from my colleagues about finishing fellowships and fall teaching. Colin and I had never discussed the fact that my fellowship was finite. We had never talked about the future at all. Most of the time I was too busy living in the past—his past.

If I didn't want the head TF job, it was only fair to give Blackburn time to offer it to someone else.

What was I thinking? If I told my friends or my parents that I was planning to stay in England and that I was planning to stay not for professional reasons but because of a guy . . .

I could already hear the howls of outrage coming down the transatlantic pipeline. Changing my plans for a man went against everything I had been raised to believe. Professional women weren't supposed to do that sort of thing. We were supposed to be strong and independent and make our own decisions without reference to the opposite sex. I could come up with a plausible excuse to stay in England through August, especially if I were able to give up my flat and live rent-free with Colin. I could make noises about needing the extra time to tie up loose ends and follow up on crucial research. But August was as far as I could push it.

Besides, Colin hadn't invited me to stay.

There was a squeak of old hinges and the brush of swollen wood against wool as the door pushed against the stained carpet.

I looked up to see the man in question standing in the doorframe.

It was warm outside, so he had rolled up the sleeves of his shirt, revealing a pair of arms already sun-browned from outdoor activity. His dark blond hair was wind tousled, and he brought with him the scent of the outdoors, garden loam and fresh-cut grass and rich new soil. It was his study, but he paused in the doorway as though waiting for me to give the okay for him to come in.

"Hey," he said, that universal male greeting that can mean anything from "hi" to "didn't see you there" to "thank you for last night." This was a decidedly dispirited "hey."

Which was a shame, because last night really had been pretty good.

"Hey," I responded in kind, trying to infuse as much sympathy as possible into the one syllable. I pushed aside my own worries about next year. We could deal with that later. Colin had enough on his plate right now. "So, um, how are things going down there?"

Colin pulled a face and jerked two thumbs downward.

"That good, huh?" Let's pretend I hadn't been listening at the window.

"The idiots wanted to cut down a three-hundred-year-old oak because it was in the way of their shot." His voice dripped with disgust. "Then they wanted to know if we could move the folly. It's only been there since 1732."

"Two days down!" I said with forced cheerfulness. If I smiled any wider, my face would probably crack in two.

Colin grimaced. "How many more does that leave?"

I tucked my legs up under me in the chair, making the ancient springs creak. "Don't make me do math."

"That's because you know I won't like the number."

Too true. The director—via Jeremy—had estimated two weeks on location. I wouldn't have put money on Colin making it through one. It was a good thing he lived a healthy, outdoor life, because his arteries were doing overtime.

I peered at him over the computer screen. "Would you—I don't know—like to go somewhere? Away? We could stay at my flat for a couple of days."

True, my basement flat was small even by London standards and Colin banged his head on the sloping bathroom ceiling every time he washed his hands, but even a week's worth of lumps on the noggin was preferable to his going into cardiac arrest every time one of the film crew wandered through the wrong door. Forget *his* nerves; I wasn't sure mine could stand another week of this.

Colin's hand rose reflexively to the back of his head. "Not your flat."

"Your aunt Arabella's, then. Or we could take a mini-break somewhere." It would have to be somewhere cheap, since neither of us was exactly flush with funds, but there had to be some moldering seaside resort that had seen better days and would be willing to take us in for the price of a large London dinner. Or we could go to one of the old Regency watering holes and I could drag Colin to Jane Austen reenactments. "It could be fun."

A loud crash and a curse resonated from the flagstone path below. At least, I was assuming there was still a flagstone path below.

Our eyes met over the computer monitor.

I sighed. "Or we could stay here and keep an eye on the film crew."

One side of Colin's mouth pulled up in something that wanted to be a smile but didn't quite make it. "Thanks. You're a brick."

I would have preferred to be something more decorative, but I appreciated the sentiment. "Look, it will all be fine. It's only two weeks and you can charge them double for every shrub they squish."

Colin didn't look convinced. He nodded towards the computer. "Anything interesting?" he asked, with forced heartiness.

I hastily moved the monitor. "Oh, just this and that."

"What is it?" Colin was way too sharp sometimes.

"Nothing!" I staggered clumsily to my feet. My legs had gone numb from sitting on them. "But I probably should get back to work if I don't want to be one of those five-thousand-year-old grad students."

Colin smoothed my hair back, turning my face this way and that as he examined it for lines and wrinkles. "You still have a ways to go yet."

Another crash. I could feel the muscles in Colin's arm stiffen under my hand. "I'm aging rapidly," I said.

Colin raised an eyebrow. "Best gather your rosebuds while you may, then."

"Smooth," I managed to say, and then his lips touched mine, and speech became a decidedly uninteresting commodity. Rosebuds, on the other hand . . . They weren't in bloom yet, and yet I could have sworn I smelled their heady scent wafting up from the garden, as much of a cliché as the stereotypical violins.

"Oh, sorry," someone said, and I realized that I did smell rosebuds, preserved in alcohol and condensed into perfume. One of the film crew was standing in the doorway, younger than me at a guess and inappropriately attired for an English spring, in tight jeans and tighter shirt. "I was just looking for the computer. It's in here, right?"

I came down to earth with a crash. Literally. Colin is a fair bit taller than I am. My heels hit carpet with a jarring thump.

"This computer is off-limits," I said, since Colin seemed incapable of saying anything at all. "This whole wing is off-limits."

"But the computer . . ."

Why does whining sound worse in an American accent?

"Is not available," I said. "Please close the door on your way out."

I'll say this for her, she did take direction. She pulled the door smartly shut behind her.

I leaned back against Colin. "We're going to hear about this from Jeremy, aren't we?"

"Bugger that," said Colin elegantly. "They're supposed to have their own Internet connection set up. Since when does 'Private' mean 'Hey! Come on in!'?" Colin's voice shifted on the last words into a parody of the film people.

His fake American accent was truly atrocious. I wondered if my fake English accent sounded as awful to him. Probably. Huh.

Colin glowered at the door, as if it had personally offended him by allowing itself to be opened. "What do we have to do, put up an electric fence?"

I decided that this was not a good time to tell Colin that amusing story about the guy who had blundered into our bathroom while I was showering. Picture *Psycho*, only without the knife and with more Herbal Essences.

"I was thinking buckets of water on the doorjamb," I said. "If I could figure out how to rig it without getting soaked."

"Pots and pans," contributed Colin. "For them to trip over."

We exchanged rueful smiles.

I stood on my tiptoes to press a quick kiss to his cheek. "Are you going to be okay in here?"

Colin's eyes drifted to the window. "I'll put my headphones on," he promised. "If I can't hear it, it's not happening."

"That's the spirit!" I cheered. I paused with one hand on the doorknob. "If you get to the point where you can't take it anymore, you know where to find me. We can drop water balloons on the film crew from the library windows. Or not."

"Hmph," said Colin, and pulled his headphones firmly down over his ears. They made him look a bit like Princess Leia.

I decided not to share that observation.

I grinned and waved and drew the door shut behind me, making my way back down the corridor, past the door to the master bedroom, over to the center of the house and the wing that housed the library. We'd taped signs that said "Private" on the door of the master bedroom, the bathroom, Colin's study, and the library, but, so far, those signs had been just about as effective as the paper they were printed on, when it came to keeping people out.

It was going to be even worse starting this evening.

The high muckety-mucks were first showing up tonight and we were all going to have a great big get-to-know-one-another shindig in the dining room, catered courtesy of DreamStone. With big names to be found, Jeremy had condescended to come out to the wilds of Sussex for it.

Lucky us.

I only hoped that whoever did the seating chart had the sense to place Jeremy and Colin at opposite ends of the table. Not that I really thought Colin was going to go after Jeremy with his fish knife . . . but, hey, why take unnecessary risks? I'd been tempted to go after Jeremy with something sharp a time or two myself.

In the meantime, we were both trying to go on pretty much as usual, Colin working on the spy novel he claimed he was writing, me making my way through his collection of family papers, taking notes for a dissertation that was turning out to be much more detailed than I could ever have dreamed.

With the threat of imminent return to America hanging over me, though, I had to force myself to focus. With all the rich resources available via Colin, I had let myself meander down some pretty random byways, researching rogue French spies, plots and schemes in India, and even an attempt to kidnap George III. It was time to get back to basics, i.e., the Pink Carnation. I knew she had been in operation in Paris in 1804. There was evidence that she had been involved—albeit peripherally—in the famous plot to assassinate Napoleon that had resulted in the execution of the duc d'Enghien in the spring of 1804.

But what had happened after?

The hallway was mercifully empty, all the crew members outside, making mincemeat of Colin's ancestral shrubbery. Someone, however, had been inside. The door to the library, with its hand-lettered sign reading "Private," was ajar.

I had closed it when I left. I knew I had.

My notebook wasn't on my favorite desk anymore. Instead, it was on the chair, and the folio I had taken out to look at before taking my e-mail break was open, when I was pretty sure I had left it closed.

Weird.

One of the film guys must have been looking for a spare sheet of paper, I decided, rearranging my materials the way I liked them. If any of them had torn out one of the precious documents in the folio and used it for scrap, I would personally tear out his masculine bits and feed them to the dogs.

Colin didn't have any dogs, but I was sure we could find some in the neighborhood.

Nope. I flipped quickly through. No sign of tearing. The neighborhood dogs were safe. And so, thank goodness, was the correspondence of Lady Henrietta Dorrington with her cousin by marriage, Miss Jane Wooliston, aka the Pink Carnation. The two ladies had constructed an ingenious code, devised around just the sort of frivolous goings-on designed to make the eyes of your average Ministry of Police employee— aka your average male—glaze over, ranging from the new cut of bonnets to the refreshments at the Venetian breakfast. Each of these terms was carefully calibrated to a double meaning designed to convey information back to the authorities in England.

Jane, the mastermind of the piece, collected her information in Paris and sent it back to Henrietta under the guise of frivolity. Henrietta passed it on to her husband, Miles, who in turn saw that it made it to the authorities at the War Office.

I had an advantage the French Ministry of Police lacked. No, not just a reliable coffeemaker. I had Henrietta's code book. I had been steadily working my way through Jane's reports through the spring of 1804, the spring of the duc d'Enghien's execution, the spring Napoleon declared himself Emperor, and the spring when invasion of England seemed imminent.

Stuck among the papers was a fragment of poetry in a surprisingly tidy hand, addressed to Jane but forwarded to Henrietta. I shook out the page and read.

> For, lo, in Cytherea's perfumed sleep
> Did she dream of the denizens of the dithery deep. . . .

Chapter 1

"Alas!" she cried, "I spy a sail
Hard-by on the wine dark sea.
I know not what it is or bides,
But I fear it comes for me!"

—Augustus Whittlesby, *The Perils of the*
Pulchritudinous Princess of the Azure Toes,
Canto XII, 14–17

For, lo!" proclaimed Augustus Whittlesby from his perch on top of a bench supported by two scowling sphinxes. "In Cytherea's perfumed sleep / Did she dream of the denizens of the dithery deep. . . ."

"Dithery? How can the deep be dithery?" A female voice, lightly accented, cut into Augustus's stirring rendition of Canto XII of *The Perils of the Pulchritudinous Princess of the Azure Toes.*

Among the smattering of people who had left the dancing in the ballroom to admire, mock, gossip, or, in the case of an elderly dowager snoring in a chair by the far wall, nap, stood two young women.

One was tall and graceful, garbed simply but elegantly in a white dress that fell in the required classical lines from a pair of admirably shaped shoulders. Her pale brown hair was gathered in a simple twist, her only jewelry a golden locket strung on a ribbon of sky-blue silk.

Jane Wooliston was, thought Augustus, all that was finest in womanly charm. He had said so quite frequently in verse, but it held true in prose as well. Not even his execrable effusions could mask her inestimable worth.

She wasn't the one who had spoken.

It had been the other one. Next to her. Half a head down.

What Emma Delagardie lacked in height, she made up for in the exuberantly curled plumes that rose from her silver spangled headdress. The tall plumes jutted a good foot into the air, bouncing up and down—like great, annoying bouncing things. In Augustus's annoyance, metaphor failed him. Her dress was white, but it wasn't the white of innocent maidens and virtuous dreams. It was of silk, sinuous and shiny, overlain with some sort of shimmery stuff that sparkled when she moved, creating the sensation of a constant disturbance in the air around her.

Emma Delagardie was slight, fine boned, and small featured, the top of her head barely level with Miss Wooliston's elegantly curved shoulder, but she took up far more room than her small stature would warrant.

"You might have the dire deep," Mme. Delagardie suggested, her American accent very much in evidence, "or the dreadful deep, but not dithery. It's not even a proper word."

"Your deep may be dire, but my deep is dithery. There is such a thing as poetic license, Madame Delagardie," said Augustus grandly.

"License or laziness? Surely, another word might serve your purpose better. The deep is a rather stationary thing."

Who had appointed Emma Delagardie the Grand Inquisitor for Poetical Excellence, Greater Paris Branch? It had been a sad, sad day for France when her uncle had been appointed American envoy to

Paris and an even sadder one when she had decided to outlast his tenure and stay.

Perhaps America would like to take her back?

"The waves, Madame Delagardie, maintain a constant flow, back and forth, just so." Augustus used the flowy fabric of his sleeves to illustrate, rocked back and forth on the bench. "And on and on they go."

With a hey nonny nonny and a ho ho ho.

Christ, he made himself sick sometimes. You're doing it for England, old chap, he used to tell himself, but the for-England bit had been rubbed bare over time, torn to shreds on the detritus of rhyme.

Oh, bugger. He was thinking in rhyme again. Was there no way to turn it off? To end the adjectives that infected his consciousness? That bedeviled his brain? That assaulted his . . .

Next time, Augustus promised himself. The next time he was recruited for a life of espionage, he was posing as a philosopher or a student of ancient languages, as someone staid and sober, someone who expressed himself in prose rather than verse, and fourth-rate verse at that.

They had warned him of this, his mentors at the War Office. Choose your persona wisely, they had said. Over time, you might just become what you pretend to be. Augustus had scoffed at it at the time. Nineteen and fearless he had been then, confident of the power of both his sword and his pen. It had seemed like such a lark, a decade ago, to couch his reports to the War Office in poetry so bad that even the Ministry of Police wouldn't want to read it. Even fanatical devotion only went so far. For the French surveillance officers, "so far" generally ended somewhere around the thirty-ninth canto.

What a stroke of brilliance, a code no one could break—because there was no code. No count-ten-letters-and-subtract-one, no book of code words and phrases, no messy paper trails to trip one up, just the information itself couched in terms of purest absurdity, truth drowned in a sea of verbiage.

Sometimes, it felt like truth wasn't the only one drowning. He had been doing this for too long; he felt the weariness of it to his very bones.

Augustus looked at Jane Wooliston, his buoy, his anchor, his island in a turbulent sea. Until she had arrived in Paris, he had been giving serious thought to throwing it all in.

Clasping his hands to his breast, Augustus looked meaningfully at Miss Wooliston. "What can one say about the sea? Oh, the sea! The inconstant sea! As indeterminate as a lady's affections and as unfathomable as the female heart."

Miss Wooliston hid her smile behind her fan. "Beautifully said, Monsieur Whittlesby, but I would urge you to credit our sex with somewhat more resoluteness of character than that."

She managed to make her voice carry without seeming to try. What a lovely voice it was, too, a fine, clear contralto, neither too high nor too low.

Augustus clapped the back of his hand to his forehead, just managing not to gag on his own sleeve. They had played this game before, he and Miss Wooliston. "Resolute in cruelty! Obdurate in obfuscation!"

"Ornate in ormolu?" It was the American again. Of course.

"Ormolu," Augustus repeated. "Ormolu?"

Emma Delagardie gave a little bounce that made her silver spangles scintillate. "Just helping out. You are doing *O*s, aren't you?"

Augustus would have loved to tell her exactly what she could do with her *A*s, *E*s and *U*s—in prose—but he had spent years perfecting his pose of poetic otherworldliness. He wasn't about to ruin it for one noisy chit from the colonies. The former colonies, that was. If Emma Delagardie was a representative example, good riddance to them.

"*If* I may continue?" he said.

Emma Delagardie fluttered her fan. Augustus sneezed. The fan was made of feathers. Feathers with silver spangles. They had a long reach.

"Oh, do. Please do," she said, far too enthusiastically for Augustus's peace of mind. No one wanted to hear his poetry that badly. In fact, no one wanted to hear his poetry at all. This boded ill.

Augustus brooded. He did it quite well. He bloody well ought to. He had spent hours practicing. "My soul shies back! To flourish, the delicate blooms of poetry must be gently nurtured and watered from the well of an understanding spirit, not withered in the harsh glare of unfeeling criticism."

"Do go on, Mr. Whittlesby," said Miss Wooliston soothingly. "I assure you, we are all attention to hear how Cytherea comes about."

"All thirty dithery cantos," added her friend cheerfully.

Did she think it was easy to consistently perpetrate works of such poetic awfulness?

He could have told Emma Delagardie a thing or two about that. Years, it had taken, years of grueling practice and downright hard work. It was a hard balance to maintain, writing poetry dreadful enough to be laughable but just credible enough to be believable.

Augustus rustled his roll of papers. "Shall I go on? Or need I fear the slings and arrows of outrageous interruptions?"

"We'll be good," promised Emma Delagardie, in a way that signaled anything but. "Mum as church mice."

The church mice he had known had been rather noisy, actually, in the walls of the vicarage of his youth, but that was beside the point. He wasn't going to let himself be drawn into yet another pointless argument.

"In that case . . ." Augustus made a show of scrolling down his page, searching his place. The gilded doors to the music room racketed open and someone skidded into the room, dressed inappropriately for an evening of entertainment, in boots with the mud of travel still on them. He was a young man, cheeks flushed, hair mussed, cravat askew. He was dressed in the glorified riding dress that the upper classes had made their common clothing, a tightly fitted coat over a bright waistcoat, tight pantaloons tucked into Hessian boots.

The difference was, these clothes had obviously been used for riding, and recently.

A few of the ladies whispered and giggled behind their fans. The dowager made a snorting noise in her sleep and burrowed deeper into her chair.

What in the hell was Horace de Lilly doing here? As a very junior sort of agent, employed for the sole purpose of his aristocratic connections, de Lilly was meant to be at Saint-Cloud, hanging about the fringes of Bonaparte's semi-regal court, not in Paris, attending a ball at the Hotel de Balcourt.

This did not bode well.

With a wary eye on his young associate, Augustus returned to his poetry. "For in the lady's youth was told / A tale of prophecies ancient and old—"

Horace began to bounce on the balls of his feet, striving to be seen over Mme. Delagardie's plumes. He mouthed something.

Augustus frowned in his general direction. Raising his voice, he proclaimed, "That once in Triton's court did dwell / And ring a nasty watery knell, / With a clangety clang and an awesome—"

"Yell?" suggested Emma Delagardie, in something that strove to be, but was not quite, sotto voce. "Knell? Mell?"

If Augustus had been holding a book, he would have slammed it. Instead, he jammed the roll of poetry under his arm. "No more! My sensitive soul can endure no further interruptions! The muse has fled. The Graces have left the building."

He jumped down off the settee, landing with a thump on the parquet floor, and had the satisfaction of seeing Mme. Delagardie take a step back. He had landed rather close to her feet, inadequately shod in Grecian sandals that showed off the diamond rings on her toes.

Augustus wafted a trembling hand in the air. "I beg you, good people! Do not attempt to follow! I must soothe myself and my muse in the only way available to one of my delicate temperament, with a spell of solitude and solitary reflection, making humble homage to the muses in the hopes that they will once again heed my call after so brutal and rude a series of interruptions of their delicate endeavors."

The excess fabric in his sleeves made a highly gratifying swishing noise as he swept towards the door.

As he passed de Lilly, he murmured, "In the study. Five minutes."

He didn't wait to see if de Lilly would answer. Casting a lingering backwards glance at Miss Wooliston—exaggerated yearning with just a hint of lustful smolder—he paused only long enough to give the footmen time to open the doors before swanning out into the throng in the next room, where refreshments had been set out among Balcourt's collection of faux Egyptological artifacts. At least, Augustus hoped they were faux. A selection of pastries had been set out on a sarcophagus that served as sideboard, while uniformed footmen scooped champagne punch from bowls constructed of Canopic jars.

Augustus was no antiquarian, but he did recall hearing somewhere that those jars had been used to contain the internal organs of the deceased. He made a mental note to stay away from the punch.

The same couldn't be said for the rest of the company. The punch was flowing freely, the party the sort that would be termed in England "a sad crush," fashionable people jostling one against the other, doing their best to see and be seen. Balcourt might not be admired, but he was known to set a lavish table and he was not without his contacts at court.

It was easy enough to waft his way through the crowd, the eccentric poet in his own private fog, with the occasional murmur of "The muse! I must set it down!"

No one would think anything of finding him in Balcourt's study. When the muse demanded . . .

Augustus closed the door of Balcourt's study behind him, shutting out the revelry without. It was quiet here, the drapes closed, the only light the candles that had been left burning, as a matter of course, in the sconces above the hearth. Balcourt was no scholar. The only thing in the room that didn't show a fine film of dust was the decanter.

The man couldn't be more different from his cousin, Miss Jane Wooliston.

The Pink Carnation.

The door racketed open as Horace de Lilly came charging in as though all the hounds of hell were behind him, the nasty, yippy ones with particularly pointy teeth.

Augustus slammed the door behind him, turning the key in the lock. "What in the blazes was that all about? Aren't you supposed to be in Saint-Cloud?"

"It is of the most urgent!" Horace declared importantly.

It had bloody well better be. Junior agents weren't meant to make direct contact with their seniors. Especially not in such an exuberant and noisy fashion. If Horace had something to report to him, there were channels for that. Quiet channels. Discreet channels. Unfortunately, to ignore the other man now would serve nothing. Whatever damage had been done was done.

"If anyone asks, you're here to commission a poem. You, lover. Me, Cyrano. Understood? You're mad with love for—someone. You can pick the girl; I won't dictate that part—"

For how can one dictate the dictates of the heart? whispered the poet in Augustus's head.

Shut up, Augustus told it.

"—but you'd better make a good show of being lovelorn. That will explain your"—Augustus looked pointedly at Horace's muddy boots, his inappropriate attire—"exuberant arrival. Everyone understands young love."

For a moment, Horace looked as though he might argue. Augustus Whittlesby was universally agreed to be the worst poet in Paris, and, like so many young men, Horace harbored vague poetic aspirations of his own. But sacrifices must be made from time to time.

"So it will be," he said manfully. "I'm here to commission a verse. Now, wait until you hear—"

"Did anyone follow you?" Augustus cut him off.

Horace shook his head. "No one suspects me."

Augustus wished that he could share the younger man's assurance. Ever since a plot to assassinate the First Consul had been uncovered last month, Bonaparte's police force had been working overtime, cracking down on threats anywhere they found them, and sometimes even where they hadn't.

Augustus knew he was lucky to have escaped the net this long. Ironically enough, that very longevity was a large part of his protection. He was like an old oak table or a particularly dingy patch of carpet; the Ministry of Police was so used to him that they scarcely noticed he was there.

Horace, on the other hand, had come over with a wave of émigrés who were being invited, in bits and pieces, back into Paris to lend aristocratic polish to Bonaparte's new court. He was new and therefore automatically suspect. Bonaparte craved the recognition of the old aristocracy, but he also mistrusted them. With reason, in this case.

"Well, they don't!" Horace said indignantly. "I have been of the most subtle."

"Right." Augustus eyed de Lilly's pink and green striped waistcoat. Not exactly what he would call subtle. "What was it that sent you running to Paris?"

Horace flung himself into Balcourt's desk chair, his spurs digging into the imported Persian carpet. "It was like this," he began, clearly determined to milk every moment of glory from the retelling. Augustus remembered when he had been like that. A very long time ago. Horace's beardless face shone with excitement. "I was with the court of the First Consul in Saint-Cloud, when the Consul received a visit from Admiral Decres—"

A sound caught Augustus's attention. A creak, as of a floorboard being depressed slowly and carefully by a person trying very hard not to be heard.

Augustus held up a hand, signaling Horace to silence.

"Edouard?" It was a female voice, raised in a questioning tone. A fingernail scratched against the wood of the door. "Edouaaaard?"

Augustus deliberately rustled the papers on the desk. "Who disturbs me?" he called out, stretching out the vowels in the most annoying way he could. "Who disturbs me in my poetic reverie?"

The scratching stopped. "Pardon?"

"Is it too much to ask for a humble poet to find a bit of peace to court the muse in private?" Augustus inquired mournfully. "Oh, the world is too much with us! Chattering and clattering, we lay waste our talents, consigning our patrimony of poetry to the wasted wind of the idle hour. Oh, woe! Woe it is to be—me."

He broke off as he heard the floorboards creak in rapid retreat.

Horace leaned forward. "Was that—?" he hissed.

"Balcourt's mistress."

"Oh." Horace shrugged off the intrusion. Mistresses were an inconsequential part of urban existence, like tavern owners or those annoying little people who collected bills. "As I was saying, I was at Saint-Cloud, when—"

Augustus cut him off. "Balcourt's mistress is an informer of the Ministry of Police."

It took Horace a moment for the words to register. "Is she?" He seemed more intrigued than alarmed.

De Lilly's insouciance set Augustus's teeth on edge. "Madame Perdite is just one of thousands, but any one of those, no matter how insignificant they may seem, can be your downfall. A landlady, a chambermaid, the boy who holds your horse. Fouché has half of Paris in his pay." An exaggeration, but not by much. "Say nothing in front of anyone, not even the servants. Particularly not the servants. Do you understand?"

Horace nodded, but Augustus could see he didn't understand, not viscerally, not in that place in one's gut that shouted danger long before the conscious senses perceived a threat. Horace had been a boy during the Terror, an adolescent in the safety of London. He had no memory of the stench of blood and sweat, the buzzing of the blood-gorged flies in the Place de la Concorde; he had never spent a night in the damp-walled hospitality of the Conciergerie, never heard the screams of a man being put to the question as he moved from begging for life to praying for death. The prisons of Paris were just names to him, names and blank facades; he had no real understanding of the true nature of the terrors within.

This was what happened of hiring boys who were still wet behind the ears and sending them out into the field with nothing more than a few vague instructions and a slightly outdated map of central Paris.

Augustus preferred not to address the fact that he had been equally amateur when William Wickham had first recruited him for covert operations, fresh out of Cambridge. At the time, he had been an aspiring poet by vocation, a fledgling clergyman by necessity, resigned to the prospect of taking a parish and sandwiching verse between his sermons. His encounter with Wickham had changed all that.

Twelve years later, Augustus could hardly imagine having been that young or that naïve. That young, that naïve, and that eager.

Augustus cocked his head, listening. After this many years in the field, he could discern the subtleties of a silence, the way a painter could distinguish between the various forms of black. There was no listening presence from behind the door; he would have known her from the breathing.

Augustus turned back to Horace. "She's gone," he said. "What do you know?"

Leaning forward, Horace braced his palms on the knees of his breeches. His hands were too large for his frame, as if he hadn't quite yet grown into his height. "The First Consul summoned Admiral

Decres to Saint-Cloud. It was a warm day, so he left the window ajar. I," he added modestly, "was beneath it."

"What did you hear?"

"The fleet. They're readying it."

"Which fleet?" There was more than one.

"All of them!" Horace said excitedly. "The plan, it has been approved at last. I heard it direct from the First Consul's lips. Save just one thing, all is readiness."

Augustus didn't need to ask, but he did. "For?"

"The First Consul, he is giving the orders for the invasion of England!"

Chapter 2

"Whither wend ye, sir?" Cytherea cried,
"And why hast thou come for me?
To drag me, O, so far from home!
Along the wine dark sea!"

—Augustus Whittlesby, *The Perils of the*
Pulchritudinous Princess of the Azure Toes,
Canto XII, 28–31

*Y*ou really must stop poking at him like that," said Jane, as the
poet made his offended way out of the room.

"I wasn't poking," said Emma.

Her friend gave her a look. Jane had a way with looks.

"Well, maybe just a little," Emma admitted. "But when he perpetrates poems like that, it's just too tempting not to poke."

Jane continued to look, her gray eyes amused.

"What?" said Emma defensively.

"There are better ways to get someone's attention."

Emma chose to ignore that. "All I did was offer a little helpful criticism."

"In the middle of his reading," pointed out Jane.

"Was it the middle? It's so hard to tell when it goes on for forty-five cantos."

"Twenty-two," corrected Jane. She would know. Whittlesby had dedicated all of them to her, his Princess of the Pulchritudinous Toes. "Haven't you ever thought of just conducting a conversation with him rather than embarrassing him in public? It might better serve your cause."

Emma wrinkled her nose at her friend. "I don't have a cause."

Jane adjusted an already perfectly aligned flounce. "You go to every single one of his readings. Poetic devotion?"

"Consider it a well-developed sense of the absurd?" Emma suggested. "For farce, he's better than the commedia dell'arte."

"Almost anything is better than the commedia dell'arte," said Jane. As Emma had learned, her friend was something of a snob when it came to theatre. It was one of the few flaws in an otherwise perfect personality. Fortunately, Emma had caught Jane reading gothic novels, or else they might never have become friends. "Care to try again?"

"It's not like that," said Emma. "Well, it's not! It's like . . . pining after an actor. You don't mean anything to come of it, but he does look so very nice in his pantaloons."

"Mmm," said Jane. "Does he now?"

Emma felt her cheeks flush. "That was meant as a general 'he,' not this 'he' in particular. Although, yes," she admitted, "he does look very good in his breeches. It's his one redeeming quality. That and his hair. He has very nice hair. And fine eyes. Oh, stop!"

"Hmm?" said Jane, but the lace of her fan couldn't quite hide her smile. "Did I do anything?"

"You know what you did," said Emma severely. "It's really just a diversion. Something safe and harmless."

There was nothing like an affair, her friends had told her years ago. How else was a young widow to divert herself? She had tried it and found it wanting. Now all she wanted was a little amusement, just a little game to play, silly and safe.

What could be sillier or safer than Augustus Whittlesby?

It hardly even counted as a *tendre*. It was just a diversion.

"If you say so," said Jane, in that maddening way of hers. "Aren't you to be writing your own magnum opus soon? That ought to engender some artistic fellow feeling with Mr. Whittlesby."

"Magnum opus?"

"I heard you were commissioned to contrive a play, for a party at Malmaison."

"Oh, that." Emma shook her head in dismissal. "Not a play, a masque, just a short piece, more spectacle than verse. Madame Bonaparte suggested it. I told her I would think about it."

"I won't accept no," Mme. Bonaparte had said in her lingering Creole drawl, tapping Emma's cheek in that way she had, that way that made her feel fifteen again, a schoolgirl at Mme. Campan's academy for young ladies, meeting Hortense's mother for the first time, surrounded by the scent of roses and the warmth of Mme. Bonaparte's smile.

They had been more family to Emma than her own family in those early days after her elopement, Hortense de Beauharnais and her mother. Hortense's mother had just married again, an army sort, a general named Bonaparte, but they found room for Emma anyway, in the crowded house in the Rue Chantereine. They had taken her in while her own family had roared with disbelief and disapproval, had sheltered her during the disillusionment of those early days of her marriage to Paul, comforted her, helped her, asking no questions and demanding no favors in return.

It was meant as a signal honor, this conferring of the writing of the masque. An honor and a politic move. As much as Hortense and Mme. Bonaparte might love her for herself, Emma didn't delude herself that the offer was tendered out of affection alone. The only reason she had been asked to contrive the entertainment was because the party was being held in honor of her cousin, the American envoy to France. Bonaparte needed the goodwill of the Americans, and Emma was about as American as they came, at least when it came to being related to envoys. Her uncle, Monroe, had been the first of the envoys to France; her cousin, Robert Livingston, currently held the post. In diplomatic circles, Emma had become known as a person to cultivate, not out of any virtue of her own but as a circumstance of the position of her relations.

She didn't want it to be like this. She didn't want to think of position and status and political advantage. Only of old friendship and good fellowship. Was that so much to ask?

"Madame Bonaparte wants the masque as a surprise for cousin Robert." Emma looked at Jane over her fan. "I suppose that means that half of Paris already knows it, and the rest will be told by nightfall."

"Three quarters," corrected Jane, with a smile. "And everyone agog to know what the subject will be and who is to act which part."

"Would you like to tell me?" Emma quipped. "I'm sure the rest of Paris will know before I do. Madame Bonaparte suggested a nautical theme, but other than that, there were no requirements, other than that there be a nice singing part for Hortense."

"Is Monsieur Talma to help you?" The famous actor regularly directed plays for the theatre-mad Bonapartes in their private theatre at Malmaison.

"If I agree to do it."

"Why not?" asked Jane.

Emma toyed with the edge of her fan. Nervous hands, her mother had called it, as if one could be scolded to serenity. "I don't mind scribbling in my spare time, but it seems cruel to inflict it on a whole audience. Just look at Mr. Whittlesby!"

"But he brings amusement to so many," said Jane blandly.

"Laughing with him or at him? Ha! My point." Emma cast around for a change of subject before Jane pressed on about the masque—or about Mr. Whittlesby. Emma pointed with her fan. "Look. That man over there. Another of your admirers? He's been staring at us for a good ten minutes."

Seeing he had caught their attention, the man moved hesitantly forward. He was dressed correctly for evening, in breeches, silk stockings, and buckled shoes, but the clothes were all slightly wrong somehow, the coat last season's cut, the shirt points too low, the cravat functionally but not elegantly tied.

He came to a stop before Emma and Jane, looking from one to the other. "If you'll pardon the interruption . . . I was told I could find Madame Delagardie here?"

His French was heavily accented, so heavily accented as to be nearly incomprehensible. Another American. That explained that, then. Emma had become something of a first port of call for American expatriates in Paris, a convenient resource for the complicated manners and mores of the French capital. "Call on Madame Delagardie," they told them back home. "She'll arrange the introductions for you and point you to a tailor who won't rob you blind." And so she did and was glad to do it. She would have been glad of such guidance once.

Emma let the fronds of her fan tickle her chin as she looked up under her lashes at the newcomer. "Your quest has been successful, then. You've found her. Me," she specified, just in case he hadn't gotten it. Poor man, he was still looking all befuddled. Paris did that to some people.

This one seemed more than usually bewildered. Twin furrows formed between his wide-set blue eyes. "Emma?" he said. "*Emma?*"

"Do I know—?" The words died on Emma's lips. Blue eyes. Very familiar blue eyes. Slim the shoulders, lighten the hair, take away a decade's worth of lines from eyes and lips. . . . "Kort?"

"Emma?"

"Gracious heavens!" Rising on her tiptoes, Emma flung her arms around her cousin's neck, enveloping him in silver spangles and causing a minor stir on the other side of the room. The rumors would be flying, but Emma didn't care. "It's you? It's really you?"

Kort untangled himself, drawing away to arm's length, clasping her hands lightly in his, his laughter making him look ten years younger again, a boy on a pier on the Hudson. "I was about to say the same to you! I've been prowling this mausoleum all evening trying to find you." He shook his head, taking her in. "Emma. Little Emma."

Emma smiled up at him. "I haven't grown so very much. In fact, I've shrunk." She turned one foot, displaying her flat-heeled slippers. The diamond rings on her toes sparkled. "The last time you saw me, I had some help from heels."

Kort blinked, dazzled by diamonds. He shook his head again. "Emma . . . I would never have known you. I expected . . ."

"A thirteen-year-old in calico?" A slight shift in Jane's stance caught Emma's attention. "Good heavens, I am being rude! Forgive me, please. Jane, this is my very favorite cousin, Mr. Kortright Livingston. Kort, I have the honor to present you to the most beautiful woman in Paris, Miss Jane Wooliston."

Jane bent her knees at just the right angle, only so far for a mister, and an American one. As far as Emma could tell, the English were born with protocol in their very bones.

"It is an honor, Mr. Livingston," said Jane, slipping into English as the others had done. "With so many cousins, to be Madame Delagardie's favorite must be a signal distinction indeed."

"You are English, Miss Wooliston?" Kort said, looking at her quizzically. Technically, travel between England and France was prohibited. Jane was something of a special circumstance. Bonaparte admired beauty.

More important, Hortense had taken Jane under her wing. Bonaparte might not respect many peoples' wishes, but his stepdaughter had a special place in his affections. Sometimes, Emma forgot that Jane hadn't attended Mme. Campan's with them; she had fit so seamlessly into their fellowship.

"English by birth," said Jane calmly. "Paris is my adopted home."

"Miss Wooliston has cousins here," Emma jumped in before the conversation could become awkward. Although some of Emma's cousins had remained Tories, her branch of the family had supported the colonies' split with Britain; even thirty years on, feelings towards the British could not be termed warm. Kort had always minded terribly that he had been born too late to take an active part in the Revolution. "You've met Monsieur de Balcourt, I think. Or if you haven't, you will." She wafted her fan around the music room, with its oversize sarcophagi and smirking sphinxes. "This is his home."

Kort looked dubiously at a mummy case. "It's all very . . . exotic."

Emma remembered the family homestead on the Hudson, decorated in the last word of pre-Revolutionary style, all clean, classical lines and plain dark wood. Her mother didn't go in for fads. Kort's mother, her own mother's second cousin, considered herself somewhat more stylish, cutting a dash in Albany, but even she would have seen nothing like this.

"It's called *Retour d'Egypte*," explained Emma, "in honor of the First Consul's expedition to Egypt."

"Hence the name," contributed Jane blandly. "If you will excuse me, there's a wounded soul I must soothe."

Emma followed her gaze to the doorway. Whittlesby clasped his scroll to his heart, looking soulfully at Jane.

Was it silly that it stung, just a bit?

"Wounded soul, indeed!" Emma turned back to Jane, the silk of her skirt swirling around her legs with a very satisfying swish. "It was only a flesh wound."

"You gouged his ego," teased Jane.

"Yes, but I left his heart alone," said Emma severely. "You'll lead him on if you continue to encourage him so."

Jane made a face. "That depends on whether you believe Petrarch really loved his Laura. I'm nothing more than a poetic object of expedience."

Emma grinned. "A muse of convenience?"

"Every poet must have one," said Jane. "Mr. Livingston."

With a cordial nod to Emma's cousin, she crossed the room to rejoin the poet, accepting the arm he held out to her.

Emma watched them as they made their way across the room. Jane was tall, but the poet was a head taller. He had to bend to speak to her, the linen of his shirt stretching across a back that was broader than it had any right to be. Hefting a quill must be better exercise than it seemed.

"What was that all about?" Kort asked.

Emma yanked her attention back to her cousin.

"Oh, nothing," she said hastily. "Just a poet."

Chapter 3

She took the key about her neck
And shook her shining head.
"You must seek elsewhere, brave my knight,
And be not daunted or misled.
My key is not the key you seek,
Nor can it stand in stead."

      —Augustus Whittlesby, *The Perils of the*
      Pulchritudinous Princess of the Azure Toes,
              Canto XII, 31–34

I know I can trust *you*, Miss Wooliston, to listen to my ode without the offense of unnecessary interruptions," Augustus proclaimed loudly.

Jane slid her arm through his, giving him a warning look under cover of her fan as she strolled with him to French doors that stood slightly ajar to allow the cool night air to reach the overheated guests. "Do come out into the garden, Mr. Whittlesby," she said. "The night is pleasant, and I find poetry is often enhanced by its surroundings."

"Ah, Miss Wooliston!" Augustus gestured extravagantly with his free arm, making the fabric of his sleeve billow like a ship under full sail. "But what rose could possibly compare to you?"

He opened the door that led down from the drawing room into the internal courtyard, motioning Jane to precede him. In the center of the garden, there would be no fear of being overheard. The musicians playing in the ballroom and the accumulated chatter of several hundred party guests masked their voices more effectively than any attempt at subterfuge.

There was nothing like conducting clandestine business in plain sight.

"Their bloom will fade; yours, fair lady, is rendered immortal, impressed on parchment by the unflagging labors of my humble pen."

"Really, Mr. Whittlesby," said Jane. "Nothing so showy as a rose."

"A rose by any other name . . ."

"Would be a different poet. I thought you were borrowing from Coleridge these days."

Mindful of potential viewers, Augustus thumped a fist against his chest. "You wound me, O cruel one. My execrations are entirely my own. With the occasional nod to Mr. Wordsworth."

"I'm sure he would be deeply flattered to hear it. Little does he realize how much he has done to secure freedom on either side of the Channel." Jane seated herself on a low stone bench in the center of the garden, in plain view of the many windows that surrounded them. "Would you prefer to stand or to disport yourself at my feet?"

Augustus flung himself dramatically onto the flagstones in front of her. It was too early in the season for flowers to bloom, so Balcourt had brought in flowering shrubs in faux porphyry tubs, scattering them strategically around the garden to create the illusion of abundance.

"I'll disport," he said. "It provides better cover."

From the windows, all anyone would see was the familiar scene of the poet lolling at beauty's feet, boring her with his latest ode.

Augustus unrolled the scroll of paper. "So, my fair Cytherea, I have tidings for you."

"From across the boundless sea?"

"Close enough. My sources claim Bonaparte's fleet is prepared to sail."

Jane turned her head away, as though abashed by his praise. "That can't be. His admirals wouldn't approve the plan. It was impracticable."

"They have now." Augustus gazed up at her yearningly over the end of the paper, the poet worshipping his muse. They had played this game many times before. "Both Villeneuve and Decres signed off on it. The fleet is due to depart in July."

He didn't tell her where he had acquired his information and she didn't ask. They both knew better than that.

Augustus looked up at her from his vantage point on the ground, marveling, not at the clean lines of cheek and jaw that were nature's gift and not her own, but at her calm good sense, unusual in anyone at all, let alone one so young.

The Pink Carnation had burst upon the scene a little more than a year before, in the spring of 1803, with the spectacular theft of the gold that Bonaparte had intended for the manufacture of a fleet to invade England. Augustus had shrugged and gone about his business. He had been in Paris since 1792. Would-be heroes came and went. One spectacular intrigue, they went all cocky, and the next thing you knew, they were in the Bastille, babbling the names of their confederates and collaborators.

Not Augustus. He was in it for the long haul. His brief was simple. Observe, record, relay. No heroics, no direct action. Just the simple gathering and transmission of information. Idiots who went swanning about Paris in a black mask seldom lasted terribly long.

But the Pink Carnation had followed up that first success with a second and then a third. There were no unnecessary heroics, no reckless bits of daring. The French press had taken note, and so had

Augustus. It had been in June that his superiors in London had ordered him to liaise with the Carnation. Augustus had gone to the rendezvous expecting a man: middle-aged, gnarled, nondescript.

Instead, he had found Jane.

In profile, her face was shadowed, the lanterns strung along the edges of the garden casting strange patterns of light and shade. There was something to be written there, something about dark and bright, her aspect, her eyes, but the words eluded him.

Augustus spared a glance at the scroll in his hands. All he had to offer was reams of endless drivel and the odd nugget of military intelligence. Quite a wooing, that. Cyrano would weep.

"But how?" she asked, tilting her head in a practiced pose of feigned interest, her face a mask of polite boredom. Her shoulders were relaxed, her hands loosely folded, her body language at complete odds with her tone, low and urgent. "A month ago, Decres said it couldn't be done."

Augustus took refuge behind his scroll. "A month ago, they didn't have the device."

"The device? What sort of device?"

"That's the rub," said Augustus. "My source doesn't know what it is. The device, Decres called it, and that was all. Whatever it is, though, they seem to set a great deal of store in it."

"Why are you telling me this?" she asked. "Aside from professional courtesy."

"You know I don't like to ask for favors—"

"But I owe you one," Jane said. "For the Silver Orchid."

He had played liaison for Jane with one of her agents, helping to spirit the woman and the duc de Berri out of Paris. Augustus had played no part in the actual escape; he had merely relayed a message when it had proved impolitic for Jane to do so herself. It had been a small enough favor, and Augustus said as much.

"Even so," said Jane. "Don't think I'm not sensible of my debt to you."

"There can be no debt between friends," Augustus said.

Didn't she know he would have done more for her if she had asked? A phoenix feather from the far ends of the earth, a dragon's horde from the depths of a flame-scorched cave, the head of a prophet on a platter.

At least, so the poet liked to think. The agent was well aware that he had compromised the terms of his own mission by doing even such a little thing for her. His mandate was to observe, not to act. Any action he took made detection more likely. Wickham had other men planted in Paris, but no one of his standing, no one who had been there as long or seen as much. He might not be indispensible, but he would be bloody hard to replace.

"What do you need of me?" she asked.

"Entrée into Malmaison," he said promptly. "Whatever this device is, they plan a final test a month from now, somewhere on the grounds of Malmaison. The trial is planned for the weekend of June ninth."

Jane looked thoughtfully over his shoulder. "They have a party planned that weekend, in honor of the American envoy."

Augustus leaned back on one elbow, lolling artistically on the flagstones. "Distraction," he said. "It provides Bonaparte with an excuse."

At Saint-Cloud, the consular court lived in state, surrounded by a growing entourage of servants and hangers-on. At Malmaison, on the other hand, the Bonapartes maintained the pretense of simplicity. Even with the addition of tents to house the servants and the consular staff, the house was nothing more than a modest gentleman's residence, its small size necessarily limiting the number of people invited. The grounds, constantly in the process of improvement, stretched out for hectares in either direction, the private preserve of Mme. Bonaparte.

It was, in other words, the perfect place to conduct a trial of Decres's mysterious device, far away from Paris and prying eyes.

"I had wondered," admitted Jane, "why he was having Mr. Livingston to Malmaison, rather than to Saint-Cloud. The excuse given was that the choice was for sentimental reasons. Mr. Livingston is Emma's cousin, and Emma is so very fond of Malmaison."

Augustus snorted. "Bonaparte is about as sentimental as a barracuda. Can you get me in?"

Jane paused a moment, then shook her head. "Not this time. I haven't been invited myself."

Augustus reacted to the tone rather than the words. "Do you think Fouché suspects you?" His mind was already racing ahead, formulating plans, ways to dodge the all-seeing eye of Bonaparte's sinister Minister of Police. He could get Jane out of Paris if he had to. The old network, stretching from Paris to Boulogne, had been eviscerated in Fouché's latest raids, but he still had connections, personal ones. "Don't be heroic."

"No, no, it's nothing like that. Nefarious behavior from the lady of the cameos? They would sooner suspect the statuary. But the group is small and Mr. Livingston is known to have little sympathy for the English. My invitation might be considered an insult." She paused, her head cocked to one side. "But there is a way."

"La belle Hortense?" Jane had become fast friends with Mme. Bonaparte's daughter from her first marriage. The two were of an age. Hortense was universally acknowledged as the best of the Bonapartes, probably because she was one only by marriage: her mother's marriage to Bonaparte, and her own marriage to Bonaparte's younger brother, Louis. "Hortense finds me amusing. Perhaps you can convince her that the weekend demands immortalizing in verse."

"Hortense has her own worries. You may have noticed she isn't here tonight." Jane spread her fan, revealing a painting of swans floating languidly on a lake. "No. I have a better idea."

"Tunneling beneath the grounds?" Augustus teased. "Fighting my way through the gates with Miss Gwen's parasol?"

"You miss the obvious," said Jane calmly. "The simplest proposition is always the best."

"I don't follow."

Jane smiled at him over the edge of her fan. "The answer was right in front of you all along. Emma Delagardie."

"*A* poet?" echoed Kort.

"Miss Wooliston tends to inspire that sort of thing." Emma wafted a dismissive hand, turning her attention back to her cousin. "Goodness, Kort. I can't believe you're really here. After all this time."

She had forgotten how big he was, or perhaps it was that he had filled out since she had seen him last. He had been only eighteen then, after all, eighteen to her thirteen. At the time, she had thought him the last word in manliness and sophistication. She had been as infatuated as only a thirteen-year-old could be, saving his dropped handkerchiefs and scribbling maudlin verse in the solitude of her favorite branch of an apple tree.

Goodness, she'd forgotten that apple tree. She had created quite the fuss by tumbling out of it and breaking her arm. She could still feel the twinge in it when the wind blew in the wrong direction.

"Cousin Robert told me I would most likely find you here. I just hadn't expected—" Kort's eyes dipped from the plumes on her headdress to the diamonds glittering at her ears, her arms, her breast.

"To see quite so much of me?" Emma quipped, and her cousin's gaze hastily snapped upwards again.

Oops. She hadn't meant to make him squirm. She had forgotten. They were less frank at home, at least about certain things. It felt odd to be speaking English again; the once familiar syllables came uncomfortably to her tongue, although not as uncomfortably as Kort's labored French.

"Something like that," Kort admitted, carefully avoiding the general direction of her bodice. He shook his head again. "I would never have known you."

It would have been nice if the statement had sounded a little bit more like a compliment.

"That's not surprising," she said, striving for sangfroid. She resisted the urge to tug at her décolletage. Her dress might be low by New York standards, but it was positively modest by Parisian ones, largely because she didn't have terribly much to display. "It's been over ten years since you last saw me. It would be more surprising if I hadn't changed."

"You've become so . . . French."

The comment surprised her into a laugh. "The French find me very American. Or so I've been told."

Refreshing, they had called her. Natural. Fruitlessly, Emma had tried to explain that her parents' home in New York was as sophisticated as anything to be found in the Faubourg Saint-Germain and the only savages on their property were her brothers, but such protestations had been unpopular with her audience. They preferred to cherish Rousseauian notions of noble savages clad in loincloths and adorned with feathers.

"When did you arrive?" she asked. "Have you been in Paris long?"

"Tuesday," he said. "Whenever I mention your name, I hear only effusions. Everyone adores Madame Delagardie."

Mme. Delagardie had made a great effort to be adored. As for Emma . . . well, it was what it was and that was all. She was Mme. Delagardie now and had been for some time.

"Almost everyone. Not everyone has come to a full and proper appreciation of my inestimable worth, but they will in time. What brings you to Paris after all these years? Surely, you could have spared a visit to your favorite cousin before this. It's just a little sea voyage. It's only a few months at sea, and I have it on the very best authorities that sea monsters have gone out of fashion."

He didn't respond to her raillery in kind. A shadow passed across his face. He paused for a moment before saying, "You will have heard about Sarah, I expect."

Oh, Lord. Emma felt like the scrapings off his boots, if he had been wearing boots. She was the lowest level of Paris gutter slime, heartless and unfeeling. She had heard. But it had been how long ago now? A year? Two? Time moved strangely in Paris, and the Atlantic divide meant that news was no longer news by the time of arrival.

"I had heard." She touched a gloved hand fleetingly to his arm. "I'm sorry, Kort."

His lips twisted with dark humor. Bitterness sat strangely on his clean-cut face. "So am I."

She had hated Sarah once. She had hated her for being older, for being taller, for catching Kort's eye. Emma had wished warts on her, or hives, with all the petty desperation of her wounded adolescent soul. She had fantasized about Sarah, always so competent and complacent, tripping on the way to the altar or ripping her wedding dress or spilling punch down her front in some humiliating and public occasion.

But not this. Never this. Emma's heart winced away from the image of Sarah and her babies, still and cold.

Sarah was the sort of woman her mother was, the sort of woman her mother had wanted her to be. She ought to be running a bustling household with a brood of children around her, all good housewifery and Dutch thrift. They had had three children, Emma had been told. She had learned of them one by one, when her mother and brothers had gradually begun writing to her again, slowly resuming the flow of family news and gossip. Two girls and a boy, all dead of the influenza, and Sarah with them, a whole family gone in one cruel blow.

"If you need distraction," said Emma, "Paris is the place to be. It's very good at helping one to forget."

Or, at least, at keeping one so busy one failed to remember. Either way, the result was the same, except in those wee, dark hours of the morning, the ones not filled with balls and the chatter of sophisticated people, when memories, regrets, and doubts came crowding in, one on top of the other, murdering sleep and shattering repose.

She had tried laudanum once, but hated the grogginess that came after. It made her feel less herself, less energetic, less alive. She was left with no recourse but to keep as busy as possible, careening from event to event in the hope that by the time the morning came, she would be tired enough to sleep.

Sometimes it even worked.

There were lines next to Kort's eyes and circles under them, attributes foreign to the carefree boy Emma had known. He looked at her soberly. "I had forgotten. You know what it is. To lose someone."

Emma shrugged, toying with the silver fringe of her shawl. It was a flimsy thing, designed more for ornament than warmth. "It was a long time ago." She didn't want to talk about Paul, especially not with Kort. It was all too complicated. She slid an arm through her cousin's, forcing herself to speak cheerfully. "I am being horrid monopolizing you like this, when there are so many fascinating people for you to meet. Shall I introduce you to the reigning beauties of Paris? Or would you rather a poet or philosopher?"

"You sound like you're offering them up for sale," said Kort bemusedly.

"Everything in Paris is for sale, in some way or another," said Emma cynically. "If it bothers you, consider it more a loan. A loan to a favorite cousin."

Emma cast about for something else to cheer him up. There was her old friend Adele de Treville in the corner, a widow, too, and a merry one. Her husband had died on the expedition to Haiti, along with Pauline Bonaparte's spouse, victim of the yellow fever that had done more to decimate the French ranks than all the efforts of the rebel army.

Adele had been part of the fellowship at Mme. Campan's, but

Emma wasn't sure Kort was quite ready for her yet. Adele was a darling, but she couldn't be called anything but fast. If her conversation made Emma blush, it would horrify Kort. Right now she was talking to—

No. Oh, no.

"You haven't met our host yet, have you?" Emma babbled, taking Kort by the arm and towing him ungently away from Adele and her companion. There were some things about her life since New York that Kort just didn't need to know. "I've been hideously remiss. I ought to have introduced you straightaway."

"No, not at all," said Kort, submitting to being tugged along, like a sturdy vessel in the grip of a particularly determined tug. "I have messages from home I've been pledged to deliver. May I call on you tomorrow?"

"You may call on me at any time," Emma promised him extravagantly, yanking him along behind her. Of all the nights for her past indiscretions to catch up with her, why did it need to be tonight? "My door is open to you at any hour of the day or night. Not literally, of course. There's a concierge for that. He opens and closes it. The door, I mean. He gets very upset when other people try to do it for him. He takes great pride in his door. I mean, his work."

Kort looked at her with concern. "Are you feeling quite well?"

"I am merely overwhelmed with the joy of your visit," Emma lied. "And champagne. Have you had any? It's really quite excellent. Here, do."

She thrust a glass at him, looking frantically for a means of escape. If there was anyone she didn't need Kort to meet . . .

"Madame Delagardie."

Too late.

Georges Marston took her hand without it being offered, took it with an assumption of intimacy that made Emma wince and Kort lower his glass of champagne.

"Madame Delagardie," he said. "It has been too long."

Chapter 4

For to the fair, all things are fair,
No ill or malice can they see;
And all the while evil's darkling hand
Descends its way towards thee!

—Augustus Whittlesby, *The Perils of the*
Pulchritudinous Princess of the Azure Toes,
Canto XII, 56–59

Emma Delagardie?" repeated Augustus. "Oh, right. Your American friend. The noisy one."

"Emma is the obvious solution," Jane said calmly.

In the dusky light, the white fabric of Jane's skirts blended with the marble of the bench, making her look even farther removed from the mortal realm than usual, a goddess on her pedestal, perfect and pure.

It was hard enough to argue with a goddess, harder when one was mute with love, tongue-tied with infatuation.

It had crept up on him slowly, over the course of months. At first, he had been aware only of admiration, admiration for her calm under pressure, for her endless serenity, for the cool, Grecian good looks that had won her a place in Bonaparte's court, and the rigorous self-discipline with which she played her chosen role. Augustus had seen so many agents come and go over the years. Some lost their nerve at the first hint of danger; others cracked through boredom, unable to sustain the pretense needed to maintain an alias over an extended period of time.

Not Jane. She made it seem so easy, as effortless and inevitable as the endless washing of waves against the beach. He had to remind himself, sometimes, that she was nearly a decade his junior. She had arrived in France fresh from the seclusion of the English countryside, with no training other than that which she had devised for herself. As far as Augustus could tell, she hadn't put a foot wrong since.

He had been instructed to liaise with her last summer, over a matter of mutual interest: the capture and containment of the spy known as the Black Tulip. It seemed a reasonable collaboration. The English government had been looking for the Black Tulip for some time; the Black Tulip had vowed to find and eliminate the Pink Carnation.

It wasn't her professionalism that caught him, or her beauty. It was the humor with which she entered into his ridiculous charades, the glint in her eye as she received his more alarming effusions. Competent, beautiful, and clever.

What man wouldn't succumb? After years of writing about love, he was finally prey to it, and it hurt like hell. It was the worst of poetic clichés: the poet infatuated, the lady indifferent. It didn't help that their professional relationship depended upon the endless perpetuation of that particular scenario, exaggerated into farce and played out before the entire audience of Paris society.

"The party at Malmaison is being held in honor of Emma's cousin, the American envoy," Jane was saying. "It's not common knowledge yet, but he's due to be recalled. This is meant by way of farewell. If anyone has the power to secure your entrée, it will be Emma."

"Yes, but will she?" Augustus dragged his attention back to the matter at hand. No use in mooning. "Emma Delagardie has no use for me."

"You mean you have no use for Emma Delagardie. Those are two very different propositions."

"The woman called my writing an expense of ink in a waste of shame."

"Clever," said Jane.

"Shakespeare," countered Augustus. "Sonnet 129."

"Is it the sentiment you object to, or the lack of originality?"

"She said my poetry was drivel."

Jane regarded him with amusement. "It is drivel. You've said as much yourself. Credit Emma with taste, at least, if not with tact. I should think you would approve of that. I'm not asking you to marry her—"

"Much obliged," muttered Augustus.

"—merely to offer her your poetic talents, such as they are, for the purpose of gaining admission into Malmaison."

"I fail to see how the one translates to the other."

"Madame Bonaparte has asked Emma to compose a masque for the gathering at Malmaison next month. Emma can turn a neat enough phrase, but she doesn't claim to be a poet. She's wary of taking on the task. You might offer to collaborate."

Augustus bit down on his automatic objection. It wasn't a bad idea, on the face of it. The theatre-mad Bonapartes weren't averse to employing professional help for their amateur theatricals. The great actor Talma regularly directed their productions. No one would think twice about Mme. Delagardie delegating the writing of her masque to a poet, nor object to that poet being on hand throughout rehearsals to tinker with the odd line or extend a soliloquy upon the request of the actor.

There were, however, some rather glaring obstacles.

Augustus gave voice to the most obvious of them. "Even if I were prepared to do so, what makes you think Madame Delagardie would accept the help of a man guilty of perpetrating unspeakable crimes against unsuspecting adverbs? That's a direct quotation, by the way," he added.

Jane was silent for a moment. "When you were young, did you ever pull a girl's hair ribbon? Or tug at her braid to get her attention?"

"Hair ribbon?" Augustus echoed. "Braid? I don't follow."

He looked at Jane with concern. He had seen this before in agents deployed too long in the field. The strain must be beginning to get to her.

Jane started to say something but thought better of it. "Never mind. Do give my suggestion some thought, won't you? Emma is less than thrilled at the prospect of crafting a masque in a month, even if it's only a short piece. She'll take help where she can find it."

"Or where it's offered?"

Jane nodded. "It might be the easiest way to get you in. Whatever you may think of her, Emma's wishes carry a great deal of weight with Madame Bonaparte." She flicked demurely at an invisible speck of dust on her skirt. "You must admit, it would be a marked improvement on creeping into the grounds in the middle of the night."

"I certainly won't argue with that." Climbing fences and dodging night watchmen had lost its charm years ago. Augustus had never been much for swinging on a rope, either. Ropes had an annoying tendency to break. "The concept is sound. It's the execution that gives me pause."

"Tell her I sent you," Jane suggested. "At the worst, she says no."

"At the best?"

"You have an invitation to Malmaison. Isn't that what you wanted?"

There was no arguing with that. "*If* my sources are correct," Augustus said darkly. "This could all be for nothing."

"You'll never know unless you try."

Why was it that cheering expressions were invariably so infuriating?

"Are you always right?" Augustus asked wearily.

Jane spread her fan, uncovering a charming scene of swans drifting on an improbably azure lake. "Only when I'm not wrong. I take it that's a yes, then?"

It was going to have to be, but there were still questions niggling. Something smelled wrong. Augustus seized on the least of them. "Why a masque? I thought those went out with the Sun King."

"Because Emma wouldn't write a play?" Jane spread her hands wide. "I know little more than you do. My guess would be that this is less about the performance and more about Emma's involvement."

"In other words," Augustus translated, "the entire rigmarole is meant to demonstrate to the American envoy how very attached his cousin is to the house of Bonaparte."

It made a certain amount of sense. For centuries, powers had risen and fallen based on a marriage here, a friendship there.

Jane perched primly on her bench, her hands folded neatly in her lap. "Bonaparte believes in personal alliances. Look at the way he married his sister off to that Roman prince. He hasn't any spare siblings to espouse to Emma, but he can show the Americans that she's a valued part of his household."

"And that way," finished Augustus, seeing the pieces fall into place, "the Americans will be less likely to cut up rough when he makes his big announcement."

Jane nodded solemnly. "It is coming," she said. "Sooner rather than later."

Neither needed to specify. The rumors had been circulating for months that Bonaparte meant to trade his consular staff for an imperial diadem. Thus far, America had remained neutral in the great struggle between England and France, the sympathies of many tending towards the supposedly republican French who had aided them in their own fight for freedom.

Their Washington had turned down a crown; Bonaparte didn't intend to. There was no telling how the volatile colonials would react when Bonaparte jettisoned the last pretense of *liberté, égalité,* and *fraternité.*

Augustus sighed. "What else did she tell you about this masque?"

Jane didn't waste time reveling in her victory. "The details were sparse. All Emma said was that it was to be relatively brief, Talma was to direct, and there needs to be a singing part for Hortense. Oh, yes," she added, tapping her furled fan against her chin. "One more thing. Madame Bonaparte requested that the masque have a nautical theme."

That afterthought was about as accidental as the Sistine Chapel.

"Nautical," Augustus repeated. "As in having to do with the water and the sea."

Jane arranged her hands neatly in her lap, looking a bit like the cat who got the cream. "One might call it just a step away from naval."

Coincidence? Augustus would have liked to think so, but it was too much. Horace's hasty report was beginning to sound more and more credible. It would be just like Bonaparte to celebrate the completion of his invasion plans with a nautically themed masque.

It might be more than that, though. One could only assume that this mysterious device had something to do with the sea. As Augustus recalled, one of the primary features of a masque as a form of entertainment was the ingenious machinery involved. A masque was as much or more about spectacle as it was about verse.

Was Bonaparte planning to conceal his precious device among the props and pulleys of his theatre?

There was, as Jane had so sagely observed, only one way to find out.

"Why that weekend?" Augustus wondered aloud. "Why the Americans? If there is a device, why choose that gathering to test it?"

"It won't do us any good to speculate. Not without further information." Jane rose, her pale skirts whispering against the marble bench. "We should be getting in. Even your poetry can only run so long. People will start to wonder."

"Don't be silly. I have at least ten cantos left to go." He reached impulsively for Jane's hand. "If I can persuade Madame Delagardie to this collaboration, I could write in a part for you."

Jane twitched her hand away. "I don't think that would be a good idea."

"Why not?" The more he thought about the idea, the better it seemed. "An extra pair of hands makes light work."

Not to mention that Mme. Bonaparte's gardens at Malmaison were justifiably famous. With the moonlight silvering the gravel, and the scent of roses heavy in the air, they would be irresistible.

Jane navigated around him, her flat slippers whispering against the flagstones. "We agreed. No more communication than necessary. It's safer that way."

"People are used to seeing me following you about." Augustus tried to make a joke of it. "It's no secret that I'm mad about you. What man wouldn't craft a role for his muse?"

"Muses work best from a distance, Mr. Whittlesby."

The thorns of a potted rose clutched and tug at Augustus's dangling sleeves as he followed after her. He could hear the rending noise as the linen snagged and tore. "Miss Wooliston—Jane—"

"Where *is* Emma?" Jane turned quickly about, making a survey of the lighted windows. "You should make sure to catch her before she goes home. She has a cousin visiting. Another Mr. Livingston. There seem to be a number of them out and about."

Bother Mr. Livingston. Bother all of them. "Jane—"

If she saw Augustus's outstretched hand, she ignored it. "Where can Emma have got to? She was in the music room when we left her."

Augustus saw Mme. Delagardie's feathers before he saw her, bobbing not far from the music room window. She was standing by a tall man in a uniform tailored more for show than combat, his dark hair brushed and curled into the very latest style, a half-cape draped rakishly across one shoulder.

Jane spoke only one word, but it was imbued with enough venom to wither all the apples in Eden.

"Marston."

"You know him?"

Adventurer, opportunist, close friend of the First Consul's brother-in-law, Joachim Murat, Georges Marston had left Paris under a cloud not long after Miss Wooliston's arrival in Paris.

"Unfortunately. What is Marston doing bothering Emma?" Jane's brows drew together with concern. "Come along. We'd best rescue her." She started busily forward.

Augustus didn't follow. "Are you sure she needs rescuing?"

Jane paused. "Emma may be fierce, but she is small. And Marston isn't beyond using force. Strength of character only goes so far against brute strength." From the expression on her face, she wasn't thinking of Emma.

That wasn't what Augustus had meant.

"Didn't you know?"

Jane frowned. "Know what?"

Augustus would have thought all Paris had heard.

Perhaps not, though. It had been two years ago, before Jane's time. For all Jane's clandestine excursions, she was still an unmarried female. Paris might be more hedonistic than London, but even in France, there were certain topics one simply didn't mention in the presence of maiden ladies.

Augustus gestured towards Marston. "That he and your Emma were lovers."

Chapter 5

"Alack! For sin will out,
Howe'er so far we flee and hide;
To light it rise and know no doubt,
'Twill engulf ye like the rising tide."

—Augustus Whittlesby, *The Perils of the*
Pulchritudinous Princess of the Azure Toes,
Canto XII, 72–75

Georges Marston possessed himself of Emma's hand, bending to press a kiss to the back of it.

"Madame Delagardie," he murmured, and, for a wild moment, Emma thought she had escaped, that he intended to be civilized and let bygones be. Marston lifted his head, his full lips curving in a sensual smile. "Emma."

Or maybe not.

"Monsieur Marston," Emma said stiffly, repossessing herself of her hand. "I trust you have been well."

Marston's gaze dropped from her eyes, to her lips, and below. "So formal . . . Emma?"

It wasn't fair. Most of Paris accumulated amours as though they were going out of style. And she? She had committed one little indiscretion, followed by two years of absolutely impeccable behavior. Well, almost impeccable, unless one counted a little bit of recreational flirting, which hardly amounted to anything by any standards.

Didn't Marston have a more recent inamorata to bedevil with his attentions? Someone? Anyone?

Emma snuck a glance at Kort. Kort, she was quite sure, wouldn't understand the culture of casual carnality that had ruled the early days of the Consulate. Nor would he take "It was years ago, really, it was!" as an adequate defense.

Emma thought of her mother and her siblings back home and repressed the urge to shudder. There were some things beyond their comprehension or their forgiving, bits of her life they would never understand. It was all so simple for them. Marry, procreate, go to church on Sundays, attend the legislature in Albany, tend the tenant farmers, and pay calls on cousins. So simple and so easy.

No, no need for Kort to know about Georges. All she could do was attempt to finesse the situation as best she could and hope—oh, hopeless hope!—that Marston behaved himself or that Kort's French would prove inadequate for nuance.

Unfortunately, a leer was a leer and Emma was Emma in just about any language.

Feathers bouncing, Emma gestured to her cousin. "Monsieur Marston, I don't believe you know my cousin, Kortright Livingston. Kort, this is Mr. Georges Marston, who occupies a very interesting position of some sort in Mr. Bonaparte's army."

Kort stepped closer to Emma. "A very interesting position of some sort?"

"Oh, you know." Emma wafted her fan. "Military matters. Marching and things that go bang. What else is there to know?"

Kort ranged himself beside Emma, a self-appointed bodyguard. "Where are you stationed, Mr. Marston?"

"Colonel Marston," Marston corrected him. When had he received so dramatic a promotion? He had been a mere lieutenant when Emma had known him, three years before. Friendship with the First Consul's brother-in-law was a lucrative proposition. "I command part of the garrison at Boulogne."

It was, his voice implied, a very important post.

"It is," he added, "a very important post."

So much for modesty.

"How utterly lovely for you!" Emma babbled. "I'm sure you'll wish to be getting back there soon. One wouldn't want to leave it unattended. Well, it was all very lovely to see you again and all that, but I wouldn't want to keep you. Not when you have Boulogne to get back to."

She sounded, she realized, like the veriest pea brain. No matter. Her brains had never been the bit of her in which Marston took an interest. As for Kort, she'd rather he think her dim than debauched.

Marston took a step forward. "One has one's duty," he said, his voice low and seductive. "But that doesn't mean one cannot also take one's pleasure."

"Pleasure in a duty well done?" Emma prevaricated, backing into Kort, who gave a muffled grunt of pain as she stepped down heavily on his foot. "I'm sure that must be vastly gratifying. Oh, dear, I am sorry. Did I just mangle your toes?"

"I believe they're mostly intact," he said, in a slightly strangled voice. "Good Lord, Emma, did you attach spikes to the bottom of your sandals?"

"No, those went out last season." Making a strategic decision, Emma took a deep breath and turned to her cousin. "I suddenly find I am parched. Kort, would you be so kind as to fetch me a glass of punch?"

He gave her a strange look, but said, "Gladly. Is there anything else?"

"Oh, no, just the punch. The heat of the rooms, you know." Emma gestured vaguely with her fan. "I'm sure you'll find it."

Kort gave Marston a hard look.

To Emma, he said, "I'll be right back."

It was both a promise and a warning.

Marston's lips parted in a wolfish grin. "Take your time."

"Thank you, Kort!" Emma called after him. She waved. Kort frowned back, but went.

Marston stepped up beside her, lowering his head until his breath tickled her ear. "I had hoped to see you here."

"How fortunate for you," said Emma brightly, twisting away. One of her plumes brushed across Marston's nose, making him sneeze. "Now that you have achieved your object, you can go home."

Marston discreetly wiped the back of his hand across his nose. It was hard to look soulful when one's eyes were tearing, but he made a valiant effort. "To empty lodgings?"

Or a well-filled brothel. Georges had never been particularly particular in his tastes. That, at the time, had been one of his attractions. Emma had wanted nothing more than to lose herself in the potent distraction of flesh on flesh, with none of the messy complications attendant on emotions, channeling all her grief and confusion into the mindless pursuit of physical pleasure. And who better for that than Marston? It had been a brief and potent madness, over nearly as quickly as it had begun.

Two years hadn't changed him. He still wore his hair long, with long sideburns that curled down below his ears to his chin. There was a bit more braid on his uniform than there had been before, but it was still closely tailored to a form maintained by a rigorous regimen of regular exercise. His batman had rigged an ingenious contraption of weights and pulleys that went with him everywhere, counteracting the effects of overindulgence in food, wine, and women.

Whatever else one thought of Georges Marston, Emma admitted, he was indisputably a fine figure of a man. He exuded animal spirits and casual carnality. That had been part of it.

But, mostly, he had been as far as she could get from Paul, muscular where Paul had been wiry, fair where Paul had been dark, broad where Paul had been slender. Not even his best friends would have called Paul handsome. His charm had resided in his lively manner and the quick intelligence in his fine, dark eyes. He had been a dreamer, a talker, a charmer. He had certainly charmed her, straight out of Mme. Campan's school for young ladies.

Even now, the memory tore at her, not with the horrible rending force it once had, but with a dull ache, like a scratch half healed.

Marston would never believe her if she told him that his attraction had been less on his own merits and more because he was Not-Paul. She had been so angry at Paul, so angry at him for dying just when it seemed they finally had a chance.

Marston leaned closer, mistaking her absorption for interest. "It's been a long time, Emma."

So it had. "Two years," she said, suddenly feeling very old and very tired. Ten years since she had left New York, eight years since she had eloped with Paul. None of her happily-ever-afters had turned out the way she had intended them. "What do you want, Georges?"

She shouldn't have called him by his first name. Marston's eyes brightened with triumph.

"The pleasure of your company, of course," he said, reaching for her hand.

Emma drew her hand sharply away.

Marston's eyes narrowed. "You found pleasure in my company once. Or do I need to remind you?"

"I also wore puce," said Emma flippantly. "Tastes change."

She had never been particularly to his taste; even at the time, she had been aware of that. He had made no secret of all the ways in which he found her wanting: too small, too thin, too flat, too plain-spoken. The affair, such as it was, had been an aberration on both their parts. On her side, purely physical. On his—well, Emma had a good guess as to what his motives had been, and they had had little to do with her personal charms.

Marston crowded forward. Emma found herself regarding the buttons on his jacket. Brass, polished to the sheen of gold. He had been hard on his valets, demanding a level of sartorial perfection that would have daunted the staff of a duke. Darns and patches were anathema to him; it was new or it wasn't used at all. He had been appalled by the state of her dressing gowns, old and worn and comfortable.

Apparently, he was prepared to put that aside.

"We had some good times. Didn't we?" His voice dropped to a husky murmur. Emma gathered she was meant to find it seductive.

Once, she even had.

"They're paste," she said.

Georges blinked. "What?"

"The diamonds," Emma said patiently. "They're paste. If you want to be kept, find someone else to keep you."

Marston mustered a halfhearted guffaw. "You will have your little joke."

Who was joking?

He followed along after her as she began to make her way through the crowded room, train looped over one wrist, nodding to acquaintances as she went.

He dodged around a dowager who had planted herself firmly in the middle of the room. "May I call on you?"

"I'd rather you didn't," Emma said honestly.

Marston's hands descended on her shoulders, holding her still. His fingers slid beneath the silver trim of her dress, seeking out the vulnerable hollows between muscle and bone. "You're still angry about Mimi, aren't you?"

"Was that her name?" She had never bothered to find out.

She had been more grateful than angry. Finding her lover actively engaged beneath the skirts of a maid had jarred her awake, out of the strange, waking nightmare in which she had been trapped since Paul's death. It had been the jolt she needed to get away from Marston and out of Paris. She had gone back, as she always did, to Malmaison, taking long walks through the sprawling parklands, as she tried to make sense of what her life had become and what she wanted to be. She had been fifteen when she eloped with Paul, too young to understand that marriage was not, in itself, a guarantee of future happiness. Just when they had finally come to terms, just when they had begun to understand each other, Paul had died. Emma had been left a widow at twenty, angry and confused, seeking easy consolation.

Marston had been easy, but he hadn't been the consolation she needed. It hadn't taken long for Emma to realize that. Mimi, or whatever her name was, had provided a much-needed excuse to break off an affair that Emma already knew to be a mistake.

"She was nothing to me," Marston insisted, misunderstanding Emma's comment. "Not like you."

"How very lowering for her," remarked Emma, and saw Marston's lack of comprehension. He wouldn't have thought of Mimi having feelings. She was just an object of convenience.

As he had been for Emma.

Despite herself, Emma felt a stirring of guilt. She had known what he was when she slept with him; she had gone to him because of it, seeking the distraction of the physical, without messy emotional ties. She had used him as much as he had used her, if not more. She owed him the courtesy of kindness, if nothing else.

Removing his hand from her shoulder, Emma pressed it briefly between both of hers. "I wish you all the best, Georges. Truly, I do. I hope you have all the success for which you could wish in Boulogne. Glories and triumphs and all that sort of thing."

"The only reward I want is right here in Paris." His eyes smoldered. "You."

"I'm sorry, Georges." Releasing his hand, Emma stepped back. "I'd get bored sitting on your mantelpiece."

There it was again, that flicker of confusion. There had been a lot of that in the brief time they had been together. She had always known he thought her a little odd. She'd never done well with being seen and not heard.

"Mantelpiece?"

Emma shook her head. It wasn't worth explaining. "Good-bye, Georges."

This wasn't what he expected. He took a step forward, crowding her back into the embrace of a garishly painted papier-mâché model of a mummy case. The mummy's crossed arms bit into Emma's back through the thin fabric of her dress.

"You don't mean that," he said.

"Ah, monsieur!"

Linen swished past the periphery of her vision. Emma sucked in a deep, relieved breath as Marston stumbled back, glaring at the source of the interruption.

Unperturbed, Augustus Whittlesby raised a hand to one ear. "What is this I hear? My instincts inform me that you are in desperate need of the offices of a poet." He smiled benignly at the infuriated Marston. "One should never try to woo without one."

"*N*o one," said Mme. Delagardie firmly, "is doing any wooing. Monsieur Marston was just leaving."

The man didn't look like he had any intention of leaving. In fact, he was quite firmly planted in front of Mme. Delagardie.

For all Jane's touching faith that the gossips must have exaggerated, it wasn't looking good for Emma Delagardie. She had got rid of the cousin. That, to Augustus, was the crucial point. No woman created the conditions for a tête-à-tête unless she wanted one, and Delagardie and Marston were very tête-à-tête indeed. As Augustus had watched, she had led Marston on a chase through the crowded drawing room, drawing him along after her, like a comet trailing its train, her spangles glittering as she glanced back over her shoulder at him.

Just friends? Augustus thought not. He had seen the way Marston's hands had disappeared beneath the trim of her dress, massaging her shoulders with the familiarity of long intimacy. He had seen the way Marston leaned in to speak to her, his lips practically devouring her ear. His pantaloons were tailored so tightly, Augustus could practically hear them squeak as he bent over.

If Marston was after Delagardie, that was all the more reason to move quickly.

Marston wouldn't be pursuing her without a reason. Marston liked them dark haired and generously endowed. Mme. Delagardie was fair and slight. It might just be that Marston was being dunned by his tailor again and thought a former lover, revisited, might be moved to generosity. The blaze of diamonds that adorned Mme. Delagardie's person bespoke a careless affluence. Marston wouldn't be the first to use a rich widow to refill his coffers; it was a trope as old as Chaucer.

On the other hand, there were plenty of other rich women out there, taller ones, bustier ones, ones more convenient to Boulogne. For Marston to have hied himself all the way to Paris to a house from which he had been banned, he must have a reason more compelling than an overdue boot maker's bill.

"Should you be in need of assistance," Augustus directed himself to Marston, "I should be more than delighted to convey your amorous sentiments into verse for the delectation of the object of your affection. For a small but reasonable remuneration, of course." He plucked delicately at one flowing sleeve. "I call it Service à la Cyrano."

"Service à la what?" Marston appeared less than overjoyed by the interruption. One might even call his tone belligerent.

To Augustus's surprise, Mme. Delagardie answered for him. "Cyrano. In Rostand's play, Cyrano de Bergerac takes on the wooing of the fair Roxanne on behalf of a handsome but . . . less verbally inclined officer."

Augustus inclined his head to Marston. "Poetry, monsieur, has long been the food of love. Perhaps you might like a small measure of assistance from a chef of long experience?"

Marston was not amused. "When I need help, I'll ask for it."

"Perhaps you ought to ask the lady." Augustus directed a flowing bow in Mme. Delagardie's direction. "A canto does more than cologne can to win the affections of a lady to a man."

A muffled snort emerged from behind Mme. Delagardie's fan.

Reddening, Marston turned to Mme. Delagardie, deliberately blocking out Augustus. "We can resume this later. Alone."

Mme. Delagardie snapped her fan shut. "You needn't bother. I shouldn't want to put you out. Good-bye, Monsieur Marston."

Marston pressed a last, lingering kiss to her palm. *"Au revoir, Emma."*

His tone was that of a lover, but his eyes were as calculating as a Cheapside moneylender's. That was Marston for you, venal to the core.

As for Mme. Delagardie, she watched her former lover go, but her expression was anything but amorous. In fact, if Augustus hadn't known better, he would have said she appeared distinctly annoyed. Her lips were tight and her fan beat an impatient tattoo against her hip.

"Bother," she said, with feeling.

"If I was interrupting . . ." Augustus fished.

Mme. Delagardie blinked, as though she had forgotten he was there. Augustus found this unaccountably annoying. He had large, flowing sleeves and carried an oversize paper scroll. He wasn't exactly inconspicuous. And yet he appeared to have entirely escaped the notice of Mme. Delagardie.

"Oh, Mr. Whittlesby," she said, confirming his initial impression. "Did you want something?"

"Me? To what wants could a humble servant of the muse possibly lay claim?" When he thought she had suffered enough, Augustus relaxed his pose. "It is not my wants, lady, but yours that bring me to your side on this fateful eve."

"I would have called it more fearful than fateful," muttered Mme. Delagardie.

"Fearfully fateful, then," said Augustus. "Flora's fairest flower informs me that you might have need of the assistance of an amanuensis for your amateur endeavors in the realm of Thespis."

"My what?"

It was late and Augustus was tired. "I hear you're writing a masque," he said bluntly. "I thought you might desire my aid."

Mme. Delagardie was silent for a moment. He had her attention now, but not necessarily in a good way. "I see," she said, and she sounded surprisingly weary. "Are you offering to hire yourself out? Is this another sideline, like the Service de Cyrano?"

Would she be more likely to collaborate with him if she thought she was meant to pay for the pleasure? Some people put worth only in those things to which they could set a price.

"Even a poor poet must survive." Something in her expression warned him that this was not a tack to pursue. Hastily, he added, "But in this case, I should be delighted to offer my expertise for the sake of art and art alone."

"What are you suggesting?" she asked.

"A collaboration. Your ideas, my verse. Together, we can craft a masque to transcend the very heavens of invention!"

"You have," she said, "a remarkable knack for statements that sound grandiose but say nothing at all."

"Precisely the talent one needs for a good theatrical production," Augustus said heartily.

Mme. Delagardie tapped her furled fan against her chin. "You might be right, at that," she said. "It's all about illusion, isn't it? Illusion and spectacle."

He had her. He could tell. Ha. He had told Jane this would be easy.

"Spectacle of the most spectacular," he promised, feeling like an unlikely Mephistopheles luring a female Faustus to his bidding. "All Paris will be talking of it for years to come."

"Years?" The tone was light, but the words were bitter. "Hours, more likely. Praise fades fast; only opprobrium lasts. Odd how memory comes and goes."

"Like a chameleon," said Augustus solemnly, "which changes color at a whim, now this, now that, no more constant than a lady's style of hat. It lights one's dreams, red, gold, and green."

"Er, yes," said Mme. Delagardie. "Something like that."

Perhaps the chameleon had been a bit much. "When shall we start?" Augustus asked. "Miss Wooliston informs me that time is of the essence."

"Miss Wooliston?" Mme. Delagardie's plumes wobbled. "Was it she who told you to speak to me?"

"She is," said Augustus reverently, "ever gracious and ever good. How could I refuse her so small a task?"

"Yes," agreed Mme. Delagardie. "She is. All of those things. But in this case, somewhat overzealous. Your offer is very kind, but I have no intention of writing the masque."

"But—"

"If you'll excuse me, my cousin wants me. Good evening, Mr. Whittlesby."

With a vague flutter of her fan, she wafted off in a cloud of silver spangles, in the direction of an ill-dressed man with his hair clubbed back in an old-fashioned queue. It was, Augustus had to admit, very neatly done. She had cut him off so quickly, he had no time to object. He was simply left standing there, mouth open on an unvoiced argument, wondering what in the devil he had done. He had been so sure he had her where he wanted her. How hard could it be, after all? She was a silly flibbertigibbet of a society matron, easily manipulable.

Only not.

Her cousin extended a glass half full of a somewhat murky liquid. He spoke in English, or the version of the language that the colonials recognized as such. "I didn't find your punch, but I managed to persuade someone to make some."

Mme. Delagardie smiled fondly up at him, but made no move to take the glass. "Thank you, Kort. Would you be hideously offended if, after all your valiant efforts, I declined to drink it? All I want is to find my carriage and go home."

"Shall I escort you back?"

"No, stay. Enjoy yourself." She favored him with a fleeting smile. "The night is still very young by Paris standards."

"But late by New York ones. I would be more than happy—"

"Please," she said, cutting him off as effectively as she had done Augustus. "I intend to curl up against the squabs and nap, and you'll only be in the way of that. Unless you're volunteering to serve as pillow?"

"All right," her cousin said reluctantly. "Before you go, though, I nearly forgot to give you this."

Fishing in his waistcoat pocket, he dragged out a piece of paper, loosely folded into thirds that promptly flapped open as he offered it to Mme. Delagardie.

"Sorry. Wrong one." He hastily stuffed it back in his pocket. Rooting about some more, he extracted a second sheet, passing it to his cousin, who accepted it with a murmur of thanks. "I'll call on you tomorrow, once you've had time to read it."

Emma Delagardie lifted a hand and touched a finger lightly to his cheek. "I shall look forward to it. Good night, Kort."

She tucked away the second paper in her reticule too quickly for Augustus to view what was written on it. He had, however, got a fairly good view of the first document, too loosely folded for privacy. It hadn't been a letter, but a drawing, marked out in brown ink with numbers and other scribbling along the sides.

In other words, a diagram. A diagram of some variety of mechanism.

Or device.

Chapter 6

There was a large device squatting smack in the middle of the dining room table.

I had taken my fair share of art history classes in undergrad, but it still took me a few moments to identify it as a projector. It was much larger and snazzier than the 1950s relics commonly used by undergrad art history departments, sleek and shiny. It emitted a faint humming noise, almost a purr.

In my own defense, one doesn't generally expect to encounter a projector on a dining room table, in between the silver and the Spode. It made a rather odd centerpiece.

But, then, it was all rather odd. I'd never actually used the dining room—Colin and I ate in the comfortably shabby kitchen, with its mustard yellow fixtures and battered pine table—but I'd wandered my way through it a time or two, admiring the elegant appointments and the paired portraits of Lord and Lady Uppington that loomed on either side of the room, presiding over the long mahogany table in paint as they must once have done in the flesh. It didn't look as it would have in their day. As Colin had informed me a while back, the house had been extensively redone in the late nineteenth century by an ancestor infatuated with the Arts and Crafts movement, which explained the heavy William Morris draperies over the windows and the Pre-Raphaelite murals on the walls—although I did wonder whether Persephone eating the pomegranate was really an appropriate scene for a dining room. What sort of message did that send? Sample the fruit plate and go straight to hell?

For tonight, that might not be so far off. Especially not with Colin and Jeremy in the same room. I didn't like to think how Colin would react when he saw what the DreamStone people had done to his dining room.

It wasn't just the projector plopped in the spot where the silver epergne usually presided. Bland, caterer-supplied china had supplanted the nicked and faded Spode pattern picked out by a late-nineteenth-century Selwick. Additions had been placed to turn the long table from an oval to a T, with microphones set in the central places at the top. Worst of all, a square white screen covered the portrait of Lord Uppington. Lady Uppington, hanging safely behind the head table, had been left unencumbered, but she looked distinctly put out at Lord Uppington's plight.

These people didn't know what trouble they were courting. I wouldn't put it past her to come swooping down from the afterlife and rearrange them all to her personal satisfaction. And direct the movie while she was at it. That was just the sort of woman Lady Uppington was.

That's the thing with reading peoples' papers. You start to feel as if you've known them personally, even if they've been dead for two hundred years.

Even with an extensive library at my disposal, it had taken me several hours to track down Emma Morris Delagardie. Fortunately, at least one of Colin's ancestors had taken an interest in American history, although books on Burr and Benedict Arnold predominated. Based on the mentions in Jane's letters to Henrietta, I knew that Emma Delagardie was collaborating with that tedious poet, Augustus Whittlesby, on a masque to be performed at Malmaison; that she was related, in some degree, to the current American envoy, Robert Livingston; and that she had a cousin named Kortright.

It was the Kortright name that gave me the clue I needed. With a little scrounging, I found the connection. James Monroe, not yet president, had been envoy to Paris in 1794. He had taken with him his wife, Elizabeth Kortright Monroe, his daughter Eliza—and his niece, Emma.

There was only one reference to the niece, a throwaway line. Monroe had enrolled his daughter, Eliza, and his niece, Emma, in Mme. Campan's school for young ladies, where Eliza formed a life-long friendship with Hortense de Beauharnais, whose portrait could still be seen at the Monroe plantation, Ash Lawn.

And that was all. For everything else, I was reliant on the incomplete tidbits of gossip in Jane's letters, the gossipy, chatty, possibly lying letters that she sent to Henrietta, designed to both convey and conceal information. Was Emma with them? Against them? What was her real connection with Georges Marston?

I'd encountered Marston before, in my original researches. He hovered on the fringes of respectable society, milking his friendship with Napoleon's brother-in-law, Joachim Murat, for promotion, while, on the side, he had been running a lucrative little smuggling ring that might or might not have been selling secrets as well as silk and brandy.

In his use of personal relationships for his own ends, Marston reminded me a lot of Colin's sister's ex-boyfriend, Nigel Dempster, curator of the Vaughn Collection. Like me, Dempster was on the trail of the Pink Carnation.

And, like me, he had been willing to date a Selwick to get his hands on it.

It wasn't the same, I told myself. Colin had been—well, an accident. I had already been granted access to a bunch of the family papers by his great-aunt Arabella before he had burst onto the scene, and the attraction between us had taken both of us very much by surprise. I already had enough material for three dissertations. I was dating Colin because I wanted to be with Colin.

But for how much longer?

I still hadn't answered Blackburn's e-mail about the head TF position. Damn. I chewed on the side of a nail. I really, really hadn't wanted to think about that.

"Excuse me." A girl with a clipboard was hovering just inside the door to the dining room. She ventured a tentative smile, an I'm-so-sorry-but smile. "You're not supposed to be in here. It's registered personnel only."

Registered personnel?

I must have given her a look, because she fidgeted with the metal bit at the top of her clipboard. "You know, production staff, caterers, people connected with the family. So I'm going to have to ask you to leave."

Unless this was like hospital admissions, where you had to be officially engaged before anyone would tell you anything, I considered myself pretty darn connected. Besides, picking up someone's socks and taking turns with the washing up had to count as a domestic partnership.

I peered over her shoulder at the chart. "I should be on there. I'm"—the owner's girlfriend? Researcher in residence? Chief cook and bottle washer?—"Eloise Kelly," I finished lamely.

She rustled efficiently through several sheets of closely printed pages, looking up apologetically as she came to the end of it. "I'm afraid I don't see you here. Unless you spell your name some weird way?"

"Nope," I said. "It's just Kelly, spelled the usual way. No Qs or silent Ns or anything like that."

She checked again and shook her head. "Sorry. Still nothing. Are you with the magazine people?"

Now there was a magazine involved, too? Colin wasn't going to like that.

"No, I'm with Colin. The owner," I specified when the Dream-Stone representative looked blank. "The one who keeps trying to make sure that no one sets the rosebushes on fire."

Comprehension dawned. "Unhappy-looking guy in a green jacket?"

"That's the one."

Her face brightened. She grinned at me, girl to girl. "He's cute."

"Thanks." I wasn't sure why I was taking the credit here, since his looks weren't something I'd had a hand in. He had his mother to thank for that, although he also had her to thank for Jeremy and the DreamStone invasion, so maybe not so much. I shrugged. "I like him."

Which, as any woman knows, is girl-speak for "I'm ridiculously over the moon about him, but not like I'm going to tempt fate by admitting to that."

Shoving the clipboard under one arm, the girl stuck out a hand. "I'm Cate, by the way. Cate Kartowsky. That's Cate with a *C*."

"A cate conformable to other household cates?" When she gave me a blank look, I said, "Sorry. I was having a Shakespeare moment. Isn't this production supposed to be—?"

"I was a communications major," said Cate. "With a minor in poli-sci. Lots of Rawls and Nozick, not so much on the Shakespeare."

"I do English history," I said. "So the Shakespeare sort of creeps in."

Cate nodded knowledgeably. These things happened. "I guess we'll all be getting our Shakespeare this week, right?"

"Help me out here. Someone told me it was *Much Ado About Nothing*, but in Regency costume?"

"You've got it," said Cate. She leaned closer, making sure no one was listening. "I know, it sounds ridiculous. But there's the whole

Austen craze, and Micah wanted to capitalize on that. He also wants cred for doing Shakespeare. There was some version of *Much Ado About Nothing* that made a big stir—"

"With Robert Sean Leonard," I said. "And Kenneth Branagh. We were all in love with Robert Sean Leonard as Claudio when I was in Upper School."

Cate looked blank. It made me feel very old. I was only twenty-seven. Should I really be feeling this ancient?

"Anyway," she said, brushing Robert Sean Leonard aside, "Micah figured that if they were each successful on their own, he could put the two together, and, bingo! Instant box office hit."

Or instant box office flop. "Is it true that there's going to be singing and dancing?"

"Only in the Regency ballroom scenes," said Cate comfortably. "Originally, there was going to be a whole rap music thing, but the execs didn't buy the Regency rap idea."

Thank goodness for that. I tried to picture Augustus Whittlesby rapping and, scarily, almost succeeded.

"We'll be doing a workshop on English country dances for the extras later this week if you want me to sneak you in," said Cate. "It should be fun."

"Thanks. I'll think about it."

She gave me a lopsided grin. "Bring your boyfriend. We're making the guys wear breeches."

It would take something a little stronger than gin to get Colin to go along with that. "Good luck with that," I said.

Cate brandished her clipboard. "What did you say your name was again? I'll add you to the list."

There's nothing like boy-talk for creating instant friendship. We were now officially Buddies.

"Eloise," I said. "Eloise with an *E*."

"Gotcha." Balancing the clipboard expertly on one forearm, she wrote down my name on the bottom of the list in firm, tidy letters. "Kelly, right? No *N*s or *Q*s."

"Right, right, and right." As she flipped up the top page to add me to the bottom, I caught a glimpse of another document below. "Is that the seating chart for tonight?"

"What? Oh, over there? Yes. You wouldn't believe the trouble we had working that out. There's all sorts of weird stuff with the family. I heard that—"

Remembering who I was again, she broke off, flushing guiltily.

Trying to salvage the situation, I said, "Trust me, you just don't want to know. This bunch makes Agamemnon and Clytemnestra look well balanced and functional." I gestured to the seating chart. "Do you mind if I take a look?"

"Knock yourself out," said Cate cheerfully, relinquishing the clipboard to me. "Just don't change anything or I'm screwed."

"That's always annoying, isn't it?" I said absently, scanning the minutely detailed chart. "When people move place cards around. I have some cousins who like to do that. It makes my grandmother apoplectic."

The writing on the chart was so tiny, it was like trying to read the fine print on a postage stamp. It took a fair amount of squinting and guesswork to make out my own name. Jeremy had put me all the way down at the foot of the table, twenty people down from Colin.

"Thanks, Jeremy," I muttered. "You're a prince among men."

"What?" said Cate, who was taking advantage of her temporary liberation from the clipboard to scroll through the accumulated texts on her mobile.

"Nothing! Just talking to myself. Occupational hazard of spending too much time in libraries."

Either Jeremy was getting back at me for Paris—he hadn't been pleased when I'd backed Colin in protesting the invitation to the film crew—or he was employing a simple divide-and-conquer technique.

I haven't said much about Colin's family, have I? To call it complicated would be to do it a disservice. Colin's family makes the tangled bureaucracy of late medieval Byzantium look like a model of efficiency and clarity.

Jeremy was Colin's mother's husband, yes (and I dare you to say that three times fast), but he was more than that. He was also Colin's cousin. It was a tangled, messy story, and no one had been particularly eager to fill me in on the details, but the bare bones of it were that Jeremy, ten years Colin's mother's junior, had run off with his cousin William's wife while William lay dying a miserable death from the cancer that was slowly eating him from the inside out.

Somehow, when it happens in fiction, it sounds better. Helen and Menelaus, Iseult and Mark of Cornwall, all those beautiful women of legend bound to older men. We cheer them on when they run off with their young lover, when Helen escapes with Paris, and Tristan and Iseult quaff their potion, even though both leave chaos and tumult behind. It's romantic. It's dramatic. And it's all once upon a time.

When it's your boyfriend's mother who's run off with the younger relative of her husband, it's not quite that romantic anymore. Instead, it just seems rather sordid.

That was all a matter of record. Then there was the other stuff, the emotional undercurrents I could only begin to guess at. There was no way of securing any sort of confirmation, but I would have been willing to wager a pretty high sum that Jeremy, the child of a cadet branch of the family, bitterly resented Colin for inheriting Selwick Hall.

Oh, I wouldn't deny that Colin didn't exactly love Jeremy either. Even if there weren't the horrible shadow of the wrong that Jeremy had done Colin's father, they were just fundamentally different character types. Colin was tersely polite with Jeremy, as the situation required, but he was still polite.

On Jeremy's side, however, it was something more. I had seen him gloating over Colin's discomfort in Paris, drinking in his distress, like a ghoul scenting blood. There had been something in Jeremy's expression, something behind his practiced social smile, that had made my skin crawl. There was hate there, real and bitter hate. If he could make Colin unhappy, he would, even in something as petty and as simple as moving me to the other side of the table.

Despite my promise to Cate, I was sorely tempted to move a few place cards around.

I didn't bother to check out the other names on the chart. Cate had finished with her text and was waiting patiently for her baby back.

I handed back the clipboard. "I'd better go change. Thanks." As an afterthought, I added, "Will you be at the dinner?"

"Me?" Cate shook her head. "I'm just the clipboard girl."

"Is that a job description? Like gaffer or best boy?" I had no idea what either of those actually meant, but I couldn't resist throwing them out there anyway. Yes, I read the credits like anyone else.

Cate grinned at me. She had a cute, chipmunk thing going, dimples in both cheeks. "Technically, my title is intern. But that generally translates to clipboard girl. Sometimes I get to make coffee."

"Are you doing this because you want to be in film?"

"Journalism. Political reporting, that sort of thing. But I have a friend who has a cousin who knew someone at DreamStone, so . . ."

"It can't hurt to have it on the résumé," I finished for her.

"I would have preferred CNN, but, hey, at least I get to spend some time in England. So it's not all bad."

"Bad plumbing, strange weather, woolly hats . . ." And Colin. England did have its consolations.

"I haven't seen the hats yet," said Cate. I couldn't tell if she was joking.

"Look, if you need anything, just let me know." On an impulse, I added, "If you'd like, I'll show you where we keep the secret Internet connection. Just don't tell anyone else."

"That would be great," she said.

"Hey, can you do me a favor? No, nothing that major. Just, if you have a chance, let the other film people know that the West Wing and the library are off-limits? We've put up signs, but they don't seem to be doing much. Someone messed around with my notes earlier today and I'd rather they didn't. There was also a shower walk-in incident," I added.

Cate winced. "I'll do what I can. I can send out a memo, if that helps. That's one of the things I get to do. Big power."

"Excuse me!" Someone was calling down the hall. "Miss! Er . . ."

"Cate," said Cate, without displaying any sign of impatience. She turned in the doorway to face whoever it was, blocking my view.

I'm lousy with faces, but I'm good with voices. This one sounded familiar. But it wasn't a voice I'd expected to hear at Selwick Hall. In fact, I would have been willing to say it was one of the last voices I'd expect to hear at Selwick Hall.

No. I must have gotten it wrong. It had been a long day.

"Cate," said the voice, all plummy rounded vowels, just a little too pointedly posh to be credible. "Can you tell me where I can find cocktails?"

Cate was all efficiency. "Cocktails will be in the long salon in half an hour." She consulted her clipboard, which included, among its other amenities, a plan of Selwick Hall, floor by floor. "That's the drawing room that runs along the far side of the house. Just go straight to the back. You won't be able to miss it."

"Thank you, . . . Cate."

The smarm was palpable even down the length of the hall. I didn't need to crane to see over Cate to know who it was. As improbable as it was, as unlikely and unseemly and any other *un* one cared to contribute, he had somehow gained admission to Selwick Hall.

Even so, I felt the need to ask. Just in case. Hope springs eternal, and all that. He couldn't be the only man with a pretentious accent in the greater Sussex area.

I poked Cate in the shoulder. "Who was that?"

"Oh, Nigel?" Cate made a face, eloquent of disapproval. "That's Nigel Dempster. He's our historical consultant."

Damn.

Chapter 7

"Come away with me," the necromancer called,
"Away across the perfumed sea.
For wonders I'll have for you there,
If only you'll come away with me."
—Augustus Whittlesby, *The Perils of the*
Pulchritudinous Princess of the Azure Toes,
Canto XII, 172–175

When Emma had given orders that Georges Marston be barred from her house, she had neglected to mention Augustus Whittlesby.

In the throng that constituted her Friday morning salon, his habitually sloppy attire hardly stood out. Morning, of course, was interpreted broadly. It was past two, but many of those present were first breaking their fast on the food set out in the octagonal salon. Friday morning at Mme. Delagardie's had become a staple for a certain sort of Parisian. There were statesmen, artists, ladies of fashion, longtime followers of the Bonaparte ascendency, and newcomers to Paris.

Since Mr. Whittlesby had never bothered to attend one of Emma's Fridays, she had a fairly shrewd guess as to what had drawn him here this time, and it wasn't her chef's pastries. He managed to make his way to her without tripping, quite the feat given the size of his sleeves and the otherworldly tilt of his head.

"Does that hurt?" she asked, in lieu of hello.

"Do you mean the endless ache of my perpetually broken heart?"

"No. I meant having your head at that angle. I'm sure the muse wouldn't mind coming down a bit, just for the sake of your joints."

"Ah, Madame Delagardie! It is plain you have never known the unremitting servitude of the muse! The grueling apprenticeship one must endure! Which is precisely why you are in such perilous need of my aid in penning your theatrical masterpiece."

"I haven't agreed to pen any such thing," Emma said, "so I'm afraid your services shan't be required. Do try the brioche, Mr. Whittlesby. I imagine even humble supplicants to the muse stand in need of sustenance from time to time."

She tried to move away, but Mr. Whittlesby stepped in front of her. "We sip on the nectar of the Graces. Can't I persuade you to join me in drinking from their cup?"

"I make it a practice to avoid all libations this early in the day." With relief, Emma spotted her cousin Robert Livingston, the American envoy, making his way across the room. "I do beg your pardon, Mr. Whittlesby. I believe my cousin Livingston is trying to attract my attention."

He wasn't, but it would do. The claims of a poet had to rate below those of the American minister to Paris, the man who had negotiated the sale of Louisiana to America for a sum that would keep Mme. Bonaparte in diamonds for some time.

She left Whittlesby standing by himself, frowning after her.

Wiggling away through the throng, Emma extended a gloved hand to her cousin. They weren't an embracing sort of family. "Welcome, cousin Robert! My humble salon is honored by your presence."

"Impertinent child," said cousin Robert equably. He didn't pinch her cheek, for which Emma was deeply appreciative. Her rouge would have come off on his glove. "Do you imagine I have nothing better to do than gad about like you?"

Emma batted her eyelashes at him. "But I gad so well."

Cousin Robert shook his head, only half jokingly. "What your parents would say . . ."

Emma tilted her fan to form a screen for them. "I won't tell if you won't."

Like so many gentlemen of a certain age, cousin Robert rather enjoyed being flirted with by a pretty young thing. All within the bounds of propriety, of course. Paris propriety, that was. At home, manners and mores were different. Emma remembered that, as through a glass darkly. She wasn't sure she would know how to get on there; not anymore.

"I know Mr. Fulton needs no introduction to you," cousin Robert said, indicating the man beside him.

"Genius never needs an introduction," said Emma, lowering her fan. Her cousin's protégé had been in Paris nearly as long as she had. His panorama had created something of a stir several years back, making him all the rage—until the next rage, that was. "How go the plans for the ship without sails?"

"Steamboat," Fulton corrected. He seemed to fizzle with energy, from his tightly curled hair all the way down to the bottom of his boots, which shifted impatiently on the faux marble floor. He bent a reproachful look on Emma. "I know *you* know better, Madame Delagardie."

"Flattery, flattery, Mr. Fulton." Emma sighed. "I should have thought a man of science would be above such things."

Fulton turned to cousin Robert. "Your cousin, sir, has the most wonderful understanding of the mechanics of hydraulics."

More hard-won than wonderful. Engineering hadn't come easily to her. She had always been more a creature of words than of charts and figures. But hydraulics had been Paul's passion. Don Quixote had his windmills; Paul had an expanse of marshland he was determined to transform into habitable and arable land, freeing his tenants of the crippling diseases bred by the swamps. It had been a noble project, but one that had absorbed so much of his time and attention that there had been little left over for the cosseting of a child bride, and a spoiled child bride, at that.

She had accused him of caring only for her dowry, of wooing her with lies, before storming off to Paris to slake her hurt feelings in a round of amusements.

Poor Paul. Poor both of them. It hadn't been all a lie, although it had taken her years to see that. In his own way, Paul had loved her. Those long afternoons in the garden outside Mme. Campan's, the poetry, the clandestine letters, he had meant them all. He had reveled as much as she in the high drama of romance. She could see that now.

Once the courtship was over, though, he had settled again into his normal life, into his estate at Carmagnac and drainage and the million and one responsibilities of land ownership, while Emma waited fruitlessly for the poetry that had gone silent. It had been easy enough to assume the worst, that he had, as everyone claimed, married her for her purse, especially as their evenings devolved from caresses into recriminations and from recriminations into full-blown fights. Later, bit by bit, she had pored over his notes and charts, puzzling over the mysterious mechanics of it all, making painstaking sense of the rough sketches of pumps and pulleys and the mathematics that went with them. Once she convinced him she was in earnest this time, that she meant to stay, he had explained it to her, Paul slowly and patiently remedying the defects of a ramshackle education, sitting hour after hour with her in his study, going over facts that must have seemed as elementary to him as the difference between Mozart and Beaumarchais was to her.

It had been a renaissance for their marriage, as well as for Paul's beloved Carmagnac. A second chance, after so much hurt and confusion and misunderstanding.

Paul's picture gazed blindly above her head from its position over the mantel, frozen forever at thirty-seven. He had been painted in his study at Carmagnac, surrounded by the implements of his vocation. Behind him, the treatises he had so painstakingly collected and shipped out across the marsh stood in neat rows in the bookcases behind him. The painter had caught Paul's surroundings, but not his expression. The black eyes that had been so bright and lively in life were flat and dull on canvas, staring blankly out at the viewer. Like a death mask.

A premonition? She had commissioned the portrait as an anniversary present, shortly before he took ill, the first present she had ever bought him—and the last.

Why did he have to go and die just as they were beginning to understand each other? He had died, leaving her with Carmagnac, a great deal of abstruse knowledge about hydraulics, and a wealth of hurt and confusion.

Fulton bowed gallantly in Emma's direction. "If I were wise, I would make it a practice to consult Madame Delagardie on all my inventions. Her observations are always invaluable."

With an effort, Emma yanked herself back to the present. "Pooh. It takes little understanding to be shown a drawing and nod one's head in all the appropriate places. I bow entirely to your expertise, Mr. Fulton, and can only extend my thanks. The new pump is a vast improvement."

Cousin Robert dealt her an avuncular pat on the shoulder. "I imagine it must be hard for you to leave Carmagnac," he said kindly. "Having put so much work into it."

"Not really," said Emma. "I never did spend terribly much time there, except when Paul—well. I'll go down to visit again at harvest. Otherwise, if there are problems, Monsieur le Maire knows to send for me here. Somehow, requests for funds never get lost in the post." She made a droll face.

Cousin Robert failed to respond in kind. "Harvest?" he said. "But how is that possible?"

Emma raised both brows. "By the grace of God and good weather? That is the usual way. Some friends were kind enough to make some suggestions for improvements, which I sent along to my steward. I've become quite the farmer. Mother would be so amused."

Something was still bothering cousin Robert. His brows had drawn together over his nose. "But you won't be here to see it, surely? Not when the ship sails in June."

"Ship?" Emma turned back to Fulton. "Are you planning to kidnap me on your steamboat, Mr. Fulton, and bear me off to a Barbary pirate's harem?"

"Quite amusing, my dear," said cousin Robert, "but I meant your return to New York."

"My—?" For once in her life, Emma found herself at a loss for easy banter. "My what?"

Cousin Robert appeared oblivious to her imminent asphyxiation. "Young Kortright told me," he said comfortably. "I'd say I was sorry to see you go, but as I'll be leaving, too, I'll be glad for it. You'll have to come visit us at Clermont once you're settled."

"I—what?"

"You'll be returning to Belvedere, I take it? Much better than setting up an establishment in the city. New York isn't like Paris, you know."

Cousin Robert should know. He had been involved in the public life of the city for years, as recorder and then as chancellor. Emma doubted there was an official capacity in which he hadn't served. But that was beside the point. Someone was obviously suffering from a misapprehension.

"I do beg your pardon, cousin Robert," she said apologetically.

"But I believe there must have been some mistake. I have no intention of removing from Paris."

Cousin Robert frowned. "Young Kortright seemed quite sure of it. He said the passage was already arranged."

"For someone else, then." Rumor spread so quickly in Paris. "I have no intention of going anywhere at all. Other than to Malmaison with you, of course."

"Best speak to young Kortright, then." Cousin Robert scanned the room, his eyes falling on someone near the door. "There he is. He seemed quite certain that you would be accompanying him back to New York in June. Said he was here at your parents' request."

Kort was awkwardly examining a statue of Venus, curved and dimpled and wearing little more than a wisp of marble veiling. He looked out of place in her salon.

Thirteen-year-old Emma would have desired nothing better than to be swept off her feet and onto a ship by her adored cousin.

Twenty-five-year-old Emma smelled a rat.

"Oh, really?" murmured Emma. She flashed a charming smile at cousin Robert and Mr. Fulton. "If you will excuse me, gentlemen, I really must have a little talk with *young Kortright*. We apparently have much to discuss."

As she swept away, with the maximum swish her morning gown would afford, she heard her cousin saying confidingly to Mr. Fulton, "Past time she went home. I can't think what she stays on for. Her mother wrote me—"

It was a conspiracy.

And it wouldn't be quite so annoying if Emma didn't sometimes wonder if her mother wasn't right. She wasn't sure what kept her in Paris. Memories? Or simply a reluctance to go home?

"Emma!" Kort seemed more happy than otherwise to see her.

Emma cut him off. "What's all this about taking me back to New York?"

Kort blinked, but recovered quickly. Of course, that might also have been the effect of her sapphires. With the sunlight streaming through the windows, they glittered rather impressively. Pity they were paste like all the rest of her jewelry, the real jewels having been bartered off to pay for hydraulic pumps and improved roofing.

"Didn't you read the letter I gave you?" he asked.

"Not yet."

It was still sitting on her dressing table. She hadn't needed to open it to know what it said. The minute she had seen her mother's handwriting, she had been able to divine the contents. It would be the usual run of family gossip, ending, as it always did, with "come home," as if she were an erring child being called in from a day spent too long at play.

Guilt made Emma sharp. "Why don't you summarize it for me?"

"All right." Her mother wasn't the only one who thought she was twelve. Kort's tone of long-suffering patience set her teeth on edge. "When your mother heard I was to be in Paris, she asked if I would escort you back. She seemed to think—"

"Yes?" prompted Emma.

"—that you were eager to return, but wary of traveling on your own. Since I was to be here anyway, I was happy to oblige."

Sharper than a serpent's tooth it was to have a scheming parent. Emma didn't know whether to be furious at her mother or rather impressed. After years of increasingly insistent letters had failed to have their effect, her mother had sent out the big guns: Kort. She was too shrewd by half, her mother. She had known—as who didn't?— of Emma's long-ago *tendre* for her cousin. And she was ruthless enough to take shameless advantage of it.

As if Emma were still a thirteen-year-old trailing along after her cousin's coattails!

"How very kind of you," said Emma, in deceptively mild tones, "to take charge of me like that. I don't know how I would possibly manage."

Kort didn't know enough to recognize danger when he heard it.

"It wasn't any bother. I had to come over here anyway. And you know I've always been fond of you," he added belatedly.

"I am so very glad," said Emma brightly, "that undertaking my conveyance wasn't so onerous a duty for you. I should have hated to have been a chore for you. Allow me to relieve your mind. My presence in Paris has nothing to do with an inability to book my own passage or entertain myself for the course of a sea voyage. I haven't left because I haven't wanted to."

"But your mother said—"

"My mother hears what she wants to hear."

"Don't you miss it?" Kort said sensibly. "Don't you want to come home?"

Miss it? He didn't know the half of it. *Home.*

Home to the Hudson and the changing patterns of the leaves in the fall. Home to long, lazy summer days where wild strawberries ripened beneath their fan-shaped leaves, and wasps buzzed about the trees in the orchard, sucking the sweetness of the peaches. Home to her old room with her shelves of battered books and the one-legged doll she had been too old and grand to admit she'd wanted to bring. Home to the swing by the lake and her initials carved discreetly into the base of the old apple tree: *E.M.* and *K.L.* in perpetuity. K.L. hadn't any idea, of course. She had eaten fallen apples and tossed the peels over her shoulders, willing them to make a *K* or an *L*, a divination of future marital bliss.

There were times when she missed it all with a horrible, visceral ache. When she missed the swing and the tree and the lake, whose quirks and shadows she had once known so well, in winter and in summer, the shallows where the carp liked to hide, the dark patch in the center where the ice never quite froze hard enough for skating, except in that one winter where it was so much more than usually brutally cold and the Albany Post Road had turned as icy as the river.

She had nieces and nephews she had never seen, adorable, chubby-cheeked children running wild across the woods and fields where she and her siblings had once played, picking wild raspberries and stumbling into ponds and getting themselves scolded and hung out to dry. Somewhere in the kitchens of Belvedere, children would be sneaking bits of bread and jam, and Annette would be dipping apples into batter for frying. Emma could still taste them in memory, the crisp, hot coating on the outside, the center disintegrating into sweetness.

The French did many things well, but they didn't understand about fried apples.

"There are certainly many things I miss about home," she said slowly. "But . . ."

"Don't tell me you'll miss all this," said Kort, indicating the red-painted walls with their murals à la Pompeii; the collection of classical vases in their specially designed cupboards; the chattering guests and their selection of accoutrements. "Paris is all very well, but it isn't where you belong."

"You haven't seen me since I was thirteen. What makes you quite so sure that you know where I belong?"

"But I know you," he said. "I've known you as long as you've known you." He raised his eyebrows at a particularly ridiculously garbed dandy, his hair combed down over his ears, his shirt points so high he couldn't turn his head, carnelian fobs jangling beneath his waistcoat. Kort gestured in his direction. "Just look at these people."

She might not wholly approve of all their sartorial choices, but Paris was her adopted city. "Those people, as you call them," she said sharply, "stood by me when my family disowned me. Those people took me in and comforted me when my husband died."

Kort's eyes focused on her. She could see the surprise in them, and it made her angry, angrier than she had felt in a long time. Did he not think she felt hurt, too? Or that her so much reviled marriage might have mattered to her, might have been more than a family embarrassment or a stir in the international scandal sheets?

She shook off the hand he held out to her. "They stood by me. Where were you?"

"Emma . . ."

His pity was the last thing she wanted. "Never mind," she said. "That wasn't fair."

He was still watching her, his eyes bent on her face. "No," he said slowly, "but perhaps neither was I. I didn't mean it as it came out. I just meant that you might be happier back among your own kind."

Emma tugged at his sleeve. "Look at me, Kort."

"All right," he said mildly, humoring her.

"No," said Emma. "Really look at me. Not at what you expect to see, or what memory provides for you, but at me, right here, right now."

She could see herself in the pier glass behind Kort, not a girl anymore, by any means. She might not be a beautiful woman, but she had learned how to be a fashionable one. No less an authority than Mme. Bonaparte herself had taught her how to apply rouge to her lips and paint to her lids, how to darken her blond brows and add the illusion of curves to a frame too thin for fashion. She wasn't the Emma who had left in 1794. There was no hiding or disguising that.

What would they make of her in New York? She didn't like to think of it.

Emma shook her head, and the mirrored Emma shook her head, too, short, feathered hair bouncing. Her straight blond hair wouldn't hold a curl, so she made a practice of threading it with ribbons or other folderol, distracting from the straightness of it.

She had tried false curls once, but disliked the sensation of wearing someone else's hair. She might divert, but she wouldn't deceive. One had to draw the line somewhere.

"You said as much yourself last night. I've changed. I'm not the girl who left all those years ago."

"I won't deny you've grown up, or that you've become fashionable, but—"

Emma cut him off with a quick gesture of negation.

If she went home, it would be home to other peoples' families and other peoples' children. Home to having her dresses and mannerisms picked over and dissected. Home to gossip and censure and those horrible hissing whispers as the good matrons of New York leaned their heads together just above their embroidery frames. "Yes, that's the one. The one who ran off with the Frenchman. No! Don't look now! She'll see you."

She could envision it now. Neither maiden nor matron, she would be used as a cautionary tale to frighten disobedient daughters. "Watch out, or you'll wind up like Emma Morris! She married without her parents' permission and look what's become of her."

"Please do try to understand, Kort. I don't want to be a cautionary tale."

"All right, so you'll have to pull up your bodices a bit. Surely that won't be too onerous."

Emma gave up trying to explain. How could she, when she couldn't entirely explain to herself? She wasn't entirely at home in Paris, but she would be even less at home in New York now. Of the two, better the devil she knew.

"Trust me about this, won't you, Emma?" Kort wheedled. "If you're too bored in New York, you can always catch the next boat back to Paris."

Something about his tone set Emma's back up. "What makes you think I can just pick up and leave like that? I have responsibilities here. I have obligations."

"Do you?" He eyed her frivolous headdress with a decidedly skeptical expression. "Such as?"

She could have mentioned Carmagnac. She could have made flippant remarks about her close, personal relationship with her dressmaker. But, instead, in that fateful moment, her gaze chanced to fall on Augustus Whittlesby.

The idea bubbled up quick as lava, and just as quickly onto her tongue. Emma lifted her chin. "Haven't you heard? Mr. Whittlesby and I have been commissioned by the First Consul himself to write a masque for his next party at Malmaison."

Let him see just how much she was wanted here in Paris. Let Kort try to argue with the First Consul!

Emma extended a hand towards Mr. Whittlesby, the bracelets on her wrists clanking together in a discord like a knell as she turned her back defiantly on her cousin and the rest of the world she had left behind.

"Haven't we, Mr. Whittlesby?"

Chapter 8

For by seeming seemed she
All that was fair,
But seeming unseemly be;
What boots it to seem,
When to seem is to show
And show deceptive be?

—Augustus Whittlesby, *The Perils of the*
Pulchritudinous Princess of the Azure Toes,
discarded fragment, presumed to be
from Canto XII

Augustus followed Emma Delagardie into her book room.
Downstairs, the guests were grazing among the last of
the cold meats, holding their glasses out to be refilled by the omni-
present footmen, gossiping about their neighbors and slandering
their friends. Mme. Delagardie had led him out of the fray, promising a quiet place where they could begin their work once the other
guests had taken their leave. Not too much work, she had specified,

but enough to make a start. With only a month until performance, they should at least agree upon their plot and their characters.

Which, Augustus thought cynically, most likely translated to her dictating the plot and his doing the work.

That was quite all right with him so long as it also translated into an invitation to Malmaison. An invitation to Malmaison and a chance to look for the paper that Emma Delagardie had so casually tucked into her reticule the night before.

Augustus had no proof that either Emma Delagardie or her cousin, the one with the strange name, had anything to do with Bonaparte's mysterious device, but the coincidences were piling up, too many for comfort. It had seemed innocuous enough that Bonaparte intended to test his device during the visit of the American envoy. The presence of the Americans might be intended only as a distraction, a smoke screen. One had the impression that they were brash and not terribly bright, thus making them perfect fodder for the role of unwitting decoy.

Likewise, it would ordinarily mean little that the American envoy's nephew had a diagram of some sort of mechanical whatnot in his waistcoat pocket. It might be nothing more than a sketch for a new patent stove or a design for an improved water closet, Yankee ingenuity once again at work. They were a strange and mercantile people, these Americans. One never knew what they might come up with next.

Last, and possibly least, it shouldn't surprise anyone that Georges Marston might wish to rekindle an old love affair with a wealthy widow. It was commonly known that Marston had expensive tastes in clothes and cheap tastes in women, both of which were best supported by a wealthy patroness. It would be unremarkable but for the fact that Marston was also linked to the fleet at Boulogne.

Which was awaiting the arrival of a device. Presumably encapsulated in a diagram. Somehow connected to the Americans.

Put it all together, and Augustus was all too glad when Mme.

Delagardie suggested she wait for him in her book room, where he might commune with the muse without interruption. He just never bothered to specify which muse was meant. There was a muse for history, for poetry, for theatre, for dance, why not one for spies?

"Please, make yourself comfortable," Mme. Delagardie said, bustling around the room, putting books on top of other books and sweeping papers off the seat of a chair. "It will just be a moment, while the rest of that lot clear out."

It was a book room in more than just name. The white painted walls were almost entirely covered with shelves, the shelves covered with books. Her books? This had never been a man's study. An octagonal carpet in a pattern of yellow and pink flowers lay in the center of the floor, the shape mirroring the pattern of the parquet. Two long windows, their drapes held back by tasseled cords, let in the afternoon sunlight, providing light enough to read without the aid of the candles in their flower-patterned sconces along the walls. Most of the candles were half burnt, suggesting that they had been lit, and recently.

It was a bright, cheerful room, and obviously much used. The chair by the fireplace sagged in the middle, the seat cushion hollowed from repeated sittings, while a patch on the left arm had been rubbed almost bare, as if the user had leaned heavily on that one side, or swung her legs over it, as Augustus remembered his little sister doing long, long ago, an apple in one hand and a book in the other.

He pushed the thought away. He didn't like to think of Polly.

Emma Delagardie's desk was a magpie's paradise of bits of paper and shiny objects, dented pen nibs lying discarded next to empty inkwells, books held open by other books, papers piled on papers.

Emma Delagardie lifted a cup off the desk, frowned into it, made a face, and stuck it on a shelf. "I really should get the maids in here." Dusting her hands on her skirt, she turned back to Augustus. "It shouldn't be long. Everyone usually leaves about this time. It's just the good-byes that seem to stretch on forever."

"I assure you, madame, I shall be well entertained in the contemplation of the mutual endeavor on which we are about to embark."

She looked a bit uneasy at that. "Consider it more a coastal jaunt than a sea voyage," she suggested. "It's really meant to be just a short piece." She looked at the roll of poetry that was never far from his arm, all twenty-two bulging cantos of *The Princess of the Pulchritudinous Toes*. "Very short."

Having gotten this far, he wasn't inclined to press his luck. "A distillation!" Augustus exclaimed. "The brandy wine of the overflowing tap of verse, refined into its purest form."

"Something like that." Mme. Delagardie cast a last look around the room. Checking the amenities? Or dispensing of incriminating materials? "There are paper and ink on the desk if you need them—not that well, that's gone dry. It was a particularly ugly color, anyway, like mud. I never cared for it. There should be another one on the other side. . . . There it is! Under that pile of papers."

Augustus could hear the clock ticking in the back of his head, precious moments wasted. As she rambled on, the guests were leaving, and, with them, Augustus's chance to examine her study unmolested.

Augustus herded her towards the door. "When the muse does command, the materials will come to hand. Forgive my impertinence, Madame, but will your guests not miss your gracious presence amongst them?"

Emma Delagardie looked back over one shoulder. Her eyes were several shades lighter than her sapphires, more aquamarine than anything else, the pale blue of sailors after long sea voyages, bleached by staring into the sun.

"That," she said, with a flash of wry humor, "is eminently debatable. But I'd best go say my good-byes. I'll be back before you know I'm gone."

Having exhausted his usual conversational effusions, Augustus limited himself to a deep bow. "Madame," he intoned.

Mme. Delagardie's heavily embroidered hem dragged behind her over the lintel. The white paneled door clicked softly shut.

Abandoning his pose, Augustus let out a long breath of relief. Alone at last. Now he could—

The door cracked open again. A blue feather poked through the gap, followed by a small, narrow-bridged nose.

"Would you like some refreshment while you wait? Coffee? Wine?"

Augustus juggled his scroll of poetry, trying futilely to maintain his grip. "Nothing," he said shortly. "Er, that is, those of us who sip from the font of poetry need no other sustenance."

"If you find yourself thirsting for anything more mundane, just tell one of the servants. They'll bring you anything you like. Well, almost anything. Just don't ask for an elephant."

The door closed again before Augustus could ask what he might want with an elephant. Augustus watched it suspiciously for several minutes, but this time it stayed closed. Apparently, Mme. Delagardie's charitable urges didn't extend to meat pies or pastries or the offer of pillow and blanket in case he felt like a short nap.

He could use a nap, at that. He had tailed Kortright Livingston last night, all the way back to the house currently occupied by the American envoy to France. All he had discovered, after several uncomfortable hours perched in a tree, was that Livingston liked his brandy neat and scorned the use of nightcaps.

Not exactly the stuff to set the War Office buzzing.

There was a connection there, though; Augustus could feel it in his bones. (Although that might have been the cramp from perching in a tree; he wasn't as young as he used to be.) Discreet inquiries had elicited the information that Livingston had an interest in the foundries in a town called Cold Spring. Foundries, in Augustus's experience, generally made munitions. Munitions might be ingeniously combined into something one might call a device.

But what sort of device? A multi-firing cannon, designed to

knock out the ships guarding the Channel? A mine of some sort, to be planted beneath the water and triggered from above? An experiment in rockets? Any might be de Lilly's mysterious device. Any might have been in that folded paper Kortright Livingston had almost handed his cousin the night before.

What had he given her? And where was it?

Augustus surveyed Mme. Delagardie's book room. If there was an attempt at concealment being made, it was of the same variety as his poetry, burying the wheat in the midst of a profusion of chaff. There were papers everywhere. Bills, letters, reminders, drawings.

The bills, Augustus had expected. They were the usual stuff of a lady of fashion—shoes, fans, gloves. Ditto the hastily scribbled notes, some still bearing the trace of a seal, arranging who was to meet whom at which box in the theatre, setting up expeditions to the dressmaker, canceling a carriage ride.

What he didn't expect were the sketches. They weren't the usual stuff of a lady's sketchbook. There were no landscapes or bowls of fruit. Augustus reached for one paper, dangling perilously off the edge of the desk. Instead, it was a diagram, a picture of a mechanism of some kind, with notes in the margins marking off size and scale.

Turn the paper though he might, he couldn't figure out what the blasted thing was meant to be.

It was at times like this that Augustus wished he had spent less time on Ovid and more time on engineering.

Was this the missing paper Livingston had handed Delagardie last night? No. That much, at least, he could determine by common sense alone. This paper was the wrong size, too long and too broad. It had also obviously never been folded, whereas the paper last night had been neatly folded into thirds and then folded again, small enough to tuck into a waistcoat pocket. Even among the profusion of debris on the desk, he could see nothing that matched those creases.

Whatever the paper was that Kortright Livingston had passed on to his cousin, it wasn't on her desk.

Augustus cursed, and was surprised to hear his own curse come back at him in echo, relayed at considerable volume.

"Devil take it!" someone bellowed from a long way below. "That can't be right."

The noise was coming from the window. Dropping the paper, Augustus made his way to one of the long windows and looked down. Georges Marston stood below, his hat jammed under one arm, his curly hair glistening with pomade in the sunlight.

He was not a happy man.

"What do you mean she won't receive me?" He muscled his way aggressively forward. "Let me in! At once!"

Augustus couldn't see the footman, but he could hear him. "Forgive me, sir," he said, "but Madame Delagardie has given orders that you not be admitted."

Augustus leaned both elbows on the sill. So Mme. Delagardie had banned Marston from her house?

"That's poppycock, sheer poppycock, do you hear?" Marston shouted, in a voice that could be heard in Boulogne. "There must be some mistake."

"No mistake, sir."

For a moment, Augustus thought Marston intended to strike the hapless servant. His hands balled into fists at his sides, and his muscles strained against the tightly tailored seams of his coat. Augustus waited for something to pop.

With an effort, Marston regained control of himself. His expression changed, an ingratiating smile replacing his previous snarl. "Women, eh?" he said, with false heartiness. "They never know their own minds. What if I were to make it worth your while?"

Marston dug in his waistcoat pocket and held out his hand, palm up, revealing the glitter of something silver and shiny.

The footman was spared the test of his morals—or deprived of the chance to earn an extra sou. Someone else emerged from the house. The footman stood aside and a man stepped down, his boots dull against the stone of the steps. Both his hat and his jacket were an unfashionable brown, his cravat simply tied. His head turned curiously toward Marston as he passed, but he didn't stop.

Marston, however, was galvanized into action. He sprang forward. "Mr. Livingston! Georges Marston. Your cousin introduced us. Last night."

Augustus wondered how much of the previous altercation Kortright Livingston had heard or whether he knew his cousin had banned Marston from the house.

Tipping his head, he said coolly, "Mr. Marston."

Marston hastily moved to get ahead of him, blocking his way down the street. "Madame Delagardie and I are good friends. Very good friends."

Kortright Livingston kept moving. "I understand my cousin has a very broad circle of acquaintance in Paris."

Marston scrambled along after him. "Paris can be confusing to those new to it. A chap doesn't know who to trust."

"I do not intend to stay long in Paris," Livingston said shortly.

"Ah," said Marston, undeterred. "Just until the business is concluded?"

Livingston stopped. He looked Marston up and down, from his champagne-blacked boots to his curly-brimmed hat. "I do not understand you, Mr. Marston."

Marston grinned. It wasn't a pleasant expression. It was all teeth and red lips, like the wolf in a tale by Charles Perrault. "I think you do, Mr. Livingston. I think you do."

Augustus's forehead hit glass. Damn. They were moving out of sight and out of earshot. He could lift the sash, but a man leaning head and shoulders out of the window was the sort of thing not likely to escape the attention of those one most wanted to avoid. Leaping down fifteen feet and running after them was equally impractical.

The door squeaked.

Augustus jumped away from the window, doing his best to strike a nonchalant pose.

"Thank goodness, that's the last of them." Emma Delagardie whirled into the room in a flurry of feathers. Fortunately, she had matters of her own to distract her. There were two red spots high in either cheek that owed nothing to rouge. "My apologies, Mr. Whittlesby, for keeping you so long."

"No matter, madame." Augustus inclined his head towards the window. Audacity always worked better than evasion. "I was just admiring the view."

Mme. Delagardie's flush deepened, but she otherwise kept her composure. "And the wildlife?" she said tartly.

"The mating calls of certain birds are particularly strident," said Augustus blandly.

Turning abruptly away, Mme. Delagardie crossed to the desk, her skirts bouncing around her ankles. "Consider that more of a swan song," she said, her hands moving rapidly among the papers, sifting, sorting, searching. "That particular bird will just have to find a different pond. This pool is no longer open."

"They are very pretty creatures, swans," commented Augustus.

"Yes, from a distance." Emma Delagardie pulled a blank sheet of paper from among the debris, clearing an open surface on the desk by dint of pushing everything else to the sides. Paper crumpled against paper and the inkwell teetered perilously on the edge. She shoved at the stack. "If you let them too close, they peck."

Augustus caught the inkwell just before it went over. Fortunately, it was empty. Inside the open container, the congealed brown ink looked like blood, like a handkerchief after a consumptive's cough, covered with matted brown stains. Augustus set the bowl gingerly aside, next to the diagram of the incomprehensible machine.

He lifted the diagram from the desk, regarding it with a studied show of indifference. "What art is this?" Augustus dangled the paper languidly in front of her. "Are you a draftsman as well as a fledgling mistress of verse, fair madame?"

"Hmm?" Mme. Delagardie glanced up from her work, her expression abstracted. It took a moment for her eyes to focus on it. She waved a dismissive hand, setting her sapphires sparkling. "Oh, that. It's all pumps and that sort of thing. Drainage was my husband's idée fixe."

She scrambled through the welter of papers for a pen with a working nib.

"You might have heard of him," she added, testing a nib against the pad of one finger, her head bowed over her work. "His experiments in drainage were much talked of at the time. The directors were very pleased with his efforts in expanding the arable land available to provide grain to the republic. They gave him a commendation for it."

Augustus had heard. Everyone had. Society had shaken its head over the spectacle of poor Paul Delagardie slaving away among the marshes while his young bride cut a dash in Paris. Opinion had been divided. Some said it was no more than he deserved, neglecting a young wife to grub in the mud. Others put the blame on his bride. Either way, the impression had been that there was little love lost in the match and little interest on Mme. Delagardie's part for her husband's besetting passion.

"A touching memento to his memory," intoned Augustus, "to preserve his papers for so long?"

"How many acts shall we have?" Mme. Delagardie twisted the lid off a new pot of ink with more than necessary vigor. "It shouldn't be a long production, but it must have some plot to it."

The discussion of drainage was officially over.

"Three?" Augustus suggested at random. "It is more than two but less than four."

To his surprise, Mme. Delagardie accepted his advice without question. "And it corresponds so nicely to the three unities." When

Augustus looked at her in surprise, she said mildly, "I do patronize the theatre, you know."

Yes, but he hadn't expected theory from her, especially not neo-classical Aristotelian derivations. "Are we to pattern ourselves on Racine, then?" he asked.

"I don't believe Racine had any singing parts," she said, "and I've been told quite explicitly that I'm meant to have one for Hortense. As for the rest, I don't see why not."

"Unity of action, time, and place?" He wasn't sure why he felt the need to push the point, but he did. It was a test, he told himself. A test of what, he couldn't quite say.

"The unity of place certainly saves money on sets," Mme. Delagardie said practically. "Although the point of a masque, generally, is to make the sets as elaborate as possible. The one is story, the other is spectacle."

It was an interesting concept, this distinction between spectacle and story. Was it a question of entertainment versus edification? The animal senses versus the more intelligent faculties? There was an argument to be made that it was a false distinction, that spectacle was a means of conveyance rather than—

Augustus pulled himself up short. He wasn't meant to be debating drama. He was meant to be insinuating himself into Mme. Delagardie's confidence, assuring his invitation to Malmaison, discerning whether she was an active player in this game or merely a pawn.

She had made one point, though, whether she intended to or not. Whatever spectacle might convey, it was also very good at concealing.

He looked at Mme. Delagardie, her fine hair topped with an absurd confection of ribbon and feather, sapphires dazzling at her neck, her wrists, her fingers, silver thread entwined with the blue embroidery on her dress, so that she shimmered when she moved.

For the first time, he wondered whether the spectacle might not, in this case, be the illusion.

Nonsense. He had masques on the mind. A bit of Aristotle and a moment of lucid conversation meant little. Emma Delagardie was a conduit, not a source.

Augustus adopted his most vapid expression. "Shall we carry on, dear lady? The muses clamor to be heard! Our audience awaits!"

"A fair point." Mme. Delagardie dipped her pen in the inkwell, tapping the nib professionally against the side.

Act the First, she wrote across the top of the page, in ink that was neither brown nor black but a very feminine violet. She looked up at Augustus, her long earrings swinging on their silver-gilt chains. "The scene . . . What shall the scene be?"

She was looking up, but Augustus was looking down, at the upside-down writing in front of him, at *Act the First*.

Her handwriting wasn't what he had expected. There were no girlish loops or feminine frills. It was an almost angular hand, impatient around the edges. He had seen it before, just a few moments ago, although not on any of the notes on the desk. Those had been correspondence directed to her, not from her.

All it took was a glance to confirm.

The hand that had written *Act the First* was the same that had made the notes in the margin of the mechanical diagram.

Chapter 9

For I shall bring you crimson leaves
And rippling wheat in golden sheaves;
A cache of berries, red and sweet,
And dappled deer on silent feet.
—Emma Delagardie and Augustus Whittlesby,
Americanus: A Masque in Three Parts

Madame Bonaparte asked that our theme be nautical in nature, but other than that, we can write whatever we like. Within reason," Emma amended.

She looked expectantly at Mr. Whittlesby.

Nothing.

Emma tried again. "We can even use your Cytherea. She lives in a casement by the sea. Doesn't she? Mr. Whittlesby?"

Mr. Whittlesby didn't answer. Eyes glazed, he was lost in poetic reverie. At least, Emma hoped it was poetic reverie. She had heard rumors about the sorts of aids to invention applied by those of artistic temperament, strange, oriental smokes and potions that dulled the mind but awakened the senses, or so they claimed.

That was all she needed, partnership with an opium eater.

It was all Emma could do not to drop her forehead to her desk and just stay there. She could burrow down among the papers and hide, hide until Kort gave up and cousin Robert went away and tangles of brambles climbed along the walls of her Paris house, leaving only a whisper and a rumor of the crazy American lady who had once lived there.

What had she gotten herself into? She didn't know the first thing about constructing a theatrical production. She didn't want to be coaxing a poet into coherence. She wasn't sure where she wanted to be, but it wasn't here. Or New York.

Perhaps she ought to find a casement by the sea somewhere.

"Mr. Whittlesby?" Emma waggled her fingers at the poet. "Hello?"

It was all Kort's fault, Emma decided. Well, maybe not all Kort's fault. Some of the blame went to Jane. If Jane hadn't set Whittlesby on her . . . If Kort hadn't gotten on her nerves like that . . .

If, just once, she had been able to curb her own impulsive tongue.

That was what really lay at the crux of it, not Kort, not Jane, not Mr. Whittlesby in his loose shirts and tight breeches, but her own silly tongue, flap, flap, flapping without any reference to rational thought, ruled always by her heart rather than her head. Something would set her off and off she would go, off to Paris, away with Paul, away *from* Paul, into the arms of Marston, and now this, ricocheting from one drama to the next, with never a moment to catch her breath in between.

Think, Emma, her mother used to say. Emma could hear her voice now, affection and exasperation, all rolled into one. *Think before you speak*.

Take a deep breath, people suggested. Count to ten. Count sheep. Oh, wait, that was for sleeping. Even in her own head, her tongue ran ahead of her brain. It propelled her into all sorts of absurd situations. Elopements. Scandals. This.

On the plus side, over the years, she had gotten very good at making the best out of bad situations. There was no cloud without a substantial silver lining—even if that lining did more often tend to be silver plate than solid sterling.

All that mattered was that it glitter.

Emma brightened at the thought. Glitter, she understood. She could make this masque glitter. She might not be a Racine or a Corneille, but she could put on a grand and gaudy spectacle with enough fireworks and mechanical effects to make the audience clap and exclaim and ignore the fact that at the core it was all fundamentally hollow.

It shouldn't be that hard, after all. People would be predisposed to like whatever they set before them, especially with Hortense playing the heroine, and the entire spectacle dedicated to cousin Robert. In fact, she thought, spirits rising, she could send everyone up on stage costumed as dancing aardvarks and this particular audience would still applaud. It didn't matter what they performed, just that they performed something. It was a very reassuring thought.

"Hark! I heard my name?" Mr. Whittlesby's words were daft, but his eyes were clear. Not, Emma decided, the eyes of an opium eater. Not that she had ever met an opium eater, but she had the idea that they were meant to be bleary-eyed and vague.

"One word about Cytherea and you were away with the fairies. Love struck?"

"Horror struck! My Cytherea to peddle her wares on the common stage?"

"It's a very exclusive stage," said Emma. They could do this. Really, they could. It might even be good, especially if she avoided the extraneous use of aardvarks. "Quite uncommon. Have you been to Malmaison?"

"The deities have yet to invite me to their fair Olympus," intoned Mr. Whittlesby.

Emma took that as a no. "There's a lovely little dollhouse of a theatre, right near the main house. It's quite new, only built the year before last."

Before that, they used to put on their plays in the house or out in the open in the field outside the house, risking rain and stormy weather. Emma tilted her head, listening to lines long since recited, songs long since sung. It boggled the memory to try to recall how many productions she had seen, how many bit roles she had acted, the laughter, the mishaps, the camaraderie. They had had such splendid times.

The new theatre might have all the conveniences, but it would never be quite the same.

"Madame Delagardie?"

Emma gave a brisk shake of her head. "If not Cytherea, who shall we press into service for our plot?"

"Have you considered as your theme," Mr. Whittlesby asked, "the New World bringing to the Old the fruits of its bounty? It would," he said grandly, "be a nice compliment to the envoy, your cousin."

"Goodness, how very courtly of you. But Madame Bonaparte wanted us to write something nautical in nature."

Mr. Whittlesby rested both palms on the edge of the desk. "The wonders of the New World," he said delicately, "would be delivered by ship."

"Of course," Emma muttered, feeling like an idiot. "Ships. Water. Nautical. Clever!"

If she kept this up, some day she might even manage a full sentence.

"With waves." Mr. Whittlesby made his hand go up and down in illustration.

Emma flushed. She had deserved that. "Well, it's certainly nautical," she said, doing her best to regain control of the situation. This was meant to be her masque, after all. Whittlesby was just the hired pen, no matter how dashing he looked in those knit pantaloons of his. Emma rested her elbows on the desk, and her chin on her hands.

"We'll need something more than that, something to provide the drama."

"A chorus of dancing gendarmes?" suggested Mr. Whittlesby blandly.

Emma sat up straighter in her chair as she was hit by an idea, a glorious, wonderful, attention-grabbing beauty of an idea.

"Pirates!" she exclaimed. "Our fleet could be attacked by pirates— nasty, vicious, scimitar-wielding pirates."

"One seldom hears those terms pronounced in tones of such glee," murmured Mr. Whittlesby.

Emma ignored him. She could already picture them on stage, vivid in their tattered finery, gold hoops swinging from their ears. Everyone loved pirates. Well, at least in fiction. The real ones were a good deal less attractive. "They can wear bandannas on their heads and carry cutlasses between their teeth, and their ship will be called . . . well, something scary and nasty. We can figure that out later."

"Pirates or privateers?" queried Mr. Whittlesby, sounding almost sensible.

"Pirates," said Emma definitively. "Our ship will be beset on all sides, besieged by the pirates, when in sails the French navy, captained by our hero, to knock the pirates' heads together, secure the treasure, and save the fair. Now, there's nautical for you!"

She beamed at Mr. Whittlesby, swept away by the brilliance of her own inspiration. Was this what it felt like to receive the muse? If so, she understood why Mr. Whittlesby spent so much time courting her.

Mr. Whittlesby seemed slightly less swept away. "It has a certain élan."

"A certain élan? It's perfect. Admit it." Emma dipped her pen in the ink, spattering violet drops on Mr. Fulton's diagram of a new hydraulic pump. "The theme is a nice compliment to both sides and we can have all sorts of fireworks and big booming noises when the various fleets collide."

"You seem to have forgotten something."

"Pardon?" Emma was scribbling away busily, her mind far away on the high seas. She hadn't actually seen the sea since her passage over, a good ten years before, but she had no intention of letting reality be an impediment to imagination. There were such things as wave machines; she had seen them. There would be a storm and a pirate attack. . . . "We'll have ships and fireworks and a battle. What can be missing?"

She looked up to meet Mr. Whittlesby's warm brown eyes. "A heroine."

"Oh." Emma ducked her head. He didn't mean her, of course. There was no reason to feel quite so flustered. "I knew I had you here for a reason. Well, that and the actual writing. You're quite right, of course. A play wouldn't be a play without a romance in it. Our heroine can be captured by the pirates. That always goes over well."

"An American heroine?"

Emma quickly shook her head. "One whose part can by sung by Hortense. But"—now there was an idea—"we might have an American hero. It will be just the thing for my cousin. The younger one," she specified hastily. Cousin Robert was a charming man, but a bit old to play the romantic lead. If he tried to pull himself up to a tower window, he would probably pull half the scenery down with him. The last thing Emma wanted was to accidentally create an international incident.

Another international incident, that is.

Mr. Whittlesby tapped a finger idly against the corner of the desk. "Does Mr. Livingston intend to remain that long in Paris?"

Sometime in June, cousin Robert had said. Sometime in June was the ship that was meant to take both Kort and Emma away. Just knowing that Kort had booked passage for her without asking her—without so much as mentioning it to her—made Emma see red.

It would serve him right if she conscripted him for a performance without telling him. After all, she just assumed he would want to.

She wouldn't, she knew. But it was still a lovely thought.

"I can certainly ask him," Emma said. "The worst he can do is say no."

"How could anyone possibly flee our shores with such an opportunity to hold him?" There was a strangely sarcastic undertone to Mr. Whittlesby's words. "Mr. Livingston's accent will lend a charming verisimilitude to the roll."

"Art imitating life imitating art? Or do I mean life imitating art imitating life?" Emma bent back over her notes. "Our American hero could be bringing a fleet filled with the bounty of the New World as a pledge to win the heroine's hand."

Mr. Whittlesby considered the idea. "Like Marlowe's promises to his shepherdess? *There will I make thee beds of roses / And a thousand fragrant posies, / A cap of flowers, and a kirtle / Embroider'd all with leaves of myrtle.*"

Emma remembered the poem from long ago, from sunny afternoons in the apple tree and stolen moments with a book of poetry among the roses at Mme. Campan's. Paul had read her Ronsard, but Marlowe she had read for herself.

She grinned at Whittlesby. "You forgot *A belt of straw and ivy buds / With coral clasps and amber studs.*"

For the first time, he looked at her, really looked at her. His eyes weren't the simple brown Emma had thought; there was a darker circle around the iris, so deep it looked almost purple. His hair fell loose around his face, too long for fashion, with a natural curl any woman would envy.

He met her line and finished it. *"And if these pleasures may thee move, / Come live with me and be my love."*

On the mantel, the clock chimed, three dulcet rings, one after the other.

The chimes struck the silence like a mallet against glass, making it shiver and break. Emma jumped up from her chair, wincing at the screeching noise it made as the legs scraped against wood.

Three? How was it three already?

She rustled through the debris on her desk, speaking and searching at the same time, avoiding Whittlesby's eyes, brown and violet. "I'm afraid I have an engagement for which I'm already late."

How did her desk manage to eat papers? After she had faithfully promised she would bring it . . . Of course, she had also faithfully promised she would be on time this time, and look where she still was.

Better to think of obligations and obligations unmet rather than shepherds and love.

She glanced fleetingly at Whittlesby. "Are you free tomorrow morning? And by morning, I mean afternoon."

"I believe that can be arranged. After some consultation with the muses, that is."

Ha! There it was. Emma snatched up the sheet of paper before it could get away again. Paul had insisted that inanimate objects couldn't have malignant motivations, but Emma had extensive proof to the contrary.

"Well, as long as your muses don't wake up too early, I'm sure we'll all deal very well together." Opening her reticule, Emma jammed the paper inside, trapping it by clicking the silver clasps shut. Rising from her chair, she held out a hand to Mr. Whittlesby, like a gentleman transacting business. That was what they were, after all, two partners embarked on a joint venture, as merchants might band together to back a ship or share a cargo. "Thank you, Mr. Whittlesby, for being so generous with your time. Tomorrow morning?"

His words were airy but his grip was firm. "I shall fly to you on the fleet feet of Hermes, madame."

"Won't he want them back?" When he looked at her, she shook her head, making a rueful face. "Never mind. It made sense in my head. Many things do."

Mr. Whittlesby stood aside to let her precede him through the door. "Shall I see you to your engagement?"

"Loath to leave my company?"

"I meant merely that we might speak more of the masque."

Why did she always say these things? "I didn't mean—"

He raised his voice, carrying on as though she hadn't spoken. "We have sadly neglected the spectacle in favor of the substance. The mechanics," he specified, when Emma looked at him blankly. "Honesty and art demand that I make full confession of my shortcomings. If spectacle there is to be, it must come from some other soul than me. These modern mechanics are beyond *my* ken."

He was rhyming again. He hadn't been before. For a little while, he had been speaking almost normally. He donned rhyme like armor, keeping her at bay. She could have told him he didn't need to. She flirted without thinking. That was armor, too.

She knew better than to let herself be lulled by the shepherd's song. *"Come live with me and be my love."* She had believed those words once; she had followed them into an early marriage. With the arrogance of youth, she had ignored the nymph's reply: *"The flowers do fade, and wanton fields / To wayward winter reckoning yields; / A honey tongue, a heart of gall, / Is fancy's spring, but sorrow's fall."*

"I had thought to ask Mr. Fulton for help," Emma said quickly. "The inventor. He created the panorama a few years ago. You must have seen it. Everyone did."

"Saw it? I wrote a poem about it! 'An Ode to the Experience of Art in the Round.' It was much admired in certain circles."

"I'm sure it was." With relief, Emma seized on the excuse offered her by the presence of her sedan chair in the courtyard, the bearers ready and waiting. There were still places in Paris where it was easier to take a chair than a carriage. "We do have much to discuss, but, as you see, my chair is already waiting."

With the ease of long practice, she climbed into her own personal chair, reciting an address to the chairmen as she did. She felt the familiar lurch of the chair as they rose to their feet.

Mr. Whittlesby's face appeared in the chair window. "You go to Madame Hortense?" he asked.

"Yes, to tell her the good news about the masque." Emma patted her reticule. Paper crinkled beneath her fingers. "And to bring her this."

Emma nodded to the chairmen and they set the chair into motion, stepping in perfect pace on the uneven cobbles.

"Until tomorrow, Mr. Whittlesby!" she called out through the window.

From the corner of her eye, she could see him standing there still, his open shirt inadequate protection against the chill of an unseasonably cool May day.

When Emma was shown into Hortense's boudoir, the others were already deep in conversation, a china pot of coffee on the table between them, two cups half full and a third glaringly empty.

Jane Wooliston smiled at Emma over her coffee cup. "Only fifteen minutes late this time. You're improving."

Hortense Bonaparte made a face at Jane. "Don't be unkind!" Rising, she embraced Emma, the differences in their height reversed from when they had first known each other, when Hortense was eleven and Emma fourteen. Now Hortense was the taller of the two, a grown woman and a mother. But she still had the same sweet nature that had endeared her to everyone at Mme. Campan's. "I'm sure there was an extenuating circumstance. Such as . . ."

"A stampede of bears across the Champs-Élysées?" suggested Jane. "Typhoons? Hurricanes?"

Emma plumped down with a thump on the yellow silk settee. "A hurricane, indeed! Hurricane Augustus, you mean. Someone"—she looked hard at Jane—"unleashed a poet on me."

" 'Unleashed' is such a strong term," said Jane.

"No one ever tells me anything," complained Hortense, to no one in particular.

It was meant jokingly, but Emma felt a twinge of guilt all the same. If she thought her own position was fraught, Hortense's was far worse. Bad enough being the First Consul's stepdaughter, but she was made doubly a Bonaparte by her marriage to Napoleon's younger brother, Louis. As the family rose in prominence, those who surrounded them were increasingly likely to be toadies, informers, or both. There were few these days whom Hortense could call friend and believe it.

Emma angled herself towards Hortense. "Trust me, you aren't missing much of anything. You know Augustus Whittlesby, don't you?"

"The poet?" Hortense perked up. She turned to Jane. "Isn't he in love with you?"

"Perpetually," said Emma, before Jane could jump in.

"Poetically," countered Jane repressively. "It isn't at all the same thing."

"Yes, yes, we've had this discussion," said Emma. And Augustus Whittlesby had been so very terrified when he had thought she might be flirting with him. Emma pushed that thought away; it wasn't a particularly flattering recollection. "What did you tell him about me?" she demanded. "You didn't say anything about my predilection for his pantaloons, did you?"

"Oh, my," said Jane, raising one brow. "One afternoon in his company and you're already away with the alliteration."

"Don't change the subject," said Emma severely. "The poor man is terrified that I intend to seduce him."

"Do you?" asked Hortense with interest. The intense scrutiny of a jealous husband left her little opportunity to seduce anyone, but she took a generous interest in her friends.

"No! Absolutely not. I'm just using him for his help with my masque." She wasn't quite sure when, but somehow, it had become her masque, hers, quite hers. Maybe it had something to do with the pirates.

"So you are writing it!" Hortense put down her cup with a delicate clink. "*Maman* will be so pleased. She was terrified she might have to ask Caroline to help instead, and you know how Caroline is." She made an admirable effort to sound cheerful, but there was no mistaking the strain beneath it.

"And Whittlesby," said Jane. "Is he . . . helpful?"

"Stop that! And, yes," Emma admitted. "He is. Or at least he might be. We'll see. If you don't stop smirking, I'll send him back to writing odes for you." She turned to Hortense. "You will be my heroine, won't you?"

Hortense took a deep interest in the contents of her coffee cup. "You know I want to be . . . but it might not be possible."

"There won't be much to . . . Oh." Emma stared at Hortense's hand, where it rested gently on her stomach as her friend's words took on new meaning. "Are you . . . I mean——"

Hortense nodded. "Yes."

"But that doesn't mean you can't perform." Women tended to go about in society up until the very last moment, a pregnancy no bar to one's usual social whirl. The masque was in less than a month. "You won't even be showing."

Hortense shook her head, not meeting Emma's eyes. "Louis wouldn't like it."

Emma and Jane exchanged a look. It was no secret that Hortense's marriage was a sham, her husband delighting in all manner of petty persecutions.

It was a hideous situation. Hortense had never wanted to marry Louis, nor Louis Hortense, but if he wanted a dynasty, Bonaparte needed heirs, and Hortense and Louis were to provide them.

Emma's heart ached for her friend.

And, just a little bit, for herself. She certainly didn't envy Hortense her situation, but she did envy her the curve of her hand across her belly, the child sleeping in the nursery, the press of small arms around her neck.

They had been planning to try for a child, she and Paul, towards the end. After all the years of confusion, of separation and reconciliation, they were going to be a family. They had gone so far as to commission a cradle.

But Paul had died. And so had gone not only that hard-won

sweetness, but all their other plans with him, all the children and hopes that might have been, leaving her to a cold and barren bed and an empty nursery. It hurt, sometimes, seeing her friends with their children, seeing Hortense, so many years younger than she, with one in the nursery and another on the way. Bonaparte's sister Caroline, bane of Mme. Campan's academy, had three.

Oh, she wouldn't trade. She wouldn't take Hortense's Louis or Caroline's Murat. But it would be nice, so very nice, to have a pair of plump little arms around her neck instead of the cold press of gems, the downy scent of a child's head instead of perfume.

"When are you due?" she asked, trying to sound cheerful, and fearing that she had failed as badly as her friend.

"In the autumn," said Hortense. She twisted in her seat to look at Jane. "Will you take my part for me? I'd rather you than Caroline."

"Won't your mother mind?" said Jane. "She intended the part for you."

Hortense tried to make a joke of it. "She would also rather anyone than Caroline. Please? It would be a pleasure for me to have you there."

What she didn't say, although the others both understood, was that she wanted allies, people outside the Bonaparte clan and the narrow circle of the court. Both Jane and Emma, aliens as they were, were safe. They had no ambitions to be satisfied, no ulterior motives to be pursued at Hortense's expense.

There was a pause, and then Jane said, "I'll hold the part in trust for you. In case you change your mind. The same costumes will fit us both."

Hortense only shook her head.

"Shall we go shopping next week?" Emma jumped in. "Surely a new baby is an excellent excuse to treat yourself to a few new hats."

"You are a dear. But that's not where the baby is!" Hortense's eyes brightened and for a moment she looked almost like her old self. Her face fell. "I can't. I have to be at Saint-Cloud. My stepfather has an important announcement to make."

"Oh?" Emma said, without interest.

"You'll hear about it soon enough. *Maman* has a surprise for you, too, but she wants to tell you herself, so it will have to wait until Malmaison." Hortense broke off at a barely heard sound, craning her neck towards the door.

It opened slowly, not Louis eavesdropping, nor one of his minions, but Louis-Charles's nursemaid, who dropped a curtsy, and said, in a low voice, "Madame . . ."

Hortense was out of her chair before the word was finished.

Emma and Jane followed suit, placing their cups on the tray as they rose.

"Forgive me," Hortense said, her attention already elsewhere, in the nursery with her child. "Louis-Charles . . ."

"Of course," said Jane gracefully.

"Malmaison, then," said Emma. "I'll bring sweets for Louis-Charles. Oh, and I nearly forgot! Stupid me!"

Opening her bag, she delved into her reticule, wondering, as she always did, how objects managed to hide in a bag no bigger than a man's fist.

Hortense signaled to the nursemaid to wait just a moment. "You did bring it, then?"

Emma held out the crumpled piece of paper. "A little the worse for wear, I'm afraid."

"Even so," said Hortense, with heartfelt gratitude. "Thank you. What are a few creases with so much at stake?"

Chapter 10

If words you doubt and vows despise,
How win I favor in your eyes?
My actions shall unspeaking speak,
Proclaim my love from peak to peak.

—Emma Delagardie and Augustus Whittlesby,
Americanus: A Masque in Three Parts

*I*t was a recipe for cough syrup," said Jane.

Augustus paused next to a statue that appeared to have misplaced its arms. They had met at the Musée Napoléon, the public art gallery housed in the former Louvre Palace. The vast marble halls provided an excellent place for an assignation. A series of antique statues, looted from Italy during Bonaparte's last campaign, stood silent sentry to their conversation.

Jane's chaperone, Miss Gwen, provided more practical protection. Ostensibly engaged in examining the art, she prowled in a continuous circle around them, poking at the statuary with her parasol, glowering at all comers, and generally providing distraction.

"Cough syrup," said Augustus. "Cough syrup?"

His revelation that Emma Delagardie was smuggling documents to Hortense de Beauharnais Bonaparte hadn't gone exactly as expected.

"Cough syrup," confirmed Jane. "Made of wild cherry bark, lemon, and honey."

Kitted out in bonnet, gloves, and pelisse, the Pink Carnation was the very image of a demure young lady scarcely out of the schoolroom, her hair swept back smoothly beneath her bonnet, her gloved hands devoid of rings or bracelets. The fichu at her throat hid the locket that she wore on a ribbon around her neck, but Augustus didn't need to see it to know that it was there. No telltale signet rings for the Pink Carnation; her seal was inscribed in the back of her locket, a delicate tracery on a lady's trinket.

Augustus admired her acumen, but omniscience was a bit much, even for the legendary Pink Carnation.

Cough syrup? How could she divine that simply from his description of a crumpled piece of paper?

"This is a new talent for you," he teased, feeling like a lovelorn adolescent as he trotted along beside her. Next, he would be offering to help her carry her hymnal, or begging her to stand up with him at the next country assembly. Ridiculous enough in an adolescent, worse in a grown man. "Walking through locked doors, seeing through solid walls, reading closed correspondence. Am I to congratulate you on the acquisition of a crystal ball?"

All his sallies won him nothing more than a smile, and a perfunctory one at that. Augustus felt reprimanded, without being quite sure why.

"No such arts were required," Jane said crisply. "I know because I saw it."

Augustus frowned. "How?"

"Hortense and Emma and I meet weekly for coffee after Emma's Friday salon." When Augustus only stared at her, Jane added gently, "I was there. I saw Emma hand Hortense the paper. I saw the contents. It was a recipe for cough syrup, nothing more."

"How do you know it was the same paper?"

"Emma had only the one in her reticule. There wasn't room for more." Jane was clearly prepared to leave it at that.

"Only one that you saw," said Augustus. "There's more than one way to transmit a message."

The bodice was an old and time-honored means of transporting illicit correspondence.

Given the depth of Mme. Delagardie's décolletage, it would have had to be a very short note. Her bodice hadn't plunged to the magnificent depths of Napoleon's sister Pauline, but it had been low enough and transparent enough to make the inclusion of a sizable epistle unlikely.

There were always garters. . . .

For some reason, it felt wrong to be contemplating Mme. Delagardie's garters, at least in front of Jane. It shouldn't have been. His interest in Mme. Delagardie's garters, Augustus reminded himself, was purely professional. It wasn't as though he were trying to imagine the contour of her thighs or the texture of her skin, the fine sheen of gold hair, or the slim curve of a calf. No. Not at all. It was entirely about papers, the conveying thereof.

Illicit papers.

Not illicit thoughts.

"There might have been another note," Augustus said shortly. "It might have been a ruse."

"Or simply cough syrup," said Jane practically. "Louis-Charles has been plagued by a terrible cough all spring. Emma's mother swears by a concoction of herbs and honey. Hortense asked Emma for the recipe. It was as simple as that."

Simple, in Augustus's experience, was a dangerous term. Look at Jane herself, the picture of innocent insipidity. The Ministry of Police had made that mistake; Augustus didn't intend to.

"Things that seem simple often aren't. The message might have been in code."

"A new code based on housewifery?" Jane arched her brows. "The idea has merit. One might substitute troop movements for the annihilation of moths or an influx of bullion for boiling with honey."

Augustus sensed a certain amount of sarcasm there.

"How is that any more absurd than a code based on frivolities?" He saw Jane stiffen and hastily moved to turn the mockery on himself. "Better anything than poetry."

The brim of her bonnet hid her face as she strolled past a row of statues, forcing him to trot along behind. "It would be a rather clever idea," she said. "No one ever pays any attention to domestic affairs. I just don't believe it to be applicable in this instance."

Augustus swallowed a hasty "Why not?" stopping himself just before the words were uttered.

Mme. Delagardie was her friend, that was why not.

How long had it been since he had called someone friend without reservation or hidden intentions? Espionage was a damnable business, not least for the effect it wrought on one's human relations, sapping trust, betraying confidences, turning friendship into a mockery and love to a ruse.

He thought of Horace de Lilly, so cavalierly spilling confidences. He had had no qualms about disabusing Horace, but what about Jane? He hated to tarnish whatever illusions she had managed to retain. This was a dirty business, no matter how one looked at it.

On the other hand, illusions could kill.

Gently, Augustus said, "Your loyalty does you credit."

"It's not loyalty, it's common sense." Jane cast him a look from beneath her bonnet, her gray eyes meeting his without fear or reservation. "Do you really believe I would allow personal affection to blind me to a danger?"

Augustus looked at Jane, her cool gray eyes at odds with the youthful smoothness of her skin, the pale pink flush of her cheeks.

Yes, he wanted to say. Yes, and it might not be a bad thing. There were times when it might be well to allow affection to supersede prudence, for emotion to trump logic. To entirely eschew human weakness was to become a thing apart. In short, Miss Gwen.

"No," he said. "I don't. At least," he added hastily, "not in this instance. We are all of us prey to the human emotions."

"That," said Jane repressively, "sounds like the poet speaking."

If it were the poet speaking, there would have been several more adverbs involved. "Not the poet," said Augustus quietly. "The man."

He needed only the littlest crook of the finger, the slightest softening of the lips. All he wanted was some indication, some sign that she had heard and understood, as a woman, not as an agent. It was a man who spoke to her, a man who had been too long alone, too long caught in this trap of his own devising, known to everyone, but known by no one, a stranger to his own mirror, a liar by his own pen. It would be nice to have just one person with whom one could be totally and entirely oneself, without subterfuge.

They could be ideally suited, if only she would just see it. She wouldn't have to play the milksop for him any more than he would have to play the poet for her. They could speak in their own voices, share their worries, exchange strategies, turn to each other for comfort when a mission went awry.

Beneath that cool facade, his Pink Carnation had feelings like anyone else. She had to have.

Augustus glanced at Miss Gwen.

Well, like *almost* anyone else.

Jane turned away. Augustus found himself contemplating the nape of her neck. A very pleasing nape it was, pale and soft, feathered with silky strands of pale brown hair, but it was still a nape, first cousin to a back, and shorthand for dismissal.

"Men," said Jane, "are fallible. We cannot afford to be."

She had a point, as much as Augustus hated to admit it. They were agents first, individuals later. There was a time when Augustus had accepted that without question, without wanting to reverse that order. Now . . . now they had a job to do.

Fine. If she wanted to discuss business, they could discuss business. "In that case, there's nothing for it but to face facts, even about those whom you call friend."

"What facts do you have?" she asked.

Augustus glanced over his shoulder. Miss Gwen was still on sentry. Her presence was all that was required to keep the area clear.

He pretended interest in one of the paintings on the wall, although he couldn't have said for sure whether it was secular or sacred, Italian or Dutch. "Diagrams," he said. "Pictures of some sort of mechanism or device."

"As in . . ." Jane let the words trail off. Neither of them were going to use the words in public, no matter how closely Miss Gwen stood guard.

"Yes. As in *that* device." The one Horace de Lilly had come stampeding from Saint-Cloud to tell them about. "The diagram was on Delagardie's desk. She disavowed it, but her handwriting was all over it. It was not," he added, "a recipe for cough syrup."

Jane appeared less perturbed than Augustus had expected. Her brow cleared. "Did the diagram involve a pair of canisters and a series of pipes?"

A vague enough description, but . . . "Yes," said Augustus cautiously. "Something like that."

"A hydraulic pump."

"I beg your pardon?"

"What you saw was a variant on a hydraulic pump. Emma's husband was experimenting with the ideas implemented by the Montgolfier brothers. That was what you saw."

Augustus might have felt better if he'd had the slightest idea what she was talking about. Montgolfier who? Someone to do with hydraulic pumps, apparently. This was as bad as the time Jane had started trying to explain to him about dephlogisticated air. Augustus's inclinations had always been more literary than scientific. Human nature fascinated him; mechanical devices left him cold.

"Unless I'm much mistaken," said Augustus, "Paul Delagardie died four years ago. You can't mean to tell me that he's engineering from beyond the grave. Also," he added, warming to his theme, "why was Madame Delagardie's writing all over it?"

He half expected Jane to make an excuse about Emma using the spare sheet as scrap paper. Instead, she said, "There's no great mystery to that. Emma continued her husband's work at Carmagnac."

If Jane had known that, why in the hell hadn't she told him that before?

Augustus puffed his chest out, fighting to retain some dignity. "Why didn't she just say so, then?"

Jane tugged lightly at one of her earrings. "In her own way, Emma is a very private person."

Ostrich feathers and diamonds so often betokened a shy and retiring nature. "Of course, she is," said Augustus. And Pauline Bonaparte was secretly a celibate.

"Don't let yourself be taken in by appearances," said Jane seriously.

Augustus stared at her in disbelief. He had managed to stay alive through three changes of government, maintaining his alias in the face of all provocation, warding off the dangers posed by double agents and false friends. Twelve years he had been in Paris, straight through the worst of the Terror, and she was advising him?

He had the greatest possible respect for her, but . . . no.

Augustus opened his mouth—although to say what, he wasn't quite sure—but, once again, the Pink Carnation beat him to the punch, nodding in the direction of the door to the gallery, to a small woman in green and gold being escorted by a man in various shades of brown. The sunlight through the long windows cast rainbows off her heavy gold earrings and the scalloped edges of her fashionable overdress.

"Ah," said Jane calmly. "There's Emma now."

"You don't sound surprised."

"Hardly," said Jane. "I invited them." Without allowing time for that to sink in, she added, "You did say you wanted to speak about Emma."

About, not to. Prepositions had been invented for a reason. When he had called for this meeting, he had envisioned it going rather differently.

But then, thought Augustus wryly, he had envisioned this all rather differently. A tête-à-tête, perhaps some wine, confidences given and exchanged, meaningful looks across the bosom of the Venus de Milo.

Jane was right. He had been playing the poet too long.

"The cousin has a controlling interest in a munitions factory," Augustus said deliberately.

Finally, he had told her something she didn't already know. For the first time that afternoon, he had Jane's full attention. But not for him. Never for him.

"They claim he's here on family business," said Augustus, speaking rapidly, keeping his voice low. "Georges Marston seems to believe it's something else. So do others I've spoken to. They think family matters are a smoke screen for business of a more businesslike kind."

"Bonaparte's device?"

"Perhaps. It would explain the timing of its testing."

Someone had taken Livingston to a barber in the past few days; his hair was no longer clubbed back but cut short, in the modern fashion, combed forward over his brow. The coat was still brown, but it had been augmented with a crisp cravat, and the man's boots looked like they might have finally seen more than a dirty rag for polish.

"See what you can do with the cousin," Augustus said roughly.

He would have preferred they play it the other way around. He could speak man-to-man with Livingston, Jane could take coffee with Delagardie.

It wouldn't work.

Jane couldn't be trusted to be objective when it came to her Emma. As for Livingston, Jane would be able to get a good deal more out of him than Augustus ever could. The thought of Jane working her wiles on another man, quiet, ladylike wiles though they might be, made Augustus's gut churn, but there was nothing else for it.

He had been a professional for too long to allow his private emotions to compromise a mission.

No matter how much he disliked it.

"You take care of the cousin," Augustus said brusquely. "I'll keep an eye on your Emma."

Chapter 11

The Garden Intrigue

With fair wind and fiery star
I've cleaved the waves to where you are,
Bringing in my foam-tossed wake,
A whole land's bounties for thy sake.
　　　—Emma Delagardie and Augustus Whittlesby,
　　　　　Americanus: A Masque in Three Parts

Y ou want me to do what?" asked Kort.

"Take part in a theatrical production," Emma repeated. This wasn't going exactly as she had intended.

"A theatrical production? As in a stage? And tights?" The last word was uttered in tones of masculine disgust.

"There don't need to be tights," said Emma soothingly. "You always seemed to enjoy our amateur theatricals at Belvedere. Remember the time you got in such trouble for stealing the rooster's tail feathers to make a Cavalier's hat?"

"Yes, but that was conducted in English," protested Kort. "Not French."

"No, it was really more of a squawk," said Emma. "Followed by loud pecking noises."

"I meant the play."

"If you do take the role, you'll be playing an American. Everyone will expect you to have an accent. It will lend verisimilitude." She didn't tell him she had borrowed the phrase from Mr. Whittlesby. Somehow, she didn't think that would help her argument. Kort hadn't seemed overly impressed by Mr. Whittlesby. It might have had something to do with all the mincing and wafting and entirely unnecessary alliteration.

Kort wasn't convinced. "It's one thing to embarrass myself in front of family, quite another to do so on the international stage."

"It's not the international stage, just a little stage at Malmaison." Emma gave him her best smile, the one she had perfected way back when, in the days of the rooster-tail hat. "And Madame Bonaparte has been all but family to me, which means that, by extension, she's family to you."

"That makes no sense at all."

"Why not?"

Kort gave her an incredulous look. "You can't just declare a family by fiat."

"Don't be silly. The law courts do it all the time. It's called adoption."

Kort wisely decided not to pursue that line of argument. Instead, he narrowed his blue eyes at Emma, asking shrewdly, "Why do you want me there so badly?"

Emma rolled her eyes. "*So* badly? You flatter yourself."

"In that case," said Kort, "why not find another leading man for your theatricals? I'm sure there are any number of them lining up in the wings."

"Yes, but none who can affect an American accent quite so convincingly." Emma linked her arm through his. "Do I have to have a reason for wanting to prolong the visit of my favorite cousin?"

"I can just see the headlines now," Kort grumbled, and Emma knew she had won. "'American Merchant Makes Fool of Self in French Farce.' And that will just be the offstage part."

"Just think of all the adoring maidens flinging themselves at your feet. No one can resist an actor." Emma cunningly played her ace. She pointed down the gallery, past a strapping Apollo garbed in the latest in fig-leaf fashion. "Speaking of which, there's your leading lady, should you choose to take the part."

Kort squinted. "The purple horror?"

Emma thumped him in the side with her reticule. "No, silliness. The other one. The pretty one."

Almost as though on cue, Jane emerged from behind the outstretched arm of the statue, a symphony in lilac linen. There was a man with her, a man garbed in tight, knit pantaloons and a shirt that billowed out at the waist and sleeves. His eyes met Emma's over Jane's shoulder, and Emma felt an absurd flutter of excitement, as though he were a lover rather than a collaborator, as though their assignations had involved something more than ink.

All nonsense, of course. Nonsense and tight breeches. Emma forced herself to attend to her cousin, turning her head deliberately away from the poet.

"I met her, didn't I?"

"Yes, at the rout at the Hotel de Balcourt last week."

Kort looked blank.

"The house with all the Egyptian bits in it," Emma translated. She fluttered her lashes at Kort. "See? Aren't you glad you've decided to take the part?"

"I hadn't said I would," Kort corrected. With studied casualness, he added, "As it happens, I'm going to be at Malmaison anyway. Uncle Robert secured an invitation for me."

"Oh." That took the wind out of her sails. So much for impressing her cousin with her French connections when he was able to obtain the same coveted invitation by other means. "Well, then! You have even less excuse not to play my leading man. I'll expect you in rehearsals next week. Once we've written it," she added, as an afterthought.

"Unless you decide not to," said Kort hopefully.

Emma struck him playfully on the arm. "Don't even think it. Resistance is futile. I will have you in those tights." Something else struck her. "Wasn't your business meant to be concluded by then?"

Kort flexed his hands in his tan gloves, manipulating the muscles to make his knuckles crack. "There have been unexpected complications," he said shortly.

"Ah," said Emma knowingly. Not that she actually knew anything about conducting business, but it was always best to assume the pretense. "You'll have to book a later passage, won't you?"

Kort looked down at her, shifting slightly from foot to foot. "Emma . . ."

"Yes?" Was that an apology she heard coming?

Kort stepped abruptly back, his boot heel connecting with a sharp sound against the marble floor. "Never mind. It doesn't matter. Come along. Don't you want to reintroduce me to your friends?"

Before Emma could argue that it did matter, that whatever he had to say, she wanted to hear it, he had started forward, tugging her along behind him, like . . . like a poodle on a leash, she thought indignantly. Just like back at Belvedere. Her flat-heeled slippers skidded against the marble floor as she scrambled to keep up.

"Emma," said Jane, her voice rich with amusement. "What a surprise to see you here. And your charming cousin as well."

Kort executed an old-fashioned bow. "Ladies."

Jane stepped forward and extended a hand to Kort. "I hear you are to be my hero."

"On the stage, at least," Kort said. His eyes slid towards Miss Gwen. Miss Gwen nodded regally, giving Kort permission to take Jane's hand.

"Hero?" managed Whittlesby, in a mangled voice.

"In our masque!" Emma's voice came out too loud and too high, waking the echoes in the corners of the room. "Isn't it above all things wonderful? Kort has agreed to take the role."

"But . . ." Mr. Whittlesby was still looking at Jane, not at her. "Miss Wooliston?"

Jane gently retrieved her hand from Kort's. She gestured to Emma, her smile never wavering. "Our ever persuasive Madame Delagardie has induced me to tread the boards. Provided, that is," she added, with mock reproach, "that you write us something fit to act in." She turned back to Kort. "What do you say, Mr. Livingston? Shall we leave them to their artistic musings? I fear we are sadly in the way."

Kort offered his arm with flattering alacrity. "I wouldn't want to be the man to stand in the way of genius."

"Lovely." It was very neatly done. Within a space of a moment, Jane was leading Kort away. Emma could hear her voice floating back, oddly distorted by the echoing space. "Have you had much experience on the stage, Mr. Livingston?"

Jane would never wink; it wasn't her way. The look she cast Emma over her shoulder, however, might as well have been a wink. It had the same effect. As Miss Gwen stalked along behind her charge, Emma realized, with growing horror, exactly what her friend had done.

She had left Emma alone with Mr. Whittlesby.

On purpose.

And it wasn't so they could discuss the masque.

It wasn't fair, Emma thought passionately. She didn't try to shove off her unwanted admirers on Jane or embarrass her friend by pointedly obvious efforts to throw her together with the object of her affections.

Of course, that was only because Jane was too circumspect to ever admit to having an object of affection. But the point still remained: Emma's hands were clean, even if only by default.

Did Mr. Whittlesby realize? He would have to be an idiot not to.

An idiot . . . or a man in love. He was, Emma realized, not looking at her at all. He was still watching Jane, his eyes following her as she led Kort along the marble hall, as her hand gestured elegantly at this painting or that statue.

Of course he didn't realize. Emma didn't register for him at all, did she? At least, not that way.

The thought oughtn't to be that lowering—she did only admire him for his breeches, after all—but it was. It clung to the back of her throat like lye, base and corrosive.

"She never told me," he said, more to himself than Emma. "Why didn't she tell me?"

"Perhaps she didn't have the chance," said Emma soothingly.

Whittlesby didn't want to be soothed. He turned on her like the Grand Inquisitor. "Was it your idea that Miss Wooliston be in the masque?"

"No." Emma realized she had sounded just as brusque as he had, and made a hasty effort at amends. It wouldn't do to sound as though she hadn't wanted Jane; she would never want anyone to think that. "Hortense suggested it—Madame Bonaparte, that is. She was to play the lead but now that— Let's just say that circumstances have rendered it unlikely. She might still, though."

Oh, good. Now she didn't sound brusque. She just sounded like the village idiot.

Mustering her wits, she said, "Either way, I'm sure it will go splendidly. How can it not with my imagination and your pen? Everyone will be shouting for encores!"

She looked expectantly at him, but Mr. Whittlesby was not inclined to match her cheerful tone. "How long have you known?"

"Since Friday."

"*Friday?*"

"I should have thought you would be glad to have Miss Wooliston in our cast," said Emma, nettled past tact. "It will save you the bother of following her from place to place."

Well, that got his attention. But not in a good way. From the look he gave her, one would have thought he had just caught her going through his jacket pockets. If he ever wore a jacket, that is. The billowy linen shirt left little to the imagination.

Emma colored. That was always the problem with fair skin—the slightest hint of embarrassment and there it came, out like a rash. But, really, there was no reason to be made to feel as though she were somehow rooting about in his private affairs. He had made his feelings for Jane entirely public.

Twenty-two cantos of public.

"You're never going to win her that way," said Emma officiously.

Whittlesby's face was a study in outrage. "I beg your pardon?"

"You ought," said Emma frankly. "All those cantos, all those readings, and all of them for nothing! It's been very tedious."

"No one asked you to subject yourself to my work," said Whittlesby loftily. "They were not intended for you."

"Please don't misunderstand me," said Emma. "I don't mean to malign your poetry. It's simply that as a technique for courtship, it leaves something to be desired. I know they say poetry is the way to a woman's heart, but it didn't work for Petrarch, either."

"Has it occurred to you, madame, that I might write verse for the sake of verse? That the creation of poetry might in itself be the object of desire rather than the fallible human form that inspires it?"

Yes, but Jane had a very lovely form, and she had several years yet before it started to be fallible. Oh, the joys of being twenty-two and in little need of corsets!

"That is nicely said," said Emma approvingly. "For your sake, I hope it's true."

"My intentions," Whittlesby said with dignity, "are as pure as my poetry."

"It isn't your intentions that are the problem, but your methods. Twenty-two cantos? There are far better ways to get a lady's attention."

"Are you offering to play Cyrano?" There was a decidedly dangerous glint in Mr. Whittlesby's eye. "Don't confuse me with your Mr. Marston. Not all men are in his mold."

"You mean, direct?" Emma wasn't quite sure why she was defending Marston, other than that, at this particular moment, she would have negated anything Whittlesby said, up to and including green being the color of grass and the sky being up rather than down.

"Direct," Whittlesby repeated. "That's one way of putting it. Direct to your door?"

Emma flushed. "At least he made clear what he wanted."

Whittlesby's eyes narrowed on her face, taking on a speculative expression. "And what might that be?"

"Didn't you know?" said Emma, with a forced laugh. "My diamonds. Pity for him they're paste."

She didn't want to talk about Marston with Augustus Whittlesby. She didn't want to talk about Marston at all.

Behind Whittlesby's shoulder, a young man was hovering, dressed richly in a deep green jacket with a waistcoat in stripes of pink and green.

"Oh, look," she babbled, waving enthusiastically, "there's dear Monsieur—"

What was his name? There had been so many people come to Paris recently, so many members of the old aristocratic families returned from exile in England and elsewhere. It was impossible to keep them all straight.

"De Lilly?" Whittlesby frowned over his shoulder at the young man.

"Yes?" At the sound of his name, the young man hastened forward. It hadn't been meant as an invitation, but he took it as such. He bowed enthusiastically over Emma's hand. "Madame Delagardie! It is a pleasure."

At least someone thought so. Emma tried to send a meaningful look at Mr. Whittlesby, but Mr. Whittlesby wasn't paying the slightest bit of attention.

De Lilly was probably roughly her own age, but he seemed like a boy, all pink cheeked and eager to please. He made Emma feel ancient.

"Do you know Mr. Whittlesby?" Emma asked de Lilly, mostly to needle the poet. She missed her fan. It was so much less effective gesticulating without one.

De Lilly glanced sideways at Mr. Whittlesby and went pink about the cheekbones. "Mr. Whittlesby and I are somewhat acquainted."

Emma looked inquisitively at Mr. Whittlesby, but the poet had assumed his most otherworldly expression.

"The muses lead many to my door," he intoned.

De Lilly dropped his gaze to his boot tops, looking sheepish and very, very young. "Mr. Whittlesby was kind enough to undertake a small commission for me."

Emma glanced archly at the poet. "Service à la Cyrano?"

Mr. Whittlesby sniffed. "If you insist on calling it that. I prefer to think of it as wooing for the romantically impaired."

De Lilly went an even deeper red.

Oh, the poor thing. Emma felt guilty for having pushed the topic. If only her mouth wouldn't run ahead of her brain! There was nothing more painful than puppy love. Emma wondered who he might be in love with. There were so many candidates.

"It's always useful to have a poet about," she said to the young man. "Everyone is hiring them these days."

"Er, yes." He dragged his eyes up from his boots, clearly eager to change the topic. "Have you heard the news?"

"News?" Emma lifted a hand in response as her friend Adele de Treville waved at her from across the room. "Oh, do you mean that story about Mademoiselle George and the tenor? Or was it a flautist? I've heard it was vastly exaggerated, especially the bit about his being tossed into the Seine naked."

M. de Lilly shook his head vigorously. "Oh, no. It wasn't the Seine, it was the fishpond at Saint-Cloud." There was a strange snorting sound from Mr. Whittlesby's general direction. M. de Lilly glanced cautiously in his direction before going on. "But that's not what I meant. Didn't you hear?"

"Hear what?" asked Emma. If it was better than the flautist in the fishpond, it was bound to be good.

De Lilly drew himself up. "The senate has voted."

As an attempted grand pronouncement, it fell rather flat.

"How nice for them," said Emma. Didn't they do that sort of thing rather frequently? "On what?"

Both men stared at her, united, for the moment, in mutual disbelief.

Mr. Whittlesby cleared his throat, shocked out of his offended silence. "Do you read anything except the fashion papers, Madame Delagardie?"

"Of course. I read *Le Moniteur* every day." More like every month, but who was counting. She batted her lashes up at the poet. "How else would I know what my friends are doing?"

Bursting with his news, de Lilly ignored their byplay. "The senate voted," he said loudly, "and Bonaparte accepted."

His words were ostensibly directed at Emma, but his eyes were on Whittlesby.

"Should you like me to compose an ode for the occasion?" drawled Whittlesby, just as Emma demanded, "Accepted what?"

De Lilly turned to her, his eyes bright with excitement. "It's official! Bonaparte is Emperor of the French!"

Chapter 12

What matter kings or princes bold?
Or belted earls with titles old?
All is mere pomp, none can display
The zeal that spurs me on my way.
　　　　　—Emma Delagardie and Augustus Whittlesby,
　　　　　　　　　Americanus: A Masque in Three Parts

What in the devil was de Lilly playing at?

Augustus tried to signal his young colleague, but it was no use. Ignorant pup, thought Augustus, too busy capering for a lady's attention to weigh the risks. Fuming inwardly, Augustus pretended insouciance and mentally began composing a memo to Wickham, listing the various reasons why Horace de Lilly was unsuitable for assignment in the field.

Whatever reaction de Lilly had hoped to elicit, he didn't get it. Mme. Delagardie blinked. And blinked again. "Emperor? As in . . . Emperor?"

Avoiding Augustus's eye, Horace de Lilly nodded vigorously, focusing all his attention on Mme. Delagardie. "I hear you're to be a lady-in-waiting, Madame Delagardie."

"A—"

"Lady-in-waiting. It's a great honor," said de Lilly earnestly.

Mme. Delagardie didn't look honored. She just looked stunned.

"My mother was a lady-in-waiting to the former queen," de Lilly said importantly, before hastily correcting himself. "I mean, the widow Capet. You'll probably have an apartment in the palace. And another at Saint-Cloud."

"Lucky me," said Mme. Delagardie, with something like her usual frivolity. "What a pity I have a home already."

Horace looked mildly horrified. "But it's not about that," he said. "It's so you can be at court. It's—oh, you're joking, aren't you, Madame Delagardie?"

"Mmm," said Mme. Delagardie.

"Darling!" Adele de Treville breezed past in a wave of perfume and burgundy silk. Like Mme. Delagardie, she was a widow about town, intimately connected with the Bonapartes and their circle. "I've been waving and waving to you from the other side of the room, but you've been too busy with this handsome thing to pay me any notice."

She batted her lashes at Horace de Lilly, who shifted from foot to foot in half pleasure, half embarrassment.

"Do you know Monsieur de Lilly?" Mme. Delagardie said, but it came out by rote, without her usual sparkle.

"Of course, I do." Mme. de Treville sent a perfunctory smolder in de Lilly's direction before turning back to Mme. Delagardie. "You've heard? We're to be ladies-in-waiting together. Once Madame Bonaparte asks us," she added, as an afterthought. "Won't it be splendid? Quite like old times. Although we do have nicer dresses now and Madame Campan doesn't supervise our gentlemen callers." She looked up at de Lilly from under her lashes. "You will call on us, won't you?"

"I couldn't imagine anything I'd like better!" de Lilly declared gallantly.

For a man supposedly dedicated to the cause of restoring the Bourbon monarchy, de Lilly appeared to be adapting rather well to the new regime. Augustus looked lofty and poetical and kept an eye on his colleague. The sort of incompetence de Lilly had betrayed might merely be incompetence—or something more sinister.

Assessing the younger man blushing under Mme. de Treville's attentions, Augustus was inclined to go with the former. It wasn't because of the blush—a man could blush and still be a villain—but because de Lilly had been promised the return of his family's estates should the Bourbon monarchy be restored to the throne. Bonaparte, while he had invited back the various émigré aristocrats, had made no such promises regarding their property, save for a few special instances.

Even so, if it was merely incompetence, incompetence could kill. They would have to have another little word. In the meantime, though, Augustus had other fish to fry.

Next to him, Mme. de Treville squeezed Mme. Delagardie's arm. "I'm so glad I found you. But I must dash. I'm dying to call on Hortense. Do you think this makes her a princess now? Or a duchess? What do you call the daughter of an emperor?"

"Hortense?" ventured Mme. Delagardie.

"Oh, *you*," said Mme. de Treville. She pressed Mme. Delagardie's hand. "Call on me soon. We need to coordinate our wardrobes for Malmaison. There's some heavenly new fabric at Madame Bertin's. Come shopping with me tomorrow? Without you, I won't be able to decide on a thing. You will escort me to my carriage, won't you, Monsieur de Lilly?"

She didn't wait for him to finish stuttering his consent. With a waft of perfume and a whisper of muslin, Mme. de Treville was gone, towing a bemused Horace in her wake.

"Is she always like that?" Augustus asked.

"Almost," said Mme. Delagardie apologetically, adding, as though it explained something, "We went to Madame Campan's together."

"Did you go to school with everyone in Paris?" Augustus asked. Forget infiltrating the government, all they needed to do was infiltrate Mme. Campan's school for girls and the entirety of Paris would be at their disposal.

"Sometimes it feels like it." Mme. Delagardie stared unseeingly at a statue of Apollo. "It doesn't seem possible, does it? *Emperor*. Emperor?"

"You didn't know?"

Augustus bent nearly double to try to get a view of her face. He could only be thankful that her tastes didn't run to the sort of bonnets Jane favored, the sort with broad, deep brims that shadowed the face. The confection perched on Mme. Delagardie's head left her entire face bare to scrutiny, exposing her every emotion for those who chose to see it.

"You truly didn't know?"

Mme. Delagardie shook her head, setting her feathers and ribbons quivering. "I do read *Le Moniteur* from time to time. I knew the senate had discussed such a measure. But . . . Emperor?"

"An emperor and an empress," said Augustus. "And a whole imperial court to go with them."

As lady-in-waiting to an empress, Mme. Delagardie would be the object of admiration and adulation; sycophants would cluster around her, basking in the reflection of her reflected glory, using her as a conduit to the imperial ear. Knowing Bonaparte, he would probably do his best to arrange a marriage for her, pairing her off with one of the more successful of his generals or one of his captive European princelings.

Pauline Bonaparte had become Princess Borghese. What might the former Emma Morris become?

She ought to have been delighted.

Mme. Delagardie turned in a slow circle, her gown whispering around her ankles, her eyes drifting over statues and bits of columns. Imagining her glorious future? Planning her gown for the coronation? There would be a coronation, Augustus had no doubt of it. Bonaparte didn't miss a trick. If Charlemagne had one, so would he.

Mme. Delagardie sounded very far away when she spoke, the sound of her voice distorted by the vast marble walls of the former palace of kings. "It sounds so antique, not something for the modern age at all."

"That is part of the idea," said Augustus. "A return to the grandeur of Rome, with Bonaparte as our Caesar."

Mme. Delagardie's skirts tangled around her ankles as she came to a halt, fixing her gaze on him. For a future lady-in-waiting, she didn't appear to be particularly exultant. Her blue eyes looked like a cloud had come over them and there were twin lines between her brows. "Didn't Caesar come to a bad end? I seem to recall knives being involved."

"That was March, not May," pointed out Augustus. "And his dynasty lived on long after him."

He wasn't sure whether she heard him. Lost in her own thoughts, Mme. Delagardie glanced away. "I thought he meant to refuse."

"Refuse?" Augustus wasn't sure he had heard quite right.

"If they offered," she said. "I had thought he meant to refuse."

In profile, the delicacy of her features was even more pronounced. She was too thin, Augustus thought, even for her narrow frame. From the side, the hollows beneath her cheekbones showed like gashes.

"Whatever gave you that idea?" asked Augustus, with genuine curiosity.

"It has been done before," Mme. Delagardie said defensively. "Like General Washington. He might have been made a king if he liked, but he refused, out of principle."

"General Washington is no Bonaparte," said Augustus. And wasn't that the understatement of the new century. General Washington hadn't voted himself First Consul for life or set up the succession among his family members.

"Yes, yes, I know. Bonaparte still has all his own teeth." Mme. Delagardie's teeth, small and even, worried at her lower lip. "Do you remember that pamphlet—it must have been a few years ago—the one claiming that Bonaparte was the direct descendant of the man in the iron mask?"

Augustus nodded.

"Then you know what I mean," she said earnestly. "I was there, at the Tuileries, when Bonaparte heard about it. He said it was laughable."

It had been laughable, but not for the reasons Mme. Delagardie meant. Someone had gone to the trouble of making an argument that Louis XIV's twin brother, the rightful king of France, had escaped from incarceration, made his way to Corsica, and begat the line that eventually produced Bonaparte—all, presumably, without removing the mask.

Personally, Augustus got a good chuckle out of the image of breakfasts in the kitchen of a Corsican farmhouse, with the chickens pecking at the legs of the table and the man in the mask reading the morning paper while little Bonapartes tumbled about in the dirt around him.

Mme. Delagardie clasped her hands together. "He might so easily have claimed to be a Bourbon and let them make him king, but he didn't. He ordered the pamphlet suppressed. He said he had no interest in being made a king." She looked searchingly at Augustus. "And that wasn't so very long ago. A man's philosophy doesn't change that much in just three years."

"King and emperor are two different things," said Augustus gently.

It wouldn't suit Bonaparte's ambitions to be just another Bourbon monarch, an offshoot of a degenerate tree. No, he wanted to be all in all, self-made and self-sustaining.

"He fought for the Revolution. Why proclaim the rights of man one day and an empire the next? There must have been some mistake. Adele must have misunderstood." Her show of bravado was belied by the anxious lines between her eyes as she added, "Don't you think?"

Bizarrely, Augustus found himself wanting to be able to comfort her.

Comfort her? He had to be mad. She was on her way to becoming one of the most envied women in France. There was no reason to lose all grip on reality.

"Don't you want to be a lady-in-waiting? There are those who would give their right arms for the position."

Mme. Delagardie twisted her face into a wry expression. "I like my right arm. I'm accustomed to it. It's quite useful."

"Are you that set against the idea?"

It took her a moment to answer. She gave a small, hopeless shrug. "I'm not made for courts and palaces. I'm too much an American for that." In a smaller voice, she added, "It feels wrong."

"You're already frequenting courts and palaces," Augustus pointed out. It was a bit late to be having attacks of republican principle.

"Yes, but . . ." She looked hopelessly up at him. "It felt different when Bonaparte called himself First Consul. It made it easier to pretend."

"Pretend what?" Augustus prompted.

She looked down at her gloved hands, worrying at the lump of a ring beneath the leather. When she spoke, it was so quietly that Augustus had to strain to hear her.

"That nothing had changed."

"Pardon?" It wasn't the most elegant question, but Augustus had no idea what she was getting at.

Mme. Delagardie's eyes were still on her hands, but she was seeing something else entirely. "Hortense was the first girl I met at Madame Campan's. We were friends almost from the first. She used to have nightmares, you know, about her mother being shut up in prison."

"No," said Augustus, since something needed to be said. "I didn't know."

"That was all before Bonaparte. Madame de Beauharnais had a little house in the Rue Chantereine, with tiny rooms up in the attic for Hortense and Eugene. I used to stay with Hortense in her room." Mme. Delagardie shook her head. "It was like living in a theatrical set. There'd always be people coming and going and never enough chairs to seat them on. There was never any food in the larder, except right before a party. Madame Bonaparte would order in all sorts of absurd delicacies, but she'd always forget something, like the bread or the milk. We'd find ourselves with wine but not the glasses to serve it in, or chocolate but no milk to mix it with. Hortense and Eugene and I would be sent off to the neighbors, to beg or borrow whatever Madame de Beauharnais needed. It got to the point that when the neighbors saw me coming, they'd meet me at the door with an armload of crockery."

She smiled at the memory, and Augustus found himself smiling with her, at the image of a small girl in a white gown staggering under the weight of plates and platters.

"It sounds . . . unique," he said.

"It was lovely," she said, in a voice that brooked no disagreement. "My family was millions of miles away and Madame de Beauharnais was all that was kind. Even after she married Bonaparte, we had such pleasant times. We used to play prisoner's base at Malmaison, and Hortense would sing in the evenings. There was no court and no curtsying and no protocol or precedence. Even after Paul—" She broke off.

"Even after?" Augustus prompted. After Paul what?

"They were very kind to me" was all she said. With a sigh, she admitted, "I miss it. I miss the informality and the camaraderie. I miss the simplicity of it all."

"Nothing can stay simple forever," Augustus said.

Unbidden, memories of the vicarage of his youth rose up before him, a churchyard and an oak tree and vines twining along the side of a house, red brick warm in the sunlight. His little sister skipped in the sunlight, twirling to make her skirts billow as she danced.

He had visited once, after the house had already passed into different hands. Polly had married, and his father had retired to Tunbridge Wells to do whatever it was that retired clergymen did. He had known it would be a bad idea, and it was. The tree had been cut down, the vines pruned away. There were fresh curtains in the window and rosebushes, scraggly with youth, planted by the door. It was a pleasant, prosperous place, but it wasn't his. Not anymore. He had gone away without going inside.

It was for the better, he told himself. "We all grow up, whether we like it or not."

"Perhaps." Mme. Delagardie didn't sound convinced. "But is there any need to make it more complicated than it needs to be? When I see what they did to Hortense, marrying her off to that—"

She broke off, catching herself before she could say whatever she had intended.

"Ambition," said Augustus softly, "can be a very powerful force."

This time, Mme. Delagardie didn't take the bait.

She fluttered a hand in an unconvincing facsimile of her usual insouciant style. "Forgive me. I'm being horrible and selfish, babbling on at you like this. What you must think of me! I scarcely know what I'm saying." Rubbing two fingers across her eyes, she said, with obvious sincerity, "I didn't sleep as well as I ought last night."

"Out carousing?"

She flashed him a too-bright smile. "Oh, naturally."

She was lying. They both knew it. But it was, in its way, a gallant lie.

Her lilac paint had smeared next to her eyes when she rubbed them. It gave her the look of a small girl caught playing in her mother's paint box, with her rouge too bright for her cheeks and a feather hanging crookedly from her hat. For the first time, he noticed how small she really was, narrow shouldered and fine boned, dwarfed by her own finery. She held herself as though she were ready to ward off an army with a smile, balanced forward on the balls of her feet, head up, shoulders back, best feather forward. An act, but a brave one.

Despite himself, Augustus felt a dangerous stirring of pity. He had discounted her before as frivolous and vapid—and perhaps she was still those things. He had suspected her of scheming, or at least of playing the role of go-between—and there was nothing to say that one couldn't look lost and vulnerable and still be a villain. Fundamentally, though, he didn't know what to make of her. Attached to the Bonapartes, yes, but not to Bonaparte. Or was that, too, just an act? And what about Paul Delagardie? The gossip had been quite clear; she had left him, possibly cuckolded him, then taken up with Marston after his death. Yet, when she spoke of him, it was with something that sounded very akin to grief.

None of it made any sense at all.

He looked up to find her watching him. "Do you know," she said slowly, "I've noticed something."

"What?"

"For quite some time, you've forgotten to rhyme."

Augustus sucked in air through his nose, feeling as though he'd just been punched in the gut. Not just any sort of punch. A punch thrown with killing force. His stomach muscles tensed, his kidneys contracted, he could feel the cold prickle of sweat below his arms. His breath jammed in his throat as panic coursed through his body. The surprise of it had him gasping. She had walloped him good and he had never ever seen it coming.

She stood in front of him still, looking small and harmless and innocent, all frills and rouge, lilac paint smeared around her eyes, one earring caught in her hair, twisted at an odd angle.

Had all of it—the confidences about her youth, the feigned dismay, her friend's interruption—been nothing more than a trap? If so, it was cleverer by far than anything Napoleon's Ministry of Police had tossed at him before.

Augustus blessed the training that enabled him to maintain a calm mask, even as his skin prickled with goose bumps, and his heart thrummed beneath his shirt.

"Madame?" he said coolly, because he didn't trust himself to say anything more.

"It's all an act, isn't it?" Mme. Delagardie was examining him as though he were a butterfly on a naturalist's table. "You're much more sensible than you sound."

He had two choices. He could launch rapidly into a stream of inanities in an attempt to convince her that his seeming lucidity was an aberration. If she were the feather wit she appeared, that might have worked. But she wasn't a feather wit, was she? She had certainly sussed him out neatly enough.

Augustus chose to go with the second option.

"And what if I am?" he said.

Mme. Delagardie shook her head. "Nothing. I just wondered . . . why?"

"People expect their poets to sound a certain way." Augustus dropped his voice and shortened his vowels, reverting to his natural voice. He lifted his shoulders in a shrug. "I satisfy their preconceptions. They commission poems. Everyone gets what they want."

Sometimes, a false admission worked better than a denial.

Mme. Delagardie looked at him with curiosity, but without suspicion, her blue eyes as guileless as a child's. "Don't you mind it? The dissembling?"

Step one: false admission. Step two: shift attention. Augustus took a shot in the dark.

"Do you?" he shot back.

"I don't—I don't know what you mean." Her words were bold enough, but her hands betrayed her, fidgeting with the ruffle on her reticule.

He had hit home. What was it Jane had said? *In her own strange way, Emma is a very private person.*

Trust Jane to get it right. Again.

Augustus folded his arms across his chest, squishing down the folds of excess fabric. He took in the kohl that darkened her lashes, the rouge that lent color to her cheeks, the powder that hid the circles beneath her eyes. "You play the merry widow very nicely. You manage to sound nearly as vapid as Madame de Treville. But it isn't true, is it?"

He had her on the defensive now, just where he wanted her, her attention focused on herself rather than on him.

"It isn't all an act," she said defensively. "I can be quite silly at times. And I do like parties and shiny things."

He cocked an eyebrow. "Made of paste?"

"I should never have told you that," she muttered. She looked up at him. "Shall we make a deal? A bargain? For the duration of our collaboration?"

Talk of deals made Augustus wary. "What kind of bargain?"

She raised her chin. "No pretenses."

"None at all?" Augustus regarded her quizzically. "Even lovers keep secrets, Madame Delagardie."

"Do you think I don't know that?" In a more moderate tone, she said, "All I meant was that we can speak sensibly to one another, rather than, oh, I don't know, trying to maintain some sort of absurd role."

"In other words," said Augustus slowly, "it will be easier to work together if I eschew some of the abverbs."

"Not all of them, but . . . yes." She favored him with a whimsical smile, the sort of smile that made one want to smile back. She did have her own charm, the little Delagardie. "It will certainly save us time. We only have three weeks until the performance."

"Ah, yes," said Augustus. "A performance fit for an emperor."

Mme. Delagardie wrinkled her nose. "I wish you wouldn't say that. It might be rumor yet," she added hopefully.

"I thought," said Augustus drily, "that we had agreed to speak sensibly to one another."

"I'm not sure I didn't like you better in your silly guise," said Mme. Delagardie darkly.

"It's too late now," said Augustus. "The adverbs are out of the bag. Unless you'd like to pretend we never had this little conversation?"

He was offering her the chance to eradicate all of it, including her careless confidences about the Bonaparte clan. That was the sort of thing that could be accounted treason these days. It took so little—a thoughtless word, an uncomplimentary comment about Bonaparte's receding hairline—to bring one to the attention of the Ministry of Police. Was she really that naïve? Or was it simply that she considered herself protected?

"No," said Mme. Delagardie decidedly. "If we are to work together, we ought to deal plainly with each other. Oh, and there's one more thing."

"Yes?" The falsely casual tone of her words sent all of Augustus's instincts humming. He had learned to be wary of *one more thing*s.

Mme. Delagardie held up both hands. "Don't look like that! It's nothing dreadful." She took a deep breath and then blurted it out. "Hadn't you best call me Emma?"

Chapter 13

From the mixed-up files of Augustus B. Whittlesby: a correspondence tentatively dated between May and June of 1804. From the absence of any address on the back of the paper, it seems likely that these notes would have been delivered by hand, on Mr. Whittlesby's side by a variety of convenient urchins (see dirt smudges), and on Mme. Delagardie's by a footman with a taste for some sort of pastry involving powdered sugar.

A. Whittlesby to E. Delagardie
Will I see you at Mme. Salpietre's tonight? We can continue our discussion there.

Cordially,
A. Whittlesby

E. Delagardie to A. Whittlesby
You will call on me tomorrow afternoon, won't you? I promise to supply the cakes if you bring a clean version of the first act. Mine is entirely scribbled over and interlined,

*and if even I can't read it, how will our actors? I do like
your idea of having our pirate king be a pirate queen
instead. It will be just the role for Miss Meadows. She does
like slashing about at people.*

*On a note only somewhat related, if you won't wear a
jacket, at least fling on a cloak. I could see the goose pimples
beneath your shirt last night at Mme. Salpietre's salon.
Admittedly, she stints on the coal, but even so. I should hate
to lose my collaborator to something so pedestrian as a chill.
Footpads, perhaps, or highwayman, or even a jealous
husband, but a mere breeze? Decidedly passé.*

With warmest expressions of esteem,
E. Delagardie

A. Whittlesby to E. Delagardie

*Am I to deduce from this that you care? Your solicitude
warms my frozen flesh.*

*If Mme. Salpietre weren't too cheap to light proper fires,
there would have been no such problem.*

*I shall be there tomorrow without fail. Bring out your
cakes.*

Warmly yours,
Augustus

E. Delagardie to A. Whittlesby

*For a man who makes his living by words, you are
remarkably stingy with them in correspondence. I would
feel quite neglected if I didn't know you had used up all
your ink composing a soliloquy for Americanus.*

*I am, however, quite obdurate on this matter of external
garments. If the temperature would deign to rise . . . if the
wind would cease to blow . . . if the sun would shine past*

midnight. You can come up with all the excuses you like. I understand that poets are particularly prone to consumption. I am convinced it is entirely on account of the wardrobe.

I don't want you dying on me, you absurd man. Who else would supply me with adverbs? In case you've forgotten, we still have two-thirds of a masque to write.

If you appear without a cloak, I shall be forced to take you shopping for one.

Unconvinced,
Emma

A. Whittlesby to E. Delagardie

Have you never heard the adage of the pot and the kettle, my dear Mme. Preachiness? Having seen you last night in what can amount to no more than a whisper of gossamer and thistledown, I can only assume that you are deliberately courting consumption in order to establish your bona fides as a member of the poetic fraternity.

By shopping . . . Is this an attempt to get me to carry your parcels again? I thought you had footmen for that.

Augustus

p.s. If it makes you feel better, I do own a perfectly serviceable cloak. If you require proof, I will even deign to wear it.

E. Delagardie to A. Whittlesby

Yes, it did make me feel better, even though you did look rather silly stalking through Saint-Germain on a sunny day all wrapped about in wool with only the top of your head showing. My footman thought you were there to rob the house and had to be soothed with a stiff brandy, even *though we all faithfully assured him that highwaymen stalk highways, not private residences.*

Why do I suspect that on the next chilly night, you'll be back to your shirtsleeves?

I've had an idea about our masque. What do you think about having Americanus run off with the Pirate Queen instead? Cytherea, while lovely, seems a bit insipid. It would be a twist that no one would ever expect!

Emma

p.s. The package contains some of those currant cakes you like so much. Please eat them so I don't.

A. Whittlesby to E. Delagardie

Not if the Pirate Queen is played by Miss Meadows. This is meant to be a comedy, not a tragedy.

A. Whittlesby to E. Delagardie

Please forgive the terse tone of my earlier missive. I wrote in haste and some horror. You were jesting, were you not? Let's just say you were, for our mutual peace of mind and the good of mankind.

Many thanks for the currant cakes. May I entice you to take some supper with me before the opera tonight? You need the feeding more than I do. Champagne, Mme. Delagardie, is not an adequate meal.

Augustus

E. Delagardie to A. Whittlesby

Scold, scold, scold. I'll mend my ways, my dear Mr. Whittlesby, when you mend yours. You're quite wrong, you know. Champagne is a perfectly lovely supper and it doesn't catch in your teeth when you're trying to talk to people.

Adele would be perfectly willing to play the Pirate Queen should you change your mind. She isn't so keen on the poetry, but she's quite eager to try her effect on the gentlemen in breeches. Her effect in breeches, that is. Not that the gentlemen wouldn't be in breeches too. You know what I mean.

All the arrangements have been made for Malmaison. We are to go up Wednesday along with the principles in the cast. Hortense has arranged for costumes, so all that will be left for us will be to make time for the final fittings in between rehearsals. The rest of the party arrive on Friday and the performance is to take place on Saturday night.

Mr. Fulton faithfully promises to send us our wave maker by Wednesday afternoon so that Americanus might be beset by waves upon the treach'rous seas, or however it is we phrased it.

My coach will call for you at eight on Wednesday.

Yes, I do mean eight in the morning. There is one. I had no idea.

In anticipation,
Emma

A. Whittlesby to E. Delagardie

There is, I have heard, a little thing called sunrise, in which the sun reverses the process we all viewed the night before. You might assume such a thing as mythical as those beasts that guard the corners of the earth, but I have it on the finest authority, and have, indeed, from time to time, regarded it with my own eyes.

While I am sure your Mme. de Treville would look very well in breeches, the entire premise behind the piece is the union of Americanus and France, in the person of Cytherea.

What message does it send if Americanus runs off with a pirate queen instead? France's feelings might be hurt. Hell hath no fury like a country scorned.

Are you pleased with the script as it stands? (Or sits or lies?) Given the restraints, I'd say we've made quite a creditable job of it. I'll say no more for fear of enraging the muses. We can gloat comfortably together in the privacy of your carriage tomorrow morning at that most uncomfortable hour.

Eagerly,
Augustus

p.s. I'll bring my cloak if you bring more currant cakes.

Chapter 14

"*A*re you sure it's okay?"

"Huh?" I was still staring after Nigel Dempster. The stripes on his suit were too close together. A little like his eyes. Not like I was prejudiced or anything. It didn't count as prejudice when it was true. "What?"

Colin was not going to be happy when he heard that his sister's snake of an ex was on the premises. Admittedly, Colin was already unhappy, but this was going to add a whole new level of awful to a week that was already shaping up to rival one of Dante's inner circles of inferno. All we needed was a frozen lake and a few upside-down popes. And maybe some little demons with pitchforks.

"About the computer," said Cate. "That would be really great, if you're sure it's okay. There's only one for the whole crew, and this sound guy keeps hogging it."

"Oh, right." It had been only about five minutes since I had contrived my cunning plan to win over a member of the film crew with extra Internet access, but it felt much longer. Back then—before Dempster—I'd only been worried about people walking in on my shower and Colin going after Jeremy with a fish knife. This was just getting more fun by the moment.

But none of it was Cate's fault.

"Of course, it's fine," I said, baring way too many teeth in an attempt to make amends for my abstraction. "Just don't tell anyone else or we'll have half the cast knocking down the door. Do you want to come with me now? I can show you where it is."

Cate fell into step beside me. "Thank you so much. I have a boyfriend at home, and this whole text thing—" Cate waved her phone in the air in illustration. "Well, it's kind of limiting."

Listening to someone else's relationship woes was preferable to trying to figure out how in the hell I was going to gently break to Colin that we had another crisis on our hands.

Or telling him that I had only one month left to live—I mean, date.

I made a sympathetic face at Cate. "How long have you been doing the transcontinental thing?"

"Two weeks." Cate regarded her mobile with disfavor. "It feels like longer."

"The whole time zone thing sucks, doesn't it?" Colin and I had played that game when I was home in New York over Christmas.

It's funny I had no problem doing math when it involved historical dating, but apply it to time zones or the calculation of a tip and I was completely lost. Hence that two a.m. call that time. His two a.m., not mine. Unfortunately, Colin isn't really a night owl. It was one of his few drawbacks as a boyfriend.

Cate's brown curls bobbed in affirmation. "I wouldn't recommend it," she said, and I couldn't tell whether she was joking or not.

My gut said not.

My gut wasn't a happy place. In one month, that would be me. Three months if I pushed it and stayed around for the summer. Our relationship would shrink to an hour at dinnertime—my dinner-time, his bedtime—and an amusing assortment of e-mail forwards, sent less for themselves and more as a placeholder, a shorthand for "Hi! I have nothing to say, but I'm thinking about you!"

We would have less and less to say. Whatever they say about absence making the heart grow fonder, a relationship lies in the daily details, not the grand reunions. Right now, Colin and I were in the process of building up a foundation of shared memories.

I don't mean the major memories, the groundbreaking moments, but the little, everyday ones that, in their own weird way, last longer and mean more. When I thought about Colin, it wasn't of our more dramatic encounters. I didn't dwell on our almost kiss in a ruined monastery or his magnificent fury (okay, fine, so it was more like midlevel pissiness, but the other sounds better for posterity) at finding me going through his aunt's papers. Instead, what I remembered was the solidness of his arm around me when I tripped on loose gravel in the pub parking lot, or the play of shadow on his face as he stood by the kitchen window, rinsing the dishes before loading them into the antiquated dishwasher.

I liked that Colin, the domestic Colin. Our conversation was less and less about the big issues—politics, religion, the inherent inferiority of the Napoleonic regime—and more and more about whether it was a pub night or a home night, or the recurring debate about who left the lid off the toothpaste tube. (Hint: It wasn't me.) I'd traded in my daydreams for domesticity. Maybe it sounds unromantic, but it had a solid feel to it. It was real.

At least for now.

"So what's the deal with Dempster?" I asked my new best friend. "What does a historical consultant actually do?"

"You mean other than demand more mineral water?" I got the feeling Dempster hadn't exactly made himself popular with Cate. "And not that brand of mineral water, the other kind."

Her English accent was even worse than mine, but I got the point.

"It's not like he really even needs to be here," she said, warming to her theme. "They mostly hired him to go over the script and make sure the historical—whatever—was right."

As someone who was a professional whatever-er, I decided to just nod rather than to take offense.

"But he insisted that he had to be here, on set, from day one. Forget day one. Day zero. The bigwigs aren't getting here until tonight. But, no, Mr. Mineral Water had to be here early."

"So that's not normal practice, then," I said. "Having the historical consultant on set."

"I wouldn't say that," said Cate hastily. She flashed me a guilty grin. "And it's not like I'd really know. I'm not really a movie person. I just got this job because—"

"Right," I filled in for her. "I remember. The cousin who knew someone."

"I'm starting at Columbia journalism school in the fall," she said proudly. "I'm doing their broadcast program. They're the only Ivy to have one."

"Congrats!" I channeled extra enthusiasm into it to hide the fact that my mind was decidedly elsewhere. "So your sense, though, is that the historical consultant wouldn't usually need to be around at this point."

"That's what I heard one of the guys on the crew saying." She shook back her brown curls. "I wasn't the only one he was trying to treat like his personal minion."

"He does do that," I murmured.

Dempster was the head archivist at a choice art collection in central London. Snooty, but not exactly lucrative. Dempster, as Cate had so aptly noted, did like the finer things in life. His cunning plan? To make his fortune by writing a muckraking, best-selling work of nonfiction about England's greatest undiscovered spy, the Pink Carnation. His efforts in that direction had been less than scrupulous, including dating Colin's sister, Serena, in an attempt to worm his way into the family archives via Serena's affections.

Needless to say, that plan hadn't gone very well.

The last time I'd had the misfortune to meet Nigel Dempster was back in November. I had hoped—if I thought of him at all—that the intervening six months would have produced new get-rich-quick schemes. Ones without a Selwick component. His presence at Selwick Hall did not bode well.

With a sick feeling, I remembered my disordered papers. Dempster had tried to steal my notes before. He had a very all's-fair approach to scholarship, at least when it worked to his advantage.

"Oh." Cate drew back, looking alarmed. "Do you know him? I didn't mean— That is, if you're friends— I'd heard he knew someone connected to the family, but I didn't realize . . ."

"No!" I said quickly. "I mean, I do know him, but we're not friends. I had to do some research in his archive a few months ago, that's all."

Plus, he had screwed over my boyfriend's sister, but it didn't seem politic to mention that bit.

"Phew." Cate visibly relaxed. "I was afraid I'd really put my foot in it. Someone said he had a thing going with someone connected to the family, and when you said . . . But you're dating the cute, grumpy guy, so that wouldn't make sense. Sorry."

The cute, grumpy guy. I liked that. I'd have to tell Colin later. And my friend Pammy, who had been watching the progress of the Colin affair from day one. We could call Colin CGG for short. Pammy was very big on the code names. Yes, we were secretly still fifth graders when it came to dealing with boys. I mean, men.

Colin's study was empty, the computer monitor tilted to the side. I held open the study door for Cate and waved her to precede me. "Someone connected to the family?"

Cate lifted her hands in a gesture indicative of the mysterious ways of the office gossip chain. "The crew guys said that was how he got the job, through his girlfriend."

What was the screen doing tilted? Colin liked it facing dead ahead. It was one of the small things that drove him batty. He was also very picky about his paper-clip collection.

I moved to draw the monitor back into place and saw something that made me pause.

"Weird," I said.

"What is it?" Cate's bouncy brown curls brushed my cheek as she leaned over my shoulder. "Is the Internet down?"

"No. No worries." I pushed abruptly away from the screen, nearly slamming into Cate. "I thought I'd closed out of my e-mail, but I guess I didn't."

There was my webmail, open on the screen, maximized to its largest size. There was a smattering of new e-mails, distinguished by their darker font, including two with the heading "Re: 10B?"

To anyone else, that wouldn't mean anything at all. It might be an apartment number or a Chinese food entrée or a new address for Sherlock Holmes. Only Harvard history department cognoscenti would automatically translate that to Western Civ, Part II. Besides, Colin and I had an honor system. I didn't go through his files—well, not after that last time—and he didn't read my e-mail. It was all about trust.

Okay, it was mostly about trust and a little bit about fear of getting caught.

"Anyway, this is the computer." Shaking off my unease, I turned back to Cate. "As long as the study is empty, please feel free to come in and use it. Just make sure not to move anything around on the desk. And Colin likes the computer monitor facing forward, so if you move it, move it back. Oh, and there are biscuits in the tin over there. Please feel free."

"This is so nice of you." Cate clutched her clipboard to her chest. "I can't tell you."

"Just knock before you come in, okay? I'll let Colin know that you might be in and out."

"Thanks." Cate glanced back over her shoulder. Even on the second floor, we could hear the sound of cars on the gravel of the drive, and voices from downstairs, steadily rising in volume. Either this was the catering crew, or some of the guests were arriving early. "I'd better get back down there. But I might sneak up later?"

"Any time," I said, sliding into Colin's desk chair. "We'll be at the dinner, so the computer is all yours. You can ward off invaders for us."

Cate brandished her clipboard. "Will do."

"Don't mind about the door. It"—there was a horrible squawking sound as she yanked at it—"sticks."

"Sorry!" Cate's voice floated back through the door panels.

My smile faded as I turned back to my e-mail. My open and maximized e-mail.

I might have just been careless and left the box open. But I didn't think so. I was paranoid enough about Colin stumbling on that stupid 10B e-mail—not that it was really a secret, and I'd have to tell him eventually, anyway, but I'd rather tell him in my own time, once I'd figured out what I wanted to do.

Well, if Dempster had looked through my e-mails, he wouldn't find anything of use to him, just details for my friend Alex's engagement party, a few amusing forwards from Pammy, and those 10B e-mails.

I scrolled down the page. There were two new e-mails, one after the other. I'd shot off an SOS to two history department friends that morning, asking for advice. This wasn't exactly the sort of dilemma with which I could go to my advisor. Archival issues, yes. Boy issues, no. Admittedly, this was a mixed issue of archive and boy, but it still smacked too much of the personal intruding onto the professional for me to share with anyone I wanted to take me seriously. So I'd appealed to Liz and Jenny instead.

Liz was my year in the history department, Jenny a year ahead of me. We had been dubbed the Triumvirate of Terror, not by the hapless undergrads to whom we had attempted to teach western civ, but by a colleague in the history department who had made the cardinal mistake of attempting to ask us each out, one after the other.

Our specialties were very different—Jenny did Charlemagne, Liz was all about madness in Renaissance Florence, and I had my thing for British spies—but we had formed a fast friendship that went well beyond complaining about undergrad essays and the lousy coffee in Robinson Hall. They were my favorite outlet shopping buddies.

They had both chimed in, Jenny from Cambridge, Liz from Florence, where she was on her research year. I checked the time stamp on Jenny's e-mail. Wow. She really needed to stop getting up so early. Surely, Charlemagne could wait until a more civilized hour. He'd been dead about twelve hundred years, after all.

She wrote: *My dearest Eloise, STAY IN England! Really, why trade London for the joys of the Coop losing your book order and undergraduates whining that the B+ you gave them is the only thing standing between them and Harvard Law? Anyway, you found original documents. It is the Holy Grail of the historian. Stay and write them up! Boy or no boy, there will be plenty of time for teaching later. Liz and I will miss you, of course, but stay. Must run to Widener before it closes and then to Daedalus for drinks. More tomorrow. Love, Jenny*

I regarded the e-mail with a warm glow. I love my friends.

I scrolled down through the e-mail chain to Liz's feedback and my glow faded. Hey, snookums, wrote Liz. Is this about the boy?

Damn. She knew me way too well. I'd tried to couch it in neutral terms, making it out to be more about extra archival research than, well, Colin. But Liz was canny that way. She could smell ulterior motives on me like cheap cologne.

Funny, I'd expected her to be more pro, but the advice was decidedly pro-10B and anti-England. . . . don't want to jeopardize your career for a guy . . . documents will still be there . . . brief research trips . . . if he really likes you, you can make it work long-distance.

Damn, damn, damn. One pro, one anti, and me still confused. I leaned my forehead against the heels of my hands, wondering how long I could reasonably put off replying to Blackburn. The sensible thing, of course, would be to talk it all through with Colin. He knew his archives better than I did. He could tell me whether there was sufficient material to make it worth my remaining an extra term—it didn't need to be a whole year. I could go back to Cambridge for spring term and pick up my teaching duties then, even though it was unlikely a deal as sweet as the 10B head TF job would come along.

He could also tell me whether any of it was an option. He was, after all, a crucial part of the equation. Without a fellowship, my staying on would be predicated on his allowing me to live with him.

I thought of the poem Augustus Whittlesby had quoted to Emma Delagardie. "Come live with me and be my love. . . ."

Did Colin want me to come live with him and be his love and go through his archives? Or was that only for weekends and holidays, too scary to contemplate for daily use?

There was no way to find out except by asking him.

Like a petulant five-year-old resisting a nap, I didn't wanna. Oh, I had any number of excellent excuses. Colin had enough on his plate, now wasn't the time, I could wait until the film people left . . . But those weren't the real reasons, sensible though they seemed. At base, I wanted Colin to say something without my having to. I wanted him to intuit what I didn't want to ask. I wanted him to want me just because he wanted me, and not because it was a choice between inviting me to stay or my going thousands of miles away.

If only real life actually worked like that. In fiction, the hero's declaration always comes just in the nick of time; the heroine doesn't have to scrounge and maneuver for it.

My friend Alex, who had been in a functional relationship longer than anyone I knew, claimed that it didn't have to do with their not caring; it was just the way they were wired. Men, that is. According to Alex, when they were least communicative was often when they were most content, happy, in ways we were not, just to take a good thing as a good thing and let it meander along its own course. In other words, the ultimate exposition of "If it ain't broke, don't fix it." We fretted about what they were feeling; they were wondering about dinner.

In this case, that was probably literally true.

Crap. How was it ten to seven already? Cocktails started on the dot and I was still in jeans and a ratty old button-down shirt. I kicked back out of Colin's chair.

Dinner and Dempster first, major relationship issues later. Fortunately, Colin's study was just down the hall from the bedroom we now shared, at least on weekends. My jeans and sweaters were slowly making inroads into the drawers, and my brush, earring collection, and deodorant had colonized a corner of the dresser.

Colin had already come and gone, judging from the clothing on the floor and the toothbrush dripping next to the sink. Damn. I had hoped to catch him while he was changing, in that intimate never-never land of shirt studs and tie loops, breaking the Dempster news to him while he was still in dishabille. Whispering it under the curious eyes of Colin's evil stepfather and assorted Hollywood luminaries was going to put distinct limits on our ability to discuss.

I glanced at the door, but it didn't obligingly open with Colin on the other side of it. Okay, I'd just have to dress like the wind and catch him downstairs. At least I didn't have much wardrobe to dither over.

I yanked my two cocktail dresses out of the closet. A life spent among the documents of dead people did not exactly prepare one for dinner with Hollywood's finest. My wardrobe choices were distinctly limited. If I had thought ahead, I could have hit up my friend Pammy for an outfit. As a PR person—and an unabashed trust-fund baby— Pammy's closet made Madonna's look tame. Don't even ask me about the hot pink yak-skin corset.

As it was, I had two choices: black or beige.

I reached for the beige. It was the closest to a designer article of clothing that I owned, made of soft mock suede with a fringed neck and hem, embroidered with a smattering of turquoise beads. A flap across the back tied at a diagonal angle, leaving a triangle of skin bare. It was a little bit Flintstones, but if all the guys I knew who had crushes on Wilma were anything to go by, that wasn't a bad thing. Plus, it had certain sentimental associations. I had worn the same dress to a certain absurd party thrown by Pammy the night I learned that Colin was, in fact, single, available, and most likely flirting.

That had been one fun night, despite having to hold his sister Serena's head over a toilet bowl when some dodgy prawns caught up with her.

I twisted my arms behind my back, struggling with the tie, which had the dual disadvantage of being leather and at an odd angle.

That had been the first night I had spent real time with Serena, who had also, because my world was that small, gone to school with my old friend Pammy. It had been the night Pammy had dropped the bombshell that Serena wasn't, as I had erroneously presumed, Colin's girlfriend but his sister, and that his solicitous attention to her was the result of her having just gone through a particularly nasty—

Oh, God.

I froze, my arms bowed out behind my back. Breakup. She had just gone through a nasty breakup with Nigel Dempster. That had been back in October. Dempster had broken up with her in September. He had made a play for me in November. Serena and Colin had functionally stopped speaking in March, when Serena threw in her vote with Jeremy in exchange for a junior partnership in the gallery where she currently worked. In the past two months, all we'd heard about her had come, piecemeal, from Pammy or from Colin's aunt Arabella, who, while disapproving, had chosen not to kick the erring ewe from the fold. But those snippets hadn't been much; Colin tended to get tight-lipped and walk away when Serena came up. He had even done that to me a time or two. Her betrayal had cut deep.

We knew she was alive and sentient and still working at the gallery, but we didn't know anything else about her. We didn't know if she was eating or sleeping or seeing a therapist. Or dating.

Serena had leaned on Colin like a crutch after her breakup. But what happened when that crutch was taken away? What happened if Dempster had decided he wanted her back? Serena was a sweet-natured girl, but she had all the spine of a bowl of tapioca pudding.

Cate had said that Dempster wrangled his job through a personal connection with the family.

Dempster had, as far as I knew, only one connection with the Selwick family, or, at least, only one I would refer to as personal, in the most personal of possible senses.

Serena.

I could hear Cate's cheerful voice, the words distinct in memory as they hadn't been in the moment. *"The crew guys said that was how he got the job, through his girlfriend."*

Ex-girlfriend? Or current?

This dinner party was shaping up to be even more fraught with treachery than a masque at Malmaison.

Chapter 15

From far across the sea I come,
Through fire, frost, and blazing sun,
That you might, with your own fair hand,
Enjoy the bounties of my land.
—Emma Delagardie and Augustus Whittlesby,
Americanus: A Masque in Three Parts

lthough the waves beset me sore, / No force shall keep me from thy door. . . ." Dropping his pose, Kort squinted at his script. "It says here that I'm supposed to be beset by waves. Where are they?"

The cast of *Americanus* had at last convened for their first full rehearsal in the theatre at Malmaison. They had arrived that morning in their several conveyances, converging on the small town of Rueil with its modest chateau, and had been sorted into their respective lodgings by those members of the staff who remained in readiness for the First Consul's impromptu visits.

Not the First Consul, Emma reminded herself. The Emperor.

Horace de Lilly hadn't lied. It was, indeed, official, voted by the senate and ratified by referendum. Modest Malmaison had become, improbably, an imperial residence. Hortense wasn't just Hortense anymore, but Princess Hortense, an imperial highness, mother of the official heir to the throne. Pushy, annoying Caroline, Caroline who had been voted least popular pupil at Mme. Campan's, was an imperial highness as well, her husband elevated to the rank of Marshal of France. The honors were descending thick and fast, all with a decidedly monarchical tang. The coins might bear the word "Republic" on one side, but they had Napoleon's head on the other.

With Francia's tower still in pieces backstage, Jane stood on a chair appropriated from the main house. With the red and gold striped cushion bowing in under her ribbon-tied slippers, and the back of the chair serving as in impromptu armrest, she looked out over the tiered seats of the theatre, largely empty except for a smattering of cast members, an abandoned script here, a discarded shawl there. So far, Jane had been a remarkably good sport about being stuck up there for the better part of half an hour. She claimed she enjoyed the view.

That was a good thing, decided Emma, because it looked like Jane was going to be on that chair for some time.

They had done a read-through of the script in Emma's house in Paris, with Hortense as audience, dandling Louis-Charles on her knee and cheering them on, but this was their first rehearsal in situ. The machinery hadn't arrived yet and the actors were discovering all sorts of problems they hadn't encountered the first time around. They weren't being shy about voicing their opinions.

At the rate they were going, theirs wouldn't be a production fit for an emperor. They'd be lucky if they had a production at all.

Kort glanced down at his feet, set slightly apart as befitted a seasoned mariner on a storm-tossed sea. The floor remained still in a very un-sea-like way. "I must say, I'm not feeling particularly beset."

"Don't worry! We'll have the waves soon!" Emma called out from the prompt box. Dropping her voice, she muttered, "At least, I hope we will."

Mr. Fulton had faithfully promised a wave machine that would make the Comédie-Française's puny efforts look like puddles in comparison. So far, however, there had been little sign of one. She had called upon him before leaving Paris. He had another commission, he said, which had set him back slightly, but the wave machine was at the very top of his list and he would be sure she had it by Tuesday.

Today was Wednesday.

A very nice man, Mr. Fulton, but he did tend to be consumed by his work. If this other project proved as engrossing as it seemed, they might be forced to resort to having footmen on either side of the stage waving bits of blue cloth, an amateurism to which Emma had sworn they would not stoop.

Augustus stooped down next to the prompt box. "Shall I get the blue cloth?" he murmured.

"No!" Emma exclaimed, as though she hadn't been thinking the exact same thing. With more confidence than she felt, she said, "Don't be silly. It's just a slight delay. You know what the roads are."

"Road-like?"

"Rutted. Why, at this very moment, a couple of sturdy stable boys might be tugging the crate down the road."

"Or your friend might have forgotten." Turning back to the stage, Augustus called out, "Lift your imagination with the lofty spirit of invention, Mr. Livingston. The absence of the baser realities should be no obstruction to the flight of fancy."

Kort folded his arms across his chest, showing off the fact that his tailoring had improved considerably since his arrival in Paris, a fact for which Emma took full credit. "In a language I can understand?"

"Try rocking back and forth," translated Emma. "And stagger a bit."

Kort obligingly staggered. "Good?"

"Excellent!" cheered Emma.

Both men gave her a look.

That made a nice change, thought Emma. Finally, they agreed on something. Emma consulted her script, even though, by now, she knew it by heart. "Americanus, you've just arrived at Francia's shores."

"Is that what they're calling them now?" whispered one of the spare pirates, one of Napoleon's younger generals.

Someone near him snickered.

Emma raised her voice. "You've come bearing all sorts of gifts for her from your native land. Shall we pick up with 'in my hand'?"

Kort consulted his script. "In my hand I hold for thee the peach, the pear, the blooming tree— How can I hold a tree in my hand?"

Emma resisted the urge to bang her head against the polished wood of the music stand she had borrowed from the main house to hold her script.

How had she forgotten how staggeringly literal-minded her cousin could be? This was the same man who told her that acorn caps couldn't be fairy teacups because they would leak.

"It's a metaphor! Oh, fine, if that makes you uncomfortable, change it to 'In my ship's hold, I hold for thee.' Better?"

"Slightly." Emma made a note of it on her master copy, and Kort returned to his script. "For I shall bring you crimson leaves, and rippling wheat in golden sheaves, a cache of berries, red and sweet, and dappled deer on silent feet."

Instead of the seductive litany Emma had envisioned, his reading sounded like a merchant ticking off items on an inventory.

"At least he has the American accent down," murmured Augustus, settling himself on the edge of the prompt box, his long legs dangling down next to her.

Emma whacked him in the ankle and poked her head out of the prompt box. "You're not inviting her to the theatre, Kort. You're trying to get her to run away with you and be your love. Surely, you can show a little more feeling than that."

"In fact," said Jane, shifting a bit from one foot to the other. The cushion beneath her feet made an unhappy squelching noise. "I am perfectly happy in my tower. I need proper inducement to entice me to leave."

"I can see to that!" called out one of the pirates.

He was abruptly silenced by the whap of thickened cardboard hitting an equally thick skull. Emma had her suspicions as to the source but preferred not to verify. If she hadn't seen it, it hadn't happened.

Kort tapped the script. "Why would I haul half of America to her shores if only to turn around and go back again? It makes no sense."

"It's a gesture," said Emma, through gritted teeth. "It's meant to be romantic."

"It's not romantic, it's impractical. I wouldn't blame Francia for turning me down flat."

A pirate popped up from behind the half-finished backdrop at the back of the stage, declaring, "First sensible thing I've heard all day!"

Miss Gwen might have traded in her signature parasol for a pirate's cutlass, but her character hadn't changed in the slightest; chaperone or scourge of the high seas, it was all the same to her, just so long as she got to lay about with a pointy implement at regular intervals.

Emma didn't like to think of Miss Gwen unleashed on the Spanish Main. It was enough to make the blood run cold. From the curl of Augustus's lip, Emma could tell he shared that view.

Undaunted, Miss Gwen stalked forward, her knee-high boots revealing a surprisingly spry figure. A gold ring bobbed in one ear as she said, with relish, "Wheat and berries? Deer? What is he? A gentleman or a gamekeeper?" She hoisted her cutlass imperiously in the air, like a ship showing its colors. "Turn him down and impound his ship, that's what I say."

"Er . . ." Emma looked from Miss Gwen to Augustus.

They hadn't even gotten to the pirate part yet and this was already turning from a rehearsal into a mutiny.

"Here." Augustus bounded up onto the stage in one fluid movement, knocking Miss Gwen's cardboard cutlass out of the way. "Watch me."

Sweeping the script out of Kort's hand, he flung himself to his knees before Jane's tower, arching his back and stretching out his arms in supplication. He looked, thought Emma, like a piece of Renaissance statuary, intensity encoded in immobility, passion quivering beneath the still surface of the tableau.

Emma wasn't sure why he had bothered to appropriate Kort's script. It dangled forgotten from one hand as he held his pose, his eyes fixed on Jane's still form with a quiet intensity that caught the attention of everyone in the room. Even the pirate Miss Gwen had so expeditiously silenced gave up clutching his head and moaning in order to watch the scene unfolding on the stage. For once, Augustus's flowing shirt and tight pantaloons didn't look silly. They were just right against the half-painted backdrop of a stormy sea. Watching him, Emma could almost imagine that Jane stood in a tower rather than on a chair, that her hair flowed freely down her back rather than being coiled neatly and practically at the back of her head. A wind seemed to stir, flowing down the length of the theatre, a wind straight from the sea, redolent of salt and brine and the tang of adventure.

Not until the theatre was quiet did Augustus speak, in a rich baritone that reached all the way to the farthest walls.

He opened his hands to Jane, palm up. "For I shall bring you crimson leaves, and rippling wheat in golden sheaves." His voice wheedled, it cajoled, it seduced. "A cache of berries, red and sweet—"

Emma could taste berries on her tongue, warmed by the sun, tartness giving way to sweetness, seeds catching between her teeth.

"—and dappled deer on silent feet." Through the woods of Emma's memory, a speckled fawn turned its funny, narrow face to stare through the leaves before breaking and running fleet-footed through the brush, leaves crackling beneath its hooves.

In a voice almost contemplative, he finished, "All these and more shall be thy dower, the woods, the winds, the sea thy bower—if my humble presents might thee move, to live with me and be my love."

The wind whistled around her, the stars circled in a dizzying whirl; on the branches of her bower, nightingales sang and leaves rustled, all the elements working in harmony to shade their lovers from all harms, leaving them safe in each other's arms.

Emma's mouth was dry and her eyes burned as though from reading too long and too late into the night. *Take me!* she wanted to cry. *I'll run away with you.*

But she couldn't, even if she could have forced her tongue to form the words. The theatre was locked in silence. Even a breath would break the fantasy.

This, Emma thought, this was why people mistrusted the theatre and inveighed against the dangers of playacting. This was why, this creation of a fantasy more powerful than reality, a fantasy that could rob one of speech and sense, bring tears to the eyes, and arouse inchoate and impossible longings.

It was Miss Gwen who broke the silence.

"Not bad," she said grudgingly.

Not bad? That had been extraordinary. Beyond extraordinary. Emma's overtaxed senses abandoned the search for adjectives. Already it was slipping away, normality encroaching. Augustus clambered to his feet, the scuff of his shoes against the boards a homely, workaday sort of noise. At the back of the theatre, the young officers resumed their whispered conversations; the birds outside dared to chirp again, and the gardeners to garden.

Had it been only a moment? It had felt like longer.

"Are you sure you shouldn't take the role?" said Kort wryly, and Emma felt a surge of affection for her cousin.

Augustus offered Kort his script back. "The poet to turn player! Never! Not for the humble scrivener the clamor of the audience's acclaim or the sweaty work of making words turn flesh." His voice was a good half-octave higher than it had been a moment before, nasal and slightly drawling. So much for not acting, thought Emma wryly. Turning to Jane, Augustus added, "Madame. As always, I am honored to declare my affections to so worthy an object."

The words were sheer absurdity; the look that accompanied them was in dead earnest.

There was acting, and then there was . . . not.

Emma cleared her throat. "I think we've all done enough for now, don't you? We can resume tomorrow morning."

Talking, laughing, complaining about their costumes, the others filed out in clusters of twos and threes. Jane went with them, her head tilted attentively towards one of the naval officers who would be playing a naval officer. Emma didn't miss the way Augustus's gaze followed them out through the door, into the last harsh glow of late afternoon sunlight.

"Well," she said, too loudly, "that went well."

The door closed, shutting out the light and Jane. Casually, too casually, Augustus clasped his hands lightly behind his back and strolled back between the rows of seats, towards the stage and Emma.

"That," he said, "is taking optimism too far. Even for you."

He offered her a hand to help her up out of the prompt box. Emma accepted it gratefully. His hand closed around hers, surprisingly strong for someone who spent the day wielding a pen, hauling her up with as little effort as though she were nothing more than a roll of paper.

"Thank you. I'm fine now." Emma self-consciously extracted her hand, making a show of shaking out her skirts and stretching her stiff limbs. "I am still worried about the ending, though."

Augustus took a step back. "Haven't we had this discussion already?"

"Yes, but that doesn't make you any more right."

"It doesn't make me any less right, either," he said mildly. "We only have a week; there's no time to start changing things around now."

"The actors haven't rehearsed that bit yet," said Emma hopefully. "And if we got them a new script by tomorrow—"

The theatre door opened and they both turned. It was a strange, hunched silhouette framed in the doorway before it resolved itself into a man in a rough cotton smock lugging behind him a large crate on a wheeled cart.

Tipping the cart, he let the crate slide with a distinct thump to the ground next to Emma, in direct contravention of the words painted on the side, advising all comers to handle with care.

Emma didn't recognize the crate and she certainly didn't know the man, but she knew that writing.

"You Madame Delagardie?" the man demanded.

Emma flung herself at the crate. "The wave machine!" She beamed at Augustus. "See? I told you Mr. Fulton hadn't forgotten." Turning to the deliveryman, she said confidingly, "It was the ruts, wasn't it?"

The man puffed out his chest, as though preparing for a fight. "We put the ruts just where we was told to," he said, "in the other place. Did you want 'em both over here? Because that'll cost extra."

"Pardon?" said Emma. She glanced back over at her crate. "There's only supposed to be the one. . . ."

Unless Mr. Fulton had felt guilty for the delay and tossed in an extra mechanism to make up for it?

"Here." The man thrust out a four-times-folded note, secured with a blob of sealing wax without a seal. It looked as though it had been dunked in a puddle a few times along the way.

The hand remained outthrust even after Emma took the note from it.

As Emma eagerly broke the wax, Augustus dug into his pocket, extracted a coin, and pressed it into the man's palm. "For your troubles," he said. "With all the ruts."

Over the top of the letter, Emma gave Augustus a look.

Having been remunerated for his pains, the deliveryman ambled off, convinced they were all crazy.

Emma bent her blond head over the letter. "It *is* the wave machine," she said delightedly. She flapped the paper at Augustus. "Mr. Fulton has even included instructions for its use."

"Good," said Augustus. "I hope you can figure it out, because I can't."

"Nonsense," said Emma in a preoccupied tone, her head bent over Mr. Fulton's scribblings. "If I can learn to make sense of these things, anyone can."

Augustus propped an elbow on the sill of Francia's tower, currently still under construction. "Why did you? I wouldn't have thought mechanics would have been your métier."

The lid had been very carefully nailed down. Oh, bother. She was going to need to find someone with a crowbar. And considerably more arm strength than she possessed.

"It's not." Maybe she didn't need a crowbar after all. If she could find something to use to pry back those nails . . . Emma looked around the crowded backstage area. She saw paint, paintbrushes, lumber, and enough rope to string up an entire troupe of highwaymen, but nothing that resembled a useful tool. "But it all reduces to simple enough principles once someone explains." She slid her fingers under the join of the lid and gave an experimental hitch. "Bother. I need something to get this lid off."

"A crowbar," said Augustus, in that definitive way men have when talking about tools, even men clad in decidedly effeminate costumes. "Your husband took an interest in these things, didn't he?"

Emma picked ineffectually at one of the nails in the lid. "Yes."

Too much of an interest. As Paul buried himself deeper and deeper in diagrams and models of mechanisms, she had accused him of wanting her dowry more than he wanted her, of marrying her merely to fund his pet project: the draining of Carmagnac.

Ironic, if that were the case, since her family had cut her off without a penny in punishment for marrying without their permission.

In retrospect, she felt distinctly sorry for Paul. He had found himself without the fortune he had been led to expect, saddled with a temperamental fifteen-year-old girl who demanded homage and went off in a huff when she didn't receive it.

If she hadn't idolized him so much at the start, they might have done better. But then, he had been just as guilty as she. He had been equally surprised when she had turned out to be not the goddess of his imaginings but a fifteen-year-old girl, spoiled and untried.

What a mess they had made, both of them.

Augustus hunkered down next to her. "You're never going to get the nails off that way," he said. "I'll find you a crowbar."

Looking at him, his long hair curling around his face, his attention innocently on the crate, Emma couldn't stop thinking of his expression as he had gazed up at Jane, as rapt as if she were the Cytherea his poems proclaimed her. It had been a joke before, his devotion, but now . . .

"Be careful," she warned.

"With the crowbar?" Still crouching beside the crate, Augustus arched a brow. "I assure you, Madame Delagardie, I am far more proficient with tools than this fragile frame would imply."

"Don't play games with me," said Emma crossly. "I didn't mean the crowbar. I meant Jane."

He went still. "What about Jane?"

Emma swallowed, trying to muster the right words. "I don't want you hurt, either of you." She bit down on her lip, concentrating on the rough wood of the crate, the places where it had cracked and splintered. "It isn't kind to idolize someone like that."

Augustus pushed up and away. One minute he was next to her, the next she had a prime view of his knees. "I don't know what you're talking about."

Emma remembered the way he had looked at Jane on her chair, as though she were the most precious thing in a million kingdoms, as though he would cross storm-tossed seas for the sake of a mere glimpse of her face.

Leaning back on her haunches, Emma laughed without humor.

"You have her up in a tower so high no man could possibly reach her, no matter how high the ladder. It's not fair. It's not fair to her and it's not fair to you."

Beneath the exuberant fall of his hair, his face was still, as still and stony as a winter's day on a barren beach.

Yanking at a nail with the pads of her fingers, Emma said, "You can't make someone into your Cytherea just by wishing it."

"I'm not trying to make anyone into anything," he said tightly.

Emma looked up from her shredded fingernails. "No? Then why the Princess of the Pulchritudinous Toes? Why twenty-two cantos?"

Why do you look at her the way you do?

But she couldn't ask that.

"That's not—" Augustus caught himself before he said whatever he had been about to snap out. He said shortly, "That's poetry. Don't you think I can tell the difference between fact and fiction?"

"No." There. It was out. There was no going back. Softening her voice, Emma said, "It's romantic and lovely, but none of it's real. Jane's not like that. She—"

"She *what?*" He stepped forward, his hands planted combatively on his hips. "I know Miss Wooliston a damned sight better than you do."

Emma held on to the crate with both hands. "That's not what I meant! Do you think I would ever say anything against Jane? I love her too. It's just that she's not like that. She's not . . . poetical."

Without another word, Augustus swung away from her. His expression of contempt seemed to linger behind him, like a sun print on the surface of the eye, creating shadow images long after the object has gone.

Emma jumped up, steadying herself against the lid of the crate. "Augustus—"

His long legs made short work of the aisle between the stage and the door. Either he didn't hear or he pretended not to. He pushed hard with both hands against the door, sending it ricocheting open. Emma held up a hand to block the sudden wash of sunlight.

For a very brief moment, Augustus turned back. Against the light, he was a dark silhouette, sinister and still.

In a hard, tight voice, he said, "I'll find you a crowbar."

The door swung shut behind him, blotting out the man and the light.

Picking futilely at the nails on the lid of the case, Emma would have felt better about the crowbar if she hadn't been quite so sure Augustus was itching to use it on her.

Chapter 16

If all the world and youth were young
And truth on every sailor's tongue,
Then these avowals might me move
To live with thee and be thy love.
But I come from a colder clime. . . .
—Emma Delagardie and Augustus Whittlesby,
Americanus: A Masque in Three Parts

Idolization, indeed!

Augustus let the theatre door slam shut behind him, the crack of wood against wood a satisfying echo of his feelings.

After all these weeks, he had thought Emma, of all people, would know better.

Certainly, he played the besotted poet in public, but that was just an act, like the adverbs and the alliteration. The verbiage was mere costuming, no more a part of him than the billowing shirt he affected in public. His real feelings for Jane weren't composed of such airy nothings; they were based on a firm foundation of mutual respect, interests, and understanding. He knew Jane for what she was, just as she knew him. Between them, there were no pretenses, no roles, no acts.

He wasn't trying to make Jane into his Cytherea; the very idea was absurd. Cytherea was the role she played in public, the princess in the tower, accepting the homage of admirers from twenty feet up, encased in a tower to protect her from elements beyond her control. If anything, he sought to liberate her from the tower, to bring her down to earth and into his arms, in a safe, protected space where they could both be what they were without the threat of prying eyes or tattling tongues.

Emma might not know the whole of it—the whole double-identity bit did make for rather a large gap—but she ought to know him better than that by now. After three weeks of working in such proximity, he had thought they had built up an understanding of sorts, even a friendship. They were frank with each other. He was blunt with her in a way he was with no one but Jane.

No. If he was being honest with himself, he was blunt with Emma in a way he wasn't with Jane. With Jane, his tongue was curbed by the vast respect he bore her, his manner softened by admiration, their interactions tinged—although not tainted!—by the echoes of their respective roles. They never knew when someone might be listening. He played the besotted poet in private as in public, half in mockery, half in earnest.

With Emma, there was no need for any of that. He could be curt, he could be blunt, he could even be crude.

That, Augustus told himself, was precisely why her absurd accusations ate at him so. There was no truth to them, of course.

Idolization, ha!

Augustus cut around the side of the theatre, toward the confusion of gardens that stretched out behind the house. Mme. Bonaparte had designed her grounds in the English manner, carefully cultivated to maintain the illusion of natural serendipity, with irregular paths circling among copses of trees, meandering over rustic bridges, wend-ing their way past bits of artfully artless statuary, planted to look like the decaying relics of a prior civilization.

Surely, somewhere in the grounds, there must be the equivalent of a garden shed. A gardener would have served equally well, but, like the shoemaker's elves, they had done their work in the morning while the house lay sleeping, scurrying out of sight by day so that the inhabitants of the house might enjoy their illusion of lonesome wilderness unimpeded by reminders of the effort that went into maintaining it.

Augustus struck out along the path to the left, past the tree Bonaparte had planted to commemorate his victory at Marengo. That information came courtesy of Emma, who had taken him on a cursory tour upon their arrival, pointing out such personal landmarks as the Best Place to Read, the Best Place to Play Prisoner's Base, and All Those New Bits That Weren't There Before.

He probably ought to have asked her where to go to find garden implements, Augustus acknowledged to himself. On the other hand, that would have ruined his exit. It was very hard to storm out and then turn meekly back around and ask for directions. It sapped all the moral force from the departure.

He would, Augustus decided generously, freely acknowledge Emma to be the authority on the estate of Malmaison and its grounds. When it came to Jane, however, she was wrong, quite wrong, and he would prove it to her.

Eventually.

The path he had chosen looped and then looped again, bringing him along the banks of a river too perfect to be entirely natural. Above the trees, the sun was beginning to set, reflecting red-gold streaks in the clear water below. Beneath the trees, though, it was already dusk. Weeping willows bent their fronds towards the banks, and swans drifted in the chill of the waters. The scene was almost eerie in its beauty, a wistful, haunted place.

Against the fronds of the willows, the woman drifting towards the bridge seemed almost a specter herself, her long gown a whisper of white in the shadow of the trees. She stepped up onto the blue-painted bridge, and the last rays of the setting sun lit upon her, embracing her with the ardor of a lover.

Augustus felt his heart leap with an answering fire.

"Well met by sunset, fair Miss Wooliston!" he called out. "You don't know how glad I am to see you."

Was there ever such a proof of fate as this? A bridge in sunset, a romantic copse of woods . . . the lady of his heart.

"Mr. Whittlesby!" Jane caught at the rustic railing as he bounded towards her, making the planks of the bridge tremble with his enthusiasm. Her eyes were bright with welcome—or perhaps merely the reflection of the setting sun. "Has there been some new development?"

"Other than my getting lost in the woods? No." Augustus thought about Dante in the middle of his life, lost in a dark wood. Then he found Beatrice, a shining figure in white, who led him forth to paradise.

Admittedly, Jane's white muslin gown was hardly the stuff of the heavenly spheres, and Augustus doubted even the most fashionable angels sported white gloves and wide-brimmed bonnets, but he liked the metaphorical resonance of it, all the same.

"These are hardly woods," Jane said practically, surveying the carefully landscaped disorder. Beneath their bridge, the swans billed the water, calling to one another in their strange, cracked voices, so at odds with their graceful facade. "If you want woods, you keep following the path to the left. This is just a wilderness."

"Is there a difference between the two?" Augustus asked, not because he wanted to know but just to keep her talking, to savor the image of a beautiful woman in a white gown against a frame of weeping willows.

"The one is designed to look wild, the other actually is."

Leaning his elbows against the rail next to her, Augustus gazed out across the brilliantly tinted waters. "So we ape nature with art and, in doing so, lose the best of both," he murmured, "just as we play at love and lose the heart of it."

Jane gave him a sideways look. "I am glad you wandered along," she said, pushing away from the railing. "I've been wanting to speak to you."

"I, too." Augustus gazed at her, trying to think how to begin. Not poetical? Emma had no idea what she was talking about. He blurted, "Have you noticed the sunset?"

"The sunset?" Jane looked more than a little perplexed. "Is that a code?"

"Of a sort," Augustus hedged. Bracing one hand against the rail, he fell back on the words of a better poet than he. *"How sweet the moonlight sleeps upon this bank! Here will we sit and let the sounds of music / Creep in our ears: soft stillness and the night / Become the touches of sweet harmony."*

He looked meaningfully at Jane.

"You should put that in the masque," she said blandly. "It might work quite nicely for Americanus."

Had she not recognized it for what it was? He couldn't tell whether she was serious or not. Sometimes, Jane's humor eluded him.

"Jane—" There was no poetic way to say it. The words were wrenched out of him. "I've had enough of this. I'm sick of masks."

Jane pursed her lips judiciously. "I understand your feelings, but it is only a week more and then you'll be done with it. Except for the commemorative volume, of course." She arched a brow, waiting for a response. When none was forthcoming, she said kindly, "Given the time constraints, your masque isn't half bad."

"No. It's fully bad," said Augustus bluntly. "But that's not the point. The point is—"

"That it got you to Malmaison." Jane nodded approvingly. "If there's any truth to your source's claims, you should be able to verify it."

"It got *us* to Malmaison," Augustus corrected. He added, more quietly, "I hadn't realized how beautiful it is here."

Emma hadn't exaggerated. It was a landscape made for lovers, all full of secluded alcoves and picturesque vistas. Even the sun was complicit, lighting the sky with the sort of sunset one never saw in Paris.

"Yes, as to that." Jane held up a hand to shield her eyes against the last glare of the sun, frowning against the purple and red magnificence of the sky, the brilliant glitter of the water. "It isn't the way I would have planned it."

"The gardens?" He could see where Jane was more of a formal parterre sort of person, but there was something about the wildness of the landscape that called to him.

Jane shook her head. "Our mutual presence at Malmaison."

"What do you mean?" Augustus recalled their prior conversation in the Balcourt garden. They spent a great deal of time in gardens, he and Jane. At the time, she had been concerned about appearances. "Are you worried about arousing suspicion? There should be no fear of that. Bonaparte's daughter herself mandated your inclusion, not I."

"Hortense didn't do us any favors." Clasping her hands behind her back, Jane glanced back towards the house, faintly visible between the fronds of the willow trees. "The party is small enough that one could effectively conduct surveillance on one's own. There's no need for both of us here."

"Maybe it's not about need," said Augustus desperately. "Maybe it's just about . . . nice. It's nice to be here together. In the gardens. In the sunset."

Jane shook her head. "We could be much more effective apart."

"Effective," Augustus repeated.

The sunset wasn't effective; the swans on the lake weren't, either. They were because they were, because they were beautiful, because they moved a man's soul.

He could hear Emma's voice in his head, saying apologetically, *She's not like that. She's not . . . poetical.*

Hush, he told her. *Hush. I will not hear you.*

The phantom Emma put her tongue out at him.

He looked at Jane, framed by weeping willows, silhouetted against the water, an objet d'art in her own right. He could imagine her with her pale brown hair streaming down her back, straight and shining as water, darker than honey, lighter than oak, defying definition, always slipping just out of reach. She was like a moonbeam, a faint gleam of light across the sky, making the throat grow dry and the heart constrict, beautiful to contemplate, impossible to hold.

No. It wasn't right. He wouldn't give up this easily.

Yes, she was beautiful. Yes, she was clever. Yes—he would admit it—she might be more than a little reserved. But there was more there. He had seen it. He had seen it in the quirk of her lip, the glint in her eye, the suppressed amusement that seemed, on more than one occasion, to be for him and him alone. They had worked together for more than a year now, and he had been sure, more than once, that he had sensed something more than a professional interest.

She was so used to his flummery by now that she probably thought it was nothing more than that, just another verse in an old poem.

"Is there nothing more to which to aspire than to efficacy?" he demanded. "What about—"

He was going to say love. He meant to say love. But his tongue refused to form the word.

"—poetry?" he finished lamely.

Jane clapped a hand to her bosom, fluttering her lashes coquettishly. "Why, Mr. Whittlesby! As always, you flatter me." Her voice dropped. "Where is he?"

Augustus's gaze immediately skittered to the side, scanning for intruders. "Who?"

Jane slowly straightened, giving him a perplexed look. "You went into role. I assumed there was someone there."

"I see," he said slowly.

And he did see. He had been right. He couldn't hide behind flowery language; she would only read it as part of the masquerade, never realizing that below his silly shirt beat a heart that beat only for her. Well, partly for her.

"What if it wasn't an act? What if I meant it?"

Jane narrowed her eyes at him. She didn't look alarmed so much as bemused. "Really, what has got into you this evening?"

It wasn't so much what had got into him as what had got away. He felt like he was clinging to the edge of a waterfall, trying, desperately, to push the water back.

"It's not this evening," he said. "It's been a long time coming. It cannot come as a surprise to you to know that I have the deepest respect and admiration for you."

"Thank you. The praise of an agent of your caliber is always a mark of honor."

Agent. The word settled on his chest like the slabs once used to crush condemned men, one stone at a time.

"I don't speak just as an agent," he said, fighting against a growing sense of doom. "I know the circumstances are inconvenient. The circumstances are always inconvenient. But if you found yourself moved . . ."

Jane's spine stiffened until she stood as upright as Miss Gwen. "We have a job to do, Mr. Whittlesby," she said crisply. "An important job."

"I know that," he said. "Don't you think I know that? I've been doing this since you were in pinafores. But there's a time for work and a time for—"

She turned her back on him, stepping rapidly away from the rail. "I made some inquiries about Mr. Livingston," she said quickly. "And about his financial interests. You were right."

"I was?" Augustus felt slow and stupid. His mouth formed the words without connection to his brain.

She stayed a careful arm's length away. Her voice had the determined cheerfulness of someone delegated to convey bad news. Cheerful voice, watchful eyes. "Your suspicions seem to have some basis in fact. I ought to have trusted your instincts on this."

On this. Only this.

Jane's mouth continued to move, conveying information that fell around him like leaves in autumn, dry and dead and brown, tainted with the scent of decay. *Munitions manufactory*, he heard, and *controlling interest*, and *business concerns*, but the rest ebbed and flowed against his ears with no discernible effect. The sky was darkening all around them. Behind Jane, the pale circle of the moon rose above the trees, crowning her head like a saint's on a painted panel.

He had got it wrong. Jane wasn't Cytherea, goddess of love and beauty; she was Cynthia, goddess of the moon, chaste and untouchable. The tower wasn't his invention; it was her choice.

Or, maybe, she just didn't want him.

Metaphor was no consolation. He could pile up classical allusions, one on top of the other, but none could hide the simple fact that Jane had known what he was saying and had deliberately ducked and dodged. She didn't want his declarations of love.

She's not like that, said Emma. *I don't want you hurt. . .*

He could smell the sickly sweet scent of Emma's pity clinging to his skin like rot. She had known and he hadn't. She had known exactly what was going to happen. Had she and Jane discussed it over their coffees with Hortense Bonaparte? Had they laughed over his ridiculous pretensions?

No, they wouldn't have laughed. Jane would have simply deflected all questions with a smile and a change of subject.

Jane had paused in whatever she was saying. She was looking at him expectantly, waiting for him to reply.

"I'm sorry," said Augustus roughly. "Can you repeat that? I'm afraid I missed the end of it."

She smiled approvingly, thanking him for what he hadn't said.

"Mr. Livingston's primary interest seems to be the munitions factory, but, as far as I've been able to tell, he hasn't conducted any business on its behalf during this visit. Instead, there's talk of a new business venture."

Augustus forced himself to frame the right words. He felt like one of those chickens that continued to career around the barnyard long after the fatal blow had been administered, too stupid to realize it was dead. "What sort of business venture?"

"That's still unclear. It appears to involve Mr. Fulton."

"Fulton?" The name drifted towards him from a very long way away, like flotsam on the river. "The inventor?"

"The very one." Jane's gaze sharpened on Augustus. "Do you know anything?"

"Madame Delagardie commissioned Fulton to make a wave machine for the masque."

Like a swimmer breaking the surface of the water, dragging in his first, gasping breath, Augustus felt his fogged brain begin to clear. There was something there . . . some connection.

"Wait," he said sharply.

De Lilly had sworn the device, whatever it was, was to be tested at Malmaison this weekend. Emma had been commissioned to produce not a play but a masque, a theatrical form notorious for its reliance on mechanical effects.

What better way to hide an incriminating device than among others? In a theatre? The backstage was clogged with ropes and pulleys and all manner of strange contrivances.

"The theatre," he said. "They're hiding it in the theatre."

Jane was instantly alert. "Are you sure?"

"No," he said bluntly. "But I can find out. Do you know where I can find a crowbar?"

"The tools are over there." Jane indicated a small building half hidden by a stand of trees.

Naturally. Naturally, Jane would know exactly where the tools were kept, even though this was her first visit to Malmaison, as it was his.

He used to find her omniscience endearing; right now, it struck him as more than a little eerie.

There was something chilling about that sort of superhuman competence.

He wasn't being fair, he knew. His colleague looked entirely the same as she had half an hour ago, the same dress, the same Kashmir shawl, the same smooth wings of hair disappearing beneath the brim of her bonnet, but he couldn't see her in the same way. The eyes that had been coolly amused were just cool, the lips that he had praised for their firmness were firmly closed against him. Her poise, her posture, the pearly tint of her skin, all seemed as off-putting as they had once been engaging.

"You should be able to persuade one of the gardeners to assist you," she said.

"I'm sure I can contrive to manage," said Augustus. His voice sounded strange and flat to his ears.

The sun had dropped below the horizon, and the wind had risen. Through the shaking branches, he could see the windows of the great house blaze into light, one by one, as the servants lit the lamps, throwing the dark outside into even greater relief. The theatre was invisible from where they stood, hidden on the far side of the house.

Augustus wondered if Emma had given up and gone away or found someone else to open her box for her.

How long had they been standing on the bridge? It might have been anywhere from fifteen minutes to half an hour. It felt like years.

He wasn't sure which would be worse, to creep in through the dark like a thief, hiding his chagrin in the shadows, or to find Emma still there, pity and understanding written all over her face.

Jane had said it. They had a job to do. It didn't matter what Emma thought of him. He just needed the contents of that thrice-damned crate.

"I should be getting back," he said brusquely.

Jane put out a hand to stop him as he strode across the bridge. He didn't stop, but he slowed, looking back over his shoulder. She was a pale blur in the shadow of the trees, insubstantial in the twilight.

A poet's dream, nothing more.

"I just want you to know," she said, and her voice sounded less certain than he had ever heard it. For a moment, in the wavering dusk, she sounded almost her age. "I do have the highest esteem for you as a colleague."

He hadn't thought he could feel any worse than he already did, but there it was.

"Thank you," said Augustus shortly. "Now, if you'll excuse me, I have a box to break."

Jane didn't ask what he was talking about. He didn't volunteer. Why bother? She probably knew already.

With exquisite pain, he recalled other conversations, other meetings, all those times he thought he was subtly paying homage. All those times he thought Jane was, in her own quiet way, sending his coded confirmation.

Instead, all the while, she had just been doing her best to keep him from declaring himself.

Had she realized? Had she known before? It must have been fairly obvious if Emma felt the need to comment on it.

I don't want you hurt. . .

Too late.

The theatre was dark. Augustus pushed open the door, his eyes adjusting with little difficulty from the window-lit dusk to the gloom of the interior. Outside, he could hear the crickets chirping and the odd hoot of an owl anticipating his evening's forays. Inside, all was still, rank upon rank of seats facing blankly forward, a phantom audience for a phantom show.

The theatre wasn't entirely empty. A narrow sliver of light fell across the stage, emanating from somewhere in the wings.

Augustus made his way quietly down the aisle between the seats, carpet muffling his steps, shadows masking his movements. The light broadened as he approached, angling into a doorway. He paused in the doorway, taking in the scene.

The crate was open. The lid was propped up against one side. Straw littered the floor. Three lanterns had been lit, set out in a semi-circle on the floor. There were bits of metal and tubing scattered about, like a child's toys left out after play.

In the middle of it sat Emma, her legs tucked up underneath her as she consulted a grimy scrap of paper, muttering to herself as she reached for a piece of metal tubing, thought better of it, and put it back again.

"But if that goes here . . ."

She had shoved her hair back behind her ears, heedless of the fashionable bandeau that was supposed to be serving that function, causing chunks of hair to bump up at odd angles. There was a smudge of dirt or grease on one cheek and straw clinging to her dress.

"Right," she said to herself. "It must be that other tube. . . ."

She scooted herself forward, adding more straw to the collection on her hem, jiggered herself up on her knees, and leaned all the way over, stretching out as far as she could to reach an errant piece of tubing that had strayed to the end of the circle. Her fingers wriggled towards the tube.

And there she froze.

She was, Augustus realized, staring at his boots. Her gaze traveled up past the tassels of his boots, to his thighs, and up to his shirt.

"Oh," she said, and did a very quick scramble back, hand by hand, to her original position, popping up flushed and disheveled in something closer to a sitting position. "Hello! You've come back."

Augustus kicked the door shut behind him. "You were right," he said.

Chapter 17

The leaves do fade and fall away,
Berries rot and sheaves decay;
The deer is fled back to the field.
That is all your promises yield.
All wind and words, your vows, I see,
Are barren as the fruitless tree.

—Emma Delagardie and Augustus Whittlesby,
Americanus: A Masque in Three Parts

"I found someone to help me with the lid," said Emma.

She heaved herself up off the floor, tripping on the end of her own skirt and trying not to career into a pile of packing straw. Lifting her hands to shove her hair back behind her ears, Emma found that her bandeau had twisted itself halfway around, listing drunkenly to the side, with her hair all bunched up underneath. There was something grimy on the back of her hand, and, oh, Lord, was that straw on her skirt?

Emma backed out of the circle of lantern light, trusting to the dark to hide her burning cheeks and disheveled appearance. Not that it mattered. It was only Augustus, after all. Still, one didn't like to be seen looking like a complete slattern—even if one was.

Emma gave a hasty tug to her bodice. "One of the nice footmen came by," she babbled, "and pried out the nails for me. It took no time at all."

"Good for you." Augustus tossed the crowbar to one side, where it connected with the side of Miss Gwen's pirate ship before clattering to the floor.

The sound echoed through the narrow room.

He wasn't still annoyed about their little spat, was he? She might have been out of line, but they had promised each other honesty.

Honesty within limits.

"Thank you for bringing the crowbar," Emma said hastily, her voice tinny in the dusty silence. "That was very . . . nice of you."

Augustus didn't look nice right now; he looked dangerous. He looked like the sort of man one wouldn't want to run into in a dark theatre. Tension surrounded him like the sky before a storm, just waiting for the right moment to crackle into lightning.

He prowled into the room, the lamplight picking out the shadows created by the folds in his shirt, dwelling lovingly on the hollows of collarbone, cheekbone, jaw. Among the coiled ropes and scattered props, his loose shirt and tight breeches gave him a piratical look. He only needed a gold ring in one ear and he would fit right in with Miss Gwen and her crew of merry marauders.

"I'm sorry to have sent you off on a wild goose chase," Emma volunteered.

Augustus propped one booted foot on the lid of a faux treasure chest from which spilled gold-painted pieces of eight and ersatz ropes of pearls. His long hair curled around his face. "Does it count as a wild goose chase when it bears fowl? Foul fowl but fowl still."

"I beg your pardon?" Fair might be foul and foul fair, but Emma didn't have any inclination to hover through the fog and filthy air to try to figure out what he was saying.

"You were right."

"That does happen from time to time. About what? The end of the masque? I told you and told you—"

Augustus kicked aside the treasure chest. Coins and chains rattled. "About Miss Wooliston."

"Oh," Emma said weakly. Of all the things she had anticipated, that wasn't one of them. "How do—"

"I have it from the horse's mouth. So to speak."

As she met his eyes, Emma felt a horrible sinking feeling in her stomach. It was one thing to inflict her opinion upon him, quite another to have him act on it.

"Oh, no," she whispered. "You didn't—"

"Just now. In the garden. She wanted none of me. You were right."

Emma wished he would stop saying that. The more he repeated it, the more she felt as though she were to blame. She had anticipated this, but she hadn't wished it on him, not really.

There were times when it was less than pleasant to be able to say *I told you so.*

Emma bit down on her lip. "I am sorry."

Augustus prowled forward, stepping neatly over a coil of rope and a discarded cutlass. "Why should you be?" His voice was as cold and hard as the fragments of metal at Emma's feet. "My folly isn't your concern."

"It's never foolish to care for someone."

Augustus gave her a look that could turn Pompeii to ash. "Don't ply me with platitudes," he said. "Didn't we promise honesty? You were honest before. Don't hold back now."

Emma swallowed hard. "What happened?"

"What do you think?"

"She does care for you, you know," Emma said earnestly. "As much as she cares for anyone. It's not you, really, it isn't. She's just not . . . romantically inclined."

Augustus nudged at a bit of tubing with his toe, sending it rattling across the floor. "I don't want to talk about it."

Then why had he brought it up?

All right. If he didn't want to talk about it, they didn't have to talk about it, even though Emma wondered, with the sort of sick curiosity that drove people to attend public executions, what exactly had been said and unsaid.

"Then we can talk about something else," she said cheerfully. "What do you think of your room in the house? You're in one of the older servant quarters, aren't you? There isn't really space for everyone, even with the new additions. Just think what it will be like tomorrow when everyone else arrives!"

Without responding, Augustus strolled inexorably forward into the circle she had made for herself. The lanterns lit his face from below, casting a demonic light across his cheekbones, creating the illusion of flame in the folds of his shirt, where the light reflected red. His eyes glittered in the lantern light.

"It's your turn," Emma said breathlessly. "To not talk about something."

"Tell me about your new machine."

"Uh . . ." For all that she had spent the past half hour playing with pieces, Emma suddenly felt unprepared and untried.

It had something to do with the way he was staring at her, eyes never wavering, moving steadily forward, like a jungle cat approaching its prey. For all the length of his limbs, he was a graceful man; he scarcely made a sound as he prowled towards her, stepping unerringly over the obstacles scattered in his path.

She backed up a bit, glancing around at the pieces lying about on the floor. "It's not one machine but four, all interconnected. I've been trying to sort out which is which."

"Four? I thought Mr. Fulton was sending you a wave machine." There was something hypnotic about those slow, steady movements, the fixed intensity of his eyes.

Emma backed up again. "Well, there is the wave machine, but Mr. Fulton wanted to try something new, so he, well, he made it more complicated. Ours doesn't just do waves; it does waves, wind, thunder, and lightning." She looked ruefully down at the debris on the floor. "At least, it will, when I figure out how to put it together."

Augustus struck a pose, parodying Hamlet. "What a piece of work is this! The power to control the elements, all in one easy box. Once you needed witchcraft to conjure storms. Now all we need is—" Leaning down, Augustus hefted a curious circle made of brass, with curved protrusions. He frowned down at it. "What *is* this? It looks like a late medieval instrument of torture."

That, at least, Emma could answer. "It's part of an air pump." She took the brass wheel from him, holding it so that the lamplight slid along the curved surfaces. "It's designed to create the illusion of wind. There are four of those circles. They sit in a frame like an artist's easel, with a string hanging down. If we pull the string, the blades will spin, creating a rush of air."

"Hmm." Abandoning the air pump, Augustus prowled the circumference of the circle of lanterns, examining the detritus from Mr. Fulton's box. Bending, he seized on another piece, a cylindrical metal drum covered with canvas. "And this?"

"That's a drum covered with canvas," Emma said helpfully.

Straightening, Augustus gave her a look. "That much," he said, "I could divine on my own."

At least he had sounded a bit more like his old self there, not the languid, versifying figure he showed to the public, but the sarcastic, short-tempered, cranky self he showed to her.

Adele was right. She really did have execrable taste in men.

"The drum is for thunder," Emma explained. She peered around the floor. "There should be a hammer here somewhere."

"Like this?"

"Exactly like that." Emma nodded emphatically. "You attach the hammer to the clamp on the side of the drum and when it strikes the canvas, it creates a sound like thunder. You'll see. It sounds surprisingly convincing."

"Not exactly sophisticated."

"It is," said Emma triumphantly, "when linked to the lightning machine!"

"The lightning machine?"

"That's the genius of it. Or it will be," she said. "According to Mr. Fulton's instructions, if we link the machines together the right way, the flash created by the lightning machine will be immediately followed by the rumble of thunder and a gust of wind, just like in a real storm."

Emma dropped to her knees and began hunting around on the ground, her fingers touching and discarding various shapes. "See this?"

"The one that looks like a pistol?" Augustus leaned over her, taking advantage of his longer reach. His shadow fell across the floor in front of her, blending with her shadow to create a strange composite creature, a fantastical heraldic beast.

A beast with two backs? Emma found herself blushing, grateful for the darkness and her bowed head.

Scooping it up, he dangled it in front of her. If she stood, she would bump up against him. Emma stayed where she was, crouched on the floor like a child.

"I suppose it does look like a firearm," she said, adding unnecessarily, "I haven't had much to do with pistols."

"No. I hadn't thought you had." The pistol-like object was whisked away.

What was that supposed to mean?

"Well, at least you don't think I spent my entire childhood fighting off savages." Emma pushed against the planks of the floor, levering herself up to her feet. She dusted her hands off against her dress. "You'd be amazed by the number of people who have asked me what it feels like to be scalped."

Augustus smiled politely but didn't take the bait. He turned over the pistol-like object in his hands. "Show me how this works."

Emma did her best to recall Mr. Fulton's instructions. "According to Mr. Fulton, the concept is similar to that of flame-throwing, only, in this case, the gunpowder in the pan, when struck by the hammer, creates the spark and the momentum that propels the flame."

"So it creates a flare."

"Yes."

"With gunpowder."

Emma looked at the mechanism in his hands. "I don't really understand it," she confessed, "but I can put the pieces together the right way and hope for the best."

She spoke with more confidence than she felt. Sketches of hydraulic pumps for Carmagnac were one thing; putting together a flamethrower was quite another. Emma didn't want to be the one responsible for burning down Bonaparte's theatre.

"If worse comes to worst," she said hopefully, "we can ask Mr. Fulton for help when he arrives. He said he wanted to see how his contrivances contrived."

"What about your cousin?" Augustus asked, and there was something in his face that she didn't quite understand. "He has some experience with munitions, hasn't he?"

"Kort?" Among his other interests, Kort's father had owned a foundry in Cold Spring, on the Hudson. Emma couldn't remember quite what it was that it made, but she did seem to recall something about ordnance. Or was that only during the war? She couldn't recall. "Something like that," said Emma vaguely.

Augustus set the piece down, more carefully than the others. "What else do you have there?"

Emma turned in a slow circle. The muslin of her dress rasped against the rough wood of the crate, catching on a splinter. "That's really all," she said. "Just waves, wind, lightning, and thunder. Isn't that enough?"

Augustus poked at another piece with his boot, this one a curved cylinder of metal. "What's this for?"

Emma dipped down to free her skirt from the crate, bumping her elbow on the way up. "I—I haven't figured that one out yet."

"Really?" Augustus's mouth twisted in a crooked smile. "I thought you had everything figured out. You certainly pegged me."

Emma started to put out a hand, but Augustus's stance didn't invite caresses. She let it drop.

"Augustus? Are you sure you're all right? We don't have to do this now. The machines will wait until morning."

Augustus folded his arms across his chest. "Of course, I'm all right. Why wouldn't I be?"

The lantern light flickered and guttered around them, creating a kaleidoscope of shifting shadows. Augustus's posture was as tense as a clenched fist. Emma fiddled with her favorite ring, turning it around and around and around. She could cede to his wishes and let it go. It was what she was best at, smiling and laughing and babbling on about nothing, letting uncomfortable truths evaporate like the bubbles in a glass of champagne.

Why dwell on unpleasantness when one could ignore it?

"Don't," she said, surprising herself. "Honesty, remember? You know exactly what I mean."

"That little scene in the garden, you mean?" Augustus waved a hand in an entirely unconvincing show of insouciance. "Forgotten already. Muses come, muses go. From Laura one day to Beatrice the next. Any interest in serving as muse? There's a pedestal going begging." He looked Emma up and down with deliberate insolence.

She was meant to be offended, she knew. Instead, she felt a painful surge of remembrance and, with it, pity.

Nothing hurt more than the disillusionment of love.

"Oh, my dear," she said softly. "You don't mean that."

He stiffened. "Why not? Don't worry," he said, "by the time I finish immortalizing you, you'll scarcely recognize yourself. It's all in a twist of the phrase."

Emma's heart ached for him. "Augustus—"

"Fair Cytherea ..." he began, and broke off again, shaking his head. "No, it shouldn't be Cytherea. We'll have to find another name for you. Would you like to be Stella? Philip Sidney used it first, but no one remembers him anyway nowadays, and certainly not in French." Dropping to one knee in front of her, he flung an arm into the air. *"Bright star! So fine, so fair! So high above where we are!"*

"Do get up," Emma pleaded, reaching down a hand to him, "and speak sensibly."

He clambered nimbly to his feet, ignoring her outstretched hand. "Would you rather be Cynthia, goddess of the moon? Astrea, patroness of the Earth, mother of all good and growing things? That was good enough for Queen Elizabeth, but she was a notoriously wanton jade when it came to poetry, posing as any goddess who came along. We can do better for you."

"I never asked to be made immortal. Augustus—"

"Make me immortal, Helen, with a kiss?" It was the least convincing leer Emma had ever seen. "No. Not Helen. You don't have that doomed look about you."

"I don't want to launch ships," she said sharply. Pity only went so far. She leaned back against the crate, feeling the scrape of the wood through the thin muslin of her gown. "Can we please—"

"Aurora!" Augustus smacked a hand against the side of the crate with such force that Emma jumped. It couldn't have done his hand much good either. "Why didn't I see it before? I'll make you Aurora, spreading light across the sky, bringing joy to the morning."

It would have been a pretty sentiment if it hadn't been spoken in tones of such concentrated sarcasm.

He struck a pose. *"Rosy-fingered dawn, all flushed with light / Bringing morning out of night ..."*

"Why do you write such rubbish?" Emma burst out. "We both know you can do better."

"Can I?" He braced his hands against the rim of the crate on either side of her. Emma wiggled back, but there was nowhere to go; she was pinned fast between him and the wooden slats. "Maybe I can't. Maybe I've written rubbish for so long, it's all I can write."

"You never know until you try." The words sounded weak and tinny on her tongue. She was sitting on the rim of the crate now, the edge digging into her buttocks. She squirmed uncomfortably. One false move and she was going to topple back inside, immured among the straw and sawdust. "I could help you!"

"Could you?"

"I could, er, listen." The box tipped precipitately under her weight, pitching her towards him. Emma grabbed at his shoulders to keep from falling. "To your poetry."

"So it's all about the poetry, is it?" They were chest to chest, pinned together by the angle of the box, his breath warm in her ear. Emma's body slid down his, muslin against linen, leg against leg, as the box rocked back into place behind them.

"What else?" Emma asked breathlessly.

"What else, indeed." He pushed away, releasing her.

Emma was left staggering, wobbly and breathless, as he strode across the room. It felt colder, suddenly. It might be June, but the nights were cool and the theatre unheated. She hadn't been cold a moment before.

She followed him, weaving erratically around the joints and hoists and tubes. "I think we should talk about this."

"We have talked. What do you think we were doing just now? Dancing?"

No wonder people thought dancing was just a step away from . . . Well. Emma didn't want to think about what they had just been doing. She rubbed her hands against her arms to stop them tingling.

"Not that sort of talking," Emma said firmly. They'd known each other too well and too long now to let him distract her like that. They were well out of the lamplight now, among the rolled-up backdrops and piles of props. Emma ducked under a painted proscenium that had been used last summer for *The Barber of Seville*. She ran him to ground against a dead end, a false doorway painted on canvas, leading into an opulent mansion designed for a southerly clime. "If not for me—I feel responsible."

"Don't," Augustus said harshly. "I was being a fool long before I knew you. Don't flatter yourself, Madame Delagardie. Your involvement is purely incidental."

That certainly put her in her place.

Emma hugged her arms to her chest. "There's no need to be a cad just because—just because it didn't go as you wished."

Augustus raised a brow, leaning back against a painted panorama of Seville that looked strangely like Venice. "It?"

"Jane." There. It was out. "A one-sided love isn't love."

"I'd forgotten." His voice dripped with sarcasm. "You have such vast experience of the world."

She refused to let herself be baited. She raised her chin. "I do, actually. I know what it's like, you see. To find out that someone isn't what you imagined him to be."

She met his gaze frankly, an eye for an eye and a stare for a stare, refusing to let herself be embarrassed or shamed out of countenance. She might be younger than he, but she knew she was right, and, deep down, he knew it, too.

Augustus broke first.

He turned his head away, dragging in a deep, shuddering breath. She could see his chest rise and fall beneath the thin fabric of his shirt. "I've been in love with a mirage," he said despairingly. "You knew it. She knew it. Everyone knew it but me. What sort of idiot does that make me?"

"A human one?"

Augustus emitted a harsh bark of laughter.

"It wasn't entirely a mirage," Emma said soothingly. "Whatever else she is, Jane is a lovely person. It's not as though . . . it's not as though you fancied yourself in love with Caroline!"

"Christ, Emma!" Augustus dropped down onto an overturned rowboat, his long limbs folding neatly beneath him. "Do you have to make the best of everything?"

He sat hunched over, his elbows resting on his knees. He looked like a little boy like that, for all that he was at least a few years older than she. Emma felt a rush of affection and irritation and concern, all mingled together. She wanted to draw his head to her bosom and rock him back and forth, murmuring soothing noises, to put her arms around him and cuddle the pain away.

"I try." Her dress brushed against his boot tops as she moved next to him. "Better that than the contrary. Wouldn't you rather a half-full glass?"

"It depends on the contents. Are you offering hemlock or fox-glove?"

Emma tentatively reached out to rest a hand on his head. His curls were thick and springy beneath her fingers, so different from Paul's short crop or her own stick-straight hair. "Surely, it's not as bad as that." She bumped him with her hip. "Scootch over."

She wouldn't call it exactly a scootch, but Augustus slid over, making room for her on the overturned raft.

He didn't look up. "I've been in love with a mirage for the better part of a year."

Emma settled herself down next to him. "What's a year in the grand scheme of things? And at least you've got lots of poetry out of it."

Augustus looked at her with dead eyes. "You think my poetry is rubbish."

"Not all of it." Taken individually, the words had promise. It was just strung together that they made no sense. "Other people like it."

Augustus sighed. "You really don't tell a lie, do you?"

"I try not to." Tentatively, Emma slid an arm around his shoulders, cuddling him as she would Hortense, or as she had Paul once, long ago. She found the hollow above his shoulder blade and pressed down with two fingers, rubbing away the pain. "It really isn't so bad as all that. I promise."

She couldn't have said whether she was talking about his romantic predicament or his poetry.

She could feel the moment he relaxed against her, letting his back slump and his head come to rest against her breast. His breath emerged in a long exhalation, almost like a sigh. He curled up against her, a tangle of dark curls hiding his face. His skin was warm through the thin muslin shirt, his body heavy against hers, curling comfortably into the hollow below her arm.

Emma stroked her fingers through his hair, focusing on the drowsy warmth of his body, the dust motes on the floor, the scents of soap and skin, as her brain turned and turned in unpleasant circles.

She wondered if she had been wrong to warn him away. He might have been happier continuing to daydream of Jane, worshipping her from an arm's length away. But what happened when an arm's length became too far? When he wanted more? He had been bound to find out sooner or later. Surely better sooner, before the hurt became even greater.

Emma rested her cheek against his hair and assured herself that what she had done, she had done out of friendship. And it wasn't that she was glad that Jane had answered as she had, not really. It was simply—simply the hastening of an inevitability. That was all. There was no other reason at all.

They sat in silence for what might have been five minutes or half an hour, no sound but the rhythmic rustle of his hair beneath her fingers, the soft susurration of their breath.

Into the dusty silence, Augustus said diffidently, "Did Jane ever mention it to you? Did she know that it wasn't—that I—"

"If she suspected, she never said anything." Emma chose her

words very carefully, stroking his hair in long, measured strokes. "I think she values you too much for that."

"Yes, but only—" Augustus mumbled something incomprehensible.

"What?"

Augustus shifted in his seat. "Nothing." But the mood was broken. He shook off her hold, drawing back so he could look at her, his hair brushing across her chest. "When you said you knew what it was like, what did you mean?"

Emma caught herself floundering, unsure of what to say. It was much easier being on the other side of it. She preferred eliciting confidences to making them.

"I—exactly what I said. That's all."

"That's not an answer."

Emma pressed his head back into the crook of her shoulder. "This is about you, not me, remember?"

She could feel his skepticism, from somewhere in the area of her collarbone. "Is it? It's only fair. I confide in you; you confide in me."

Emma peered down at the top of Augustus's head. "Appealing to my sense of fair play, are you?"

His voice rose sepulchrally from her chest. "You brought up the topic."

"I—oh, fine." Was it possible to feel both very protective and very irritated at the same time? Fair enough. "I was very young when I met my husband," she said, striving to put a sensible face on it. "I had all sorts of romantic images about him. Don't misunderstand me! Paul was a wonderful man, really he was. He just wasn't the person I thought he was."

"What was he?" Augustus's voice was a brush of breath against her bosom. She could feel the tingle of it straight down to her toes.

Emma shivered with something that wasn't cold.

"Human," said Emma, pushing away and twitching her bodice

more firmly up over her shoulders. She made a droll face. "You can't believe what a disappointment that was."

Augustus hoisted himself back into a sitting position. "You were fairly young, weren't you?"

"Fifteen."

It would have been so easy to use that as an excuse. Emma contemplated her knees, twin bumps beneath the thin lawn of her gown. Nine years. Had it really been so long? Five years with Paul, four years without him. In a few months, he would have been gone longer than they had been together. It was a curious sensation.

Her skin prickled as she felt Augustus's hand come to rest on the small of her back, rubbing in small, discreet circles. He was offering her the same promise of comfort she had held out to him. She wanted, so very much, to let herself curl into the crook of his arm, to rest her head against his shoulder and feel his lips on her hair and allow herself the solace of touch. It would be so nice to be cuddled and comforted, all the worries of the last nine years soothed away.

If she did so, it would be under false pretenses. She might have been young, but she ought to have known better, just as she ought to know better now.

Sighing, Emma straightened. "I don't think age has anything to do with it. We're all prey to our emotions, whether we're fifteen or fifty."

"Which you know," Augustus said drily, "because you turned fifty when?"

"When we started writing this masque," she said and waited for him to laugh.

He didn't. "Has it been that onerous for you?"

"Not onerous, no." She looked at him, at the long hair curling around his thin face, at the tiny lines at the sides of his eyes, at the long, flexible mouth that could crimp into absurdity or relax into gentleness. He had become so familiar to her in the past month. Familiar and dearer than she cared to admit. "Against all my better judgment, I actually like you."

"Just not my poetry."

"If I were you, I would take what I can get." The minute the words were out of her mouth, Emma realized how they sounded. "I didn't mean—"

His brown eyes shaded to violet at the edges, warm as velvet. "I know." His thumb rubbed against her cheekbone. "Honest Emma."

Of all the epithets he had offered to provide her, that had to be the least flattering of the lot.

Emma grimaced. "*Make me immortal, Emma, with plain speaking?* That doesn't have much of a ring to it."

His fingers found a bit of hair that had escaped from her bandeau. He smoothed it back behind her ear. Emma closed her eyes and let herself lean into his touch, just a little bit. Just for the moment.

"You said you didn't want to launch ships."

No, but that didn't mean she didn't want to be just a little bit of an object of romantic desire. Someday. For someone.

Oh, well.

Emma abruptly sat up, her hair tangling in his fingers. "No, I just—"

She had been about to say *sit on them*, and maybe make a silly comment about something to do with not launching ships, but the words caught in her throat as her nose bumped his.

She went very still.

She could feel his fingers caught in her hair, the muscles of his arm tense beneath her hand, frozen, just as she was. She should, she knew, wiggle away, move back, laugh, say something.

Her voice came out half whisper, half squeak. "Augustus?"

"Emma?" he said, and she could feel the brush of his breath like a caress against her lips.

It wasn't, she thought, entirely reassuring that he sounded as entirely befuddled as she felt.

"I—" she began, and broke off, because she didn't have the least idea of what she was trying to say, or why she was trying to say anything at all.

His lips brushed hers, so softly she might have imagined it.

She should open her eyes, she knew. But there was something terribly seductive about the darkness, something drugging and dreamlike.

As in a dream, her hands moved without conscious volition, threading up through his hair, as tentative as his lips, learning as they went, following the curve of his scalp like someone embarking in twilight on an unfamiliar path through winter woods, warm and cold at the same time, fascinated and hesitant, white snow and dark trees, light and shade all mixed up together.

His hands cupped her face, not coercing or forcing, not pushing or demanding, but cradling. If he had pushed or demanded, she might have pulled away.

But he didn't.

Chapter 18

Close your lips; don't speak me fair;
Those wordy vows are but pure air.
My port is yours, my friendship free,
In simple camaraderie.

— Emma Delagardie and Augustus Whittlesby,
Americanus: A Masque in Three Parts

She smelled like violets and musk, innocence and experience, all rolled into one.

Augustus nuzzled the side of Emma's face with his nose, breathing in the scent of her, so familiar and yet strangely heady at such close quarters, like perfume in its purest and distilled form, or spirits drunk straight.

She blinked at him, like one half asleep, eyes blurred and unfocused. She looked adorable that way, hair tousled, cheeks flushed. He had seen her flustered before, flustered, tousled, blustering, but never like this, soft around the corners.

"I don't think—" she said hoarsely.

Augustus put a finger to her lips. "Yes, you do," he said fondly. "All the time."

Gently, he brushed his finger across her lips. For a moment, he thought she might argue, her lips parted as though to speak, but only air came out. Her eyelids flickered closed, lilac paint making purple shadows.

"Emma," Augustus said, tasting the name on his tongue, invocation and question all in one. This was Emma and it wasn't, commonplace and strange all at the same time, like a familiar landscape viewed from a new angle. What was the line? *Suffer a sea change to something rich and strange.*

Rich and strange, indeed. Her lips were soft and slightly parted beneath his finger, her breath a benediction on his skin. So many discussions they had had, so many conversations, so many arguments, and he had never imagined her lips would feel like this, like crinkled satin, smooth and soft to touch.

How had he known her without knowing this?

In fact, all of her was soft, from the whispery fabric of her dress to the bare skin of her arm beneath the small, puffed sleeve of her dress. The costly muslin of her dress felt coarse next to the silk of her skin, coarse and crude, the clumsy work of man a poor second to the wonders of nature. He skimmed his hand lightly up her arm, feeling the goose pimples rise beneath his fingers. He had dismissed her as skinny once, but there was flesh on her bones, soft, feminine flesh that quivered with the passage of his touch.

He ran his knuckles along the border of her bodice, once so seemingly low, now far too high.

"Emma," he said again, and leaned in to kiss her.

"Don't." Emma jerked sharply sideways. Augustus's lips grazed hair. "Augustus—don't."

Augustus spat out a blond hair that had attached itself to his tongue. "Emma?"

Using both hands, she held his head away from her. Her small hands had surprising strength in them. "No. Please."

Augustus pulled back. "Of course. Whatever you say." Seeing her look at him that way made him feel like the meanest sort of cad. Worse than a cad. Someone like Marston. "I didn't mean—"

"I know you didn't." Clumsily, she scrambled off his lap, her elbow digging hard into his chest as she pushed away. Her voice was muffled by the movement. "That's just the problem."

"That's not—" Augustus broke off, befuddled.

He'd been going to say that wasn't what he meant, but he'd be damned if he knew what he did mean. All he knew was that his lap felt very empty without Emma in it. His mind was still scrambling to catch up with his body.

His body, meanwhile, wanted to catch up with Emma.

"Emma, I don't know what to say. I—"

Turning away, Emma yanked at her bodice. A few tugs, and she had hoisted the fabric higher than it had ever been meant to go. "It's quite all right," she said. She wouldn't look him in the eye but concentrated on righting her bodice. "You don't have to say anything. I understand."

He was glad someone did. He sure as hell didn't.

Augustus shoved himself up off the rounded keel of the rowboat, his movements stiff and awkward. "Emma—"

Turning, she shook out her skirts, rousting out creases with unnecessary force. "Shall we go back to the house? It must be nearly time for supper. Are you hungry?"

Hungry? Food was the last thing on his mind.

Emma kept up a steady flow of chatter. "It won't be anything fancy; it never is at Malmaison. Bonaparte likes to be simple in the country—the Emperor, I mean. I can't seem to remember to call him that."

"*Wait.*" Augustus plunged desperately into the gap left by a semi-second's silence. "That's it?"

"What's it?"

"This. Us. Now." It wasn't his most articulate moment.

"There isn't an us." She fiddled with her rings, turning a cluster of diamonds around and around and around. "It's all right. You don't have to pretend. I know this isn't about me."

His body disagreed. It thought it was very much about her. He could still feel the press of her against the crook of his arm and more distracting places, like an impression left in wax.

Emma took his silence as assent. "It's just that I was here," she said earnestly. "I do understand, you know. You were hurt. You wanted comforting."

No. Yes. Maybe?

Augustus shoved his hair back away from his face. "Emma—"

She smiled a rueful smile. "Right now, I imagine any warm body would do. Mine just happened to be here." Turning, she ducked beneath a painted proscenium, maneuvering around a miniature version of the leaning tower of Pisa. "Shall we take the side door? It's faster."

Augustus grabbed for her, catching her hand. "Not so fast."

Her hand felt painfully frail in his, tiny bones in tiny fingers, the massive stones of her rings biting into his palms, the last defense of a kingdom unprepared for siege.

"Yes?"

Now that he had her attention, he didn't know what to do with it. What was he supposed to tell her? *You're not just a warm body? In fact, you're rather chilly?* Or *Yes, this was all about Jane, but you're not so bad yourself?*

Brilliant, Augustus, brilliant. One could launch ships with that.

Brusquely, he said, "Don't sell yourself short."

Emma's eyes fell to their joined hands. "I'm not." She closed her eyes and then opened them again. "I'm just being . . . realistic. It's a natural reaction, to seek consolation. How can I fault you for that? I've done it too."

"Have you?" Augustus's reaction was visceral and negative. He didn't like the thought of that, not one bit. It had probably been Marston, the bastard, based on all accounts. He had never heard Emma's name linked with anyone else's, not in that way at any rate. Flirtations, yes; courtships, naturally; but an affair? Only Marston.

He hated the thought of Emma in Marston's arms, her tiny form engulfed in his embrace, Marston's hands in her hair, on her shoulders, her breasts.

She nodded, but didn't elaborate. "So you see, I do understand."

Augustus wished she would stop understanding. "Yes, but . . ."

"Well, then," Emma said, as though that answered everything. She smiled at him, the smile she wore in Paris, the bright, fake smile that went with her paste jewelry and glittery garments. It looked very out of place with her snagged gown and tousled hair. "We only have two days left to rehearse. I do hope Kort manages to remember his lines this time."

Damn Kort and his lines. "It doesn't matter what he says," Augustus said shortly. "They would applaud if he recited the alphabet."

"I don't think we're quite so desperate as all that." Emma twisted open a door Augustus hadn't even seen. It opened onto a short path between the theatre and gallery that ran along the right side of the house, a faster and more convenient route than going all the way around to the front. "We should have some semblance of a play by Saturday."

Augustus caught the door just before it closed. He twisted through, hurrying after her. For a small person, Emma moved quickly, her dress whispering against her legs, her sandals slapping gently against the close-cut grass.

"Emma, *wait*." Augustus caught her just as she reached for the door handle. He twisted himself into the gap, wedging himself between her and the door. "Shouldn't we"—he couldn't believe he was saying this—"talk?"

He caught her off her guard. The eyes she lifted to his were vulnerable, confused. "Talk?"

"About what happened."

Whatever she was looking for, she didn't find it. Her mask clamped down again, more effective than any amount of maquillage.

"Oh, Augustus. You *are* sweet." It was her fake voice again, the society voice, like too-sweet champagne, sweet on the surface but cloying in quantity. Rising on her tiptoes, she pressed a quick kiss to his cheek. He caught a whiff of her perfume, musk and violets. "There's no need, though. Friends?"

"Friends," he echoed.

They were friends, friends in a way he hadn't been friends since his early days at Cambridge and maybe not even then. He hadn't counted anyone as friend for a long, long time. Not even Jane. Jane had been a poet's fancy. A poet's fancy and a very reliable colleague. They had trusted one another with their lives, but never with their inner selves.

They were friends, but that wasn't the heart of it, what had happened between them here, now.

"Emma—"

"Good. I shouldn't have wanted to lose you." Her eyes seemed too large for her face, the kohl rimming them jarringly dark against her fair skin. With an attempt at a smile, she said, "Who else would provide me with adverbs?"

With that parting shot, she swung away, yanking open the door to the gallery with a decidedly dramatic flourish.

And froze.

Rather than the empty room they had anticipated, the gallery thronged with a collection of women in expensive evening dress and men in brightly colored uniforms. Servants scurried to lay out refreshments, while empty glasses were already accumulating on all available surfaces.

It wasn't just the cast of the masque anymore. Their brief interlude of privacy was over.

Over Emma's shoulder, Augustus saw a woman in white raise a languid hand in greeting, calling out, in an unmistakable Creole drawl, "Emma, my dear! We had wondered where you had got to."

Chapter 19

Beset, besieged from every side,
I run, I flee, I look to hide
But where shall I some shelter find?
What solace from my own weak mind?
—Emma Delagardie and Augustus Whittlesby,
Americanus: A Masque in Three Parts

"Madame Bonaparte!" Emma dropped into a curtsy. The door swung shut behind her as she released it, banging her in the backside. "I hadn't thought you were to be here until tomorrow."

A dozen or so sets of eyes turned in her direction, identified the new arrival, and slid away again, back to their own conversations and pursuits. Adele gave a wave before turning back to the man at whom she was fluttering her lashes, one of the naval officers who had been impressed into the production to play a naval officer. Jane was at the far end of the room, in conversation with Kort.

Jane, whom Augustus thought he loved.

Did love. Had loved? Emma wasn't sure of anything anymore, least of all the untrustworthy ramblings of the human heart.

Behind her, the door remained closed. Augustus must have slipped around the other way, leaving her to greet Mme. Bonaparte alone.

That had been good of him, she told herself. He had done the prudent thing. To have entered the room together, looking as she did, would have been tantamount to an announcement of an affair. Neither of them wanted that. It would be embarrassing for her, more embarrassing for her than for him. In the eyes of the insular circle that had formed around the First Consul and his wife, she would be either the predator, the bored matron who had taken a poet for a lover, or the prey, the wealthy widow being seduced for her patronage.

Why, then, did she feel quite so shunned?

She felt cold. Cold and tired and strangely wobbly. It had taken more strength than she would have thought to laugh and smile and pretend—because it was pretense—that she didn't care. It had been even harder to make him stop.

She hadn't wanted him to stop. Not one little bit. Not at all. It wasn't just in her lips that she still felt his touch; it was everywhere, memory blurring with memory, awakening desires she thought she had pushed aside long ago, blurred memories of lips and hands and panting breath, sweat and skin and tangled hair.

Only this time, it wasn't Paul's face or Paul's hands that memory provided to her.

Idiot, Emma told herself, and crossed the room to lower herself into the curtsy that the new court etiquette made de rigueur, even at harum-scarum Malmaison, the curtsy that once would have been an embrace.

Mme. Bonaparte raised her up.

"Emma." A powdered cheek drifted across hers, bringing with it the distinctive scent of roses and rouge that always made Emma feel as though she were fourteen again, accompanying Hortense home from school for a rare weekend away. It had always been a treat to come stay with Mme. Bonaparte, in a house with no routines and no rules, where one might breakfast on sweetmeats and spend the day lollygagging with a novel or grubbing in the garden, just as one chose. "My dear girl."

Emma felt tears well up in the back of her throat, silly, pointless tears. She had come to Mme. Bonaparte and Malmaison when her marriage with Paul had failed and then again, seeking peace and solitude after the brief madness of her affair with Marston. And here she was again, nearly twenty-five and no wiser, with the scent of roses and rouge, entangling herself where she shouldn't, playing roulette with her heart and making a general mess of everything.

"Of all surprises, this is the most pleasant," Emma said, making no effort to hide the moisture in her eyes. Mme. Bonaparte cried easily herself, although only when she stood in no danger of ruining her rouge. She would think they were tears of joy, and be flattered. "I've missed you so, madame."

Mme. Bonaparte beamed the warmth of her famous close-lipped smile on Emma, well pleased. "We came down early. I couldn't wait to see how you were getting on."

"Famously," Emma said quickly. "We're getting on famously, especially with Mr. Whittlesby to help with the verse."

Why had she felt the need to mention him? She might as well take out a column in *Le Moniteur*, with the heading, "Lady kisses poet. Both agree it meant nothing."

That wasn't entirely true. If there had been any kissing, it had gone the other way. He had kissed her, not the other way around.

What did it matter? It had been an aberration. It wasn't happening again. Friends. They were friends, that was all. Friendship meant more than passion in the long run; she of all people should know that.

Mme. Bonaparte didn't seem to notice anything amiss. "It was terribly clever of you to hire a poet," she said complacently. "So much more sensible than trying to write it all yourself. But, my dear, what have you been doing to yourself? You look as though you've been playing in the dirt!"

Emma ducked her chin, trying to see down her own front. Her white muslin dress was no longer quite so white. "Oh. Dear." She looked up at Mme. Bonaparte. "I was backstage in the theatre, trying to put together one of Mr. Fulton's machines. I'm afraid the floor wasn't the cleanest."

Mme. Bonaparte swallowed the story without question. Perhaps, thought Emma, with a dull sense of surprise, because it was true. She had got herself into this state even without Augustus's ministrations.

Her struggles with Mr. Fulton's machine seemed like a lifetime ago.

"I'm so very glad you decided to abandon your labors and join us," Mme. Bonaparte said, drawing her aside with the effortless skill of the accomplished hostess. "There's something I've been wanting to ask you."

"Yes?" There were people coming and going, the usual gay and glittering crowd who attended on the First Consul's wife—the Empress, now, Emma reminded herself—but no sign of Augustus.

Perhaps, she thought gloomily, he had fled back to Paris, horrified at his own almost indiscretion. Or maybe he was up in his garret, writing long poems of pain and loss to his inconstant Cytherea.

But why? Why inconstant Cytherea? It was Augustus who had kissed her. Inconstant Augustus, then. In fact, thought Emma, with a twinge of indignation, why was she worrying about Augustus's feelings? Shouldn't he be worrying about hers? She encouraged the indignation, nursing it. She was the one who had offered him comfort, just comfort, nothing more. He was the one who had taken advantage of that, seeking a sort of solace she had never offered.

The fact that she had craved it—had welcomed it—was entirely beside the point.

Mme. Bonaparte was looking at her expectantly. Emma realized that the other woman had stopped speaking and was waiting for her to answer.

"I'm sorry," she said contritely. "Forgive me. I was woolgathering."

Whatever Mme. Bonaparte's other vanities, she wasn't the sort to account inattention a sort of petty treason. "What are we to do with you?" she said fondly. "When you join us at Saint-Cloud, I hope you will pay better attention."

"At Saint-Cloud?"

Mme. Bonaparte's face lit like a child's. "You, my dear, are to be one of my household. A lady-in-waiting! That way, I shall have you with me always."

"But—" Emma found herself caught, caught off guard, caught in the web of Mme. Bonaparte's enthusiasm. "But I hadn't—"

"Thought to be asked?" said Mme. Bonaparte gaily. "My dear girl, how could I leave you aside? Hortense would never forgive me. When I think of the two of you playing in my paint pots and ruining my best hat . . ."

Emma let the words wash over her, bringing with them a host of rosy-tinted memories of carefree school days and adolescent romps. Would it be such a very bad thing to say yes? She didn't have anything else she wanted to do or anywhere else she wanted to be. They didn't really need her at Carmagnac. All the improvements that needed to be made had been made; it was all progressing according to Paul's plans and M. le Maire had matters well in hand.

If she said yes to Mme. Bonaparte, she would have, in the space of one word, a place and a purpose. Mme. Delagardie would become lady-in-waiting to the Empress. Even Kort couldn't sneer at that.

Kort and who else? Emma tried not to think about poets.

"We couldn't possibly go on without you." Mme. Bonaparte squeezed Emma's hand languidly in her own. "You're all but a daughter to me."

She had married her own daughter off for her own advantage,

consigning Hortense to a miserable marriage with a man who despised her.

The reminder acted on Emma like the proverbial bucket of cold water. She didn't doubt Mme. Bonaparte meant it. But she also didn't doubt Bonaparte had advised it, or that, while Mme. Bonaparte might be motivated by affection, there was also a sturdy dollop of policy behind it.

Get the American girl, Bonaparte would have said. *You mean my Emma*, Mme. Bonaparte would have replied. *Lovely. We all like Emma.*

If she said yes, it meant an end to the autonomy she had earned for herself. It meant curtsying and attending and jumping into a carriage at an hour's notice whenever the Emperor decided on one of his impromptu migrations. It meant guarding her back and watching her tongue and never being able to know whether any profession of friendship, any amorous overture, was for her own sake or that of her proximity to power.

If she were a daughter, Mme. Bonaparte wouldn't hesitate to use her as she had her own. She would find herself married off for Bonaparte's advantage, locked in a loveless marriage, forced to play go-between in the endless games between nations that had somehow supplanted their old and carefree games of prisoner's base.

This would be a very different sort of prison, but still a prison.

"I can't," Emma blurted out. "I'm so sorry, Madame Bonaparte."

"Can't?" Mme. Bonaparte appeared genuinely confused. She had forgotten to shade the lamps in her usual manner. The too-bright light picked out the cracks in her rouge.

How embarrassed Uncle Monroe and cousin Robert would be by her, letting diplomacy fly to the winds like that. Two diplomats in the family and she couldn't even muster a graceful refusal to an offer meant to shower her with honor.

Mme. Bonaparte should count herself lucky not to have Emma in her household.

Emma hastily gathered the remnants of her wits. "Please don't think I'm not entirely sensible of the great honor you do me, Madame Bonaparte, and you do know that under most circumstances there is nothing I would rather have than the privilege of being near you, but I find myself incapable of accepting. Forgive me. Please."

Mme. Bonaparte's face cleared. Her lips curved in that enigmatic smile that had driven countless men wild. "Ah," she said. "I understand."

She did?

Mme. Bonaparte leaned forward, her eyes bright. "It's that handsome cousin of yours."

"Kort?" Emma had lost the thread of the conversation somewhere.

"Kort." Mme. Bonaparte tried out the name. It sounded very strange in a French Creole lilt. Her nose wrinkled, but she brushed that small matter aside. "Whatever you call him, he is a fine figure of a man. And I imagine your parents will be so pleased."

"They would be if we—I mean, that is . . ."

Mme. Bonaparte squeezed her arm. "I should have known we would lose you sooner or later."

"But I'm not—" Emma broke off, stymied in the face of Mme. Bonaparte's firm conviction. What could she say? Better to have Mme. Bonaparte think she was turning her down for Kort than that she was rejecting her in her own right. Hating herself for it, she hedged. "Nothing has been decided."

So much for honest Emma.

"Of course not," said Mme. Bonaparte knowingly. "All the same, when the time comes . . . You must let me be the first to congratulate you." She looked sentimentally at Emma. "After all your troubles, it will be nice to see you settled."

There was a lump in Emma's throat that hadn't been there before. She knew that charm came easily to Mme. Bonaparte, but even so, she was moved, both by the sentiment and the memories it invoked, of those difficult days when Emma had fled her marriage and taken shelter at Malmaison.

"Thank you," Emma said feelingly. She wondered if she was making a terrible mistake. So many people would give their eyeteeth for an offer such as this. In her own way, Mme. Bonaparte did love her, Emma knew she did.

She also knew that Mme. Bonaparte's affection, sincere though it might be, wasn't enough to protect her if Bonaparte decided her marriage would serve his ends.

"My dear," said Mme. Bonaparte, touching a finger lightly to her cheek. Lightly, so as not to further disarrange Emma's rouge. "I just want to see you happy."

"It's not just for that that I owe you thanks," said Emma, guilt lending her extra fervor. What would Mme. Bonaparte say when the promised betrothal to Kort never materialized? "But for all your many kindnesses to me over the years. No matter what happens, I would never want you to think me ungrateful or insensible of how much I owe you. You and Hortense and Eugene"—dimly, she was aware that she was babbling, and that, in this strange new world, such sentiments might be accounted lèse-majeste, but this was more important, this was her heart scrubbed raw—"you have been more than family to me and I will never, ever forget that."

"How sweet," said someone behind her.

Emma turned, slowly, to see Caroline Murat, all satin and feathers. The cloying sweetness of her smile only emphasized the acid beneath it.

Caroline. It would be.

The other woman strolled forward. "What a terribly charming sentiment, Madame Delagardie."

Emma took a deep breath, hating herself for being caught in a moment of vulnerability before Caroline. Caroline, of all people.

Emma could feel Mme. Bonaparte stiffen, but her voice was

pleasant as she said, "Good evening, Caroline. How nice of you to join us."

"Madame." Caroline Murat didn't bother to hide the disdain she felt for her sister-in-law. She turned her critical gaze on Emma, taking in every aspect of Emma's tousled appearance. "Your lip rouge is smudged. And is that *straw* in your hair?"

Hortense had tried to befriend Caroline when she first arrived at Mme. Campan's. Caroline had never forgiven her for it. Emma was an enemy by extension. Caroline took her enmities very seriously. It must, Emma decided, be the Corsican in her. Vendetta was a concept that Caroline not only understood but cherished.

"I've been in the theatre," said Emma defensively, "trying to sort through props."

"Props," repeated Caroline, looking pointedly at Emma's smudged lip rouge. "Is that what you call them in the Americas?"

Caroline raised a gloved hand, ostensibly to toy with her cameo necklace, but really to better display her impressive figure. She looked pointedly at Emma's comparative lack of endowment.

Yes, yes, Emma knew. Nature was kinder to some than to others. Georges had been quite clear on that front, during the period of their entanglement. Lithe, Paul had called her, with his happy facility for turning any phrase to advantage.

And then there was Augustus. She had no idea of Augustus's thoughts on the topic or if he thought about it at all. Or if he would have fled if she hadn't fled first.

"Yes, props," said Emma, more sharply than she ought. "For the masque the First Consul commissioned."

"You mean the Emperor," Caroline said snippily, and might have said more but for the clatter of spurs against the parquet floor of the drawing room that led into the gallery.

The sound arrested Caroline's attention. She listened for a moment, and then smiled, the slow, smug smile of the cat who got the cream. "As it happens, I've brought a prop of my own."

Caroline crooked a finger imperiously at the doorway.

A man strode forward, slightly the worse for travel. His boots still bore the dust of the road, and his buttons lacked their usual sheen. But his teeth were as white as ever. He had them all bared in a smile as he crossed the room towards them.

Caroline extended a languid hand. "Whatever took you so long?" Turning back to Emma, she said, "Madame Delagardie, I don't believe you need any introduction to Colonel Marston."

Chapter 20

Sussex, England
May 2004

$\mathcal{I}$ hightailed it to the library.

I'm not sure what I had been expecting to find. Dempster and Serena in flagrante delicto? Dempster going through my notes, chortling like a stage villain? Instead, the library was as it always was, an oasis of evening calm, the setting sun streaming through the long windows, picking out the worn patches on the red and blue carpet, and highlighting the dust that collected in the long grooves of the ornamental pilasters between the bookshelves. My notebook lay where I had left it, the research books I had been using scattered around in my usual cheerful disarray. It all seemed normal enough. . . .

I ventured closer. Why was I walking like a member of the bomb squad from *Law & Order*? This was silly. I marched briskly up to my favorite table. A folio of letters from Jane to Henrietta, detailing Jane's role in the masque at Malmaison, all present and accounted for. Copy of the masque, printed in a vanity edition with red morocco covers, check. The spiral notebook I used when I didn't feel like lugging my laptop, check. Four assorted volumes on American history, used for background research on the Morris/Monroe/Livingston and Fulton connections, all there.

My reference books had verified what I'd found in Jane's letters. I'd never known that Mr. Fulton, the inventor of the steamboat, had lived in France for a number of years, working on his steamboat and various other devices before teaming up with Mr. Livingston and going home to New York. But it appeared that he had. He had also come up with the first-ever panorama, which caused a rage in Paris. Theatrical equipment must have been a no-brainer for him after that.

If it was theatrical equipment, that is, and not the early-nineteenth-century equivalent of a weapon of mass destruction.

Wouldn't that be an interesting double fake! What if Fulton were, in fact, working for the French Royalists? There were various groups floating around, often at odds with each other, seldom in sync with the English and Austrian agents who purported to be working in their interests. Someone had tried to assassinate Bonaparte on his way to the theatre in Christmas 1800—why not in his own theatre in 1804?

Because it hadn't happened, I reminded myself. That's the weird thing about reading history through peoples' papers and documents. You forget that you do know how it all turned out. Charles I was beheaded, Marie Antoinette never made it past Varennes, Bonaparte wasn't assassinated in 1804.

That didn't mean someone might not try. Maybe Marston was a double agent.

Huh. That was weird. Not Marston—although he was peculiar enough all by himself—but the folio on the desk, next to the biography of Fulton that I hadn't quite got around to finishing (or starting). The folio I had thought was the one I had been reading—well, it wasn't. It had been replaced with another. They all looked the same, those folios, from the outside at least. A late Victorian member of the Selwick clan had catalogued the family papers, albeit in a rather haphazard fashion, pasting them in chronological order into large folio volumes, all of which looked alike, but for the labels on the spine. The one I was holding wasn't the correspondence of Henrietta Dorrington (née Selwick) and Miss Jane Wooliston, 1804–1805. It was Henrietta Dorrington and Lady Frederick Staines (née Deveraux), 1803–1806.

I'd been through those papers before. They had to do with various intrigues in India, although they weren't much use without the corresponding documentation from the archives of a now defunct Indian administrative province, fortunately preserved in the notebooks of Colin's great-aunt, in her flat in London. In short, nothing to do with anything I was doing.

So what was it doing on my desk?

I lifted the folio, turning it this way and that, but it told me nothing. Not as if it was going to pipe up like an item out of a fairy tale and sing, *"Folio, folio on the shelf / Dempster is an evil elf!"* or something like that.

What would Dempster want with Henrietta's India correspondence? His interest, like mine, was in the Pink Carnation and her league. If he wanted that, the Delagardie affair was a positive gold mine. But that folio, the folio dealing with Jane's summer sojourn at Malmaison, sat chastely on my chair where I had left it, seemingly undisturbed.

Now that I looked for it, I could see the marks of hasty turning on the pages of my notebook, the bent paper, the tiny tears. Okay, well, maybe some of those had been me, but it still made me feel like Sherlock Holmes. And was that a smear of blood on one corner? Oh, coffee. That had been me, then. Oops.

I closed the red plastic cover of my notebook and, defiantly, left it sitting in plain sight on the desk. No point in closing the barn door, right? I jammed my feet harder into my tottery stilettos and marched purposefully towards the library door. Dempster and I were going to have to have ourselves a little talk. I was historian, hear me roar!

Or not.

The library door yanked open just as I put my hand to it, causing me to wobble dangerously on my three-inch heels.

"Steady there," said Colin, grabbing me just as I pitched face-first into his chest.

There were worse places to be. "Hi," I mumbled into his shirt-front. "Looking for me?"

"Do you know what time it is?" he said, but I could hear the annoyance fading away even as he said it, in the softening of his tone and the way his arms wrapped around me. "I thought you had done a bunk rather than go down to dinner with me."

I rubbed my nose into his chest, smelling his familiar scent of detergent and deodorant. "And miss the fun?" I said. "I'm thinking of going down to dinner like this. It's very comfy."

He slid a finger beneath my chin, tilting my face up. "You might have some trouble eating that way."

It would have been nice to just stay that way, but guilt and knowledge lay heavy upon me. By the lurching of my tum, something Dempster this way come, and Colin didn't know it yet.

"Hey," I said, reluctantly peeling away. "Is Serena supposed to be here tonight?"

Maybe that hadn't been the best opening gambit. He let me go. I felt very wobbly without his hands on my arms, wobbly and cold, the crisp air biting into that exposed triangle at the small of my back.

"Why?" He started down the hall to the stairs, me trailing along-side.

I hated the shuttered look on his face. Serena was a closed topic as far as Colin was concerned. Efforts to get him to Talk About It resulted in one of two things: diversion, i.e., kissing that sensitive spot behind my ear, pointing out a rare yellow-billed redheaded warbler through the window (I still wasn't convinced there was any such bird, but if there was, it clearly responded to the sound of Serena's name), or simply smiling and changing the subject. Or this. Complete shutdown. No one home, admittance interdicted, beware of dog.

There was nothing to do but blurt it out. "Dempster is here. He's DreamStone's historical consultant."

"What?"

"I know, that was my reaction, too. And it gets worse." Catching a heel on the worn carpet that ran down the center of the hall, I stumbled in my too-high heels.

"Worse?" He caught my arm, drawing it through his for support, mine or his.

"According to Cate—no, you haven't met her yet," I added, before he could ask. "She's their clipboard girl, and I've told her she can use our computer if she likes. Don't worry, you'll like her."

Colin was beginning to look a little bewildered. "What does this have to do with Dempster?"

"Right." I took a deep breath. "Anyway, according to Cate—you know, the clipboard girl—Dempster got the job through personal connections. Apparently, he's dating someone connected to the film."

The carpet came to an end just at the landing. We stood at the top of the stairs, the polished wooden banister stretching along in front of us. One of Colin's ancestors had redone it all during the height of the Arts and Crafts movement, getting rid of the old white moldings and pale paint, replacing them with heavy walnut and shiny brocades. Small golden gargoyles on a dark green background snarled down at me from the wall.

Colin turned to me, his sun-streaked hair bright against the hunter green backdrop. "Do you think—?"

I shook my head. "I don't know. She didn't say." I didn't like this any more than he did, but there was no ignoring the evidence. "Who else could it be?"

Colin pressed his eyes closed. I could see the network of fine lines around his eyes, pale against his suntanned skin. There was more than one way to save the world. Colin might not be a swashbuckling double-oh-something, but he had his own variety of hero complex. He had single-handedly held up his sister through the trauma of their father's death, their mother's defection, and Serena's own romantic disasters.

I squeezed Colin's arm. "She's a grown woman." Serena was a full two months older than me. Right now, I felt positively ancient. "She's old enough to make her own decisions."

"Yes. She has done, hasn't she?" Colin nodded towards the stairs, his face showing nothing, revealing nothing. "Shall we go down?"

I thought of and discarded at least half a dozen saving phrases. *She didn't mean it; she does love you, you know; that's not what I meant.* None of them would do the least bit of good. It would only draw us both further into a conversation neither of us really wanted to have. Sometimes, talking about it doesn't make it better.

There was also the selfishness factor. My relationship with Colin still felt, even six months in, too new and fragile to risk, even for a good cause.

I wrinkled my nose at him. "Unless you want to order takeout and have it delivered up to the second floor? Right. I didn't think so." We made it about two steps before I tugged him to a halt. "There's one more thing you should know."

"Don't tell me," Colin said flatly. "They've decided to rebuild the whole house as a Disney castle and staff it with singing Martians."

"Er, no. Jeremy's seated us at opposite ends of the table." I did my best to dispel the image of a kick line of musical Martians pouring our after-dinner tea. That was probably DreamStone's next movie, with Micah Stone as the kick-ass alien hunter. "The joke will be on him when we spend the whole evening communicating in semaphore. Like that Monty Python sketch with Cathy and Heathcliff."

Colin slid his arm around me for a quick squeeze. "Whatever Jeremy might think, it is still my table. No one's seating arrangement is set in stone."

"Except for Micah Stone!" We paused on the landing where the stairs turned. "That was a joke."

Colin scanned the arriving guests from the safety of the balustrade. "Do you see Dempster?"

From the landing, we had an excellent view of the center hall. The house had never been a grand mansion, only a modest gentleman's residence, but, to my apartment-bred eyes, the hall was still a generously proportioned one. It might not be Blenheim or Chatsworth, but it could still hold a good thirty people with room for catering staff to circulate with their faux silver rent-a-trays. The door kept opening and closing, admitting more and more people as cars made hash of the carefully combed gravel circle outside, some veering off onto Colin's precious lawn.

They were a mixed bag, the guests. I amused myself by playing Spot the Americans. It wasn't a fail-safe game, but I prided myself on a fifty percent accuracy rate. It wasn't just the clothes, but something about expression and carriage. My theory has always been that different vocal constructions shape our facial muscles differently, so that you can tell an American face from a British one simply by the way the person holds her mouth.

Not a fail-proof system, but reasonably reliable. In this case, there was the added clue of the Curse of the American in England, the attempt to out-British the British, the Americans wearing what they presumed Brits wore for a country house weekend, while the Brits themselves, a far flashier and more glamorous crowd than the gang at the pub or the academics of my acquaintance, were dressed in the latest of Madison Avenue couture. DreamStone backers, I imagined, or friends of Colin's mother and her husband. They moved in moneyed circles, hobnobbing with the artsier end of the international jet set—and by artsy, I mean those who bought art, not those who produced it. That was Jeremy's job. He sold high-end art, acting as agent to a series of prestigious modern artists, among them, Colin's mother.

I didn't see Colin's mother. I gathered, from what I had heard, that she had a phobia about Selwick Hall. The phrase "gives me hives" may or may not have been used. Besides, this production was Jeremy's baby, not hers. It didn't matter to her that her only son might be involved or that his life might be disrupted by it.

My fingers had curved into claws on the timeworn walnut of the banister. I forced them to unclench and went back to scanning the crowd.

Below me, I could hear someone saying in cut-glass tones, as pretentiously posh as Dempster's, that, heavens, no, she wasn't here with the film crew, she was the representative from *Manderley;* hadn't they heard of *Manderley?*

I looked down and saw a perfectly coiffed blond head, not a hint of telltale roots showing, highlighted to feign a vacation in St. Barth's, cut in a kicky sweep not unlike my last haircut, the one that had now grown out into straggles. Oh, damn. Unconsciously, I reached for the ends of my hair, too short to put up, too long for style.

Even up half a flight of stairs, Joan Plowden-Plugge still had the power to make me feel like a mugwump.

I tugged at Colin's sleeve. "Hey. What's Joan doing here?"

"I didn't invite her," he said quickly. I believed him. Not out of consideration for me and my feelings, but because Joan had made no bones about her desire to become mistress of Selwick Hall, or at least of its master. "She's here for *Manderley.*"

"And you're okay with that?" Colin had been quite clear about wanting to keep a lid on publicity, at least as it pertained to Selwick Hall. The movie itself he couldn't do much about. That was Dream-Stone's province.

Colin's lip twisted. "I'm not okay with any of this."

Fair point. That wasn't what I'd meant, though, and he knew it.

He leaned a hand on the other side of the railing next to me, boxing me in. "Look, if I have to have reporters in my home, I'd rather it be *Manderley* than one of the tabloids."

I wasn't sure a periodical that looked down its nose at *Town &
Country* as hopelessly plebeian counted as a substitute for the gossip
rags. But if Colin thought doing a piece in *Manderley* would stave off
the tits 'n ass crowd, then so be it. I had my doubts. Where Micah
Stone went, there went the paparazzi. And nothing would suit Jeremy better than a double-page spread of himself in front of "his"
ancestral home, complete with wellies and a gun propped over his
shoulder.

Colin looked down at me, his hazel eyes concerned. "I know Joan
isn't your favorite person—"

"I can't imagine where you get these ideas," I muttered. Just because she had all but hired a coyote to drop an Acme anvil on my
head.

"But I've known her since we were children. I trust her not to say
anything . . ." Colin paused, searching for the right phrase.

"Libelous?" I'm not the child of two lawyers for nothing.

Colin pushed away from the railing. "Embarrassing."

"Right. That, too. Do you think we should go down, or shall we
just stay up here and keep staring at people? I'm fine going either
way."

"Was that a hint?" Colin asked.

"It was more of a directive." I took his arm in a proprietary grasp.
Take that, Joan Plowden-Plugge! She might have two names, but I
had one Colin, and, by gad, I wasn't sharing, not for all the cupcakes
in kindergarten. "I could use one of those glasses of bubbly."

"Only one?"

"Do you really want me to get blotto and start singing show
tunes?"

Colin's lips brushed the top of my head. "You're cute when you're
blotto," he said.

I noticed he didn't say anything about my singing ability.

"You're just hoping I'll lose it and say horrible things to Jeremy so
you won't have to." Oops. Did I say that out loud?

Colin didn't seem too perturbed by the prospect. "That would be a plus, yes."

I poked Colin in the arm. "There's Dempster."

We weren't the only ones who had spotted him. Joan's carefully highlighted head turned and, with just the right words of good-bye, she excused herself and maneuvered her way through the crowd, her black dress narrow enough not to make so much as a whisper as she passed. Her heels were a modest inch and a half. Sling-backs. Unlike me, she wasn't relying on the shoemaker's art for lengthening and slimming.

Toad.

How did she know Dempster? The Vaughn Collection, I guessed. It made sense that the editor of a fine-arts magazine would be on more than nodding terms with the archivist of London's answer to the Frick Collection.

But this looked like a hell of a lot more than nodding terms. Holding her champagne glass out to the side, Joan leaned in, not for the traditional air kiss but for a solid peck on the lips. As she leaned back, Dempster's hand settled in a proprietary way just above her waist.

What?

I looked at Colin, gawping like a child catching Mommy with Santa Claus. If Santa Claus was evil, that is. And if Mommy were the wicked stepmother. "Did you—?" I said.

Colin shook his head, looking just as befuddled as I felt. "No. I— No." He looked down at them, a man at sea. "They are colleagues. . . ."

"His hand is still on her ass," I pointed out. "That's not collegial behavior." A little lightbulb went on in my brain. "Do you know what this means? Serena didn't invite Dempster. Joan did."

Colin seemed insufficiently excited by this revelation.

I tugged on his sleeve. "Don't you get it? Serena isn't back together with Dempster!"

Not to mention that now Joan was safely off the market, so maybe she'd stay out of our hair for five minutes. And by ours, I meant mine. It would be nice to go to the pub without Joan throwing darts at me instead of the board.

"I got that," said Colin slowly. I followed his gaze and saw what had caught his attention. Oh, damn. There was another corollary to Serena not being back together with Dempster, one I hadn't quite thought through.

Serena stood in the shadow of the front door, looking like someone had just run a knife straight through her heart.

Dempster had been using Serena, and the odds were that he was probably using Joan, too. He had even made a play for me. I didn't think the man was capable of decent, disinterested affection. But I doubted that would make much of a difference to Serena right now. All that mattered was that the man who had broken her heart was in her home in the company of another woman.

I had spent months privately griping about Colin cosseting Serena, about our relationship being crowded with three when it ought to have been cozy with two. And let's just say I hadn't been too happy with her when she had sided with Jeremy, flinging Colin to the wolves. But now . . .

"Go to her." I gave Colin a little push. "She needs you."

Colin did his best imitation of an Easter Island statue, nothing but the finest granite.

"Fine," I said. "I'll go."

I started down, slipping and skidding in my inappropriate heels, only to find myself checked four steps up by Dempster.

"Eloise!" he said volubly, for all the world as though he were the host. I could see Serena over his shoulder, looking shadowed and fragile. It wasn't lost on me that even though she had grown up in this house, it was Serena who was coming in from outside. Some people, it seemed, were doomed to be perpetual outsiders, like a moth at the far side of a lighted patio, always hovering just out of reach of the light.

I was too generally pissed off to bother with the amenities. "I see you've found another way of getting into Selwick Hall."

Dempster's chest expanded. "I'm the historical consultant for the film," he said.

From what I'd seen, calling it a film seemed like a stretch. "I wasn't talking about the movie. Excuse me."

"I'm glad you're here," Dempster said suavely, ignoring my attempt to get around him.

"Why? So you can steal my notes?"

I had to give him this much. He put on a good show of confusion.

"What's this?" Colin had come down behind me. We might be having our own tiff, but it was a solid front when it came to barbarians at the gate. Colin's fingers fumbled for mine.

I slid my hand gratefully into his.

"Ask Dempster," I said, nodding at the other man. "Ask him just what he's looking for at Selwick Hall."

Chapter 21

What use is compass, map or chart,
Or any of the mariner's art?
My mast is broke, my rudder gone,
Darkling I drift, and all alone.

—Emma Delagardie and Augustus Whittlesby,
Americanus: A Masque in Three Parts

He couldn't shake the image of her face.

Augustus slipped away around the side of the house, moving with a stealth that had been ingrained by time and brutal training. He had good cause to be grateful for that training. It was all that was keeping him from barreling headfirst over the nearest shrub. He felt entirely disoriented, adrift, at sea. Gravel crunched beneath his feet, the only sign he was still on a path. The curtains had been drawn in the house, but enough light leached through them to provide a vague illumination, a strange echo of light, worse than no light at all.

What in the hell had just happened in there?

To his left lay Bonaparte's dollhouse of a theatre, smug on its own patch of ground. Dark now, all dark, entirely dark, no Emma inside playing with props or rocking back on her heels to look up at him with her hair all any which way and a smudge on her face.

He could still feel the texture of her hair beneath his fingers, thicker than he would have thought, thick and sleek and straight, blunt at the ends where it had been cut short, frizzled in bits where her maid must have experimented with the curling iron and failed. He could feel the silk of her hair and the delicate shape of the scalp beneath. She had a mole behind one ear, just a little bump in the skin, but his fingers remembered it, mapping it onto the landscape of her body, familiar terrain made unfamiliar, discovered and rediscovered.

Weeks they had spent together, bent over a desk, passing at a party, sending notes back and forth with a speed that made the messengers drag their feet and ask with palpable reluctance, "Is there a reply?" in a way that suggested they knew the answer would be yes but hoped for no.

No, no reply. Augustus had nothing to say. He was muddled, befuddled, baffled, perplexed, kerflummoxed. Confusion robbed him of the facile phrases that rose so easily to his lips, left him only with a cacophony of image and emotion, none of it reducible to the simple parameters of prose or even the lying truths of poetry.

No matter, she had told him, or something to that effect. She understood. Augustus was bloody glad someone did. Perhaps Emma might deign to explain it to him.

This was Emma. Emma! Emma of the too-low dresses and too-shiny jewels and too-bright smile and too-late parties. Emma who flitted and frolicked and sent him tea cakes and made sure he wore his cloak. Emma, who had somehow wiggled her way into his life, tucked securely next to his heart like a talisman in his coat pocket, a comfortable presence only to be noticed in its absence. One didn't take it out and play with it or consider the purpose of its existence; it was simply there.

He couldn't fancy Emma. She was just . . . Emma. Always there, always in motion, always running half an hour late. He admired the statuesque, the stately, the serene, Grecian goddesses made flesh, alabaster without the pedestal.

Then why couldn't he stop thinking about Emma? And why in hell wouldn't she stop to talk? She had certainly been eager enough to talk when it involved *his* emotions.

Augustus stubbed his toe on a bit of loose gravel and cursed. It did little to relieve his feelings.

The graveled circle in front of the house was crowded with carriages in various stages of unloading. Servants swarmed over them, disentangling the luggage that had been roped to the roofs, handing down boxes and trunks, while the aristocracy of the serving world— ladies' maids and manservants—hovered to ensure the correct dispositions of their masters' belongings, complaining loudly about clumsiness and protesting as trunks came tumbling down. Farther along, empty conveyances were being led down the trail to the carriage house, the horses to be unhitched and taken to the stable for grooming and feeding. It was a scene a world removed from the genteel gathering in the gallery, noisy, boisterous, busy.

Augustus paused in the lee of a miniature potted plant, watching, as from a world away, the bustle in front of him.

What if, just what if, the reason she hadn't wanted to talk about it was because she had meant exactly what she said?

Two unpleasant facts impressed themselves upon his consciousness.

Item the first: He had kissed her. They could quibble about accidents and chance encounters and primal instincts and so forth, but when it came down to it, his lips had been the ones to seek hers.

Item the second: She was the one who had called halt. He hadn't been thinking terribly clearly at that point. Blame it on fatigue, blame it on emotional exhaustion, blame it on the rain in Spain; whatever the cause, he would have been happy to go on kissing Emma indefinitely. And by kissing, he meant . . . well.

Until she had kindly but firmly put him back in his place. Friend.

"Aaarrghh!" Augustus let out a strangled cry as a vise slammed down on his throat.

His soles scuffed against gravel as he was yanked backwards, ineffectually scrabbling for purchase against the sliding surface. His fingers fumbled at the bar hampering his breathing. He stamped down with one foot, but missed his target. Instead, his heel caught fabric.

There was a tearing sound, and the weight abruptly lifted from his throat.

"Really!" said Miss Gwen. "Was that entirely necessary?"

Augustus clutched his aching throat and turned to glare at the older woman, who was regarding her torn hem with a frown of displeasure. The instrument of torture, her parasol, dangled from one hand.

"Was *that* necessary?" he choked out. He was going to have bruises for a week.

Miss Gwen examined her skirt and dismissed the damage with a sniff.

Sod her skirt, what about his vocal cords? He had never so deeply regretted that his costume didn't allow for a cravat. At least it would have provided a little extra padding.

"Shoddy, Whittlesby, shoddy," she said smugly, tapping with her parasol against the ground for emphasis. Augustus prudently took a step back. "If I were an assassin, you would be dead by now."

Augustus tilted back his chin. "Here's my throat. Care to finish me off?"

Miss Gwen emitted one of her infamous "hmph" noises. "There's no need for melodrama, Mr. Whittlesby. Just see that I don't catch you daydreaming on the job."

"I wasn't—"

Oh, hell, what was the point? Just as there was no point to reminding Miss Gwen that, in point of fact, she was more likely to work for him than he for her. Augustus had his appointment directly from the War Office. Miss Gwen was a country spinster turned spy, a hobbyist who had got lucky. She had a bit of nerve lecturing him.

It didn't help that she was right.

"Was that the sole purpose of this exercise," Augustus asked coolly, "or did you have something you wished to say to me?"

"Hmph. Not everyone pants after a ruffled shirt, young man." A fact for which Augustus could only be grateful. "While you were wandering about in poetic reverie, I was doing what you were meant to be doing."

"Which is?"

"Listening!" Augustus jumped as the parasol landed dangerously near his left foot. "In case you haven't noticed, we have a number of new arrivals, including"—Miss Gwen's steely eyes glinted in the torchlight—"Mr. Fulton."

"We knew he was expected," said Augustus. "How is that news?"

"A day early?" countered Miss Gwen. She played her trump card. "He was asking after a crate."

"Emma's wave machine," Augustus said shortly.

"Emma, is it?" Miss Gwen's eyes narrowed speculatively, but she forbore to comment. For the moment. "As it happens, Mr. Whittlesby, you are wrong. Quite, quite wrong. Mr. Fulton was most specific about it. There is a second crate."

"A second crate," Augustus repeated. From far away, a very long time ago, he remembered the deliveryman mumbling something about the ruts. No, the rest. If he hadn't been so busy being lovelorn, he would have noticed. He should have noticed. "Another device?"

"That would be the logical conclusion," said Miss Gwen crisply. "Another device. One he doesn't want anyone to see. But someone knows about it."

"The Emperor, presumably." And most of the naval higher-ups.

Assuming this was the device they sought. Assuming such a device existed.

"Livingston," said Miss Gwen, with relish. "The younger one. He came out asking after it."

"What did he say?"

Miss Gwen looked mildly miffed. "I couldn't hear," she admitted. "There was too much noise. It's over to you now."

"To me?"

"Where is your brain, young man? Have you been playing the idiot for too long? Think!" *Thump.* "Who would know what Fulton and Livingston have been planning? Who has access to both?" With withering sarcasm, she added, "I assume this is why you've been frittering away your time dallying with the Delagardie chit."

"I wasn't—" Augustus broke off. "You, of all people, should know how important it is to win a contact's confidence."

Miss Gwen looked skeptical. She generally preferred more direct methods. Her interrogation techniques were of the Torquemada variety. Had Torquemada been in possession of a large collection of parasols.

She poked him with the point of her parasol, herding him beneath the striped awning at the entrance and into the house. "You've done with winning. From what I've seen, you've won it. Now use it."

Not use it. Use her. Augustus had never scrupled to use any means at his disposal to get information. He had dallied, he had flirted, he had even feigned passion when the situation required it. But Miss Gwen's blunt directive left a nasty taste in his mouth.

"What makes you think she knows?" he hedged.

"I'm not the only one," said Miss Gwen portentously.

Her heels echoed against the black-and-white tiles of the front hall. Even with the candles lit, the room looked gloomy, the light reflecting dully off the porphyry columns, like a muddy lake by moonlight. The classical statues on either side of the glass doors onto the garden looked down their marble noses at them as they entered.

Miss Gwen looked superciliously down her nose at him, and said, in the hectoring tones of a governess, "If you don't get the information out of her, someone else will."

She didn't need to specify who the "her" in question might be.

Augustus unclenched his hands, finger by finger, each one a slow, deliberate act of will. "What do you mean?"

Miss Gwen nodded towards the French windows. Augustus could see the shadows of their own reflections, his and Miss Gwen's, like ghosts in the window. Beneath them, though, if he squinted, he could make out other forms, just beyond the French doors, on the wide bridge that spanned the moat at the back of the house.

It was the man he saw first, or rather, the gold epaulettes on his shoulders, the insignia of a colonel, glittering in the torchlight. The woman with him seemed insubstantial in comparison, the filmy material of her gown as fine as mist, barely visible around the solid bulk of her companion. He blocked her from view, like an eclipse of the moon, only the faintest glimmer revealing her presence.

That was all the view Augustus needed.

Miss Gwen spelled it out for him anyway. "If you're not careful," she said, "Colonel Marston will steal a march on you."

She might have said more, but Augustus didn't hear it. He was already halfway to the door.

"*Y*ou didn't answer my letters." Georges took a step closer, so close that his buttons brushed her bodice.

Emma smelled a rat and she didn't just mean Georges.

Caroline had made herself scarce. In another person, Emma might have ascribed it to tact. Given that it was Caroline, it reeked of collusion. Georges was close friends with Caroline's husband, Joachim Murat. That was, in fact, how Emma had met him, those years and years before, at a party chez Murat, the sort of party a widow might attend but not a debutante, a party for the fashionably amoral, for widows, for bored matrons, for handsome hangers-on.

"Why are you here?" she asked flatly.

Georges attempted to exude innocence and secreted smarm instead. "Madame Murat brought me."

Not as a lover. Caroline was too possessive to cede her property that easily.

"You asked her to, didn't you?" said Emma wearily. This was all the day needed: a confrontation with a lover she had never loved and to whom she had ceased to make love a very long time ago. It wasn't the sins of the fathers one had to worry about, but one's own indiscretions.

"What else was I to do?" Georges smiled with his teeth but not his eyes. He had smiled like that often when they were together, his mind always busy, calculating his next move, his next woman. The lips would curve, but the eyes were empty. Emma hadn't minded terribly. It hadn't been for his mind that she had wanted him. "You've been avoiding me."

"I've been busy," Emma countered. What was it about early training that made her hedge, when the truth was that she had been avoiding him? She wished she could just come out and say it, but that was the problem with manners; they came back to haunt one at the most inconvenient times.

"How fortunate for me," said Georges silkily, "to find you less busy now."

There was an unmistakable edge of menace behind his words.

"Hardly!" Emma fluttered one hand. A mistake. Georges's eyes followed the glitter of her rings. "I'm in the midst of producing a masque for Madame Bonaparte. There are a thousand things to be done before Saturday, not least the composition of all the ridiculous machines required for the effects."

"Oh?" There was a speculative gleam in Georges's eye, the sort that in many men would be accounted lust, but in Georges's spelled profit. "Perhaps I might be of assistance."

This from a man who deemed buttoning his own breeches unacceptable manual labor? He must truly be desperate if he thought to put actual physical effort into winning her good graces.

"No, no," said Emma breezily. "It's very sweet of you to offer, but I'm sure I have everything quite under control."

"In which case," he said, taking possession of her arm so neatly that Emma hadn't even time to see it coming, "you will have no objection to taking a bit of a stroll with me."

No objection? She had every objection. But it would cause more of a stir to protest than to accede. His grip on her arm wasn't tight enough to be punitive, but it was firm enough to require a concerted yank to free herself. All around her, Mme. Bonaparte's hangers-on whispered and gossiped, saying one thing while meaning another, eyes roaming the room, constantly searching for the latest and greatest *on dit*. If she created a scene, even a small one, half the room would dine out on it for a month.

Georges knew that as well as she did. She could tell. He had the smug air of a man who had his opponent's king in check.

Part of Emma wanted, oh so badly, to make that scene, to behave like a small child in a temper tantrum, to pull free and run and run until she reached the sterile silence of her room. She was so sick of being obliging: smiling at Mme. Bonaparte, soothing Kort, telling Augustus that it didn't matter that he had kissed her because he was in love with her friend.

Wouldn't that surprise them all! But she wouldn't do it. She knew herself well enough for that. She had had enough of scandal years ago.

Fine. Let Georges have his petty victory. Once out of the room, she could extricate herself as loudly and firmly as she pleased. He wasn't really dangerous, Georges, just a bully. She would hear him out, tell him no to whatever it was he wanted, and go. All civilized and simple.

"A very brief stroll," she said, and he smiled, a real smile, all the more terrifying in its intensity.

"You won't regret it," he said.

"I already have," muttered Emma, but if Georges heard, he professed not to, leading her smilingly through the drawing room that adjoined the gallery, making light conversation about the large paintings from the poems of Ossian that leered down from the walls.

Emma nodded and smiled and wondered where Augustus had got to. Licking his wounds over Jane? Hiding from her? She was thoroughly fed up with mankind. It was a pity she wasn't Catholic. She might have joined a nunnery.

She let Georges lead her through the billiard room and out into the marble cool of the entryway, elegant in the daytime, funereal in the dusk. When he would have led her outdoors, she balked.

"Whatever you have to say, can't it be said here?"

"Just outside," he urged. "We won't go any farther. See? The night is warm."

It wasn't, actually. It was rather chilly.

"Fine," said Emma, and stepped onto the bridge that led across the moat to the gardens. She wrapped her arms around herself. "What do you want, Georges?"

"You, my sweet." He essayed a leer, but it was purely perfunctory.

"Yes, yes," said Emma, and propped herself against the base of one of the two statues that guarded the bridge. Her dress couldn't get any dirtier, after all. "Let's pretend we've done that part. What is it you want me to do for you?"

"It's not for me," he said. He would have reached for her hands, but Emma planted them firmly on the plinth. "It's for us."

Emma could have pointed out there was no such entity, but that would only have prolonged the exercise. Somewhere in the gardens, a bird was singing. The night breeze bore the scents of June flowers:

roses and hydrangea and lily of the valley and other scents her nose wasn't sophisticated enough to identify. This was a night made for romance, a night for lovers to whisper sweet nothings and pledge their troth.

For whatever that troth was worth.

Emma felt, suddenly, entirely irritated with it all. With the birdsong, with the moon, with the false promise of the flowers, which bloomed for a season and then withered away. And with poets, like Augustus, who rolled it all up in verse and dangled it like a lure in front of unsuspecting maidens. Not that she had been a maiden for a very long time. But the principle remained the same.

"—to your cousin and that Fulton," Georges was saying pettishly, "but neither of them would listen. But you can do it."

Emma shifted against the cold stone. "Do what? Speak to them on your behalf?"

There was something dark and unpleasant in Georges's countenance. "No. We're past that. There isn't enough time." He laughed a nasty laugh. "It's their loss. If they'd cut me in, they might have had a share. But you can do it. You know where he keeps them."

"Keeps what?"

"The plans," said Marston insistently. "The plans. I have a buyer lined up. He'll pay dearly for them."

Emma blinked up at him. "You want me to steal Mr. Fulton's plans?"

"Not steal," Marston hedged. "Borrow. Do you realize how much they're willing to pay? I'll be set for life. I mean, we'll be set for life. It's for us, my darling. For our future."

Emma gaped at him. "You are joking."

Marston dropped to his knees in front of her. "Would I joke about this much money? I mean, about our future? They want those plans. Badly." His hands were crushing hers; she could feel her bones protesting the pressure. "Which means I want those plans. Badly."

"Georges—" Emma tried to extricate her hands.

"They trust you. They'll tell you where they are." He levered himself up, looming over her. Emma could feel the sharp edge of the plinth biting into the backs of her legs as she strained backwards. "I know he has them. I saw them with him in the carriage. He'll tell you."

His hands were on her shoulders, crushing, insistent.

"One small thing, Emma," he urged. "Just this one small thing."

"Oh, dear," someone drawled loudly, loudly enough that Marston cursed and let go. "Do I wander unwelcome into Eros's amorous domain?"

Chapter 22

These sails I spy upon the main
Might offer succor, risk or pain;
Are they mirage or do I see
What my eyes are offering me?

—Emma Delagardie and Augustus Whittlesby,
Americanus: A Masque in Three Parts

Yes, you bloody well do," snarled Georges.

Augustus lounged in the doorway, picking at the lace on his cuffs as though the entire matter were one of extreme indifference to him. Emma felt her chest contract with a dangerous combination of relief and confusion and irritation.

"No," she said firmly, and stepped around Georges. "Colonel Marston was just going. Weren't you, Georges?"

Augustus's eyes narrowed at her use of Georges's first name, but he didn't let it spoil his act. Gazing vaguely into the air, he declaimed, "Far be it from a humble votary of the muses to disturb the worship of Venus, but that the pressing concerns of Thespis demand Madame Delagardie's prompt and immediate assistance."

Georges cracked his knuckles. "I'll tell you what you can do with your thespian. . . ."

Emma felt an absurd bubble of laughter rising in her throat. Naturally, Georges would think it had to do with a prostitute. "Not a thespian, Georges. Thespis. The muse of the theatre."

Augustus looked pained. "Dear lady, much as it pains me to contradict one so fair, I must not, I cannot, be silent when the honor of the magnificent muses rests upon the witness of my humble tongue. Thespis, although a prime mover in the origin of our art, was a mere mortal, an actor. The muses with whom the playwright pleads are Thalia, the queen of comedy, and Melpomene, the dark lord of tragedy, spring and winter, the Persephone and Hades of our theatrical scheme."

He paused, either because he had said his piece, or because he had run out of breath.

Emma jumped in before Georges decided to end the agony by throttling him. "Mr. Whittlesby requires my help with the masque," she translated.

"With the burning urgency of a thousand suns," Augustus assured her solemnly. His eyes met hers. He quirked an eyebrow in unspoken question. Beneath the vapid mask, she could see the concern in his eyes.

Emma shook her head slightly, although what he was asking and what she was answering, she wasn't quite sure. Part of her wanted to take him by his artfully disarranged collar and shake him. It wasn't fair. Why did he have to come barging in, being all heroic and concerned, just when she most wanted to resent him?

Georges was brooding over his own wrongs. "If that's the case, why didn't he just say so?" He turned imperiously to Emma, dismissing Augustus with a shrug of the shoulder. "Whatever it is, it can wait."

Emma touched her fingers to Georges's sleeve, tilting her head coquettishly up towards him, ignoring Augustus for all she was worth. He wasn't the only one who could play a role.

"I'm afraid it can't," she said with false regret. "One would hate to have the Emperor disappointed in our entertainment, don't you agree?"

No one could argue with the Emperor. It was the trump card to trump all trump cards.

Georges looked at the hand resting on his sleeve, eyes narrowed. Emma wished she were wearing gloves; she felt strangely vulnerable without them, her fingers bare and very pale in the cold, making her rings loose on her fingers.

His other hand closed over hers, tightly. Not so tight as to be punitive, but tight enough to send a message. Emma could feel Augustus shift on the balls of his feet.

"Another time, then." Georges raised his hand to her lips, deliberately reversing her hand so that his lips touched her palm. "Think about what I told you."

Turning on his heel, he strode towards the door, only to go sprawling in a most undignified fashion as his shin connected with Augustus's calf. He let out a bellow of shock and rage as he stumbled, arms flailing, catching himself just before he crashed into Mme. Bonaparte's French windows.

"Oh, dear," said Augustus, the malicious glint in his eye belying his vague tone. "Was I in your way?"

Georges didn't bother to answer. Favoring Augustus with a look of extreme dislike, he wrenched open the door to the hall. He looked back over his shoulder at Emma.

"Remember," he said, and was gone.

He didn't slam the door. It might have been less disconcerting if he had.

Bother, bother, bother.

"You shouldn't have made him angry," she said shortly, watching Georges's distorted form in the glass as he made an abrupt turn towards the billiards room, ostentatiously favoring his left leg.

Behind him, in reflection, she could see Augustus, his white shirt misty pale against dark panels.

Instead of responding, he asked, "Are you all right?"

That was all. *Are you all right?* But something about the way he said it, his voice low and serious, his eyes intent on hers in the glass, tore right through to the depths of her composure. There was no doubting the genuineness of his concern. Conversely, that almost made it worse. It would be easier to brush off if there were no caring there, if she could dismiss him as just another acquaintance, another chance meeting, another accidental kiss.

To know that someone did care, really cared, but just didn't care enough . . . That was worst of all.

Emma took a deep breath, tucking up the ragged ends of her pride. "Perfectly all right," she said tartly, turning away from the glass.

It was almost a shock to see him in the flesh rather than in reflection, startlingly, corporeally real. Too real. She knew the texture of his cheek, the shape of his scalp, the scent of his skin, so close and yet so far.

"It was very kind of you to intervene," she said primly. "But there was no need."

"That's not the way it looked to me."

"Georges wouldn't hurt me. He just wants what he wants." She added pettishly, "There was no need to come charging in like that. Now he'll only seek me out and we'll have to have the whole tiresome conversation all over again."

Augustus folded his arms over his chest, looking as forbidding as a man in a ruffled shirt could look. "And what if you were in the way of what he wanted?"

"He would be too loath to get blood on his uniform to do anything violent," Emma said lightly. "Really, Augustus, there's no need to worry. I can take care of myself."

"You're a third of his size."

Emma self-consciously straightened her spine. "There's no need to harp on my height."

Just because Jane was tall . . . Emma banished the unworthy thought. This wasn't a competition.

If it was, she wouldn't win.

Augustus scowled. "It's not about height; it's bulk. He could squash you with one hand."

"Give me some credit," she said. "It would take two hands at least. Though I be small, I be fierce. How *does* that line go?"

"*Though she be but little, she is fierce.*" He looked over his shoulder, frowning, more serious than she had ever seen him. "This isn't a joke, Emma."

Emma's eyes stung. With fatigue, that was all. "No," she said quietly. "It's not. Nor is it any of your concern."

He stood entirely still, the stillness of a dark pond on a dark night, uncanny in its silence, strange things moving beneath the surface. "*You* are my concern," he said in a low voice.

Fine words, and she was sure he meant them, too.

As a friend.

"Don't worry," said Emma flippantly. "If Georges murders me and drops my body in the river, I'm sure you can find another collaborator."

He stared at her as though trying to divine whether she meant it. She could see his fingers curl into his palms. It was a good thing his nails were short, or they would leave marks. "That's not what I meant."

If he wasn't going to explain, she wasn't going to ask. She held his gaze until he broke. He turned abruptly away, swinging towards the glass doors through which Georges had exited.

"How did you ever come to take up with that cretin?" he demanded.

Half a dozen excuses bubbled to Emma's tongue, the same ones she had trotted out before in half a dozen imaginary conversations. It had been a difficult time. . . . She hadn't been happy. . . .

What was she doing? Emma pulled herself to an abrupt halt.

What right had he to ask? Or to judge. It was none of his concern. She was under no obligation to explain herself to him or anyone else.

Emma folded her arms across her chest and glowered. "Have you never taken to bed someone you regretted later?"

Augustus gawped at her.

She could practically see the wheels in his head turning. His stance relaxed. He said, with a quirk of the lips, "Fair point."

It would have felt more like a victory if she hadn't wondered exactly who he might be thinking of, if Emma would know her, and, if so, what the circumstances had been.

If Georges was none of his business, that was none of hers.

"Please," he said softly. "Let's not argue."

Emma regarded him warily.

"Truce?" he urged.

Emma held out a hand. "Truce."

He wasn't wearing gloves either. His hand engulfed hers. She could feel the calluses on his thumb worn by a pen and other calluses on his palm, made by something else entirely.

She made to draw her hand back, but instead of releasing it, he looked down at her, his expression thoughtful. "May I ask you something else?"

Despite herself, Emma's pulse picked up. The play, the theatre, the kiss. *Nothing at all*, she could imagine herself saying, *it was nothing at all. Unless you . . .*

"Provided it's nothing to do with multiplication tables," she said flippantly.

Augustus's hand tightened and then let go. "What is it that Marston wants from you?"

"What?" It was so far from what she had been expecting that it took her a moment to comprehend the words. "Georges?"

She had the small satisfaction of seeing Augustus scowl at the name. "Yes," he said. "That."

"*That*," said Emma, tucking her hands under her arms, "was a fascinating exercise in venality and wishful thinking."

Wishful thinking. Emma resisted a hysterical urge to laugh. She knew a thing or two about that. What a fool she was, what an addlepated fool. Kort was right; she shouldn't be allowed out on her own.

"I heard a bit of it," said Augustus cautiously. "Something about . . . plans?"

Emma shrugged, wishing she had had the forethought to wear a shawl. She was cold again, colder than she had been before. She assumed Mme. Bonaparte wouldn't mind if she made it an early night and sought the solace of her own quilt. "Georges wanted a share in a business venture between my cousin and Mr. Fulton. They turned him down."

Augustus cocked an eyebrow. "So he wants you to steal their plans?"

Emma wafted a hand. "That's Georges for you, always out for the easy sou. Shall we go in?"

Augustus made no move towards the door. He looked at her, his brows drawing together. "Be careful, Emma," he said abruptly. "This— You don't—"

He broke off, broodingly. He had never looked more like the poet he pretended to be.

"Goodness, Augustus," said Emma, "there's no need to look like that. No matter who Georges thinks he's found to pay for them, I can't imagine they're worth that much. Even if it works, it will take ages and lots of investment before it can be profitable."

Augustus's dark eyes were intent on her face. "It? You know what it is?"

"Well, yes." Why was he looking like that? Did he really think Georges would murder her out of frustrated greed? "It's not exactly a secret."

"Isn't it?"

"They've kept it relatively quiet," said Emma, "but that's just because they were waiting until Mr. Fulton built a proper model. But everyone will know about it by tomorrow. They're doing a demonstration on the river."

"A demonstration?" Augustus looked dazed. "A public demonstration?"

"For the Emperor," said Emma. "He wanted to see it—or Mr. Fulton wanted him to see it. I think he was hoping the Emperor might invest. Mr. Fulton, I mean."

"Are we—are we talking about the same thing?"

"The steamship," said Emma matter-of-factly.

"The—" Augustus blinked at her.

She had heard so much about it that she had forgotten that he might not have.

"A ship propelled by steam," she translated. "The French call it a *chariot d'eau mu par le feu*. They're holding a demonstration of it tomorrow."

Mr. Fulton had a lovely day for his steamship exhibition.

The imperial couple had made an event of it. Servants had spread silk cloths to protect the ladies' dresses from the turf. They lolled in little clusters along the bank, some reclining like Mme. Récamier, others with their legs tucked beneath them like children at a picnic, leaning forward to exclaim over a freshly picked flower or stretching to pluck a sweetmeat from the tray of a circling attendant.

Mme. Bonaparte's personal china service was spread in opulent array on a low table laden with all the delicacies a sophisticated palate might desire. Ladies picked delicately at candied chestnuts and hothouse peaches, munching sweetmeats and flinging bits of cake to the ducks on the river. The sunlight glittered off cut-crystal glasses dangling idly from the hands of young gallants as they pressed their suits with the prettier of Mme. Bonaparte's ladies-in-waiting, all giggles and coy fans.

Over it all, the imperial couple presided, seated on twin chairs. Augustus recognized the chairs from the gilded drawing room, incongruous in the rustic idyll in which they purported to participate. Many of the ladies, in keeping with the rural theme, had twined flowers in their hair, but Mme. Bonaparte wore a tiny gilt diadem, a token of the status she had yet to formally attain. She might be Empress by courtesy, but she hadn't yet been crowned, a fact of which everyone was very much aware. A silk canopy held by four poles had been stretched above them to protect Mme. Bonaparte's delicate complexion.

In the place of honor beside Mme. Bonaparte sat Robert Livingston, with his nephew, still under the canopy but less favored, standing beside him. Likewise, Robert Fulton had a place beneath the canopy but no chair. He stood by the Emperor's left hand.

Augustus lounged on the grass, flirting idly with Mme. de Rémusat, and wondered what in the hell was going on.

A demonstration, Horace de Lilly had said. Bonaparte's secret weapon awaited only a demonstration. But this public demonstration, held for a full audience of giggling ladies-in-waiting and yawning courtiers, was nothing like what Augustus had imagined.

Then why, if this wasn't the device, had the flower of France's admiralty been summoned from their various obligations to cluster behind Bonaparte's chair?

They were all there: Rear Admiral Decres, openly fidgeting; Vice Admiral Bruix, looking tired and ill but standing nonetheless; Admiral Latouche-Tréville, commander of the Mediterranean fleet, summoned summarily from Toulon, travel strained and weary; Vice Admiral Truguet, at the very verge of the group, being punished for his public stance in opposition to the imperial title; and, with them, but slightly behind, a protective cluster of aides and lesser commanders. France's best—or at least its most prominent—naval minds stood beneath a silk canopy sipping champagne punch and waiting as Robert Livingston, at a sign from the Emperor, heaved himself to his feet and raised his champagne glass in the air.

"My thanks," he began, "to His Excellency the Emperor for making my stay in France such a pleasant and productive one."

The Emperor inclined his head curtly in reply, striving for imperial dignity, and missing.

"Together," said Livingston, "we have strengthened the bond between our countries and accomplished great things."

An appreciative murmur from the crowd. He referred, Augustus knew, to the purchase of New France, which he had brokered the year before, refilling Bonaparte's anemic coffers and vastly increasing the size of the fledgling American republic.

"My tenure here," said Livingston, "is sadly at an end. But before I go, it pleases me to share with you the fruits of my latest endeavor—"

At a gesture from Mme. Bonaparte, a lackey obediently moved towards the river to remove the shielding cover from whatever it was that rocked on makeshift moorings. The lackey yanked the cover off, revealing a boat about three feet long and two feet high, with a cylinder, instead of a sail, sticking out of the middle.

"—the steamship!"

There was an entirely inappropriate giggle from one of the blankets. Everyone twisted to look. The lady-in-waiting in question flushed and hastily moved away from the gallant who had been murmuring salacious nothings in her ear.

"As I was saying," said Livingston.

Augustus let the words wash over him and looked about for Emma. He found her on one of the blankets, safely sandwiched between Mme. Junot and another one of her Mme. Campan's comrades, picking at a candied chestnut. Her eyes met his and she looked away, biting with unnecessary vigor into her sweetmeat. Her lips puckered at the rush of cloying sweetness.

Augustus held himself back, resisting the urge to go to her. He had made a right muck of it, hadn't he? And he didn't know what to say to set it right. He wanted things back the way they were, the way they had been before, when they had been comfortable and happy with each other. He wanted her fussing over him and arguing with him, popping up at his elbow to murmur idiosyncratic observations. He wanted—

Augustus caught himself short, but not soon enough, not before the image of tousled hair and parted lips, the memory of her skin against his palm and her lips against his lips left him staggered and short of breath, as though he had been sprinting instead of standing. His chest felt tight and his head ached from the sun. The glare from the river offended his eyes, too bright, too brassy.

". . . partnership," Livingston was saying, and Augustus squinted in their direction to see the younger Livingston standing at his uncle's elbow, looking properly modest. "It takes over a week for goods to make their way from New York to Albany by ship. With Mr. Fulton's steamship, we believe the same journey can be undertaken in under sixty hours."

"Or fewer!" chimed in Mr. Fulton.

Goods? Sixty hours from New York to Albany instead of a week? This was all very exciting, Augustus was sure, but it wasn't exactly the warship of his imagining. He might have believed that Horace de Lilly—young, overeager, still wet behind the ears—had misunderstood, but for the fact that the accumulated force of the admiralty was all gathered on the banks of the small stream.

What was he missing? What was there about this boat that didn't meet the eye?

Something glittered at the corner of his vision, and Augustus felt his pulse pick up. Emma's diamonds? No. Just Mme. de Treville raising a glass to her lips, sunlight scintillating off crystal.

"It will be better, bigger, faster," declaimed Robert Livingston. He raised his glass to the model ship bobbing at its makeshift moorings. "We have lived long, but I can only believe there are greater works still to come. Ladies and gentlemen, I present to you the face of our future—the steamship."

"The steamship." Some of the assemblage obediently raised their glasses.

The bulk of them kept on with their picnicking and their gossiping, deeming the progress of commerce far less interesting than who had disappeared with whom into the shrubbery last night and was it really true that the princess Borghese had already abandoned her husband and was on her way back to Paris, bringing an honor guard of new lovers, a dancing bear, and, quite possibly, the Pope.

Even the admirals standing in phalanx around the chair of their Emperor looked bored. One or two seemed intrigued, on general principles, but it was an academic interest, not the focused attention of men whose careers might rest on the success or failure of this venture.

"A pretty toy," Augustus heard Truguet murmur to Decres.

"It might be valuable," said Decres sharply, moving away from Truguet, as though disgrace were a disease that might spread.

Truguet essayed the classic Gallic shrug, redolent of disbelief.

"If you would be so good as to do the honors?" With a bow, Robert Livingston handed the glass of champagne to Bonaparte.

"Only a glass, not a bottle?"

"It's only a model," Fulton hastened to explain. "The impact of an entire bottle of champagne would likely sink it before it ever got under way!"

Bonaparte looked at him from under beetled brows. "I hope your other projects are more hardy, Mr. Fulton."

Other projects?

The Emperor poured the champagne over the ship, and the audience mustered a polite cheer as Mr. Fulton bent over his creation, coaxing it into motion. There was handshaking and backslapping and congratulatory noises made as those more politic rose to congratulate the Livingstons on their ambitious venture.

Someone joggled Augustus's elbow, making him spill his punch. "It's a sensible match," said a voice in Augustus's ear.

"Pardon?" His mind elsewhere, Augustus looked vaguely around him. His gaze settled on Horace de Lilly, decked out in a rose satin waistcoat with jade buttons. His fair-skinned face was pink with the heat of the day and, perhaps, from the glass he held in his hand.

"Madame Delagardie and Mr. Livingston." De Lilly nodded towards the tent. Under the ruched canopy, Kortright Livingston was smiling down at an animated Emma. "Don't you agree?"

She had gone up to congratulate him, of course, just like the others. "Emma and—"

Horace de Lilly rummaged around in his sleeve, producing a monogrammed handkerchief. "Didn't you know? I would have thought you would, with your spending so much time together over the masque. The rumor is that they were childhood sweethearts. I hear the cousin has a good estate in—well, wherever it is that they're from."

"New York," said Augustus flatly. Emma had never said anything about being childhood sweethearts, never intimated that her cousin was anything more to her than a cousin. Other than the obvious joy with which she had greeted him. And the enthusiasm with which she was speaking to him now, her hand familiarly on his arm. "What makes you think—"

"Why else would she turn down a position at court?" De Lilly dropped his voice, leaning avidly forward. "Do you have it yet? The device?"

Augustus held up a hand to silence him. "She turned down a position at court?"

De Lilly shrugged. "So my mother says. Madame Bonaparte asked her last night and Madame Delagardie said no. There is," said the Royalist agent, "no conceivable reason for it unless she intends to leave the country. Why else refuse the font from which favor flows?"

A curious sentiment from a man pledged to bring down the regime. Or, perhaps, not so curious after all, decided Augustus, watching Emma sparkling up at her cousin. De Lilly, after all, was engaged in a variant of the same scheme, working to restore a monarch in the hopes that said monarch would be sufficiently pleased with his efforts to return the family estates and provide him a place at court. Emperor or king, the basic principle was the same. De Lilly wasn't in it for political philosophy.

"No one turns down that sort of opportunity," said de Lilly decidedly. "It *must* be the cousin. Just look at them."

Augustus did and wished he hadn't. Standing on her tiptoes, Emma brushed her lips across her cousin's cheek. Kortright Livingston's arm folded protectively around her waist as he bent his head for her convenience. There was a comfort to them, the comfort of old and easy acquaintance.

And something more?

"Don't they make a handsome pair?" said de Lilly blithely.

Chapter 23

A road once lost cannot be found;
A tie untied can't be re-bound;
So true it is, that love once spurned
Cannot be borrowed, begged or earned.

—Emma Delagardie and Augustus Whittlesby,
Americanus: A Masque in Three Parts

"Congratulations, Kort." Emma stood on her tiptoes to press a kiss against her cousin's cheek. "You must be very proud."

He squeezed her waist in a perfunctory half hug. "Proud *and* privileged. Just think, Emma. No more relying on winds or tides. We'll open up the whole country for commerce! And I get to be part of it."

Kort's enthusiasm reminded Emma of summers long ago, of a fair-haired boy squatting over a fallen birds' nest, marveling over its construction. He was more in his element here than he had been in the salons of Paris or treading the boards in Bonaparte's theatre. This was Kort as she knew and remembered him, not the uncomfortable, stilted man of the past month.

Some people, reflected Emma, just weren't meant for the Old World. It wasn't good or bad; it just was. She had taken immediately to the more leisured pace of life, to the endless and pointless arguments of the salons, the debate for the sake of debate, the idea of life lived as art for its own sake, with no need to actually go about producing anything at the end of it. Kort hadn't.

"What if you run out of rivers?" she teased.

Kort grinned at her. "Then we'll dig canals. Where's your Yankee initiative, Madame Delagardie?"

"Left at the altar with my old name," quipped Emma. "I'm a slow study these days."

"Not if what I've heard about Carmagnac is true." The name sounded strange coming from Kort. Kort and Carmagnac? The two just didn't go together.

Emma rolled her eyes. "Mr. Fulton has been telling tales out of school."

Kort wasn't ready to let it go. "He told me that you had kept up your husband's plans and improved on them. He's not a man easily impressed."

"He means I took his suggestions," said Emma wryly. "Isn't that enough to convince most people of one's intelligence?"

Flying high on champagne and success, Kort caught her hand. "Come back with me, Emma. There's so much to be done at home, so much you could do."

Emma looked down at their joined hands. She had convinced Kort to invest in new gloves. They were tan, elegantly cut and stiff with newness. It might have been that that accounted for the awkwardness of his touch, but she thought not.

Emma gently freed her hand. "Why did you come to France, Kort? Was it because of the steamship?"

He nodded, a reminiscent expression on his face. "Uncle Robert wrote me about it. He thought it would be just the venture for me and he was right." The very thought of it made him glow with industrial fervor. Belatedly remembering Emma's presence, he added, "And your mother was delighted that I could come and badger you in person. She gave me very specific instructions."

Emma didn't doubt it. "How specific?"

Kort suddenly discovered an interest in the flattened grass on the verge of the river. A little farther along, Mr. Fulton was bending over his model, feeding small pieces of coal into a miniature furnace. "Pretty much what you would expect."

"Which might be?" Emma prompted.

Mr. Fulton's steamship let out a long, stammering, huffing noise. A few yards away, a duck turned up its tail feathers in indignation.

Kort's eyes followed the duck as it flounced up the bank. One of the children was throwing cake crumbs at it. "She urged me to do whatever it would take to convince you to come back with me."

"Up to and including proposals of marriage?"

She knew she had hit home when she saw her cousin wince. "Proposal. One proposal."

She gave him credit for not pretending he didn't know what she meant. He had never been able to tell a lie, not even when it would have saved them all from being sent to their rooms without supper.

"Quite a sacrifice to make for the family," she said neutrally. "I hope you told my mother that familial devotion goes only so far."

"Familial devotion, yes." Kort didn't meet her eye. Something in his voice made Emma look up. He was staring at the river still, his face in profile, his expression abstracted. His hands flexed at his sides. Clearing his throat, his eyes fixed on the river, he said awkwardly, "Have you ever thought that it might not be such a bad idea?"

Had she? At twelve, she had thought it was an excellent idea. But that was over half a lifetime ago and half a world away.

"You don't really mean that," she said. She poked him in the arm. "Kort? Hello?"

He focused on her with difficulty, blinking as though coming back from somewhere very far away. His Adam's apple moved up and down in his throat. "I do, actually." He looked down at her, his face serious. "There have been worse matches."

"Yes, the Prince of Wales and Caroline of Brunswick, or Henry VIII and just about anyone," said Emma spiritedly. "I'm flattered, Kort, really I am."

Kort pressed his eyes closed. "I deserved that, didn't I? I didn't mean it the way it sounded."

Emma looked at her cousin's troubled face. It was not that of a man about to propose to the woman he loved. It was that of a man set to do his duty, no matter how unpleasant that duty might be.

He had said exactly what he meant. It was expedient and it could be worse. That was Kort for you, always honest to a fault, even with himself. It was a rare but not necessarily comfortable commodity.

"Do you know," said Emma thoughtfully, "I rather think you did."

Kort ignored her. "It would be a sensible match," he said, almost as much for himself as for her. "We've both had losses. We would be kind to each other."

It was a very odd way of framing the sentiment. In fact, it was a very odd proposal. Not that Emma had received that many, but she couldn't imagine that any of her favorite plays or novels would ever have included such an avowal as this one.

Emma voiced the truth her twelve-year-old self had had such trouble stomaching. "You really loved Sarah, didn't you?"

Kort's face was bleak. "More than I ever want to love anyone again."

"And I'm safe." She didn't need the sudden tightening of his lips to know she had hit it, the real reason for Kort's proposal. "You know exactly what you're getting with me. You won't ever have to feel about me the way you did about her. I'm the perfect compromise option."

Kort's shoulders sagged. "It's not as cold as you make it sound. We understand each other. We're comfortable with each other."

No, he was comfortable with the memory of her. It was a very different thing. And even if it weren't, there was one major flaw to the plan.

"I think," Emma said slowly, "that I want something more than comfort. We both should."

Kort did his best to rise to the occasion. "I do love you, you know." He sounded like a man offering bonbons when he knew he ought to have brought rubies.

Once, that might have been enough for her. Not anymore.

"And I love you. But not in the right way." Emma released her pent-up breath in a long, gusty sigh that ruffled the folds of her cousin's cravat. "No, Kort. It wouldn't work, for either of us. Trust me."

For a moment, she thought he was going to argue. But whatever it was he saw in her face, it made her argument for her better than any number of words could.

Kort let out his own breath. "All right," he said, sounding easier and more natural than he had since the conversation began. Reaching out a hand, he ruffled her hair as he used to long, long ago. "Come back anyway. I promise not to importune you with proposals."

Emma hastily readjusted her hair ornaments. "Why are you so keen to get me out of Paris?"

"Not just Paris," Kort said. "France."

Emma narrowed her eyes at him.

Kort locked his hands behind his back. "Uncle Robert thinks that once Bonaparte gets the crown on his head, he's going to put aside his old wife and take a more nubile one. I know you're friends with the old one. If your safety here rests on that friendship . . ."

He didn't need to fill in the rest. With cousin Robert gone back to America, what official clout she had had as the cousin of the American envoy would be gone. If she lost her voice at court or, even worse, was actively associated with a discarded and disgraced faction, her place in Paris could become very precarious.

Precarious and possibly even dangerous.

Emma glanced back at the canopy. Bonaparte sprawled in his chair, clearly bored. His wife leaned towards him, her hand on his arm, her body fluid and pliant, her smile designed to charm. In her white dress and gilt diadem, she made a charming picture still, the shadow of the canopy protecting her from the too-honest light of the sun.

Bonaparte might have his mistresses, but it was always his wife he came back to. She knew how to coax him out of his sulks, how to soften the rough edges of his life. The idea of his being married to someone else was unthinkable.

"No," said Emma decisively. "He wouldn't. Whatever his other shortcomings, he adores her. He *does*."

She sounded like a child and she knew it.

Kort looked at her with infuriating patience. "That has nothing to do with it. If it's politically expedient . . ."

"Like your proposal to me?"

All right, that hadn't been fair. But if he was going to go all know-it-all at her . . . What did he know, in Paris for all of two months? She had been here far longer than he. He knew nothing about the French court and the political games they played.

Even if he might be right.

The thought sent a chill down Emma's spine. No, it couldn't be. "Excuse me," she said abruptly. "I shouldn't be monopolizing you."

"Don't storm off."

"I'm not storming." If she were storming, he would know it. She did a good line in flounce and stomp when the occasion called for it. Emma mustered a strained smile. "I'm not doing my duty as guest. We're meant to mingle and be charming."

Looking down at her, Kort's expression softened. "You don't have to be charming with me. You only have to be yourself."

Emma recognized it for the olive branch it was. She touched her fingers lightly to Kort's arm. "I'll take that as it was intended," she said, and slipped away before he could respond.

It was always best to have the last word, especially when there were discussions one wanted to avoid.

It was absurd, of course. The Emperor would never put Mme. Bonaparte aside. If he were, why would she be collecting ladies-in-waiting? Unless, of course, she, too, was avoiding unpleasant truths.

Emma thought of the open disdain with which Caroline had greeted Mme. Bonaparte last night. It didn't mean anything. Caroline had always treated Mme. Bonaparte like that. But it did mean that she felt safe in doing so.

Caroline and all the rest of the Bonapartes would be lobbying for Mme. Bonaparte's replacement.

Emma smiled and nodded as she went. She hadn't thought she was going anywhere in particular, but she found her steps slowing as she approached a familiar bend in the river, where a young woman sat with a child in her lap, watching the steamship begin its progress down the river.

Hortense raised a hand in warning, jerking her head towards the sleeping child in her lap.

Emma nodded to show that she understood, and lowered herself awkwardly onto the blanket, taking care not to bump Louis-Charles. Hortense's husband was on the other side of the clearing, pointedly ignoring his wife and child.

Emma folded her legs beneath her, wondering how to ask what she needed to ask.

Before she could, Hortense said quietly, "Remember our old games of prisoner's base?"

She was looking out across the river at the undulating vista of green grass and artfully artless trees, the scene of their old revels and games. "Yes. You always won."

"My legs are longer than yours." Hortense had always been generous in victory.

Emma couldn't take it anymore. "Is it true?" she blurted out. "Is the Emperor planning to divorce your mother?"

Emma expected shock, outrage, denial. There wasn't any. Hortense didn't seem the least bit surprised. Bending her head over her sleeping child, she said carefully, "It is possible."

Emma felt as though she had had the wind knocked out of her. "But—why?"

Hortense glanced over her shoulder to the canopy where the Emperor sat. Caroline stood by his side. He was dandling Caroline's son, Achille, on his knee. The three-year-old squirmed, wriggling to be let down. Mme. Bonaparte looked on, a strained, fixed smile on her face.

Behind them, among the rest of the hangers-on, she could see Augustus in conversation with Horace de Lilly. He didn't seem happy about whatever it was. In fact, he didn't seem happy. Emma wondered, unhappily, if he were still brooding over Jane.

They hadn't spoken since last night, not since the incident with Marston.

"They want him to put *Maman* aside," Hortense said quietly.

"What?" Emma guiltily turned her attention back to her friend. Now wasn't the time to dither over Augustus, not when the whole world was falling to pieces around her.

"They want him to divorce her," said Hortense. "Before the coronation. Theirs was only a civil marriage, you know."

"Who wants it? The Bonapartes?" The Bonapartes had hated Hortense's mother from the very beginning, holding against her her age, her past, her effortless elegance.

Hortense shook her head. "Not just the Bonapartes. His advisors, too. They say the succession is unsure. They want him to make a dynastic marriage."

"A dynastic marriage?" Dynastic marriages were for kings and dukes and the scion of ancient houses, not jumped-up generals turned rulers. Hadn't they fought a revolution to be done with dynasties? The very idea was ludicrous. "He's not exactly King George."

"No," said Hortense quietly. "He rules far more territory than King George, and will rule still more if his plans go as he intends them. They usually do," she added.

It wasn't an indictment, just a statement of fact.

"What plans?" asked Emma suspiciously.

"There are always plans," said Hortense wearily. "This time it's the invasion of England. He's always wanted to conquer England. If he manages that . . ." She shrugged. "He'll have achieved what none of his predecessors could. France will rule England. For that, he'll need an heir."

Emma couldn't care less about England, but she did care about Hortense. "But he has an heir," Emma said stubbornly. "What about you? What about Louis-Charles?"

The very purpose behind Hortense's disaster of a marriage to Bonaparte's younger brother had been to provide Bonaparte with that heir, an heir of both his blood and Josephine's. Louis-Charles had been intended for that position from birth. If the Emperor had changed his mind now, it meant that Hortense's sacrifice and all the pain she had endured since had been for naught.

It was, thought Emma passionately, unthinkable.

"He won't go back on his word now," she said, wishing she could believe her own words.

Hortense smiled without humor. "It's not the same. If he is to be an emperor, he must have heirs of the blood. Or so they say."

Emma bit down on her lower lip. "What about your mother?"

Hortense didn't even need to think about it. "It will devastate her," she said simply.

Emma could remember when Bonaparte had been the one clamoring for Mme. Bonaparte's attention, suing for such crumbs of affection as she might choose to toss him. She had treated him, then, with a sort of abstracted fondness, and chosen her lovers elsewhere.

Emma wasn't sure when the balance had shifted; she had been preoccupied with her own affairs, with Carmagnac and Paul and her own wounded feelings. It had been a blurry and confused time, and, at the end of it, she had come to Malmaison to find that the world had shifted, that it was Mme. Bonaparte begging her husband's affection, biting her lip and looking the other way as he chose his mistresses from among the actresses at the Comédie-Française, and sometimes even from among his stepdaughter's friends.

Once, Mme. Bonaparte might have had her own way with a single, softly spoken word. Not anymore.

Emma had a very bad feeling about this.

"What can you do?" Emma asked her friend.

Hortense looked down at her son's head. "I've done everything I can do," she said, and there was a touch of bitterness in her voice. "What else, I don't know."

They sat together in silence, each caught in her own thoughts. The sun shone brightly on the river, but it seemed dim to Emma's eyes, too much light turned dark, like a black spot on one's eye from staring directly at the sun.

Emma looked at Hortense's familiar face, at the new hollows between her cheekbones and the shadows below her eyes, prettier, in some ways, than she had been as a girl, but so much sadder. They had sat so often like this, she and Hortense, in this same spot, watching the play of light on the water, tossing crumbs to the ducks, and talking of books and dresses and life and love. Here Emma had told Hortense of her disillusionment with Paul, twisting her hands in her lap, hour slipping into hour as the sun set over the water, and here Hortense had confessed her love for a young general, Duroc, one of the set that had flocked to Malmaison in those long-ago halcyon days.

Hortense had been so certain her stepfather would give his consent.

Emma jerked around as a sudden clatter erupted from the river. Bored with the adults, Caroline's child had wiggled free and was pelting Mr. Fulton's steamship with pebbles. The noise battered against Emma's skull, shattering the illusion of peace. The ducks squawked in protest, their feathers ruffled.

Plink, plink, plink went Achille's pebbles against the side of Mr. Fulton's ship. Crowing to himself, he scrambled along the bank, looking for more powerful ammunition. Something, Emma thought bitterly, of which Achille's uncle Napoleon would approve.

Emma's hands balled into fists in her lap. "It didn't need to come to this," she said.

She didn't need to explain what she meant; Hortense always knew.

The Emperor's daughter smiled wryly. "Didn't it? My stepfather is the comet and we are the tail. We must follow where he leads for better or ill." Her smile twisted, like a theatrical mask, half comedy, half tragedy. "I imagine the comet's tail doesn't much enjoy it either."

Emma's heart ached for her friend. She held out a hand. "Hortense—"

Hortense waved her away. "Forgive me. I can't think why I'm being so melodramatic! It must be the child. It wreaks havoc with one's emotions. You'll see."

"But you're not being melodramatic. Not at all! Not if you really believe—" Emma would have pressed the topic, but her words were drowned out by a resounding crash.

In the shocked silence that followed, she could hear an ominous cracking noise.

As the crowd stared in mingled horror and delight, the chimney of Mr. Fulton's steamship cracked, sliding slowly sideways. The ship skewed sideways, a sad, ruined thing.

"I sank it! I sank it!" crowed Achille.

Mr. Fulton looked ill. Kort gaped, as though he couldn't quite believe what had just happened. Hortense sighed, and shifted her own sleeping son on her lap.

"Yes, you did," said the Emperor genially. He pushed out of his chair, gesturing brusquely to his staff. "Enough entertainment. To work!" He jerked his head in the direction of Mr. Fulton. "You, too."

With one last, wordless look of dislike at Achille, Fulton joined the stream of naval commanders following the Emperor to the summerhouse he employed as an office in good weather.

The party was over, at least for some. Emma could see Mme. Bonaparte moving graciously through the crowd, smoothing over her husband's gaffe, urging everyone to stay where they were and enjoy the refreshments and the fine weather. Most people didn't need to be asked twice. Someone began plucking at a guitar, singing in a pleasant tenor voice about flowers blooming, bloomed too soon, ducking and striking a false chord as a candied chestnut sailed past one ear. In Hortense's lap, Louis-Charles stirred fitfully.

"I should take him in," Hortense said, just as a shadow fell over their sunny spot.

Emma didn't need to look up. She could see the silhouette stretched across the blanket, the full sleeves, the curling hair, the long legs, distorted and caricatured by the angle of the sun, and, yet, still recognizable. Or maybe it was the other things that she recognized: the smell of fresh-washed linen and ink, the elaborate clearing of the throat that preceded a grand oration.

Augustus addressed himself to Hortense. "Might I beg your indulgence, O Our Madonna of these Riparian Banks?"

"You may," Hortense said graciously. "Provided that you never call me that again."

Augustus bowed with a flourish, his head nearly scraping grass. "My dear lady, your lightest wish is my commandment. I crave only the counsel of your companion, should you be so very good as to release her into my custody for a brief colloquy."

"Her custody is her own," said Hortense. "Emma?"

Emma looked up at Augustus. "I need to talk to you," he said in a low voice, intended for her ears alone.

"What is it?" she mouthed, but he only shook his head.

"Are you sure you don't mind?" Emma asked Hortense.

Hortense mustered something akin to a smile. "Go," she said. "I'm quite content to doze by the river now that the excitement appears to be over."

Was it? Emma's pulse picked up as Augustus held out a hand to

Emma. Against her better judgment, she took it, letting him draw her up off the blanket.

"A thousand thanks, O benevolent ladies." As he waved an enthusiastic farewell to the Emperor's stepdaughter, Augustus bent close to Emma's ear, sending a shiver down her spine as he murmured, "Come with me. We need to be private."

Chapter 24

Hold not a mirror to my heart;
The truth's a very poisoned dart.
That same mote that you claim to spy,
Becomes a beam in thine own eye.
— Emma Delagardie and Augustus Whittlesby,
Americanus: A Masque in Three Parts

Private?" Emma echoed.

Behind her, on the blanket, Hortense studiously pretended not to listen. She was not listening so hard, Emma could practically hear it.

Emma scowled at Augustus. "Surely, whatever it is, you can tell me here."

"There are some things one prefers to discuss without an audience," Augustus said circumspectly.

That was certainly informative.

"You plan to abandon poetry and set up as a mantua maker," Emma extrapolated extravagantly. "No, no, wait, don't tell me. You have a sudden desire to go prospecting for gold in the outer Antipodes, accompanied only by your faithful bearer, Calvin."

"Calvin?" If she had hoped to annoy Augustus into an admission, the strategy failed. Her companion conducted a leisurely survey of the grounds, his gaze moving impartially over the revelers, some lounging on blankets, others, less daunted by the warmth of the sun, playing an impromptu game of tag.

"What would you prefer?" Emma grumbled. "Hobbes?"

"Solitary, poor, nasty, brutish, and short?" Augustus raised a brow. "Why not? We have a fine exhibition of the state of nature here before us."

One of Mme. Bonaparte's younger ladies stumbled on the hem of her skirt, tumbling into the grasp of the gallant who had been chasing her. She squeaked as he squeezed her, and dealt him a resounding slap.

Oh. Emma grimaced. Maybe that hadn't been tag.

"Hardly poor," she said. There were enough jewels in evidence to fund a small revolution. "Or solitary."

"You didn't say anything about brutish." Augustus regarded the assemblage with a jaded eye. "This lot won't go in until the food runs out. We'll have no privacy back here."

As if in illustration, the guitar struck up again, discordantly. Oh, dear, Lieutenant Caradotte had gotten hold of it. He would insist on playing, despite being tone-deaf. Emma winced as he struck a chord that sounded like an offended feline on a bad day. There was a thud and a squawk as someone tried to wrestle the guitar away.

"Madame Delagardie!" Someone came jogging up. It was another of Bonaparte's aides—no, not an aide anymore, but he had been three years ago during one of their endless summers at Malmaison. He was something important now, but Emma couldn't remember what. To her, he would always be the aide whose pantaloons had split during a game of prisoner's base. Sans Culottes, they had called him for weeks. "Come join us for blindman's buff!"

Emma waved back, all too aware of Augustus's hand on her other elbow. Privacy, he had said. Privacy for what? They had agreed there was nothing to talk about. It might be nothing more sinister than plans for the masque, an addendum to the script, a change of cast. There were a hundred and one innocent reasons he might want to speak to her.

"Later," she called back to Sans Culottes. What *was* his name? "It's too warm."

"See?" murmured Augustus. "You're far too much in demand. I won't have five minutes without someone dragging you away for a game or a gossip."

"I'm not so much in demand as all that. We could speak here. There's no place so private as among a crowd."

A yard from them, Caradotte crashed onto the turf, triumphantly raising the guitar in both hands. "Nice try!" he yelled back.

"Doesn't someone want to call him out?" a lady called out from her semi-prone position on a blanket.

"Lutes at ten paces!" shouted someone else.

Augustus didn't need to say anything. His point had been made for him.

Emma sighed. "We could go to the theatre."

The minute the words were out of her mouth, she knew she had made a mistake. They stared at each other for an awful, frozen moment. The last time they had been in the theatre together—well, the less of that, the better.

"The front of the theatre, I mean," Emma babbled. "The large part with the stage in it."

"Er, yes," said Augustus, and Emma felt her cheeks going even redder. What was wrong with her? She had managed to conduct an entire affair with Georges with complete sangfroid, and an accidental kiss had her bumbling and babbling. "I did rather get that. Miss Gwen is rehearsing her pirates. Remember?"

"That's right." Emma seized on the distraction with relief. "What was it she called them? She said they were insufficiently fearsome."

"I believe the exact phrase was *couldn't pillage their way out of a wet paper parcel*," said Augustus delicately.

They grinned at one another, completely in accord.

Emma felt something catch at the back of her throat. She had missed him. She had missed this. Which was absurd, she knew. How could you miss someone when you hadn't been apart?

"I never understood why they were in that wet paper parcel," Emma said, her voice constricted. She cleared her throat. "It sounded like a very uncomfortable venue."

"Perhaps they couldn't afford a proper ship," suggested Augustus. "They might be penurious pirates."

"You're alliterating again," Emma pointed out. "You needn't do that with me."

They had been strolling rather aimlessly along the side of the house, but at that, Augustus paused. "No," he said. "Not with you."

There was a strange note in his voice. Emma let her own steps dawdle to a halt. She looked up at him quizzically. He was looking at her, none of the usual mockery in his face. There were twin furrows between his brows, and he suddenly seemed older than she had thought him to be.

"What is it?" she asked. "What's wrong?"

Whatever it was, he thought better of it. He shook his head, moving briskly along. "Where shall we go? The back of the house is occupied and the house itself is swamped with people."

Oh, yes. Their mysterious talk. Despite her growing unease, Emma strove to keep her voice light. "I draw the line at the stables. And the gardeners are very protective of the greenhouses."

Augustus didn't look at her. "What about the rose garden?"

It wasn't an unreasonable suggestion. Leaving aside the romantic connotations of roses, it was well away from both the revelers in the back and the pirates in the theatre. A long alley of trees led down one side, shading the area and separating the roses from the bustle of the drive. It was as private as they could hope to be, with only one small caveat.

"Is the Emperor working in the summerhouse?" Emma asked, as they turned their steps in that direction. "If he is, we might want to stay out of the way."

"Summerhouse?"

She'd forgotten that Augustus didn't know Malmaison. Sometimes, it felt as though he had always been there. "It's at the end of the alley," said Emma, "just past the roses. On fine days, the First Consul—I mean, the Emperor—brings his work out there. As long as the windows are closed, we should be all right, though."

"Mm-hmm," said Augustus, which might have meant anything from yes to no to maybe. Emma took it as yes.

Emma glanced at Augustus's shuttered face, doubly screened by the long fall of curly hair. One thing was certain: She wasn't getting anything out of him until he was good and ready to speak.

They cut around the far side of the house from the theatre, along an alley of trees leading towards Mme. Bonaparte's famous roses and the nondescript, octagonal façade of the summerhouse. Some of the roses, the earlier sorts, had already unfurled their petals to the sun. The leaves were stiff and glossy. There were rare and exotic varieties, Emma knew, smuggled in from all around the world, whisked into France in direct contravention of the blockades. The authorities knew to turn a blind eye when it came to Mme. Bonaparte's garden.

Emma knew she ought to know more about it, to be able to appreciate the distinctions of this rose versus that, but her knowledge of horticulture was limited to "Ooh, aren't the pink ones lovely!" A connoisseur might appreciate the niceties of specific species; Emma had only a jumbled impression of color and the heavy, heady scent of roses, all the more intense in the hazy heat of the day.

The low buzz of the bees was broken only by the sound of voices from the summerhouse, too low to be distinguishable, just loud enough to jar the peace of the garden. Emma could hear the earnest tones of Mr. Fulton's voice, followed by the Emperor's sharp bark, then another voice, softer, interceding. It must be very hot in there, with that many people crammed inside around the small table.

A bee bumbled past, drunk with pollen.

Emma looked at Augustus, who wasn't looking at her. "All right," she said. "We're here now."

Augustus clasped his hands behind his back. He paced towards the summerhouse, head bent, body angled forward, pausing for what felt like a very long while. The silence stretched between them, broken only by the staccato rhythm of voices from the summerhouse and the low hum of bees among the roses.

Emma's skirt brushed against a rosebush, catching on thorns. She yanked it free again, making the flowers shake. The bee buzzed angrily and zigzagged away.

She knew how it felt.

The day was humid, despite the hot sunshine. Drops of sweat dripped down beneath her bodice, catching between her breasts. There would be a storm soon, if she wasn't much mistaken. She could feel it in the prickling of the skin below her gloves, in the frizzled hairs at the nape of her neck.

"Do you have something to say," Emma burst out, "or would you rather just stand there?"

For a moment, she thought Augustus might choose the latter. Then he turned abruptly on one heel. "Are you marrying your cousin?"

Emma gawped at him, the minor irritants of sweat and skin forgotten. "What?"

"Livingston," Augustus said flatly. "The younger one. Are you marrying him?"

"It would be very hard for me to marry the older one," said Emma sharply, "given that he's been quite happily married since 1770."

Augustus gave her a look. "That's not an answer."

"I'm not sure you deserve one." Emma clawed at the itch on her arm, thwarted by her own gloved fingers. She squinted at Augustus, the sun full in her eyes. "I thought you were dying of a mysterious disease—or at least on the verge of fleeing the country. Instead, you drag me all the way out here to ask that?"

Augustus was dark against the sun. "Horace de Lilly told me you refused the Empress's offer of a position in her household. Is it true?"

Emma raised a hand to shield her eyes. "What is this? Let's interrogate Emma?" She was hot and itchy and irritable and unaccountably aggravated at Augustus, for reasons she didn't quite understand and didn't want to. "Yes. Yes, I did."

He looked like Cotton Mather ready to cast out a sinner. "Because you're going back to America."

"Don't worry," said Emma flippantly. "I'm not going anywhere until after the masque is done. It won't affect you."

"So you are—" Augustus stumbled a step back, his expression a study in confusion. "I didn't think—I didn't imagine you would really—"

"Ever go anywhere?"

That was her, everyone's friend, Mme. Delagardie, always there, always available, excellent for confidences, fine to kiss when one was disappointed in love, but have a life or a love of her own? Not likely.

"You didn't imagine I would really what? Marry? I may not be your vision of Cytherea, but that doesn't mean that no one wants to scale my tower."

Lies, all lies, but she was too angry to care.

Augustus's mouth opened and closed. Twenty-two cantos and she had rendered him speechless. "I never said that. I never meant—"

"You never mean anything," retorted Emma. "That's just the problem. Words, words, words, all sound and fury signifying nothing. Heaven help you if you ever had to shout for help. You wouldn't be able to put it in less than five cantos. You'd be drowned before you got out the cry."

Augustus ignored her ramblings. "Does he love you?" he asked in a low voice.

"Who?" She wasn't sure why she felt the need to draw this out, but she did. Revenge, perhaps. Revenge for dragging her out here, for making her worry, for peppering her with inconsequentialities, for pretending he cared who loved her and who didn't. What did it matter? He wasn't offering to take up the torch himself.

"Livingston." Augustus took a step forward. "Does he love you?"

Oh, Lord, why was she doing this? Emma pressed her eyes together so she wouldn't have to look at him. The sun made strange patterns against the lids.

"As a cousin. He loves me as a cousin. That's all. I'm not marrying him. I'm not going to America." She forced out the words, tasting dust on her tongue, at the back of her throat. "Everything is exactly as it was."

Augustus drew in a deep breath, a long, rumbling breath that was a paragraph all of its own. "I'm glad," he said softly.

Was she meant to be glad he was glad? Emma felt her stomach clench with hurt and loss and confusion, all mixed together like cheap punch, the sort that burned the back of your throat and gave you a headache the following morning.

"I'm so glad my life has been arranged for your convenience," she said tartly.

Augustus looked at her, relief written plainly across his face. "You've become one of my closest friends. Hell, you are my closest friend. I would have hated to lose you."

Emma couldn't find it in her to respond. She knew he meant what he was saying, and meant it with all the fullness of his heart, but it scraped at the raw edges of her emotions. He pronounced it as though it were an honor to be bestowed upon her, the Order of the Most Excellent Friend, as though his feelings were all that mattered, his friendship, his loss. What about hers? What if she had wanted to marry Kort? Was his friendship alone meant to be compensation enough?

She should be glad, she knew, glad he cared, glad he counted her a friend, glad he didn't want her to go away, but, instead, she was tired and frustrated and dangerously out of sorts.

Now that he had her life arranged to his satisfaction, Augustus was free to indulge his curiosity, "If you're not leaving, why not join Madame Bonaparte?"

Emma didn't want to talk about it. If she were being honest, she didn't want to talk to him. She shrugged. "I didn't feel like it."

Augustus raised a brow. "You didn't feel like it."

"If Madame Bonaparte was satisfied with my reasons, what is it to you? I wasn't aware that I owed you an account of my actions."

Oblivious and undaunted, Augustus studied her face with the sort of curiosity usually reserved by naturalists for their specimens. "If you're not marrying your cousin and you're not joining Madame Bonaparte's household—what are you doing?"

Emma's lips pressed together. "I am taking a lover and moving to Italy, where I intend to join a traveling commedia dell'arte troupe. All right?"

Her voice veered dangerously high on the last word. She needed to leave. She needed to leave now, before she said something ridiculous or, even worse, started crying for no reason at all other than the sun and her aching head and the drops of sweat like slow torture, dripping, dripping, dripping between her skin and her chemise, making her itch and ache and want to stomp on something.

She turned on her heel, prepared to stomp back to the house, when Augustus said something that stopped her in her tracks.

"You're running away," he said.

His voice was soft and low, like the prickle of sweat against her skin, barely there, but impossible to ignore.

She should ignore it, she knew. Just ignore it and walk away. She was in a foul, foul mood and anything she said right now she would only regret later. She knew that, in the sensible, rational part of her brain.

But she turned anyway. Turned and said, incredulously, "What?"

Augustus folded his arms across his chest, looking offensively cool and comfortable in his billowing linen shirt, surveying her with all the superiority of his extra inches.

"You're running away," he repeated. "You won't marry your cousin and you won't join the court. You won't go back to America, but you won't settle at Carmagnac. You didn't even want to write the masque until someone cornered you into it."

"A pity I didn't trust my judgment about that," Emma shot back. "We might have been spared a great deal of bother."

"No risk, no reward," said Augustus coolly. "You aren't willing to take the risks, so you forgo the rewards. You play with people and ideas, but you drop them before they get too serious—in the nicest possible way, of course. You wouldn't want to upset anyone."

"You might want to give that some consideration." Emma could feel herself shaking, literally shaking, from her slippers right up to her sleeves. The buzzing of the bees had become a buzzing in her ears. "Not upsetting anyone."

"You want everyone nice and calm and at a safe remove." He was looking at her as though she were a butterfly pinned to a paper. It made Emma want to scratch him. "You won't even have it out with that cretin Marston. You won't tell him no, will you? You just placate him and put him off and hope he won't cause a scene."

Emma's voice was shaky with rage. "My relationship with Georges has nothing to do with you."

Augustus took a step forward, holding her in his gaze like a duelist with his opponent in his sights. "Your relationship with Georges has nothing to do with Georges, does it? You only picked him because you knew you wouldn't have to keep him."

The smug certainty in his voice made Emma want to slap him. "You know nothing about it," she said coldly.

"I know you," he said, and then, unforgivably, "you're hiding."

"Hiding?" Emma echoed. There was a red haze in front of her eyes. "*I'm* hiding? What about you?"

There was an old adage about hornet's nests. Augustus had the uneasy feeling that he had just kicked one.

"This isn't about me," Augustus said hastily.

In fact, this wasn't supposed to be about either of them. This was supposed to be about Mr. Fulton and his mysterious plans. For the mission, he had told himself, all for the mission. It would arouse suspicion for a man alone to be loitering by the Emperor's summerhouse. But a man and a lady, in a rose garden . . . who would remark on that? Not to mention the niggling little matter of Horace de Lilly's bombshell about Emma's supposed betrothal.

It had been such a nice, tidy little plan: eavesdrop on the Emperor, reassure himself that this American marriage was just another nonsensical rumor.

Until it wasn't. Tidy, that is. In fact, it was starting to feel distinctly out of control. What in the blazes had he been thinking? He hadn't been thinking. It had just all followed, one thing after another. It had rattled him, thinking she might actually be going back to America, marrying that taciturn cousin of hers. The rest had just . . . come out.

"This isn't about me," he repeated.

"Oh, isn't it?" said Emma. Her gloved hands were clenched into fists at her sides and there were two bright red spots in her cheeks that had nothing to do with rouge.

"You're going to get sunburnt, standing out here like this," said Augustus solicitously. "Perhaps we had better—"

"And whose fault would that be?" In her anger, Emma seemed to grow a good three inches. It took Augustus a moment to realize she actually had. She was standing on tiptoe in her ridiculous, frivolous, ribbon-trimmed slippers. That was going to hurt in a moment or two, but for the moment, she was buoyed up with rage. "But, no, you had to drag me out here to ask ridiculous questions and cast aspersions on my character. Heaven forbid you tear me to bits in the comfort of a shady drawing room. No. It had to be out here."

"I wasn't trying to tear you to bits," Augustus said soothingly. "I just wanted—"

"I know," said Emma viciously. "To talk. Fine. We can talk. Do you want to talk about running away? Let's talk about you. A grown man and you don't even own a waistcoat!"

That wasn't fair. "I own a waistcoat," he said defensively. "I don't see where that—"

"Don't you? You can't even commit to an outer garment, much less anything else, and you talk to me about running away?"

It was time to get this conversation back where it belonged. "I was simply pointing out," Augustus said in the most reasonable tone he could muster, "that you have managed to dodge every single commitment that's been presented to you. If not hiding, what would you like to call it?"

Emma went off like a grenade. "You. You have the nerve to stand here and ask me that? What do you know about commitment? I've kept Carmagnac going all these years. I have a house. I have dependents. I have *responsibilities*."

Did she want to talk about responsibilities? He'd say saving England from invasion was a jolly big responsibility. Knowing that if your messages were intercepted, people would die—that was responsibility. Knowing that lives depended on the insipidity of his poetry, on his eschewing the bloody waistcoat—that was responsibility. Knowing that he could damn himself by a chance word, by a slip, by a murmur in his sleep, that was responsibility.

He had eschewed friendships, family, outer garments, all for this, and she told him he had no sense of responsibility? If it weren't a matter of both personal and national security, he could pin back her ears with responsibility.

But he couldn't.

Emma was still in full spate. "And you? You live in rented lodgings. You have no friends that I've seen. And what about family? No wife, no children, no parents, no siblings . . ."

"I had a sibling. A sister."

That got her. Emma broke off mid-rant. "I'm so sorry. I didn't mean—Was she— Is she—?"

"Married," said Augustus grimly.

She had dwindled into a country housewife, counting the chickens, making soup for the poor, more interested in the pantry than poetry.

Emma settled her hands on her hips, her lips set so tightly, Augustus was amazed she could get the words through them. "That's what normal, grown-up people *do*, Augustus. They don't go around posturing from salon to salon, spouting ridiculous bits of verse. They get married. They grow up."

He had never heard that tone from her before, not even in the most acrimonious of their debates about the final act of the masque.

"You should talk," retorted Augustus. "Is there any ballroom that's safe from you? When was the last time you refused an invitation? Or a glass of champagne?"

Emma's voice rose. "Do you think I enjoy this—limbo? I was married. If Paul hadn't died, I would still be married. I would have a nursery and children and something more to think about than the next dress and the next ball. But Paul died."

Augustus was caught up short by the raw pain in her voice. This was an Emma he had never seen before.

He had never thought that she might have loved her Paul, not like that. She had been fond enough of him, she had made that much clear; she had missed him, that was fair enough; but with all the ups and downs and gossip and scandal, Augustus had just assumed, as everyone else had, that it couldn't have been a terribly deep emotion. As she had said herself, she had been young.

He was an ass. A complete and utter ass.

He was also, alarmingly, bitterly jealous of a dead man.

Emma's fingers twisted together, like snakes in a Greek sculpture. Her words tumbled out, one after the other. "He couldn't help dying and I couldn't stop it. Neither of us had that choice or that chance. But you do. You have every chance in the world and you chose to be what you are."

Augustus's lips moved with difficulty. "What am I?"

He could see Emma's throat move as she swallowed. "A fainéant. A do-nothing." She blinked away tears, tossing her head defiantly back. "Do you know what I think?"

Augustus had the uncomfortable feeling that he was going to.

"I think you wanted Jane because you knew she would never have you." Her eyes glittered with a strange, fierce light. "I think you wanted her because she was safe. Cytherea is only Cytherea because she doesn't leave the tower."

"I—" Augustus couldn't think of anything to say.

He didn't have to.

The door to the summerhouse rocketed open, hinges screeching. A man stormed onto the stairs, red faced with heat and anger.

"Can a man get no work done?" raged the Emperor.

Chapter 25

Journeys perilous, risks, and hazards,
Man-high waves and mutinous laggards,
Are easy tasks to undertake
Compared to facing one's own mistake.
—Emma Delagardie and Augustus Whittlesby,
Americanus: A Masque in Three Parts

A ugustus and Emma froze in the face of imperial wrath, arrested mid-argument.

Had they been speaking that loudly? From the expressions of amusement and derision, Augustus could only assume they must have been.

It wasn't just Bonaparte on the steps but the entire flower of France's navy ranged behind him, staring over his shoulder in varying degrees of annoyance, curiosity, and yawning indifference. Even the bees on the roses seemed to have stopped their buzzing to pause and stare.

Augustus had forgotten, at some point in their discussion, that Bonaparte was just a window away. He had forgotten about everything except Emma and the words pouring from her lips. They buffeted him like the wind and waves of Mr. Fulton's machine, sending him racketing about as helplessly as Americanus in his ill-fated barque, his mast broken, his defenses down. He felt like a necromancer who had summoned a storm only to find it turned against him, scourged with lightning, deafened by thunder.

Metaphor again, always metaphor. If he clung to metaphor, he wouldn't have to think about the meat of it, what Emma had actually told him.

She wasn't the only one who knew how to hide.

Next to him, Emma sank into a deep and hasty curtsy. Augustus could see only the very top of her head, gilded by sunlight. "I beg pardon, sire. We were just . . . talking. About the masque."

"Practicing the love scenes, were they?" murmured one officer to another.

Augustus could see the tips of Emma's ears go red. It was the only bit of her he could make out. It made him feel like the worst sort of cad. Exposing himself to scorn and derision—well, he was used to that. To expose her to the amusement and censure of Bonaparte's entourage, that was another matter entirely.

Bonaparte made a grunting noise. "The production had better be worth the trouble."

Trying to draw attention from Emma to himself, Augustus said loudly, "We strive to amuse, sire. We trust the mellifluous meditations of our meandering marauders shall be to your certain satisfaction."

"Yes, yes," said Bonaparte impatiently. "Next time, confine your scenes to the theatre."

"Sire," said Emma, and bowed her head still farther.

"Enough, Madame Delagardie, enough." The Emperor was inclined to be benevolent. Chucking her under the chin, he raised her to her feet. He wasn't a large man, but she looked very small in his grasp. A moment ago, Augustus would have sworn she was the size of the Athena Nike, able to overleap buildings and shake the foundations of empires with the volume of her voice. "There's no need for that. We were done here anyway. Weren't we, gentlemen?"

There was a decided note of challenge in his voice.

Admiral Villeneuve opened his mouth and then closed it again.

Robert Fulton stepped forward, holding himself stiffly. "I do not imagine we can have anything more to say."

"Come back to me when you have made the changes," said the Emperor dismissively. He turned to Villeneuve, turning his back on Fulton. "Where did you leave the other plan?"

"In the council room, sire."

"What are we waiting for? Come!" With a wave of his hand, Bonaparte motioned his minions onward. They surged forward, making for the house, leaving Emma, Augustus, and Fulton in their wake, the summerhouse abandoned but for the detritus of paper and one red jacket that someone had tossed carelessly across the back of a chair and forgotten in the race to the house. Mr. Fulton's portfolio was sprawled open on the table.

Somewhere, in the back of his mind, the bit that sounded strangely like Miss Gwen, Augustus dimly remembered that this was what he was here for, that he was meant to discover what Mr. Fulton had devised and how Bonaparte meant to deploy it.

Right now, though, all that felt curiously insubstantial. Emma's words still rang in his ears. He had been in the midst of a cannon fusillade once, caught in the wrong place at the wrong time. It had felt something like this, the explosion followed by a painful, ringing silence, with the black soot griming his face and clouding his eyes. He had felt it then, too, this curious stillness. The senses faltered before the enormity of the bombardment.

Augustus opened his mouth to speak, but the words clogged in his throat. For once in his life, he had no idea what to say.

A fainéant, she had called him. A do-nothing.

Emma's back was to him, the line of her spine showing clearly through the thin fabric of her dress.

If Paul hadn't died, I would still be married.

Was that what she agonized over, behind that fake, bright smile? Did she pretend that Paul was still alive, that they had a nursery of children together at that estate of his, the one with the drainage issues? Was it Paul she still dreamed of at night, Paul whose name she murmured in her sleep?

Augustus felt as though the world had just been picked up and dropped again, all his certitudes and convictions lying in pieces around him. All these weeks of working together, laughing together, being together, and he had never suspected, never even imagined. Emma was what she was, the widow Delagardie, so long a widow that her widowhood was a fact rather than an event. It had never occurred to him that to her, the late Delagardie was more than the precondition to her widowhood, or that she might, despite the time, despite the rumors, despite it all, still mourn him.

Should he offer sympathy? It was a bit late for that, and the stiff line of Emma's back denied it.

Besides, why would she want the sympathy of one such as he, a fainéant, a do-nothing? Augustus tried to muster anger and failed. Indignation sparked briefly and sputtered out again. It had been easy to be angry yesterday, over Jane. But this? He was too dazed for anger.

I think you wanted her because she was safe, she had said. *Cytherea is only Cytherea because she doesn't leave the tower.*

There was a sick feeling at the pit of Augustus's stomach. What if yesterday had resolved itself differently? What if Jane had turned around and told him she shared his feelings and loved him in return? Would he have held out his arms to her?

Or would he have fled in the opposite direction?

"Months of work!" Augustus jumped as Mr. Fulton whacked the side of the summerhouse with an openhanded slap. Mr. Fulton was having no trouble mustering all the rage that Augustus lacked. "A full-size model . . . a full trial . . . and he . . ."

Ignoring Augustus, Emma went to the inventor, placing a hand on his shoulder. "Are you all right, Mr. Fulton?"

Mr. Fulton was too busy with his own grievances to notice her flushed cheeks or strained voice. "Perfect, just perfect," he said bitterly. "Changes, he says! And yet he still wants it by July!"

They had both forgotten Augustus was there. At least, Mr. Fulton had forgotten. Emma was quite studiously pretending Augustus didn't exist.

"Oh, dear," she said, in her soothing voice. Augustus knew that voice; it was the one that went with the head tilt and the arm pat. Emma had sympathy down to an art. "How trying for you."

With an effort, Fulton got hold of his emotions. "I'm sorry, Madame Delagardie. You can't want to hear this. You said you needed help with the wave machine?"

Emma threaded her arm through the inventor's. She didn't look at Augustus. Not once. He might have been invisible. "If you wouldn't mind . . . ?"

"No, not at all." Mr. Fulton visibly squared his shoulders. "Just show me where you've put it."

Her back was to him. She was moving already, moving away, as if he weren't there at all. He could hear her say to Fulton, in her society voice, "You're so kind. It's the lightning bit. . . ."

Augustus watched her walk away, the words all jammed up in his throat. She had handled it very neatly, in her own Emma way. If he ran after her now, there would be explanations to be made, a reproachful look in the direction of Fulton, a "But, Augustus, Mr. Fulton has offered to share his valuable time," all civilized and pleasant, papering over what had just occurred as though it had never happened, just as she had papered over the kiss the night before. Pretend it wasn't there, pretend it had never happened, pretend everything was light and easy and just fine.

He had thought he knew her, but he had been just as taken in as everyone else in the end, hadn't he? Fooled by a frivolous exterior and an easygoing air. The pain in her voice etched into his memory like acid. *Paul died.* He had seen, in her haunted eyes too large for her face, the ghosts of all those children that never were, the domesticity that was not. Augustus wanted to wrap his arms around her and press the pain away, as if one embrace could cancel out another. He wanted to tuck her head under his chin and pretend he had never seen that, or the exasperation on her face as she said, *That's what normal, grown-up people* do, *Augustus. They grow up.*

He had thought he had grown up. He had been pressed into Wickham's service nearly as young as Emma had been a bride.

Well, all right, not quite as young, but still at an age when most other chaps were still bedeviling their tutors or betting on who could balance a chamber pot on the spire of the chapel. He had thought himself very noble.

A decade later, what did he have to show?

He had told himself that Jane was the answer to the question. But when he had imagined Jane, it was always poetry and moonlight, always set pieces, like something out of an opera. It was impossible to take the image and turn it into flesh, to make the fire crackle, to conjure the scent of food on the table. He couldn't envision Jane's hair unbound. It was all pasteboard, like the scenery in the theatre, the mere semblance and substitute of life.

If he loved and loved hopelessly, he never had to make room for messy realities. He never had to genuinely care.

In the relentless sunshine, the summerhouse seemed to shimmer. The glare from the windows hurt his eyes. Augustus could only be glad there was no mirror. He didn't think he would like what he saw in it.

This was what Emma had seen, what she had seen and he hadn't, shortsightedness and cowardice and, above all, selfishness, all slicked over with poetry.

All was fair in espionage and war.

He didn't want to live like that anymore.

The door to the summerhouse stood open, and, inside, Fulton's plans still lay on the table, momentarily forgotten. Someone would be back for them soon enough. Whatever Fulton's feelings, Bonaparte had made it clear he considered his changes only a delay, not a denial. Augustus regarded the open door without enthusiasm. Whatever else, it would be a dereliction of duty not to see this through. One last mission. And then?

And then he would make it right with Emma. He wasn't sure why, but the very thought of it made his spirits rise.

Augustus turned and slipped into the summerhouse.

*A*ugustus would say she was running away.

Emma could hear her own voice saying things like *It's the lightning bit*, and then, in response to something else, *I can't figure out how to attach it to the thunder. I'm deathly afraid of burning the building down. I should hate to be the one responsible for destroying the Emperor's theatre*, and then Mr. Fulton's voice in reply, uttering words that pattered against her ears like pebbles on a windowpane, just a distant clatter from somewhere far outside. She could feel the grass beneath her slippers, her skirt slapping against her legs, the sun on her head as Augustus and the summerhouse receded farther and farther into the distance.

Running away, indeed!

What business was it of Augustus's whether she married her cousin or moved to America or set up house in the outer Hebrides? What concern was it of his whether she slept with Georges Marston or half the imperial guard? As for this business of her playing with people and ideas—well, that was simply absurd. If he asked any of her friends from Mme. Campan's, they could tell him that. To be fair, most of them she saw only for quick, whispered gossips at parties, or for casual chatter over chocolate, but at least she *had* friends.

This idea that she couldn't commit to anything was pure nonsense. She had committed to Paul, hadn't she? *Nine years ago, on a whim*, whispered a nasty little voice at the back of her head. And she had gone running as soon as the going had gotten rough.

Well, yes, but she had gone back to him. They had been trying to make it work that last time. She had made compromises, she had learned, she had tried, really tried. *Yes, for all of four months.* But that hadn't been within her control, the fact that they had only four months. It wasn't her fault that Paul had died.

The familiar refrain grated on her ears. Not my fault, not my fault, not my fault. She had been saying it for so long, and, yet, what did it really mean? Her fault, his fault, Fate's fault, the outcome was the same. It was going on four years now. Soon Paul would have been dead longer than they had been together, and they had been together only for a fraction of the time they had officially been together.

Fine, so perhaps she had been using Paul as an excuse. And perhaps Augustus had a bit of a point when it came to Marston—or a lot of a point. But that didn't mean she shirked her duties or hid from obligation or whatever else it was that he was trying to accuse her of. After all, there was Carmagnac, thought Emma, brightening. Always Carmagnac.

Only there wasn't, really. For all that she took credit for it, all she had done was complete Paul's plans in the most minimal possible of ways. She might have used her friendship with Mr. Fulton to improve upon those plans a bit, but it had still been Paul's work, not hers. It had taken very little effort to take Mr. Fulton's sketches and dispatch them to Paul's old steward at Carmagnac. She dispensed funds when asked and went down once a year to survey the fields and think Profound Thoughts about the life that hadn't been, but that was the extent of her involvement in Carmagnac. She could get along very well without Carmagnac, and Carmagnac could get along very well without her.

What had she done that was hers? Hers and not someone else's? When had she taken a step that was entirely of her own choosing and, having stepped it, stayed with it?

"Madame Delagardie?"

She couldn't even commit to a conversation. Mr. Fulton was looking at her expectantly, waiting for her to say something.

Emma shook her head ruefully. "I'm sorry, Mr. Fulton," she said. "I didn't catch a word of that."

"It will be easier to show you," he said kindly, absolving her of inattention. His lip curled. "Apparently my powers of description leave something to be desired."

Emma attempted to make up for her lapse with an excess of sympathy. "I am sorry your venture proved unfruitful."

Fulton grimaced. "So am I. It's been months in the planning, months of back and forth, a full demonstration in Boulogne, and now . . . He's angry because I didn't bring a full-size model with me! That silly little river behind the house isn't deep enough."

"It was deep enough for the steamship, wasn't it?" Until Achille sank it. Only to be expected of a son of Caroline.

Fulton dismissed that. "Yes, but this isn't a steamship. It's a—well, it is what it is." His face set in hard lines. "I've had enough of France anyway. I had a much better time of it in England. They, at least, knew how to appreciate the power of innovation. They didn't string a man along from committee to committee and then tell him he has to add an extra torpedo."

"I can see how that might be rather wearying." Emma had no idea what he was on about, but the venting seemed to be doing him good.

"If Bonaparte doesn't like my *Nautilus* as it is, I'm sure I can find someone else who will."

"Of course," said Emma soothingly. "I'm sure it's a brilliant machine. But what is it?"

"It's a submarine," he said abruptly, and pushed open the door of the theatre. "A ship that sails under the water."

Chapter 26

> By stealth, they stole upon her tower,
> At the very witching hour;
> Using all their treacherous art
> As rakes will steal a maiden's heart.

—Emma Delagardie and Augustus Whittlesby,
Americanus: A Masque in Three Parts

Wasn't the point of ships to stay above the water? A little thing about not drowning? Emma shook that aside. "Whatever it is, I'm sure you'll be able to reach some accommodation with the Emperor."

"Or not," said Fulton. He straightened his shoulders and ostentatiously examined his surroundings, deliberately putting an end to the discussion. "Now, where have you put the wave machine?"

"It's back here," said Emma, leading him down the aisle between the seats. On the stage, a number of men in tights and red bandannas cowered in various stages of abject subjection as their fearless leader exhorted them on to bigger and better piracy.

"Remember!" shouted Miss Gwen. "Always pillage *before* you burn! Desmoulins, that means you!"

Desmoulins toyed with his gold earring. "I just thought . . ."

"Don't!" Miss Gwen snapped. "Less thinking, more plundering!"

"She does know that it's all make-believe, doesn't she?" whispered Fulton to Emma.

Emma looked at Miss Gwen decked out in a tunic-type costume, complete with purple sash and what Emma was fairly sure was a real rather than a pasteboard cutlass. The cutlass blade flashed dangerously close to the ropes holding up the scenery for Act II.

"I do hope so," Emma said. She led Mr. Fulton through the door at the side of the stage, where a confusion of props littered two long tables, none of them in their proper places. The wave machine was still in pieces on the floor, although someone had moved the pieces to one side, jumbling them any which way in the process. "There's your machine, all in bits still, I'm afraid."

"I have the plans in my room," said Mr. Fulton. He began rolling up his sleeves. "But I believe I can manage this from memory."

"You're very kind," said Emma, and stepped back to let him pass.

The room looked very different in daylight. Dust motes danced in the sleepy sunlight, giving the space a hazy air. Last night, it had seemed endless, an Aladdin's cave of treasures, filled with dark alleys and treacherous corners, a mysterious and slightly dangerous place. Now it was simply itself, a reasonably large storage room, blocked off into bits by tottering piles of old scenery.

In the corner, Mr. Fulton began sorting busily through bits and pieces of machinery, muttering to himself and wiping off stray parts on the tail of his coat. Emma left him to it and wandered in the direction of the painted backdrop of Venice behind which she and Augustus had sat last night. She felt uneasy and slightly sick, the way she had when that first letter had arrived from her parents after the elopement, knowing that steps had been taken that couldn't be untaken, that there was no way to smooth everything over and make it all pleasant again.

What was said couldn't be unsaid.

"Emma?"

Venice undulated, the houses collapsing in on themselves.

As Emma caught her breath, Jane ducked neatly beneath the canvas, Venice bunched up in one hand, a script in the other.

"You scared me," Emma said. "I didn't realize anyone was there."

Jane indicated her script. "I was going over my lines while Miss Gwen puts her pirates through their paces. It's much quieter in here than out there."

Emma couldn't argue with the wisdom of that. Through the partition, she could hear Miss Gwen's voice, raised in harangue. Behind Jane, she could see the rowboat she and Augustus had shared last night, mundane now in the afternoon light, nothing but a rowboat.

Jane let Venice fall. It swung back into place, shrouding the boat once again in obscurity. The Campanile looked down its bell tower at Emma.

"Is something wrong?"

Emma made a face. "I had a row with Mr. Whittlesby."

"About the masque?"

"What else?"

"He can be rather flighty, can't he?"

"I wouldn't say that." Not in so many words, at any rate. She thought back over their long association. "We met nearly every day for over a month and he was never once late. Not once."

In fact, for a man who couldn't be trusted to wear a waistcoat, he had been remarkably reliable. Reliable, patient, hardworking. . . . Oh, for heaven's sake, Emma told herself. Enough. Just because she was feeling guilty was no reason to canonize the man.

"The poetry does get to one after a while," said Jane in commiserating tones. "All that rhyme and metaphor and so forth. You've been very good to put up with him for as long as you have."

Put up with him? She and Jane had happily mocked Augustus before, laughing over his exaggerated rhymes, his melodramatic airs.

But he hadn't been Augustus then. He had been Mr. Whittlesby. And it seemed, somehow, unkind for Jane to be standing there, serene in white muslin, casting judgment on Augustus when she had so recently crushed his hopes. Callous, even. Emma hadn't thought her friend could be callous.

Emma wordlessly shook her head.

For a moment, Jane was silent too. She said, with unaccustomed hesitation, "Was it anything to do with me?"

"Why should it be about you? You don't want him anyway."

The horrible words came out before she could stop them. Emma pressed a hand to her lips. She could feel her fingers trembling.

"Emma?" said Jane. She didn't stare—Jane would never do anything so graceless as stare—but her attention fixed on Emma with a great deal of concern. "What is this?"

Oh, what was the use?

"I know about yesterday," Emma said despairingly. "I know about the two of you."

"About the two of—" For a moment, Jane looked as near to perturbed as Emma had ever seen her. "About what?"

"Your conversation," said Emma, which was just another way of saying the same thing without saying anything at all. "Augustus told me he had—"

"He had what?" Jane's face was entirely remote. She might have been a stranger, rather than the woman with whom Emma had gossiped and laughed and compared bonnets.

"You knew how he felt about you," said Emma wretchedly. "Couldn't you have been a little kinder about it? Not that it's all your fault. I didn't mean to imply that. I know we all made fun—and he did make such a show of it—but that doesn't mean there wasn't real emotion there. Of some sort."

Whatever she had expected, it wasn't Jane's reaction. Jane's face relaxed. She seemed almost amused. "Is that all this is about?"

"All?" Emma's voice was sharper than she had intended. "I know this may seem comical to you, but you didn't see him last night, Jane. He was hurt, genuinely hurt."

"Hmm," said Jane. "I'm sure he'll get over it. A few cantos, and he'll feel quite the thing again."

Emma bristled. It didn't matter that she had said much the same thing, and crueler. She wasn't the one he had been in love with.

"One doesn't just get over a broken heart."

"I wouldn't know," said Jane simply. "Matters of the heart aren't my area of expertise."

For a moment, Emma was distracted from the question of Augustus. She looked at her friend, so sought after, so feted, and yet, in her own way, so very alone.

"Don't you miss it?" Emma said. "Being in love is—" How to explain it? Terrible and wonderful all at once. Messy, unpredictable, occasionally dreadful, and yet so incredibly vital.

Jane brushed the question aside. "Whatever it is that Mr. Whittlesby might have wanted or needed of me," she said matter-of-factly, "I doubt love was at the heart of it."

Memories of breath against her cheek, hands in her hair, lips against her neck, two feet away and a century removed.

"You don't mean to imply—not Augustus!"

It took Jane a moment to catch Emma's meaning. When she did, her eyebrows shot up so high, they nearly touched her hairline. "Heavens, no! Mr. Whittlesby is no Marston." Completely oblivious to any implications that might have for Emma, she went blithely on. "I simply meant that Mr. Whittlesby's interest in me is primarily"— she considered for a moment before settling on the appropriate word—"professional."

"Professional?"

"His poetry," Jane specified, in case Emma needed specification. "Every poet needs a muse."

"That doesn't mean he might not fancy himself in love with his muse," said Emma. She felt, suddenly, very weary.

What a tangle. Jane couldn't help not being in love with Augustus any more than he could have helped fancying himself in love with Jane, or Emma could have helped—

No. Emma pushed the thought from her mind. What was the use of adding another hopeless passion to the pile?

"Nonsense," said Jane firmly, so firmly that Emma wondered, fleetingly, whether Jane really had been quite so unaware of Augustus's intentions. "If it is a fancy, it's a passing one. I imagine sculptors fancy themselves in love with their statues, but that doesn't mean they expect the marble to reciprocate."

"But you're not marble," said Emma. "And neither is he."

"Why this sudden interest in Mr. Whittlesby's emotions?" Jane's voice changed as she looked at Emma's face. "You're not— Emma?"

Emma pressed her lips together, not trusting herself to say anything. "We're friends," she said. "We had a row."

"You always said it was only the breeches," Jane said softly. "Pure aesthetics, you said."

"That was before I knew him," said Emma, in a very small voice.

Jane set down her script very carefully, tapping the pages into order. "Are you sure you know him now?"

"What do you mean?"

Jane didn't meet Emma's eyes. "I mean," she said carefully, "that Mr. Whittlesby is a very attractive man. And he can be a very charming one. But he isn't . . ."

"Isn't what?"

"Exactly steady," said Jane, with the air of one navigating choppy waters. She reached out a hand to touch Emma's sleeve. "There are better places to trust your heart."

Emma twitched away. "I thought matters of the heart weren't your expertise."

"No, but I do know Mr. Whittlesby," said Jane.

"Do you?" Emma thought of all the times she had seen Augustus kneeling in tableau at Jane's feet, all the verse he had addressed to her, all the overblown sentiments, and, far worse, the private looks of longing. Something dark and nasty unfurled in her chest. "Or are you just afraid to lose your acolyte?"

"I just don't want you to be disappointed," Jane said reasonably. "Mr. Whittlesby is all very well for a—a drawing room flirtation, but he's not settling-down material. He's a poet."

"You say poet as though it were akin to pirate! It's not a crime against society to write poetry."

"That depends on the poetry," snapped Miss Gwen, coming up behind them.

"I do wish people would stop doing that," said Emma crossly.

Miss Gwen went on without paying any notice. "If you mean that Whittlesby fellow, it's not piracy, it's leprosy. At least piracy is a trade with a bit of dignity to it."

Emma looked at Miss Gwen's purple sash, broad black hat, and large gold hoop earring. Dignity wasn't the word that came to mind. "Poetry is a noble profession," she said, lifting her chin. "Think of Spenser. Think of Shakespeare."

"Ha! Think Shakespeare is all it takes to win an argument? The man could turn a phrase, I'll grant him that, but when you get down to it, he was nothing more than an actor."

Given that Miss Gwen had just stepped off a stage, Emma wasn't sure she saw the logic of that indictment. "Nonetheless," Emma said coldly, "people still quote him to this day."

"Is that what you want?" said Miss Gwen. "Immortality via Whittlesby? You won't have much luck in that direction. Lining boots, that's all those poems of his will be good for in ten years."

"I'm not interested in immortality," said Emma.

Miss Gwen's dark eyes narrowed. "Then it's the man you want? More fool you. You'd best go for the verse, then."

Emma folded her arms across her chest. "What's so very wrong with Mr. Whittlesby?"

Jane and her chaperone exchanged a look.

"Aside from the lack of waistcoat?" offered Jane.

"And jacket and cravat and hat . . ." enumerated Miss Gwen. "Hmph. The boy might as well appear in public in his nightshirt!"

"Our own dresses are just as revealing," argued Emma. Well, maybe not Miss Gwen's. Even as a scourge of the seas, the older woman was fully covered. Emma resisted the urge to cover her own chest as the chaperone looked pointedly at her décolletage. "A decade ago, we would have been wearing piles of petticoats. Who's to say that fashion won't shift again, making Mr. Whittlesby the forerunner of the new mode?"

"The open shirt and looking-silly style?" riposted Miss Gwen. "What next? Breeches for women?"

"It's not so much the aesthetics of it," Jane intervened, "as it is—well, his suitability."

"One flirts with poets," barked Miss Gwen. "One doesn't fall in love with them. And one certainly doesn't marry them."

She made it sound like an inalterable law. Somewhere in the Napoleonic Code was buried a provision banning matrimony for all purveyors of verse, to be defined under subsection 62(a)(iii), not to be confused with subsection 62(a)(iv)—minstrels, traveling.

"I said nothing about marriage," said Emma hotly. Or love. In fact, she had said nothing at all. It was all being assumed.

"You're not the not-marrying kind," said Jane. And then, before Emma could argue, "I've seen the way you look at Louis-Charles."

Hortense's baby. Emma bit down hard on her lower lip.

"You need someone reliable," said Jane. "You need someone who can make a home with you. What about your cousin?"

"I wish everyone would stop trying to marry me off to Kort," said Emma, so vehemently that Jane took a step back and Miss Gwen cackled, either in approval or just on general principles. "I have no interest in Kort. Kort has no interest in me. Shall I put it in verse?"

"Please don't," said Jane hastily. "I think we've had enough of that. But—Mr. Whittlesby?"

"He's not what you think," said Emma hotly.

"You don't know the half of it," muttered Miss Gwen.

Jane shot her chaperone a look.

"He's not the dilettante he pretends to be. He's clever, truly clever." Too clever sometimes. She remembered the way he dealt with their poetical meanderings, precise, analytical, entirely at odds with his public persona. And then there was the rest of it. "And he's kind." She looked at Jane's and Miss Gwen's uncomprehending faces, both in their own ways so cloistered, so little acquainted with the world. "Kindness isn't so common as you might think."

"So the man's neither a cretin nor a brute," said Miss Gwen. "My faith in mankind is restored."

"I don't need a hero," said Emma. She pushed aside the memory of Augustus neatly tripping Marston. "I don't want someone who will conquer kingdoms or bestride the globe like a colossus or whatever else heroes are supposed to do. I don't want flowery professions." She had had that once, from Paul, and look how that had turned out. She took a deep breath. "I can't claim to make any sense of it, but I'm happier when I'm with Augustus than I have been since—well, for a very long time."

It was true. When she was with him, she didn't worry what people were thinking or whether she was going to be able to sleep at night. She didn't brood about the past or fret about the future. She was happy simply to be, and to be with him.

At least, she had been. Emma pinched the fabric of her skirt between her fingers.

Into the silence, Jane said quietly, "People aren't always what they seem. Are you sure this is what you want?"

If someone had asked her that nine years ago, on the eve of her elopement with Paul, she would have blithely declared yes. Now? She knew Jane was right, even if she might be right for the wrong reasons. It had taken her years to know Paul, truly know him, with all their false starts and willful misconceptions. She wouldn't even vouch for her ability to know herself.

She had a sense of the Augustus-ness of Augustus, his quick, restless intelligence so at odds with the languid air he cultivated; his brusque displays of affection—pulling her cloak around her shoulders, taking her champagne glass from her hand—so very much the opposite of his flowery odes; the fundamental honesty that forced him to admit his own flaws and misconceptions, even when she knew he was burning to believe otherwise.

All these were Augustus, but she knew they weren't the sum of him. She knew instincts could deceive, that perception could be warped by desire or pride or sheer stubbornness. She could feel herself being stubborn now, could feel her toes curling in her slippers, digging into the floor.

It would be so easy to say yes, to say it defiantly and wield it as a weapon.

But it would be a lie. She didn't know what she wanted. To know what she wanted implied a degree of certainty she couldn't claim. She had thought she knew what Paul was and what their life together would be; she had been sure, then, that she knew what she wanted. Now—she had no idea. She had no idea when she would have an idea. And where did that leave her? She could go on as she had been, cocooned in her house in the Faubourg Saint-Germain, making the same rounds of parties, drinking enough champagne to get to sleep, waiting for enlightenment to strike, waiting for a divine voice to boom out and tell her to get on with it, whether getting on with it meant marrying Kort or joining Mme. Bonaparte's household or taking up missionary work in the outer Antipodes.

Or she could take a grand gamble. There had been a rope swing over the river at Belvedere. Year after year, Emma had picked her way carefully down the bank, easing into the water bit by bit as the others went flying over her head, releasing the rope to land with a cry and a splash. *No risk, no reward*, said Augustus.

Emma wasn't sure what she wanted, but she thought she knew what she needed.

"No," Emma said honestly. "But I would rather take the chance and risk being disappointed."

"Fools will be fools," Miss Gwen said austerely.

"Be careful," said Jane.

*F*ulton's plans blurred in front of Augustus's eyes.

He couldn't make heads or tails of them. The body of the device was almost, but not quite, cylindrical, coming to a point on one side, fitted with a curious sort of propeller on the other. There was a bump with a stick protruding out of the top, not at the middle, but all the way over to one side, and two rectangular, letter-labeled devices at the bottom. An octagonal structure of some sort billowed above the whole. It looked almost like a kite, but far too large and oddly shaped. Across the whole were additional markings and scribbling: levers, pulleys, dimensions.

Augustus turned it upside down, then sideways. It made no sense in any direction. Hell, he couldn't tell if it was an elongated and oddly shaped form of grenade, a means of conveyance, or a perfume atomizer designed for Mme. Bonaparte's boudoir.

Emma would know what it all meant.

Pushing away from the desk, Augustus briskly shuffled the plans back into their folder. Short of divine engineering intervention, staring at the plans wasn't going to lead to enlightenment. He stuffed the whole beneath the coverlet of his bed. Only an idiot attempted to hide contraband beneath a mattress or a pillow. But no one ever thought to try the simple expedient of lifting up the counterpane.

He needed to get the plans back to London. It would be even better if he could deliver the inventor with the plans. Fulton had seemed less than pleased with Bonaparte that afternoon. Fulton was a native of Pennsylvania, yes, but not of the rabidly anti-English variety of colonial. Fulton had spent time in England before, trying out one of his inventions on the estate of the Duke of Bridgewater.

Augustus would deliver the plans to England. Personally. Not by courier. And once back in England . . . He smoothed the blankets over the folio, arranging them so that no telltale bump showed. Once back in England, he would stay there. He had overstayed his time in Paris. His heart wasn't in it anymore. He was growing sloppy. Sloppy killed. True, Wickham would be disappointed to lose his longest-term man in Paris, but that would be more than balanced out by the delivery of the plans for Bonaparte's secret weapon.

He didn't want to go on as he had, caricaturing himself into the mere mockery of a human being.

Emma had been right.

Emma. There was the drawback to his plan. Grow up, she had told him—well, not in so many words, perhaps, but the implication had been clear—but to do so meant England, so near geographically, and yet so far away in every other sense. He wouldn't miss the salons or the taverns, but he would miss those afternoons in Emma's house, sprawled across a too-small chair in Emma's book room.

He would miss Emma.

He could picture her as she had walked away, her back very stiff beneath the thin fabric of her dress, damped with sweat until he could practically see the skin beneath. Her arm had been threaded through Mr. Fulton's, her head tilted at her listening angle, but he knew she had been no more listening than he had been capable of concentrating.

Was she at rehearsal? In her room? Sticking pins in a poet-shaped doll?

He had to find her and set things right.

Augustus crossed his cubbyhole of a room in two steps. The theatre was the most likely place to find her. Hadn't Fulton said something about repairing the wave machine? They had only one more day until the masque.

If he wanted to leave with Fulton's plans—and, preferably, Fulton—the ideal time would be tomorrow night, while everyone else was focused on the play. Which meant he had only one night and one day more with Emma. One night and one day to beg her pardon.

Quickening his pace, Augustus yanked open the door. One night and one day to—

"Oh!" said a very familiar voice.

Augustus blinked. Yes, his eyes were sore after staring at those plans, but he had never experienced a mirage before, and certainly not one so precise in every detail.

Emma stood in the open doorway, her hand poised as though to knock.

Her hair was shoved behind her ears in that way she had when she was either deep in thought or trying to work up her nerve. Her dress was wrinkled, splotched slightly with sweat stains and dusted in places with pollen from their interlude in the garden.

She stared at him, as shocked as he, her hand suspended in the air. If she continued the motion, she would hit him. If she did, he would probably deserve it.

"I am so sorry," he said, just as Emma dropped her hand and said all in a rush, "I was just looking for you."

"What I said before"—Augustus jumped in, anxious to say his piece before she could—"I had no right."

Whatever she had meant to say to him, his words shocked her silent. Her eyes searched his face. Augustus felt as though he were being sized up and unconsciously drew himself up straighter.

Emma regarded him intently, her expression serious. "You had no right," she agreed. "But that doesn't make you less right."

They stood on either side of the doorway, each waiting for the other to say something. Without her usual armor of frivolity, there were hollows in Emma's cheeks that Augustus had never noticed before. She still wore her paint, but he felt, somehow, as though he were seeing her scrubbed bare.

Augustus's throat worked. He had been on delicate missions before, missions in which life or death hinged on the turn of a phrase, but never before had he felt as though quite so much depended on the choice of a word.

"Perhaps," he said, and watched her eyelids flicker, watched her brace herself as though for some anticipated blow.

He held out a hand, his palm turned up, his fingers relaxed. It took all his will not to let them tremble.

"Perhaps," he said, and cleared his throat, "this might better be discussed inside?"

Emma's hand hovered for a moment at her side. He could see her eyes slide past him, to the tiny room beyond, assessing what he had said and what he was asking. Augustus held his breath and counted the seconds. He didn't know what he wanted, but he did know that if she dropped her hand and turned away, his life would be the poorer for it. He might have tried persuasion, patter, poetry, but some things were too important for words. He could only stand frozen, his hand outstretched.

Her lips pressed together and she dipped her chin in a movement barely recognizable as a nod.

"Yes," she said, and placed her hand in his. "Yes, I think that would be . . . best."

Closing his fingers around hers, Augustus drew her into the room, letting the door click shut behind her.

Chapter 27

The fierceness of the raging tide
Oft throws up treasures waves do hide;
In tempest-calm, these gifts we glean,
Through water darkly, now fully seen.
——Emma Delagardie and Augustus Whittlesby,
Americanus: A Masque in Three Parts

*H*is room was much smaller than hers.

It was scarcely large enough to contain a narrow bed, a spindly writing table, and a dressing stand with basin, ewer, and the mysterious accoutrements deemed necessary for the male toilette. The walls had been whitewashed rather than papered and there was no covering on the floor. A former dressing room or servant's room, it had only the smallest pretense of a window, allowing in just enough natural light to expose the dinginess of it all. Her own room, a floor down, was petite to say the least, but boasted fresh, patterned paper and a vaguely Pompeii-esque border along the ceiling.

Emma stepped inside, forcing herself to concentrate on the spindly legs of the writing desk, the graying white of the walls.

Behind her, she heard the door swing shut. It made the small room seem even smaller. The four walls closed in around them, boxing her and Augustus together, too close for comfort, the bed blocking them on one side, the dressing stand on the other. The heat of the day shimmered around her, trapped beneath the attic roof. She could feel the warmth of it in her cheeks, in her breast, in her hand. There was nowhere else to lead her. Why hadn't he let go?

Emma wriggled her wrist and Augustus released her hand, taking a step back, a movement that pressed him almost flush to the writing table. The chair wobbled on its narrow legs.

Emma made a show of looking about. "So this is how the bachelors lodge," she said.

The words sounded tinny in the expectant silence. Augustus accorded them all the attention they deserved. None.

"I was on my way to find you. To apologize."

Emma locked her hands loosely at her waist. "It seems we were on the same mission, then."

She would have liked to sit down, but the only options were the chair, which would have required wiggling past Augustus, or the bed.

The bed was far too much a bed.

"You? You have no need to apologize." Augustus rested a hand against the back of the chair, bracing himself. "Under the law, truth is always a defense to an accusation of defamation of character."

"In that case," Emma said, "you have no cause to apologize either. Everything you said about me, it was true." She hated saying it, but she forced the words out anyway. "You were right. I don't know what I want or where I want to be. I only know what I don't want."

"Marston?" suggested Augustus. His tone was light, but his eyes were intent.

"You were right about that, too. When it comes down to it, what do I have to say for myself?" The words tore up out of her chest, giving voice to truths she hadn't wanted to acknowledge, the sorts of truths that kept one up at four in the morning and took headache-inducing amounts of champagne to drown into slumber. "I have no useful function in anyone's life, least of all my own."

"Don't say that." Augustus took a step forward. His voice was low and urgent. "If anything I said made you think that you have no worth—then I deserve to be horsewhipped. Never, ever say that. Don't even think it. Don't you know—"

"It's not you, really," Emma said quickly, before he could blame himself further. "It's me. It wouldn't have hurt so much if I didn't already know it for myself." She made a face. "I know what I am."

"No," said Augustus flatly. "You don't." Somehow, he was holding her hands. Emma hadn't been aware of his taking them. "Shall I tell you what you are?"

"A flibbertigibbet?" volunteered Emma.

"A comet," he countered, his eyes burning as brightly as any flaming star. "Whatever you do, you make it blaze. You have more energy, more joy, than anyone else I know. What sort of function would you like to have? Do you want to meddle in politics, like Madame Murat? Have a brood of babies, like the younger Madame Bonaparte? What do they add that you don't? You can take even a third-rate masque and make it sparkle."

The passion in his voice unnerved her, made her warm in some places and wobbly in others and thoroughly disconcerted in all of them.

"I think that was Mr. Fulton's lightning machine," Emma said. "The sparkle, I mean."

Augustus gave her a quelling look. "Haven't you noticed the way people gather around you? Everywhere we go, everyone clamors for Madame Delagardie, to join in a game, to judge a contest, to read a poem. The only way to get you by yourself is to find you in your book room, and even then, the notes and flowers keep coming. You need an army of footmen to keep your acquaintances at bay."

Emma wordlessly shook her head. She was a habit with people, that was all. They knew her. She was convenient.

"You don't think so? You don't realize how much joy you give simply by being yourself?"

"So does a statue," said Emma stubbornly. "Or cut flowers in a vase."

"Marble collects moss. Flowers wither. They're decorative, passive. You're the least passive person I know. I'd like to see someone try to put you on a pedestal. You'd be off before you were on. They'd be left with an empty base and a deserted gallery."

Was that a good thing? Emma wasn't sure.

"Well . . ." she said, but Augustus wasn't done.

"You told me earlier that you're not my vision of Cytherea." Augustus's hands tightened on hers, holding her fast before she could pull away. "You were right. You're not Cytherea. Cytherea is—she's cold. If she shines, she shines the way ice shines. Her beauty chills what it touches. She's essentially untouchable. As for you . . ."

He paused, searching for the right words. Emma knew she should say something, should intervene, should potentially be offended, but she seemed to be frozen, caught in breathless expectation in the heat of the shimmering air, half fire, half ice, hot, then cold. If Cytherea was untouchable, what did that make her? She had never felt so touchable in her life. Her skin ached with it.

"Yes?" she said hoarsely.

"You . . ." Augustus's eyes slithered away from hers. "You transcend towers," he said grandly.

"Thank you," said Emma. "I think."

Augustus looked at her tenderly. "Just because I didn't render it in rhyme doesn't mean it wasn't a compliment."

"You did alliterate a bit there," said Emma shyly. Why did she suddenly feel shy? This was Augustus, for heaven's sake. Augustus. She ducked her head. "I shouldn't have called you a fainéant. It was unkind."

Augustus released her hands, straightening. Emma found herself with a very good view of the breast of his shirt. "Unkind, but not untrue."

"You work very hard at your poetry," protested Emma.

"My poetry is rubbish," he said brutally. She could see his chest move beneath the thin linen of his shirt as he shrugged. "It's not worth the paper it's printed on."

"That doesn't mean that you are," said Emma tentatively. "Rubbish, I mean."

"Aren't I?" His hair fell around his face as he looked down at her. Emma thought, absurdly, of fallen angels chained to rocks in hell. "Once I wanted to be a gadfly of the government. I was going to start a journal, write satirical political pieces, maybe even run for Parliament. Whatever I did, my words were going to count for something. And now, I find, they've come to this." His gesture encompassed his attire, the unfinished page on the writing desk, the narrow room.

"There's still time," said Emma. "I hear *Le Moniteur* is hiring."

"No," said Augustus. "If I were to do it, it would have to be back in England."

England. The thought of it took Emma aback with a force she hadn't expected. What would it mean for Augustus to go? No Augustus reciting silly poetry, no Augustus sprawled on the spare chair in her book room, no Augustus looking at her as though she were a comet who lit up the sky.

As a good friend, she could encourage him to go. But . . .

"Oh," said Emma.

"It's not on," said Augustus. "And do you know why? Because I'm too much of a coward to try. I've written nothing but this . . . doggerel for years now." His face twisted with self-mockery. "My pen's gone limp."

"You never know unless you try," said Emma softly, and couldn't help thinking that they might be talking about something more than politics or poetry. "No risk, no reward."

Augustus shook his head. "You were right, in every respect. I've become estranged from my family, shunned my friends, mooned after rainbows, and"—he paused, his face unreadable—"most unforgivable by far, I've done everything I can to offend and alienate the best thing that's ever happened to me."

Emma looked up at him, quizzically. "Jane?"

His lips quirked in something that was almost a smile. "You."

She was the best thing that had ever happened to him?

"You haven't alienated me," she said dumbly.

"But I have offended," he said. He looked down at her, his expression serious. "I don't even know where to begin begging your pardon."

Emma pressed a hand to his lips. "Don't. Please. There's no need."

Augustus caught her hand in his. "You have a generous spirit, Emma Delagardie." She could feel his breath against her palm, more intimate than a kiss. "But even generosity only goes so far."

"If this is about—if this is about that kiss . . ." Emma floundered.

There was a strange light in his deep brown eyes. "That kiss," said Augustus, "is the one thing I won't apologize for. I know I should say otherwise, but I can't. I'm not sorry I kissed you."

After weeks of working together, debating phrasing and parsing words, it wasn't wasted on Emma that he had said, "I kissed you." Not, *we kissed* or *the kiss happened* or any other twist of semantics that might absolve him from at least part of the responsibility.

"You're not?" said Emma.

"No." They were standing, she realized, very, very close together. His hand was still on her wrist, holding her fingers just away from his lips, his thumb resting on the point where her blood had begun to pound with betraying speed. "It may break all the rules of friendship and make me the worst sort of cad, but, no. I can't be sorry. I'm glad I kissed you. And if I had the chance, I would do it again."

The blood was pounding in her ears, turning his words to sounds heard through a seashell. She could feel them in her lips, her hands, her skin. This was what the poets couldn't put in their poetry, she thought dumbly, the rush of desire so fierce and pure it made one shake, all on the force of a word.

"You would?" she said breathlessly.

Augustus's lips turned up at the corners. "Is that an invitation?"

What if she said yes? Emma wondered wildly. What then?

He was so close, all he had to do was bend his head. There was no mistaking the light in his eye. It was something she hadn't seen in a very long time, desire and tenderness and uncertainty, all mixed together. It wasn't just the wanting that was making her fingers tingle and her chest tight, it was the caring.

And that was the truly scary bit.

"Do you want it to be?" Emma blurted out, and winced at her own gaucherie.

"What do you think?" he said.

"I don't know," Emma floundered.

She put out a hand to touch his arm, a gesture she had made a hundred times, a thousand times, but this time she flinched away from it at the last minute.

"I'm scared," she admitted. "I haven't felt this way about anyone since—"

No, not even with Paul. She had been young and naïve then, and dalliance had been a game, desire a toy to be played with. She hadn't known, as she knew now, the pleasures involved. And the pitfalls.

She looked wordlessly to Augustus, but he had no answers for her.

"I've never felt this way about anyone. Ever," he said. "You have me in terra incognita."

He wasn't the only one. Here be dragons, Emma knew. Dragons and sea serpents and monsters poised to swallow a heart whole. She could stay snugly on board, steering her barque back to safer waters—but, then, who knew what wonders she might miss? *No risk, no reward*, Augustus had said earlier. The words circled through her head like a nursery rhyme, in rhythmic cadence, like the pounding of her heart, beat by beat, thump by thump. No risk, no reward. No risk, no Augustus. What would happen if she embarked on an *affaire* with him? There would be storms, she knew, storms and tempests and doubts and broken compasses, but there might be marvels, too.

Emma very slowly lifted her head, gathering all her courage to meet his eyes. "Sail off the edge of the world with me?"

"I'm already there," he said, and his arms went around her, which was a very good thing, since Emma's knees didn't seem to be doing their duty anymore.

She reached up to him, her arms locking around his neck, his hair caught beneath her fingers, his chest pressed against hers, linen to linen, the thin fabric damped with sweat, hardly any barrier at all.

His kiss wasn't tentative at all, not this time. He kissed her as though he had always meant to kiss her, his body warm and steady against hers, keeping her from falling, keeping her safe. She tasted the lingering tang of coffee on his lips. He felt so solid, much more so than his languid disarray had suggested. Emma spread her hand flat against his back as he bent her backwards, feeling the play of muscles, the broad strength of him. His skin burned through the thin fabric of his shirt—or maybe she was the one burning.

Hands moved, tongues twined, bodies pressed together. Emma felt the writing desk at her back, the edge pressing into her buttocks. Without breaking the kiss, Augustus hitched her up, so that she was sprawled across his latest effusion, her back against the window, his tongue in her mouth and his fingers in her hair.

Augustus brushed kisses across Emma's closed eyes and down the bridge of her nose. Her familiar features were pinked with passion, hair tousled, lips swollen, cheeks flushed, her face turned trustingly up towards his. The sun fell from behind her, lighting her hair like a halo. An angel. His angel. He traced the curve of her cheek, the whorls of her ear, lowered his lips to echo the motion and felt her quiver at the touch. His America, his newfound land. Donne had known what he was about when he wrote that.

She is all Kings, all Princes I . . . Fragments of poetry—other people's poetry, good poetry—swirled around Augustus's brain. *If we had world enough and time* . . .

Only the Cavalier poets would do. Augustus pressed his lips to the sensitive spot behind Emma's ear and felt her shiver. The writing desk wobbled. How had they missed this for so long? How had they spent hour after hour together, writing, talking, and never thought of this? This had been right below his nose all this time. This, the little freckle beneath her right ear. This, the delicate line of her throat as she arched her neck. This, the way the breath sang between her lips as she sighed.

"An hundred years should go to praise, / Thine eyes and on thy fore-head gaze," Augustus murmured, brushing his lips across her closed eyes, along her cheekbones, down to her jaw.

Making a low, murmuring noise deep in her throat, she obligingly arched her neck for him, baring the delicate path along the side of her neck, down past her collarbone, all the way to the first swell of her breasts, where her bodice did more to tease than to cover.

Augustus grazed a knuckle along the low neck of her bodice, watching as her breasts rose and fell against the taut fabric, practically bare already. All it took was a twitch of the fabric—all right, perhaps a little more than a twitch, a slight wriggle—and she went from being daringly décolleté to bare. She was small but well formed, perfectly in proportion to herself.

"Two hundred to adore each breast," Augustus quoted hoarsely. He leaned down and touched a tongue to one nipple, feeling it pebble in response.

His hand began the long, slow slide from ankle to knee, beneath skirts, beneath petticoats, traveling along her silk stocking to the ribbon that held her garter in place. *"But thirty thousand to the rest—"*

He leaned in to kiss her again, but Emma pulled away, saying, very clearly and distinctly, "Marvel."

His finger traced the top of her stocking, the band where silk met flesh. "Yes," he agreed. "Quite marvelous."

She pulled back against his arm, pushing his hand away. "Andrew Marvel. 'To His Coy Mistress.'"

Not exactly in keeping with the mood, but, all right, points to her for knowing her seventeenth-century poets.

"Well spotted," Augustus murmured, and leaned forward to kiss her again, since her lips were so temptingly red and rosy and this had all been going quite well until . . .

"It's not your own," Emma said. The writing desk wobbled as she pushed back. She shoved her hair back behind her ears. "Those aren't your words."

"Not my words?" Augustus's brain was still keeping company with his libido. He couldn't help but notice that her bosom heaved very nicely and that she hadn't bothered to pull up her bodice.

Emma yanked up her bodice. Damn.

"You wrote poetry for Jane," she said, and bit down on her lip as though to keep herself from saying anything else.

Oh? Oh. A glimmer of comprehension broke through the fog of desire.

He took a deep breath. "My own words aren't good enough for you. My doggerel was good enough for—well, for an adolescent infatuation, but it's not good enough for you. You deserve better. You deserve the best."

"Marvel?"

"And Shakespeare and Donne and Scève and Ronsard."

Emma pressed her lips together in that way she had when she was thinking. At the familiar gesture, Augustus felt a rush of tenderness as disconcerting as it was surprising. Something in his head stirred and whispered, *Emma?*

"I've been wooed with Scève before," Emma said thoughtfully. "And Ronsard and du Bellay. I'd rather just have you. In prose, if need be." She looked up at him with that peculiar sort of frankness that was entirely hers, saying, "We did promise each other honesty."

I'm a British spy and I've been using you to get to your friend's plans.

There was a mad moment when Augustus was almost tempted to blurt it out, the whole damnable tangle. He wanted to tell her that he had been using her, but not anymore. That whatever that was, it had nothing to do with this. That he hadn't ever felt like this before and wasn't quite sure what he was feeling, but whatever it was, it meant that he wanted her with him for a very long time, not out of ploy or policy, but because she was Emma, and he had got rather accustomed to the Emma-ness of her, to the tilt of her head and the cadence of her voice and the sparkle and glitter of her paste jewels as she blazed her way through the room. He wanted to tell her that he thrilled to the crystalline ring of her laughter, that her bluntness intoxicated him, that her lack of self-deception was a revelation and an inspiration.

And then what? his thwarted libido murmured. Would this all happen before or after she told him he was crazy and/or stomped out of the room?

She looked so good, all warm and pink and tousled. All she was waiting for was the word, and all that could be his, the flushed flesh above the low neckline of her dress, the reddened lips that pressed together as she waited for his reply, the blue vein that flickered in the hollow of her throat, just waiting for his lips.

Revelations could wait.

"It's prose you want, then?" Augustus said huskily. "I can give you prose."

"That would be . . . nice," said Emma. Her eyes were dilated and her chest rose and fell rapidly beneath the barrier of her bodice.

Augustus brushed a finger lightly across one cheekbone, tracing the lines of her face. "You fascinate me," he said softly. "You confuse me. You intoxicate me."

Emma made a breathy little noise that wasn't quite a laugh. "I don't seem to have done anything to your vocabulary."

"Haven't you?" They were practically nose to nose. "I don't have the words to describe what you do to me, what you're doing to me right now. Do you want me to tell you how much I want you?"

Emma made a little noise in the back of her throat, and for an awful moment, Augustus thought she meant to say no.

She leaned forward, setting the desk wobbling. Her voice was husky as she said, "I'd rather you show me."

Lightning flashed and thunder rumbled, even though the sky outside was still blue and the sunlight, unconcerned, dawdled lazily on the corners of the desk. Augustus grabbed her so hard that he heard the breath rush out of her lungs in a whoosh.

"All right," croaked Emma. "That's one way."

She was laughing. Augustus had never seen anything so wonderful as that laughter.

"Hush, you," he said, and leaned forward to kiss her. "Don't you know mockery isn't conducive to passion?"

Emma wrapped her arms around his neck, pressing her body against his. "Really?" she said, and the bit of Augustus's brain that could still comprehend language vaguely registered the word.

"Mmm," said Augustus, into her neck. "I might be wrong."

She made a little mewing noise. Augustus reclaimed her lips as they staggered unevenly in the direction of the bed. There wasn't far to stagger.

"Bed?" he murmured.

"Bed," she agreed, and dropped down onto the coverlet, pulling him with her.

Something crinkled. And crinkled again.

Oh, hell.

Augustus froze as Emma rolled over and said curiously but without any of the alarm that was steadily mounting in his own chest, "Is there something under here?"

"It's nothing," he said quickly, and reached for her, but it was too late. Emma drew down the coverlet and pulled out Fulton's plans.

She looked up at him with confusion. "But aren't these . . . ?"

Chapter 28

I don't know what you're talking about," said Dempster.

Oh, didn't he? "My papers," I said, as much for Colin as Dempster. "Someone's been going through them. And my e-mail."

"I don't know why anyone would want to read your e-mail," said Joan, joining us on the stairs. I should have known she couldn't stay away. Her long skirt whispered against the stair treads. She smiled at Colin over my head. "It must be the strain of the academic life. Scholars are such . . . special people."

Delusional, that smile seemed to say. Americans. What can one expect of them?

I'd show her special.

"Ask your boyfriend," I said, my voice cold and hard. "Ask him what he's looking for. Ask him why he used you to get in here."

Just as he had used Serena before.

"Colin!" exclaimed Joan. "Tell her—"

"I warned you," Colin said to Dempster. "Not again."

"The film—" Dempster began, just as his girlfriend said something that included the phrase "obviously disturbed," before both were drowned out by a clangorous knell that echoed in my ears and made me catch at Colin's arm for balance. It was a horrible, metallic sound, and it seemed to go on and on, catching the guests in the hall in shimmering waves of sound.

In the corner of the hall, Cate, sans clipboard, was wielding a mallet against a brass gong with considerable vigor and more than a little relish. The tinkle of a fork against a glass would never have been heard in that din. The gong swept everyone away in its wake. The guests stopped gossiping, the waiters stopped circling. Even Joan shut her mouth, although she shot me a look that promised retribution later—and another one, at Dempster, that made me think that the extra-connubial bed wasn't going to be all that cozy that night.

An expectant hush settled on the room, broken only by the swish of fabric against the floor as someone shifted weight, the click of a glass against someone's ring, and then even those sounds ceased.

Dinner?

No. It was Micah Stone.

The film star sauntered into the room. The hiss and whisper of conversation faded to nothing beneath the click of his cowboy boots against the marble of the entryway. I was reminded, for no discernible reason, of Charles II making his way between bowing courtiers at Whitehall. Micah Stone had that same sort of lanky grace, that same indefinable saunter, the saunter of a man confident enough to lope rather than stride.

Stone was taller in real life than he appeared on screen. I'd thought it was usually the other way around. Maybe it was just that they paired him with particularly leggy leading ladies. Either way, he made Jeremy, clinging to his left elbow, seem short, stocky, and overdressed, even though Jeremy was a reasonably tall, reasonably fit man, dressed up by dressing down in dark slacks and sport coat. No sport coats for Stone. He was wearing jeans—acid washed—and a

T-shirt. It was, appropriately enough, a DreamStone T-shirt, emblazoned with the company's logo of a large rock. A dreaming rock, presumably.

"Hey!" he said, and everyone in the hallway gazed at him with rapt attention, as though that casual "hey" were the modern answer to "Friends, Romans, countrymen." His voice was low and deep and very generically American, neither the surfer drawl of the West Coast or the pseudo-English affectations of certain portions of the East. "I see a lot of familiar faces here. Thanks for making it out here—"

"To the ass end of nowhere," I heard someone whisper.

"—to historic Selwick Hall." Micah Stone grinned self-deprecatingly, to show he was being silly. Strangely, I felt myself grinning along. Maybe this was what they called charisma? "Where we'll be filming *Much Ado About You*. I hope you're all as excited about this project as I am."

"Very!" Jeremy assured him enthusiastically.

What a douche bag.

With a nicely calculated head tilt that indicated Jeremy without acknowledging him, Micah Stone said, in that same relaxed, carrying voice, "I'd particularly like to thank the Selwick family, who opened their home for all of us. We all know that having a bunch of film people around is no picnic"—polite titters, some simpers—"but the Selwicks have been nothing but generous."

Generous? That was a debatable term. The Selwicks were, in fact, being paid a hefty fee for the use of the hall, somewhat less impressive by being divided three ways, a fact I found massively unfair, given that Colin was the only one put out by it. Colin's share was being plowed back into the hall; Serena's to purchase a partnership in the gallery at which she worked; and Jeremy's—well, let's just say I didn't know what Jeremy did with his money and I didn't particularly want to know, although I'd be willing to bet a lot of it went to designer clothing and first-class airfare.

"I'd especially like to thank—"

Micah Stone paused, conducting a leisurely survey of the crowd. Jeremy drew himself up, pre-preening.

"I'd especially like to thank Colin Selwick, for taking us all in and doing it so graciously. Colin? Where are you, Colin?"

Wishing himself anywhere but here, if I knew my Colin.

Colin raised an unenthusiastic hand. He said flatly, "Think nothing of it."

Fifty-odd pairs of eyes lifted in our direction. But soft, what movie star from yonder hallway beckoned? We were only a modest five steps up, but it was enough to create a potentially unflattering angle. I resisted the urge to pull my skirt closer to my legs. Next to me, Joan lifted a hand to her perfectly coiffed hair, putting her best profile forward, sidling closer to Colin. Trollop.

Micah grinned up at the landing. "What are you doing all the way up there? Come on down so we can all give you a hand."

I made to step back, but Colin clamped my arm in his, leaving me with no choice but to come along with him. His grip was like a vise. Okay, I got it. He wasn't doing this alone. As we made our way down the stairs, I resisted the urge to do a QE II wave. Royalty might be trained to wave and walk at the same time, but I didn't trust my own small motor skills. Even if that might take some of the tension out of the evening, my doing a pratfall down the stairs.

We made our way through the hall, and the crowd parted for us as it had for Stone, celebrities by extension. I saw Serena press back into the doorway, making herself as small as possible. Joan's mouth was pursed in a moue of distaste. She was still elevated above the crowd, on the stairs, but the crowd had shifted and their attention with it.

"Is this Mrs. Selwick?" Micah Stone asked easily, holding out a hand to me.

"No," I said quickly, before Jeremy could. "I'm Eloise Kelly, official girlfriend in residence."

Micah Stone took my hand. "Nice to meet you, official girlfriend in residence." From the fringe of the group, Cate grinned at me and gave a little salute with her clipboard. Stone turned back to Colin. "Nice to finally meet you. Are you sure you wouldn't like a cameo in the film?"

Colin kept his smile in place, but it was the most unconvincing smile I had ever seen. "I don't perform to strangers."

"We're not strangers here," Jeremy rushed in. "We're family! And we'd like to think of DreamStone as part of that family."

"Uh, yeah," said Micah Stone, and I found myself liking him more and more, not just because he was a fellow American in a sea of Brits, but because he managed to cut through Jeremy's pretensions with two nondescript syllables.

If we were playing happy families, though, there was someone they'd forgotten.

"There's one more Selwick you still have to meet," I said.

Fine, I knew it wasn't any of my business, but hadn't the poor girl been squished enough by seeing her ex here with a new woman? The least I could do was make sure she was introduced to a dashing movie star. Even if Colin was still Not Speaking to her.

Stone leaned towards me, American to American. "Is this the one they keep in the attic?"

Give her a few more hours of this. . . . "No, this is the pretty one," I said firmly. I waved a hand in the air. "Serena!"

Serena detached herself reluctantly from the doorframe and made her way slowly forward. Even in the depths of despair, there was a grace about her. There was something about the bruised look around her eyes that made me think of fairy tales and the princesses condemned to dance night after night in the goblin hall beneath the castle. She had the same bewildered air about her as those poor, dancing princesses in my storybook, going through the motions under compulsion, but doing it very prettily all the same.

I could see Dempster behind her, on the stairs, watching. I marked

him down for later. If he thought he was getting off the hook for rifling through my notes, he had another think coming.

"My cousin, Serena, is part owner of the Selwick estate," Jeremy
jumped in, oozing confidentially towards Stone. Cousin . . . stepdaughter . . . But who was counting? He slid an arm around Serena's
shoulders, staking his claim. "Without her, DreamStone wouldn't
be here."

He had to remind everyone?

"Thanks, Serena," said Micah Stone. In his deep voice, the name
was a caress. I could just hear the squealing teenyboppers. "Nice to
meet you. I'm glad they saved the best Selwick for last."

Serena murmured something inaudible, but socially correct.

"Nice place you have here," said Stone.

"We like it," said Jeremy, stepping in front of Colin. "And we
hope you do, too."

I had to give Colin lots of credit. He kept his mouth shut and held
on to his temper, even though he was so tightly wound that if you had
put a cuckoo in his mouth, he could have struck the hour. As for
Serena, she seemed to shrink in on herself even more. Next time I
looked, there would be nothing more than a walking pashmina,
with no Serena in it at all.

I looked around longingly. Where was that champagne, again?

Stone looked from Colin to Jeremy and came to his own conclusions. Gesturing to Cate and her clipboard, he cut the meet-and-greet
short with a seemingly casual, "Shall we head to dinner?"

Under that laid-back exterior, Stone was bright enough to be
aware that something was going on, and he didn't want any part of
it. As he raised his hand, I spotted a hemp bracelet on one wrist, the
rough strands woven into a braid, like a child's lower school art project. The entire outfit was designed to make him look young, un-
threatening, laid back. But, so far, he was doing a pretty good job of
handling Jeremy. I wondered how much of him was for real.

I looked at Joan, artificially blond, clinging to Dempster's arm; at

Serena, so weak and yet strong enough to sell Colin down the river; and then, of course, Jeremy, our own private Mephistopheles. Everyone putting on a false face, playing a role, perpetually engaged in a masque without a script. There was only one person I could trust to be exactly what he was: Colin. I felt a surge of gratitude towards him. He might not always be the easiest person to deal with, but I knew that he was what he was. Always. Whatever he said, he meant.

At one point, I had wondered if Colin, like Augustus Whittlesby, was a secret agent, feigning one thing, doing another. I had searched for clues and double meanings. But Colin? I couldn't believe that of him. He was, whatever his silences, too fundamentally honest.

I glanced at Colin's profile as we all moved down the hallway, clustered around the lanky form of Micah Stone, trailing PAs and party guests behind us like streamers. I was going to have to tell him about the job offer, sooner rather than later. If he was honest with me, I should be with him. Wasn't that part of the growth of the relationship, sharing problems rather than keeping them to oneself? I was very good at the whole getting-him-to-share-his-problems-with-me bit, not so good at confiding my own.

After dinner, I promised myself. When we were both mellow with good wine and the relief of the hideous evening being done. Then I would sit him down, tell him my dilemma, and see if he could help me find a way out of it. As I knew from Augustus and Emma, waiting for these things to come out of their own accord was always a mistake.

"Huh?" I said. Someone was talking to me.

I looked around and saw various expressions of horror and disbelief. Cate was stifling a nervous giggle behind one hand. Jeremy looked miffed, but, then, Jeremy generally looked miffed where I was involved.

Oh. It was Micah Stone. And he wasn't used to being ignored.

Of course, of the lot of them, the one person who didn't seem to mind my not paying attention to Micah Stone was Micah Stone.

"Sorry!" I said brightly. "I was thinking about something else."

"Eloise," said Jeremy, "is an academic. Her mind is often elsewhere."

"Yeah?" said Micah Stone. "What do you study?"

"English history," I said. I made a gesture that encompassed the hallway down which we were walking. "This."

"Eloise," said Jeremy again, "is only here for a short time."

For some reason I couldn't quite explain, the hairs on the back of my neck prickled. I know it's a cliché, but clichés exist for a reason. Sometimes they're true.

"I'm here on a fellowship," I explained to Stone. A fellowship that was about to run out.

"I imagine you'll miss all this," Jeremy said meaningfully. "When you go back to America."

"That's not for some time yet," piped up Serena, the first thing she had said. I felt a surge of gratitude towards her. "Isn't it?"

I could feel Colin looking at me. I didn't know what to say. "Um . . . The lease on my flat runs out pretty soon," I admitted. "I need to do something about that. Anyway. This is the first time I've ever seen a film crew!"

As a diversion, it didn't do much to divert.

"When?" asked Colin.

"June. June 1." Only two weeks away. I scratched at a suddenly itchy patch on my arm. "I'm sure I can get them to let me renew. Are most on-location places like this?" I asked Stone desperately.

"Some have worse plumbing," he said, and we all obediently laughed. He turned to Colin, having correctly marked him out as the man of the house. "We'll try to stay out of your hair as much as possible while we're here."

Jeremy looked distinctly displeased.

"And we'll try to stay out of yours," I said.

"Thanks," said Stone, and seemed to mean it.

"Do you have to redo a lot of takes because of people waving at the camera?" I asked curiously. Thank goodness for the change of subject. Whatever Stone's next movie, even if it was kung fu meets Marlowe with rappers, I was going to watch it. At the theatre. For full price.

"You don't even want to know," said Stone.

"Will you be able to stay that long?" Jeremy broke in.

Both Stone and I looked at him.

"Being in the movie, I kind of have to be here," said Stone, as to a slow child. I could see Colin's lips twitch. Phew. A few more digs at Jeremy, and Colin might even be reconciled to the presence of the film crew. I could have hugged Micah Stone. That is, if I hadn't thought that would make Colin become unreconciled.

"I meant Eloise," Jeremy said, his voice smooth, so smooth that one almost missed the ratty edge underneath. "I hear congratulations are due. On your teaching position."

"Teaching position?" said Colin.

"At Harvard," I said distractedly. How in the hell had Jeremy known? "I've been offered the head teaching fellow slot for 10B. Modern Europe. I haven't said yes," I added quickly.

"Or no?" said Jeremy. In his black turtleneck and dark gray sport coat, he reminded me of a modern update of a medieval woodcut of a demon taunting some hapless soul. He had that same sort of smug look about the mouth. If he had a pitchfork, he would have been poking me with it.

"You're the one," I said. "You're the one who's been going through my notes."

"I don't know what you're talking about," said Jeremy, just as Dempster had, but whereas Dempster had been genuinely confused, Jeremy seemed just a little too pleased with himself.

Micah Stone moved slightly sideways, disassociating himself from the lot of us.

"Yes, you do," I said with confidence. There was a sick feeling in the pit of my stomach. I didn't want to look at Colin, not now that he knew I had been lying to him—well, if not lying, then not being to-tally forthcoming. "You went through my notes. You read my e-mail. Why?"

Jeremy said nothing. He just kept smiling.

"Christ," said Colin, and we all looked at him, even Micah Stone. Colin was staring straight at Jeremy, disbelief and disgust writ large across his face. "You're still looking for it, aren't you?"

Whatever it was, Serena knew what they were talking about. She edged out from under Jeremy's arm. Cate raised both eyebrows at me over her clipboard. I shook my head. I had no idea.

"It?" I ventured, not quite touching Colin's arm.

Colin looked down at me, and I felt my breath release in a silent sigh of relief. Whatever else, his disgust wasn't for me. I put my hand on his arm and his hand closed over it, warm and solid.

"Why don't you tell her, Jeremy," he said. "Since you find the topic so absorbing."

Jeremy wasn't having any of it. For the moment, he seemed to have forgotten the imperative to suck up to Micah Stone. He folded his arms across his chest. "It's as much mine as it is yours."

"If it existed," countered Colin. "Which it doesn't."

"It?" I repeated.

"Don't look at me," said Micah Stone.

"Why else would you bring *her* here?" Jeremy nodded at me. "I know what you're after."

"Oh, do you?" What went on between us in our bedroom was strictly between me and Colin.

Jeremy dismissed me with a glance. "The old woman's in on it, too."

"That 'old woman' is your grandmother," Colin said tensely. "The woman who raised you. You might show a little respect."

"This is all very entertaining," said Stone, "but we have food get-ting cold. Anyone want to tell me what's going on?"

Colin looked at Jeremy. Jeremy looked at Colin. Serena looked at her shoes. They were very cute shoes—Manolos, unless I missed my guess—but, still.

I sighed. "He," I said, pointing at Jeremy, "has been going through my notes and my e-mail, looking for something."

"For the plans," said Colin.

For a weird moment, past and present collided.

"The plans for the submarine?" I blurted out.

"Er, no," said Colin, giving me a weird look. "The plans to the house."

"O-kay," said Stone.

"Not just any plans," said Jeremy. "*The* plans. Why else would you bring in a historian, but to find them? I know what you're after."

"I'm after dinner," said Micah Stone pleasantly. "Anyone else coming?"

"I am!" said Cate, waving her clipboard. "And I have the seating chart."

"You just want it for yourself," Jeremy sneered. "That's what this is all about."

"For the last time," said Colin, his voice cracking with frustration. "It. Doesn't. Exist."

I couldn't take it anymore. I stepped between the two men. "What doesn't exist?" I demanded.

They were too busy glaring at each other to answer me. Serena's voice piped up, unnaturally high in the sudden silence.

"The lost treasure of Berar."

Chapter 29

Betrayed, betrayed, and all dismayed,
Filled now with fears not soon allayed,
For treachery at last will out,
And with it pain and hurt and doubt.
—Emma Delagardie and Augustus Whittlesby,
Americanus: A Masque in Three Parts

ut aren't these . . . ?"

Emma's brow wrinkled as she drew out the papers from beneath the coverlet. She didn't recognize the specific mechanism, but she knew Mr. Fulton's distinctive hand. Her muddled brain was slow to make sense of what she was seeing. It wasn't the sketch for the wind machine, and it certainly wasn't the steamship, but it was quite decidedly Mr. Fulton's.

What were Mr. Fulton's plans doing in Augustus's bed?

If they were back at Mme. Campan's, she would assume it was someone's version of a practical joke. Not that Augustus would have been at Mme. Campan's, being male, or that they would have been in this position.

"How bizarre!" she said, and looked up at Augustus. "These are Mr. Fulton's. I wonder how they got—?"

"Emma," Augustus said.

He wasn't smiling. He wasn't perplexed. Instead, there was a grim determination on his face that Emma had never seen there before. It made him look like a different person. Like a stranger, wearing Augustus's face.

Emma drew back, holding the plans to her chest.

"What is it?" she asked. "Why are you looking like that? It's just someone's joke, I'm sure."

He levered himself up into a sitting position, with a brusque, abrupt motion. "It's not a joke." There was a note of grim finality in his voice entirely at odds with the situation. "Emma—"

"Yes?" It was still stifling hot in the room, but Emma felt cold, cold and alarmed without being quite sure why. She looked up at him hopefully, far too conscious of her own disarray, of the sudden removal from intimacy to distance. "Whatever it is, surely it can't be all that bad."

"Mmph," said Augustus enigmatically.

Emma heard paper crinkle and realized she was crushing Mr. Fulton's plans between her fingers.

"You're beginning to scare me," she said, only half jokingly.

"What I have to tell you," Augustus said, "places the power of life or death in your hands. Not only my life," he added, "but those of others as well."

The words ought to have sounded melodramatic. They didn't. He spoke them in a simple, matter-of-fact tone that sent a chill down Emma's spine.

Pressing her lips together, she nodded to show that she understood, even though she didn't understand, not one bit.

Augustus looked at the documents in Emma's lap. "Those papers didn't get there by accident. I put them there."

"But why?" she asked.

Augustus took a deep breath and lifted his eyes to hers. "Because I am—and have been for some time—an agent for the English government."

"An agent," Emma repeated. Her mind scrabbled uselessly with the word. She had an agent. He managed her property for her. Somehow, she didn't think that was the sort of agent to which Augustus referred, not given the way he was looking at her, as though he had just dragged his guts out to be pecked by particularly vicious vultures. Not just an agent. An agent for the English government. Under ordinary circumstances, that might mean any number of things. But not now, not in a time of war, with all official diplomatic and commercial communication between the two countries forbidden. "You mean a spy?"

"I prefer master of inquiries," said Augustus.

Emma gaped at him. There he sat, his long hair curling around his face, the neck of his shirt untied where she had untied it, looking so normal, so familiar, and yet so ineffably different. It was something in his expression that had changed, something in the way he held himself.

"You're not—this is not—" Emma floundered. "You mean it."

"Every word," he said.

"But—" How could that be? He was a fixture of the Parisian scene. He had been here a good ten years or more. Did that mean for ten years, he—Emma's mind shied away from the thought. "Then, your poetry . . ."

"A front," he said quietly. "And a code."

Through a glass, darkly, she could remember standing with him in Bonaparte's new gallery in the Louvre Palace. She could hear her own voice, in echo, saying, *It's all an act, isn't it? You're much more sensible than you sound.* He had been taken aback, but only for a moment, before he had answered, oh so glibly, that patrons prefer their poets poetical. And she had believed him.

"That's why you sound one way in public and another in private. It's not just because your patrons expect a poet to sound poetical."

He bowed his head in acknowledgment.

"When I realized that you weren't what you claimed to be, weren't you afraid I might find you out?"

Augustus studied her face for a moment. "No," he said gently.

The word hit Emma like a slap across the face.

"No?" she echoed, knowing that in it was encapsulated a worse insult than she could immediately comprehend. She forced out a laugh. "No, of course not. Why would I? Not silly Madame Delagardie? You must have thought me such a fool."

"I don't think you a fool."

Didn't he? Emma pressed back against the wall, the thin pillow bunched against her back. He had known she would never figure it out on her own. And she hadn't. She wouldn't have. Not even now. He might have given her a ridiculous story about the plans—no idea how they got there, part of a prank, insulation for the cold nights—she would have believed any of it, just as she had believed him before. Emma wrapped her arms around herself to stop herself from shaking.

"Why are you telling me this now?" she asked shrilly.

"Because we promised each other honesty," Augustus said simply.

Honesty? Emma stared at him, at his familiar-strange face, at the deep brown eyes regarding her so steadily and so sadly, and felt a burning rage boil up inside her. He had lied to her. He had lied to her about everything and he dared to speak to her about honesty?

Nothing, nothing at all was as she had thought it to be. Her life, her life as she had known and experienced it, wasn't what she had believed it to be. It was all upside down and inside out and all because this man, this treacherous, lying, treacherous—she had already used "treacherous," hadn't she? It didn't matter. The outcome was the same, whatever she called it. She had been deliberately deceived, deceived and misled.

Seen through this new lens, seemingly innocuous events took on a sinister hue. She remembered Augustus, uninvited, offering his services with the masque. Augustus, again uninvited, invading her salon. Augustus, always attentive, always solicitous, hinting that their best work would be done if he was to accompany her to this salon or that party.

"You were the one who sought me out about the masque," she said, her voice shaking. "Not the other way around. You were the one who insisted we needed to work together. Why?"

He didn't even try to deny it. "I had been told that Bonaparte had a new weapon he was testing. Here. This weekend."

"I see," said Emma, and for the first time she finally did. "You needed me to get to Malmaison."

Augustus nodded.

Emma's voice went up. "All of this"—the weeks of work, the cozy tête-à-têtes in her study, his supposed concern for her health and well-being—"you did all of this for an invitation to Malmaison."

"Not all," said Augustus, and his voice was so low she could hardly hear it.

"You used me," Emma said wonderingly. "You used me and I didn't even know it." It would be amusing if it weren't so awful, so awful and so painful. She lifted her chin and said, conversationally, "You're much better at it than Georges."

Augustus flinched. "It's not like that, Emma. I promise—"

"*Don't.*" Her voice crackled through the room, surprising them both. Emma pressed her hands together, so hard she could feel her knuckles crack. "Don't promise me anything. I don't want promises. Not from you."

Augustus leaned forward. "You have every right to be angry. But at least hear me out. There were reasons—"

She held up a hand to forestall him, her mind working furiously. "You wanted Mr. Fulton's plans. You knew they would be in the summerhouse. That's why you wanted to talk to me today, wasn't it? Not because you were worried I might be marrying Kort. You just needed me to get to the summerhouse."

The guilt on his face was all the answer she needed.

Emma felt tears stinging her eyes and blinked them fiercely away. She wouldn't cry for him. He wasn't worth crying for.

"I'm right, aren't I?"

"That was part of the reason." There were lines on Augustus's face that hadn't been there before. "I shouldn't have involved you. I know that. At the beginning, yes. That was different. But now, once I—" He broke off, seemingly at a loss. "I shouldn't have done it. It wasn't fair to you. It wasn't fair to us."

Us? What us? There was no us. "I wouldn't have wanted our friendship to get in the way of your plans," said Emma politely.

"It's not—" Augustus pressed his palms against his eyes. She had him on the defensive now. Shouldn't that make her feel better? There was a lump in Emma's throat that wouldn't go away when she swallowed. Augustus drew in a deep breath. "Today at the summerhouse, you had me turned so topsy-turvy that I completely forgot why I was meant to be there. I forgot the plans. I forgot everything but you."

Emma drew her legs up under her. "How very inconvenient for you."

"I didn't want to deceive you," he said. "Trust me that far, at least. There were things I couldn't tell you, things I wasn't allowed to tell you. But everything else—everything we've done together, everything I've said to you—Emma, that much is real."

"Everything we've done together?" Emma hugged her knees. "You mean when you were pretending to be a poet in need of employment? When you were lying to me about your motives? When you were using me to get into Malmaison?"

"It's not like that," Augustus said. He dashed his hair out of his eyes. "I mean, it was like that. In the beginning. But not since I've got to know you. Not since you've come to mean so much to me."

Emma lifted her chin, contempt dripping from her voice, as much for herself as for him. "You don't need to lie to me. I'll keep your secret for you."

Augustus blinked as though she had slapped him. "This isn't about that. I wouldn't—"

He caught himself, by which Emma inferred that, indeed, he would, and probably had. The thought made her feel vaguely queasy. How many other women had he romanced for the sake of the information they might bring him? How many lonely widows had he kissed into adoring silence?

"Everything I said about you is true. Our time together, in your book room—working together—I've never felt— Oh, Christ. I'm making a muck of this."

Augustus leaned forward, his eyes earnest on her face.

A lie, Emma reminded herself, just like everything else. Men could lie with their eyes as well as their lips, and Augustus was an expert at both.

"You feel like home to me," he said. "I've never been happier than I've been with you. You have a way of making everything—well, better. Brighter."

"But not bright enough to see through you," Emma said brittlely.

Fulton's plans lay discarded on the coverlet, reminding her forcibly of her almost-lover's real objectives. Not love, but politics and policy and the great games of nations.

"Emma," he said, and the sound of her name on his lips made something curl up and whimper inside her. "No matter what else, I think you're wonderful."

With that and ten sous, she could buy a ride down the Seine.

"Georges thinks I'm wonderful, too," said Emma woodenly. "When he wants something from me."

Augustus drew back. "Don't compare me to Marston."

"Why not?" asked Emma harshly. "I fail to see any difference."

Why was she even still here? Eve must have been equally intrigued by that blasted serpent. And Augustus—Augustus didn't even have an apple to offer her. Only his regard, and now she knew what that was worth.

She scrambled off the bed, being careful to steer clear of Augustus in the process. The sight of the tousled sheets made her feel obscurely soiled. Used. Did he really think she would believe him, after that? Did he think she was that gullible, that easily led? That starved for the pretense of affection?

The answer to all of which, of course, was yes.

Folding her arms across her chest, Emma looked down at him. "These plans of yours might be quite important, indeed, for both of you to think I'm wonderful in one week."

Augustus's head lifted, suddenly alert. "Marston knows about the plans?"

"Oh, yes," said Emma airily, shaking out her dress with more than necessary force. "He wants them, too. He told me it's so he can fund our future together. I seem to be very much in demand these days. Such a pity it's all about Mr. Fulton's submarine."

"His what?"

Somehow, that was the last straw. Emma suppressed a wild urge to laugh. "You didn't even know. All this and you didn't even know what it was for." He looked at her and she said, "It's a submarine. A boat that sails under the water."

There. She hoped he was happy.

No, actually, she hoped he was very unhappy.

He didn't look it, though. He was a million miles away, his eyes unfocused, his mind turning. "A boat that sails under the water," he repeated.

She should have been immune to betrayal by now, but something about it made her stomach twist. She didn't exist for him anymore, she could tell. His mind was entirely on the information, the information he had bought off her so carelessly and so cruelly.

He slapped the coverlet with the flat of his hand. "That's what it is. That's how they were planning to get rid of the ships guarding the Channel. They send a boat under the water, where no one can see it. It's brilliant."

Emma pasted on her most brittle social smile. "So delighted to have been of assistance. Good day."

"Wait!" Augustus grabbed for her hand. Emma jerked out of reach. "Emma, please, try to understand. This is larger than you or me."

Yes, she imagined the completed submarine probably was.

"There are lives at stake," he said. "You know Bonaparte. You've seen where his ambition has led him. He won't stop. He's marched over half of Europe, laying it to waste. He's looted Italy for its treasures. He's made himself Emperor. England is the last defense against his ambitions."

His words brought with them an unsettling echo of her conversation with Hortense. It caught Emma off guard, it made her doubt—but just for a moment.

She looked at him coldly. "What do I care for England?"

"If England falls," said Augustus, catching her gaze and holding it, "what next? How would you feel to see your own New York overrun by French soldiers, your family tossed from their home, your property confiscated, and your government reordered? Bonaparte must be stopped."

He spoke with such absolute confidence that, for a moment, Emma could almost see it. She could see Bonaparte on the patio of Belvedere, the Consular guard lolling about the cookhouse, Caroline greedily sorting through her mother's jewelry, lifting grandmother's brooch to watch it sparkle in the sunlight, then tossing it aside as a trumpery thing, hardly worth looting.

Absurd, of course. Bonaparte was a friend to America. At least, for the moment. Emma felt a vague and unjustifiable sense of unease. But that was just what Augustus wanted, wasn't it? To shift the blame onto someone else.

"Because the cause is honorable," said Emma slowly, "or because you believe it to be so, does that mean the means are justified?"

Augustus lifted his eyes to hers. "I thought so once. Sometimes, though, the cost is just too high."

Emma's eyes slid past him, to the tousled bed, where, only half an hour before, they had dropped, entangled.

"But you paid it anyway," she said.

She could see his Adam's apple move up and down as he swallowed. "I had no choice. What would you have me do?"

You could have chosen me, she wanted to say, idiotically, illogically. You didn't have to lie to me. You didn't have to use me.

At least, she told herself, averting her eyes from the bed, at least she had found out before they brought matters to fruition. Better to know before she made herself truly vulnerable by going to bed with him.

Who was she fooling? Emma would have laughed if she could, but she was afraid the bitterness of it might burn her, bubbling up like acid, eating through her chest. She was already vulnerable. She might not have slept with him, but she had opened herself to him in every other way. She had confided in him, shared with him, trusted him.

How naïve she had been! And how very foolish she was. Even now, wanting to believe him, wanting to exonerate him.

All lies.

"Give me a chance to redeem myself," he said hoarsely. "Please, Emma."

Emma looked down at him. He was still seated on the edge of the bed, his hands pressing hard into the mattress on either side of him, leaving impressions like wounds, Fulton's plans crumpled and abandoned on the coverlet behind him. Such flimsy things to cause so much bother.

"I won't betray you," she said. "But don't expect me to talk to you."

Her legs felt like lead as she turned and moved towards the door, concentrating on every step, every movement. Her body felt unfamiliar to her; the walls and floor were out of proportion; everything was awkward and strange.

The bed rustled. "Emma. Emma, wait." She could hear the bed

ropes creak as Augustus levered himself to his feet. "There's something else I have to tell you."

Emma didn't turn around. "There's nothing else you can possibly have to say to me."

She twisted the knob of the door. The metal was warm beneath her fingers, worn smooth with use. Time did that, they said. It smoothed off rough edges and healed wounds. Or so they said. What they didn't talk about were the scabs it left behind.

"Wait, please," Augustus pleaded. "Just a moment. Is that too much to ask?"

Emma didn't wait to see if he would follow. She pulled open the door of the room. The hallway was empty, the rooms lining it deserted as their occupants frolicked in the sunshine.

"Emma—" Augustus's voice sounded very far away. He spoke in English in his urgency. "Emma, I think I might be in love with you."

"Too late," she said, and sent the door swinging shut behind her.

Chapter 30

When plots we lay and plans we set,
The more we feign, the leave we get;
When first we practice to deceive,
Our lies catch us in a tangled weave.
—Emma Delagardie and Augustus Whittlesby,
Americanus: A Masque in Three Parts

"Mr. Whittlesby?" It took several moments for Augustus to realize that someone was speaking to him, and still more for the source of the voice to register. Jane's serene smile was beginning to look a little ragged around the edges as she said, "You had promised me a word about my lines."

"Of course, my pulchritudinous princess," Augustus said mechanically. Emma was on the other side of the room, sharing a coffeepot with the soon to be former American envoy to France, the elder Mr. Livingston. She was not looking at Augustus. It had been nearly twenty hours since they had last spoken. Not that Augustus was counting. "Nothing would give me greater pleasure."

"One would never be able to tell," murmured Jane.

"I beg your pardon." Augustus fluttered his sleeves in the old style, but the move felt forced. "Affairs of verse have weighed heavily upon me."

Affairs, but not affairs of verse.

Emma had kept her word; there had been no midnight raids on his bedroom by the Ministry of Police. She had kept her word in other ways as well. With the masque rapidly approaching, she had managed to ever so subtly pretend he didn't exist. Oh, yes, she said the right things, made the right noises about being terribly excited about the performance and so very grateful to Mr. Whittlesby for his expert assistance with the script, but she said it in her society voice, glib and meaningless, as if he were merely the hired poet the world believed him to be.

There was only an hour left until the masque. The primary members of the cast, with the exception of Jane, had already made their way to the theatre, to be outfitted and assume their roles each in their own individual style. Miss Gwen had last been seen marauding somewhere out back, a ragtag band of pirates trailing along behind her. Bonaparte was in his council chamber, closeted with the cream of the Admiralty, while the remainder of the party, those involved in neither playacting nor policy, partook of coffee and cakes in the drawing room prior to the evening's promised spectacle. There was to be an alfresco supper served after the performance, supper and a fireworks display reputedly a secret but already known to everyone.

The younger Mr. Livingston was already in the theatre, assuming his theatrical breeches, but the elder Mr. Livingston was partaking of coffee. Marston, Augustus noticed, was also hovering near, but never quite next to, Emma. Augustus scowled. It went unnoticed by either party. Emma had her gaze resolutely fixed on her cousin Robert, as he waxed lyrical about the benefits of the territory of Louisiana, the purchase he had negotiated with Bonaparte.

Blast it all, no one was that fascinated by the Mississippi River.

Jane shook out her script, wafting it underneath Augustus's nose.

"It's this rhyme," she said loudly. "It doesn't quite scan." In a softer voice, she added, "I have promising tidings."

"Of what?" murmured Augustus, rubbing his nose. "My dear lady, you have got the pronunciation wrong. If you simply change the stress on the last vowel, you will find it rhymes perfectly well."

"How inventive!" exclaimed Jane, then dropped her voice. "Our inventor. He is, it seems, dangerously disaffected with the current regime." And then, more loudly, "But doesn't that change the meaning of the word?"

"Oh, fair one, have you not heard of the term poetic license?" Augustus bent his head over the script. Good God, they had written drivel, he and Emma. But what fun they had had doing it. Those long afternoons in her book room, laughing over a particularly ridiculous turn of phrase . . . Augustus yanked himself back to the present. "Will he defect?"

"I grant you no license, Mr. Whittlesby, poetic or otherwise, save those accorded by good manners," said Jane severely. "All it will take is a word in his ear. I heard him speaking to Emma yesterday."

Emma. Automatically, Augustus's eyes sought her out. She was still seated by the elder Mr. Livingston, partaking of coffee from one of Mme. Bonaparte's delicate china cups. She wore one of her extravagant costumes, white satin decorated with silver flowers embroidered around glittering diamond centers, but, for once, her demeanor failed to echo the sparkle of her costume. There was an unaccustomed fragility about her, in the delicate bones of her shoulders, in the hollows below her cheekbones.

"Yesterday," Augustus repeated. "Yesterday?"

"Yes, in the theatre," said Jane, frowning at him. Inattention was not acceptable. Jane preferred to say her piece only once. "He reiterated his concerns to Mr. Livingston this morning."

Yesterday. Augustus remembered Fulton's mutinous expression as he stormed out of the summerhouse. If he hadn't been so rattled by Emma, if he had stopped to consider the ramifications of that then . . .

"Livingston," added Jane, "counseled caution, at least until his official term as envoy is done. Mr. Fulton seemed disinclined to heed him."

If he had had his wits about him, would there have been any need to steal the plans?

If he had spoken to Mr. Fulton then—subtly, cleverly—there would have been no need to steal the plans. There would have been no need to puzzle over them. There would have been no need to hide them beneath his coverlet. If the infernal plans hadn't been beneath his coverlet . . .

Emma would have needed to be told sooner or later, Augustus argued with himself. Given his imminent departure for England, the operative word was "sooner."

But did it have to be just then?

His body was firmly of the opinion that it had been very poor timing, indeed.

"I infer that," said Jane, "from the fact the Mr. Fulton was already packing his baggage, even though the party does not end until tomorrow. When I saw him, he was tearing apart the summerhouse, looking for his plans."

Augustus straightened. "Looking for his plans?"

Jane regarded him levelly. "They seem to have gone missing."

The careful construction wasn't wasted on Augustus. He had just been scolded, in the most imperceptible of fashions.

"No, they haven't," Augustus said grimly. They would have to find Fulton, find him and bring him over before he could make a scene. "But if you think he can be—"

"Insupportable!" The door to the drawing room banged open. "Utterly insupportable!"

Mr. Fulton was far from his usual dapper self. His curly hair was in disarray, his jacket misbuttoned.

"You were saying?" murmured Jane.

"Damn," muttered Augustus.

Fulton made a beeline for the older Mr. Livingston. "I wish to make a formal complaint," he announced.

With his jowls jowly and his coat pleasantly creased, Livingston looked like an affable country squire, but the warning look he gave Fulton belied his easygoing air. "Let's just discuss this ourselves, shall we?" he said comfortingly. "Have a cup of coffee, Robert. Or would you prefer chocolate?"

"I don't want coffee, or chocolate. My plans." The word came out as a lament, Hecuba crying for Troy. "My plans. They're gone."

Emma sat silently, her head down over her coffee cup, her face hidden. Horace de Lilly paused in his game of cards. Marston drifted closer.

"I call this a travesty," said Fulton, refusing the chair Livingston offered him. "Our negotiations may have come to a standstill, but simply to appropriate the fruits of a man's labor— Not that it should surprise anyone! The very art on the walls—"

Livingston neatly cut him off before he could say anything that might cause an international incident. "Are you sure they're gone, Robert?" he said soothingly. "Might you not have misplaced them?"

"No," said Fulton firmly. "I know where they were and they're not there anymore."

Emma lifted her head. "I have them," she said flatly.

Both men turned to look at her in surprise.

"You?" said Mr. Livingston.

Emma set down her coffee cup with a distinct clink. She had missed the center of the saucer. Augustus could hear it rattling as it rocked back and forth.

"Yes," she said.

Having made her decision, she wasn't going to do it by halves. Her back straightened and her eyes fixed on her cousin, wide and blue and guileless. She didn't look at Augustus, but Augustus knew she was aware of him, as he was of her.

As Augustus watched, she went on, "I am so sorry, cousin Robert,

Mr. Fulton. You must have left them backstage when you helped me with the wave machine. I stumbled upon them and put them away for you." She made a self-deprecating face. "And then I forgot to give them to you. I feel so terribly foolish."

It wasn't a brilliant performance. She was too stiff, too self-conscious, but Livingston and Fulton were too caught up in their relief over the safe return of the plans to notice. Did anyone else? Jane, certainly. Her eyes flickered from Augustus to Emma and back again, her expression assessing. But other than she . . . No. Augustus didn't think so. They were safe. Because of Emma.

"In that case . . ." said Mr. Livingston, obviously relieved. It was no small thing to have to accuse an emperor of appropriating other peoples' property, even if he had and did. "Crisis averted, I believe, Robert?"

"Hardly a crisis." Slightly red about the ears, Mr. Fulton tucked his chin into his cravat. "I shouldn't have reacted so strongly. But it is a relief to know they haven't gone astray. I spent a great deal of time on that project."

"I could get them for you now if you like. . . ." Emma pushed back her chair and made as though to rise.

Mr. Fulton put out a hand to forestall her. "There's no urgency. I know you have a great deal to do in the theatre before tonight."

"Don't you mean *you* have a great deal to do in the theatre to-night?" Emma teased. "I'm relying on you to run that brilliant mechanism for me, Mr. Fulton. I shall just sit in the audience and applaud wildly at every clap of thunder."

"And drown out my thunder, clap by clap?" protested Mr. Fulton. As an attempt at banter, it was weak. Mr. Fulton's mind was clearly elsewhere.

"Yes," murmured Augustus to Jane, intuiting her unspoken question. "I'll speak to him."

"Good," said Jane.

"Thank you for retrieving my documents," Mr. Fulton was saying to Emma. "I really should be——" He wafted vaguely at the door, the one that led through the billiard room to the entrance hall.

"Yes, and so should I," agreed Emma, standing. "I have actors to herd. They're worse than cats."

"We look forward to the fruits of your labors," said Mr. Livingston kindly.

"Don't look forward too much," warned Emma.

With that parting sally, she set off in the opposite direction, towards the long gallery and the side door that opened to the theatre. Augustus looked from Fulton to Emma and back again—Fulton moving one way, Emma the other.

Drawing a deep breath, he moved to follow Fulton.

*E*mma managed to make it across the drawing room into the gallery before tripping over her own feet.

Everything felt strangely out of shape, her perspective skewed, her own perceptions no longer to be trusted. The edges of objects softened and twisted; shadows masqueraded as substance, and substance as shadow; and there was no way of being sure that anyone was what he or she seemed.

She wasn't even sure about herself.

Why had she done that just now? She might have kept her head down and let events play themselves out. They probably wouldn't have traced the plans to Augustus. Mr. Fulton was an inventor and everyone knew that inventors were crazy anyway, nearly as crazy as poets. She had done her bit—and more!—in the name of their former friendship by the simple act of not betraying him. He, after all, had betrayed her. He had betrayed her and he had used her—or was it the other way around? Not that it mattered. She had been over it from every angle, tossing and thrashing in her bed, knowing that no amount of champagne would ever put her to sleep this time.

He had betrayed her. She kept having to remind herself of that, like a child's lesson learned by rote. It should hurt more, shouldn't it? She should be angry, angry as she had been at Paul. Instead, she felt curiously numb.

Emma pushed open the door that led out of the gallery to the side of the house, the narrow path along which Augustus had pursued her only two nights ago, wanting to talk about the kiss. How mammoth that had loomed then and how insignificant it seemed now. She had been fussing and fretting over a kiss while Augustus played with the affairs of nations.

Had she been nothing more than that to him? Something small and insignificant, a pin on a map?

This much is true, he had said. But how could she believe him? She had lost all faith in her ability to distinguish between truth and illusion.

"Emma!" A hand closed over her shoulder, hard, jerking her to a halt. "There's no need to run away like that."

Emma blinked up at Georges Marston. His ruddy face was bent towards hers as he oozed self-satisfaction out of every pore.

"Surely," he said smugly, "there's no need to be shy now. I knew you weren't indifferent. I knew you were just playing coy." He gave her shoulder an affectionate squeeze.

Emma wriggled out from under his hand. "I beg your pardon?"

"Just now. Covering for me like that. Just playing hard to get, weren't you, you clever thing, you?"

Emma wondered when the world had gone mad. Had it always been this way, and she just hadn't noticed? "I don't understand."

"Come now, Emma," Georges said exuberantly. "You can drop the act now. I know why you did it. And you won't regret it. Once I sell them, you'll be set up like a queen—no! Like an empress. Not this empress," he amended. He gave a derisive laugh. "She's not going to last long."

Emma gaped at him. Georges, being Georges, took it for admiration.

Leaving aside the obvious insult to Mme. Bonaparte . . . "Just what are you talking about?" Emma demanded.

"The plans!" said Georges. "The plans! Tucked safe away in my—well, you don't need to know that." He tapped the side of his nose. "Least said, soonest mended."

The more he said, the less sense it made. "You have the plans."

"I got them last night. From Fulton's room. He didn't even bother to hide them." Georges's voice was rich with contempt for people too stupid to know when they might be burgled. "They were right there in the open."

Emma's mind raced over the possibilities. It wasn't entirely impossible. What if Augustus, struck by a fit of remorse—a not entirely displeasing prospect—had replaced the plans in Fulton's room after she had left him? What if that had been his way of trying to earn back her good judgment? Or, said the more cynical part of her mind, simply a means of protecting himself in the event that she broke her word and set the authorities on him. It would be very hard to prove anything without the files actually in his room.

The more she thought about it, the more plausible it seemed. In which case—if she could have, Emma would have banged her head against the side of the building—by oh so nobly and foolishly protecting Augustus, she had, in actuality, been protecting Georges.

Who said there was no justice in this world? She had just been served it, twice over, with a garnish of sour grapes.

"I have a buyer all set up," Georges was saying smugly. "My contact in Kent. Usually, I would send a courier, but with a package this important, I plan to escort it personally. Along with a few cases of third-rate brandy. They'll drink anything, those English, if you tell them it's French, and pay through their teeth for the privilege."

He grinned wolfishly at his own cleverness.

"You're selling Mr. Fulton's plans to the English?"

"Not so loud! Who else did you think would pay so well? I offered them to the Austrians, but they had no interest," he added.

Emma could see where they wouldn't, being largely landlocked.

There appeared to be one obvious issue. "Isn't that treason?"

"Treason is such a nasty word. Good business is what I call it. Besides, it would never have worked anyway, that machine. I'm doing the Emperor a favor by seeing it diverted. He should be paying me to rid him of it."

Mr. Fulton was many things, but he wasn't a hopeless dreamer. If he said something worked, it generally did.

"What's wrong with it?" asked Emma cautiously.

"It's meant to be a ship that sails under the water." Marston's expression showed just what he thought of that crazy idea. "But these plans I found, they don't look like any type of ship I've ever seen."

Emma remembered the plans she had seen in Augustus's bed. She would have a very hard time forgetting them. There had been a long, tubular structure, certainly not her image of a sailing vessel, but anyone with some imagination and some experience of the sea could imagine how it might be intended to work. And Georges, for his sins—especially for those sins enjoyed in the company of Bonaparte's brother-in-law—was in charge of a regiment at Boulogne, overseeing Bonaparte's prized new naval base.

"It was all little pieces," he complained. "A box and a drum and a pistol. Is the drum meant to float? At that rate, we can just close a man in a crate, hand him a pistol, drop him in the Seine, and see what happens."

"It would have to be a waterproofed crate," said Emma, but her mind was busily turning over the elements Georges had just described.

A box, a drum, a pistol. Lots of little pieces.

Georges had stolen the plans for the wave machine.

Chapter 31

If berries rot and crops decay,
What hope have we for longer stay?
A pledge is fair, it warms the heart,
But makes no light to see by dark.

—Emma Delagardie and Augustus Whittlesby,
Americanus: A Masque in Three Parts

Emma would have laughed if it hadn't been quite so absurd. And quite so awful. Georges's Kentish contact would be receiving the very latest in theatrical equipment.

She hoped whoever it was had a masque to perform.

"Well, this was all very cunning of you," she said, patting his arm. "But I'm afraid I must be getting on to the theatre. There's so much to do, with the performance in less than an hour."

In fact, there was very little for her to do. But Georges didn't need to know that.

"I'll be back for you," he said, with a very credible smolder.

He really was a fine figure of a man, thought Emma objectively. Tall, broad, strong-featured. And completely lacking in any moral sense.

Did he mean to marry her to make her keep her silence? Probably not, decided Emma. It was more likely that he simply intended to dangle the prospect of his wonderful self before her, confident that his professions of devotion would keep her from running to the Emperor before he had departed with the plans. Amazing what people were willing to do for those plans. Mr. Fulton had no idea how popular his plans had made her, or what lengths men might be willing to go in order to obtain and keep them.

She could hear Augustus's voice, forlorn in memory: *Emma, I think I love you.*

"Lovely," said Emma. "I look forward to it."

"My carriage leaves at eight," Georges murmured. "The boat sails at dawn. So this must be . . . farewell."

He made as if to embrace her, but Emma stepped back out of the way. "I'm sure you must have a number of arrangements to make," she said politely. It was always easier to humor Georges than to argue with him. "I wouldn't want to keep you. Not when our future depends on it."

Georges gave a forced laugh. "That's my practical Emma," he said. If he meant it to be a compliment, it didn't quite come out that way. "Best to keep one's eye on the prize, yes?"

"Oh, absolutely," Emma agreed. "You wouldn't want to let it slip away." Someone, somewhere, was bound to be in need of a wave machine. "Safe journey."

Keeping his eyes on hers, Georges pressed a lingering kiss to his own palm and released it in her direction.

Emma waggled her fingers farewell.

With a final smolder, Georges flipped his coattails and slipped back around the house, presumably to collect the plans, harry his valet, pack his luggage, and disappear into the night. If his carriage left at eight o'clock, he only had an hour. The masque was scheduled to begin somewhere in the vicinity of seven thirty.

It wasn't, reflected Emma, the journey Georges needed to worry about. It was the people on the other end. They weren't going to be best pleased when he arrived bearing the designs for a piece of expensive theatrical equipment rather than a weapon of war. She doubted that "go away or I'll make thunder noises at you" would go far on the field of battle.

Crosses, double crosses, and Georges outsmarted by himself. Emma would have gone so far as to call it poetic justice if poetry hadn't been such a sensitive subject just then.

If Georges didn't have the plans, did that mean Augustus did? And if he did, just what did he intend to do with them?

I think I love you, he whispered again.

Damn him, damn him, damn him. Emma reached for the back door of the theatre.

Someone touched her shoulder. Emma ground her teeth in irritation. Oh, for all that was holy! Hadn't that tender parting scene been enough for Georges?

Shaking off the hand, Emma whirled around, barking, "What?"

"Emma," said Augustus, and she felt the handle of the door bite into her back as she took a step back.

He looked much the same as always, hair unbound, shirt properly disordered, breeches just on the acceptable end of tight, but there was a seriousness about him that hadn't been there before. Or, perhaps, it always had been, and she just hadn't seen it. She hadn't seen a lot of things.

"Would you like to explain what just happened in there?" he asked.

"No," said Emma honestly. His nearness was more distracting than she would have liked to admit. She could feel the warmth of him, just a thin layer of clothing away. Even now, even after all that had happened, she wanted him, so badly. She wanted to twine her arms around his neck and slide her fingers into his hair and . . .

Flushing, Emma tucked her hands under her elbows, out of harm's way.

"You lied for me," he said.

"It wasn't entirely a lie. I did stumble on the plans."

"Less stumble, more sat," said Augustus fondly. His glance was a caress.

Emma's red cheeks turned redder. "Well, anyway," she said meaninglessly, as she groped for her wits. Betrayal, she reminded herself. Intrigue. Plans. Georges. "Stumbling, sitting, either way, it was a form of the truth. I did come upon them unawares." Very unawares. "And while I may not have the plans in my possession now, I will once you give them to me to give back to Mr. Fulton. Won't I?"

Folding her arms across her chest, she raised her brows at him.

Augustus didn't take the bait. "That's not the point. The point is that you lied for *me*."

That was a poet for you, parsing every word. Emma glowered at him. "It would have put a damper on the performance if we had had to pause to guillotine you."

"Emma." He planted his hands on the doorframe to either side of her. They were in trouble, thought Emma vaguely, should someone try to come out. She was pinned to the door like someone's archery target. "Emma, I have something to tell you."

He looked so earnest. But hadn't she seen that before? He did earnest quite well. "What might it be this time? Do you have nine wives in the attic? A taste for women's undergarments?" Emma made to duck under his arm. "Forgive me if I have very little interest in hearing."

Augustus blocked her by the simple expedient of lowering his arm. Trapped. She was trapped. "Emma, Mr. Fulton is coming back to England with me."

Emma stopped wiggling. "What?"

Augustus dropped his arms. "I spoke to him a few moments ago. He's not happy with the reception of his submarine. He believes it would fare better in England."

Emma slowly assimilated the new information. "So you're not only stealing the plans, you're stealing the man."

"Hardly stealing when he comes willingly," said Augustus reasonably. Why did he have to be reasonable? Emma was feeling anything but. He had this all turned around, so that, somehow, he was in the right. It made no sense. "There's something else."

"Are you taking cousin Robert, too?" asked Emma crankily. "Perhaps England could use a lightly used envoy."

"Now you're being silly." She was being silly? Emma would have expressed her indignation had she the breath to do so—and if Augustus hadn't surprised her by suddenly making a grab at her hands. "Come with me, Emma. Come to England with me."

Emma wasn't quite sure she had heard him right. "England? Me?"

Augustus looked at her tenderly. "England. You."

No. This wasn't right. Not any of it. Emma snatched her hands away, her mind a muddle of plans and deceptions and unlikely seductions.

"Why? So I won't reveal your secret?"

Augustus didn't seem offended or alarmed by the question. He shook his head. "As soon as I leave France with Mr. Fulton, my identity is already compromised. I'm not coming back to France, Emma. This is it for me. I'm going back to England and starting over. Just as you said I should." He looked down at her, his eyes locking with hers. "But I can't do it without you."

Emma cleared her throat as best she could. "I don't understand."

"Yes, you do," said Augustus. She could feel the panels of the door hard against her back, blocking her egress. "You just don't want to. And I can't blame you for it. I understand why you're angry with me. If circumstances were different, I could make it up to you in a million different ways. I could woo you slowly, token by token. I could find ways to make you trust me again, hour by hour and day by day. But we don't have that kind of time."

Emma said the only thing she could think of to say. "When do you leave?"

"As soon as I make the arrangements. Three days at the outside. Fewer, if anything goes wrong."

364 of Lauren Willig

"That soon." It wasn't enough time. She needed time to think, to make sense of it all.

Augustus's hands settled on her shoulders, massaging the tense muscles at the base of her neck. "Come with me, Emma."

Come live with me and be my love / And we shall all the pleasures prove. They had discussed that poem together, a very long time ago, all the shepherd's seductive promises to his love.

"There'll be a reward for this," Augustus was saying. "Not a large one, but enough to set up that journal I've always wanted, maybe make a run for Parliament. There'll be no more deceptions, no subterfuge, no playacting." He looked down with a rueful grin. "No more shirts like these."

He looked so much younger when he smiled like that. So much younger and more carefree, as though he were already sloughing off the weight of carting around a second identity, so much more wearing than a waistcoat.

Emma's throat was tight. "And will you make me beds of roses and a thousand fragrant posies?"

Augustus's expression softened. "A cap of flowers and a kirtle, embroidered all with fragrant myrtle, and silver dishes for thy meat, as fragrant as the gods do eat. Well, maybe not that," he amended. "English cuisine isn't known for its Lucullan qualities. But the flowers are lovely in the meadows in springtime, as lovely as the poet claims. I'll make you crowns of daisy chains and beds of violets."

"What about the frosts?" asked Emma. "It can't be always summer."

"Even better," said Augustus. "There'll be sleighing and skating and hot chocolate on cold days, with the steam rising to make patterns in the cold air. We can go down to the Thames and watch the apprentices skid on the frozen river or go out to the countryside and cut holly for the color of the berries. Or we can stay warm inside, with no place better to be than with each other. Outside, the winds will batter and blow, but we'll have long nights in front of the fire, as the sparks fly and crackle, and crisp mornings buried beneath the quilts."

Emma could picture it, their own little refuge against a cold world, with firelight brightening the windows against the winter dusk. A sofa—not a spindly, narrow French construction, but something comfortable and deep—and a good fire in a proper hearth, sending slicks of warm light pooling along the surfaces of the furniture and reflecting off the panes of the windows. The winds would batter, but inside they would be warm, curled up together on the couch, his papers on one side, her books on the other.

It wasn't the shepherd's promise of endless summer or Americanus's pledge of boundless plenty. But Emma found it all the more seductive for all that.

"A new life in an old world," said Emma, testing the concept.

"It's a new life for me, too," said Augustus. "It's been a good decade since I've been back. We'll learn it together, the two of us, our own demi-paradise."

He was switching poets on her, from Marlowe to Shakespeare. But it wasn't either of them who spoke to Emma. It was another one of those Elizabethan courtiers, whichever of them it was who had written the nymph's reply to the shepherd.

If all the world and love were young and truth on every shepherd's tongue, these pretty pleasures might me move to live with thee and be thy love. . . .

If. It was a horrible and powerful if. She had felt that way nine years ago, with Paul, when the world and love were young, and look how wrong she'd got it then. The first hint of frost, and all his pretty flowers, all his vows and protestations had withered, and her love along with them. She was older now, and hardier, and there was no telling whether this might not be a sturdier plant, a tree rather than a shrub, but how could she possibly know? Especially with so little time?

No matter how honorable Augustus's intentions might be at this particular moment, there were no guarantees.

It had hurt enough last time, watching love crumble to dust, picking up the pieces of her life and trying to go on, and that had been with the love and support of her old schoolfellows. She wasn't sure she could do it again.

No matter how tempting.

"I . . . can't," Emma said, and watched Augustus's face fall.

"Can't?" he said carefully. "Or won't?"

"What difference does it make?" asked Emma despairingly. "Can't, won't. I am willing to believe"——Emma glanced down at his waistcoat, fighting with the words—"that you might actually care for me. That you might even think you love me." She hurried on before he could interject. "But how can I know? What if this is only another matter of policy, too deep for me to understand?"

Augustus tucked a stray lock of hair behind her ear. "What policy would be served by taking you with me?"

"That's just the problem," said Emma. "I don't know. I know nothing of this whole world of yours. I can't imagine the rules by which you play, or the goals for which you scheme. It's all foreign to me. Until yesterday, I had no idea any of this even existed. It's all unfathomable."

"You don't have to fathom it," said Augustus determinedly. "I'm getting out. There'll be no more of this. No more lies. We'll even make peace with my father. He's a clergyman, you know. You can't get much more straight and narrow than that."

"So you say," said Emma. "But how do I know what's truth and what's lies? How do I know even that?"

"Those are strong words," he said slowly.

Emma tilted her head up to him. Tears blurred her vision, presenting him to her as through a glass darkly, the outlines and details vague and uncertain. "What you ask of me is no small thing."

"Trust," he said.

Emma nodded wordlessly. She didn't need to enumerate his deceptions. They stood between them like a palpable thing.

"I have never," he said, his voice low, "lied to you in anything to do with you. Nor about how I feel for you. The pretext might have been a lie, but the substance never was."

"Say I believe you," she said, and her voice wobbled. She forced herself to rush onward before she lost her ability to speak entirely. "Say I believe that you mean it, that you believe it to be true, what if you wake up two months from now to find you mistook your feelings? It's happened before."

With Jane. She didn't say it and neither did he. She didn't need to. He knew exactly what she meant.

"It is," she said, "a great deal you ask of me."

"What assurances can I give you?" His eyes searched her face. "What can I say to you that will make you believe?"

Emma bit down on her lower lip, caught in a struggle between common sense and desire. Nothing, her mind declared, there was nothing Augustus Whittlesby could say that could reassure her. How could there be? He was a proven liar, a deceiver by trade.

And yet . . . Foolish as it was, stupid as she knew it to be, deep down, she believed him.

Did she believe him enough to stake her future on it? Emma's teeth worried at her lower lip as she stared at him, torn, a storm of contradictory arguments whipping her now this way, now that.

Augustus took pity on her confusion. He touched his knuckle gently to her cheek, a gesture that almost undid her.

"After the masque," he said. "We'll talk after the masque."

After the masque. Everything had been about the masque—until the masque, plans for the masque—and now the masque was upon them, and Emma felt as though she had reached the very end of the earth, the bit guarded by sea monsters, where the land ended in an abrupt drop.

"Will it make a difference?" she asked.

"That," said Augustus, "is up to you."

He stepped back, honoring their bargain, leaving her free to go.

His every instinct clamored to him to stop. Fool, he called himself. Fool, to embrace a belated and costly honor. How much more effective it would be to embrace away her indecision. He could quell her misgivings with caresses and stop her doubts with kisses. She wanted to be persuaded, his lesser self argued. She was practically begging for it. Why not take the decision out of her hands? It would be a kindness.

"Enjoy the performance," he said, and reached past her to push open the back door of the theatre for her.

"Our performance," Emma said, her voice low. Ducking her head, she hurried past him into the theatre.

Their performance. No matter what, they would always have that. Augustus stared at the closed door. Three acts of mediocre verse and a month of memories.

Damn.

Augustus kicked the wall of the theatre and succeeded only in stubbing his toe. They had made it so much easier for Americanus, he and Emma. All Americanus had to do was rescue his lady from a band of rascally pirates. It wasn't his persuasions that won her from her tower, but a chance abduction.

Augustus doubted that a band of pirates was going to come marauding through Malmaison just for his convenience.

In this version, he couldn't prove his devotion with pretty speeches or daring feats of rescue. Instead, he had no choice but to wait for his Cytherea to come to him, flawed and false though she knew him to be. He had to trust to the strength of the strange rapport between them to overcome all the objections of reason and all the fears that came with making oneself vulnerable to another. No tricks, no gimmicks, no deceptions. All he could was hope that love would prove stronger than reason.

It was not a very comforting thought.

"Mr. Whittlesby!" Someone was bouncing towards him around the side of the theatre. It was Horace de Lilly, pink of face and green of waistcoat, looking disgustingly healthy and happy and far too eager to see Augustus. "What luck! I was hoping to have a chance to speak to you."

"Now is really not the time," said Augustus quellingly.

The last thing he needed right now was another round of "I want to be just like you when I grow up." Hell, he didn't want to be just like him when he grew up. Horace de Lilly could just find another agent to idolize. He was done.

Horace, unfortunately, wasn't. He bounced to a stop in front of Augustus, quivering with excitement. "You've done it! You've done it, haven't you?"

"Shouldn't you be reserving your seat for the masque?" Augustus said shortly. "I hear it's to be the theatrical event of the summer."

Horace wasn't to be deterred. His boyish face shone with excitement. "You have them, don't you? The plans? I knew you would do it!"

"Your confidence overwhelms me," said Augustus. "Not now."

Of all the ill-chosen agents, de Lilly was about as subtle as a cartload of monkeys. The concept of "not in public" appeared to have passed him by. At least after this week, he would no longer be Augustus's problem.

But he would still be someone else's.

Augustus took a deep breath. "A word of advice, de Lilly. Curb your enthusiasm. I know you're terribly excited about the poetry you commissioned from me," he placed heavy emphasis on the words, "but unless you want to tip your lady off to your purpose, I would advise a modicum of discretion. Hell hath no fury." Like an emperor betrayed.

De Lilly's brow wrinkled. "Er, right. But you do have the, um, poetry? Where is it? Was it what we thought it was? Can I do anything to help?"

Augustus kept a careful rein on his temper. "If you want to make yourself useful, look into fast carriages. I look to leave in three days' time."

In fact, he looked to leave in one. It didn't matter whether de Lilly's erratic behavior was simply youth or something else; either way, he was a danger. Better to send him off on a useless errand, believing himself to have time to spare. If he were a double agent, he would wait to pounce until the last minute. They generally did. If he weren't, his energies would be safely and uselessly expended examining horseflesh and racing curricles. Either way, by the time de Lilly moved, Augustus would be gone.

With or without Emma.

That was all he had. One day. One day to convince Emma of his good intentions and persuade her to leave behind everything she knew for an uncertain future in an unfamiliar country, all for love of him.

Put that way, it sounded pretty damn improbable. Improbable? Try impossible.

From inside the theatre, thunder rumbled.

Chapter 32

All the world may not be young
Nor truth on every sailor's tongue,
But this tongue, this truth, these I trust
Because my heart says I must.
——Emma Delagardie and Augustus Whittlesby,
Americanus: A Masque in Three Parts

"For I shall bring you crimson leaves."

On the stage, Kort was doing a credible, if not an inspired job as Americanus. From her tower, all that could be seen of Cytherea was her long blond wig as Kort declaimed to her the list of wonders that awaited her in the new world.

"And rippling wheat in golden sheaves."

It wasn't Kort's fault that he sounded like he was reading off a ship's inventory—which, when one came down to it, was rather what he was. Not everyone could take those words and make of them what Augustus had, imbuing them with magic far beyond their basic form. He had taken them and turned them from an inventory into an incantation.

Just as he had now. Emma's fingers tightened on her fan, so hard she could feel the delicate wood slats begin to crack beneath the strain. Crowns of daisies and beds of violets. Warm fires on cold days. Apprentices skidding on the frozen Thames. Like Americanus's leaves and berries, they were humble and homey items, a far cry from the usual enticements of jewels and money, position and power.

Emma ached for that simple hearth as she never had for diamonds or status.

On the stage, Kort held up his hands to Cytherea, bearing in them a bowl laden with crimson fruit. "A cache of berries, red and sweet . . ."

Like pomegranate seeds. In the myth, the fruit lured Persephone to Hades. In their masque, Americanus dangled them in front of Cytherea to entice her to the new world, that new world that was Emma's old world, so familiar and rich and well loved.

If she went with Augustus, it would be only to the other side of the Channel. There was no threat of strange diseases or Indian attack or any of the other fears that might have bedeviled her ancestors going from the Old World to the New.

No, the only risk was to her heart.

Mme. de Rémusat's shrill voice broke into Emma's thoughts. She twisted in her seat to look back at Emma. "How wonderfully rustic!" she gushed. "Is that what they all wear back where you're from?"

It took Emma a moment to realize that she was referring to Kort, all tricked out in buckskins and ragged shirt. To Emma, the ensemble looked palpably like the costume it was. The closest Kort had ever come to the frontier was Albany.

"Oh, all the time," said Emma. "I used to sew my own skirts from skins. It was the scraping them that was so tedious."

Mme. de Rémusat's mouth pursed. "There's no need to make fun," she said, and settled back in a huff.

Next to her, Mme. Junot cast Emma a quick grin. Part of the

Bonapartes' old Corsican connection, Mme. Junot felt that Mme. de Rémusat put on airs.

"Is silence too much to ask?" demanded the Emperor loudly.

The chorus on stage abruptly stopped singing.

"Not you!" barked the Emperor.

The chorus resumed, somewhat raggedly, having lost their note in the interim. Talma, veteran of the Comédie-Française, buried his head in his hands. In her tower, Jane continued to look ethereal and lovely, the only one unperturbed.

Emma could only be grateful that the Emperor's interruption hadn't occurred during Miss Gwen's pirate chorus. There was no telling what might have happened.

Bristling, Mme. de Rémusat sent an "I told you so" look over her shoulder at Emma. All too aware of the Emperor sitting two rows ahead, Emma found herself in the annoying position of being unable to point out that she had started it.

Good heavens, they were all behaving like five-year-olds.

This, thought Emma, sinking down in her seat in the back of the imperial box, was what she had to look forward to if she stayed in Paris. The Emperor and his wife sat in the front, with cousin Robert in the place of honor at the Emperor's right. It helped to be the envoy of a foreign power, even a not so very powerful power. Behind them, in a phalanx armored in feathers and jewels, sat Mme. Bonaparte's ladies-in-waiting. The Emperor's aides, less privileged, were left to crouch on stools along the sides, casting glances at the ladies and occasionally the stage. Guards—once consular guards, now imperial—ranged themselves at the entrance to the box, controlling access to the Emperor.

At the back sat Emma. The Emperor was cross with her, she knew, for refusing Mme. Bonaparte's offer. As the American envoy's niece, however, and the author of the masque, she couldn't be entirely slighted. So here she sat, at the back of the box, simultaneously honored and chastised, her silk skirt neatly arrayed around her legs, her hands folded demurely in her lap, and her mind in turmoil.

Emma cast a longing look at the back of Hortense's head. Imperial princess that she now was, Hortense was seated on Mme. Bonaparte's left, too far away to whisper or gossip or drag outside for a hurried consultation.

But what would she say to her if she could say it? I think I'm in love with an English spy? Who also happens to be a truly awful poet? And he's going to leave within the next few days and he wants me to go with him and I don't know what to do.

Yes, that was going to go over well.

What would Hortense say? Emma realized that she didn't know anymore. Her old friend, the one who had helped pack her belongings for her flurried flight with Paul, had cares and worries and divided loyalties she could only begin to understand. She would never doubt Hortense's friendship or her love, but what would she say if Emma told her she was in love with a man sworn to bring down her stepfather's empire?

From long ago, as clearly as though she were sitting next to her, Emma could hear her best friend's voice.

Yes, yes, said Hortense. *But do you love him?*

But it's not that simple, Emma argued with the phantom Hortense in her head. We're older now. She was sure there were other considerations, if only she could remember what they were. Family? Hers was thousands of miles away, estranged long ago. Friends, then. Adele, careless and restless. Hortense, ever more a part of Bonaparte's new imperial circle.

Carmagnac? Carmagnac practically ran itself, the fields drained, all of Paul's reforms accomplished.

Emma could feel her excuses running through her fingers like straw. She frowned at the back of Mme. de Rémusat's head. When she broke it down into its component parts, this life she had built for herself in France proved a surprisingly ephemeral thing. Cousin

Robert was due to return to America; Mr. Fulton was going to England. Her structure of friends and acquaintances was collapsed around her as neatly and noiselessly as a Gypsy tent.

Which left her, then, with that one, crucial question: *Do you love him?*

On the stage, Americanus had retired for the night, and the pirates were beginning to creep around Cytherea's tower. Emma found herself envying Cytherea, not for her beauty, but for the fact that her decisions were made for her. Carried off by pirates, rescued by the hero, she never had to wrestle with her heart or her conscience. There was a divinity that shaped her end: her author.

Whereas Emma . . . Emma was dithering, and she knew it.

She could toss a coin, she thought wildly. Heads, I love him; tails, I love him not. On the new coinage, the head was Bonaparte's. That would be an amusing bit of irony right there, the Emperor unintentionally blessing her elopement with his enemy.

"But I must!" came an urgent whisper from the curtains that blocked the entrance to the box.

Emma twisted in her chair, grateful for any distraction. All she could see was a hand being waved about for emphasis, a hand and a bit of lace on the sleeve.

Whoever it was sounded as though he were in a high state of excitement, so excited that he was tipsy with it. "I must see the Emperor right now. I have urgent tidings for him. *Important* tidings."

The guard was unimpressed. "The Emperor is not to be disturbed until after the performance."

"But you don't even know what my news is," said the other man indignantly. "I assure you, the Emperor will want to know."

The curtains moved and Emma could see him at last, Horace de Lilly, in a green waistcoat with cameo fobs. His light brown hair was charmingly tousled around his face, his cheeks pink.

He tugged at the guard's arm. "Wouldn't the Emperor want to know about . . . treason?"

The imperial box was warm, but Emma felt a chill prickle along the skin of her arms. Her nails dug into the arms of her chair. There were many treasons in France, she reassured herself. Georges for one. Treason didn't necessarily mean Augustus.

De Lilly's connections were with the aristocratic émigré community. If he were going to denounce anyone, it would be one of his childhood playmates. Perhaps someone had slighted his waistcoat or taken one of his toys away.

The thought didn't bring the relief it should. Even if not from de Lilly, Augustus was in danger every moment he remained in France. Emma felt a sudden, impetuous need to urge him to flee, flee now. But that was foolish, wasn't it? He knew what he was doing. He knew the risks.

Even so. Her eyes took in the guards stationed all around the theatre, seeing them as though for the first time. Guards at the imperial box, guards by the stage, guards on the stage, dressed as pirates. The new emperor didn't stint on precautions, even at his wife's beloved Malmaison.

The guard at the door took in de Lilly's youth, his waistcoat, the slight English accent that persisted from a childhood in exile in England. Emma could see him arriving at the same conclusions she had, placing de Lilly in a compartment roughly labeled *trouble-making aristo.*

"After the performance," said the guard implacably.

Horace jiggled with frustration, setting his watch fobs jangling. "But by then the poet may have got away!"

The guard pointedly let the heavy velvet curtain drop, right in de Lilly's flushed face.

On the stage, the first signs of the storm were brewing. Emma could hear the distant rumble of thunder, and the pattering sound of raindrops, cunningly created by pebbles in a jar. Thank goodness for it. It masked the frantic pattering of her heart, clattering a mile a minute. The poet. There was only one man at Malmaison who could, with confidence, be called *the* poet. The gray silk storm clouds drew together, eked out with a fine haze of mist. At any moment, the full force of the storm's fury would be unleashed.

Right on Augustus's unwitting head.

Energy crackled through Emma like lightning; she could feel her fingers tingle with it. The masque was half done, proceeding unevenly but inevitably towards the storm, the sea battle, the reconciliation and happily-ever-afters.

They had an hour.

Leaning forward, she whispered in Mme. Junot's ear, "There's something not quite right with the storm machine. I'm going to get someone to fix it."

Mme. Junot nodded without looking at her. "Good luck," she whispered back.

Emma appreciated the sentiment. She rather thought she would need it.

She forced herself to move slowly, even though every instinct urged her to run. Her silk skirts dragged on her legs; her fan weighed on her wrist like an anchor. She wanted to shake free of them and sprint, but she confined herself to a measured saunter, smiling and nodding at her acquaintances as she went.

Augustus was standing at the back of the theatre, in the section reserved for those not favored enough to deserve seats. She saw him look up at her, his eyes eager, hopeful.

"The wind machine isn't working properly," she said, loudly enough that the people on both sides could hear it. "I need you to fix it. Now."

The wind machine? They both knew he couldn't tell one end of a machine from another.

Augustus cloaked his surprise. Her expression was imperious, but her eyes were watchful, her nails digging into the palms of her gloves. All his instincts immediately went on the alert. Something was wrong.

"Immediately, madame," he said, with a deep bow, following her through the door, between the laughing courtiers, who were reaching their own conclusions about the urgent summons. Their comments about ballast might not be original, but they certainly made their point.

Emma signaled silence, drawing him several yards away from the theatre, into the lee of a potted tree.

"If this is a seduction attempt . . ." Augustus began hopefully.

"It's Horace de Lilly," Emma said abruptly. "He knows."

"Of course, he knows. He's—" Augustus's brain belatedly kicked back into service. "Wait. How do you know about de Lilly?"

Emma's face was very pale in the starlight. "He came to the Emperor's box. He demanded to speak to him. He said he had great tidings to impart. About treason."

A double cross. He might have suspected it, but much as one played with the idea of drowning on a crossing. It wasn't out of the realm of possibility, but no one ever expected it. Augustus conjured up the image of old Mme. de Lilly, the spider in her web. She wanted the de Lilly estates back. How better to prove one's loyalty to the new regime than a bit of double-dealing.

Augustus faced Emma. "What did he tell the Emperor?"

"He didn't have the chance," she said, and Augustus felt the weight on his chest lighten. "The guards wouldn't admit him. They made him wait until after the performance."

"Which means," said Augustus, glancing sideways at the theatre, "that I have an hour. At the most."

An hour. An hour to grab the plans, steal a horse, and get well away before Bonaparte could hear the news and snap into action. He would have to abandon any hope of taking Fulton with him. Fulton might come later, of his own volition. Or not. That wasn't the worst of it.

Augustus looked wordlessly at Emma, struck silent by the sheer hopelessness of it all. What was there to say? He couldn't ask her to come with him, riding pillion, on a midnight flight through the night. There wasn't even time for a proper good-bye.

"Emma—" he said brokenly.

"I have a plan," Emma blurted out.

"What?"

Diamonds dazzled his eyes as she waved her hands about. Her eyes blazed brighter than the jewels, excited and anxious all at the same time. "I have a plan," she repeated rapidly. "It may not be the best plan, but—can you trust me?"

"No one better," he said, and meant it.

Emma lifted her chin. "I'll get the plans and you find Mr. Fulton. Here's my idea. . . ."

As the clocks in the hall chimed eight, a heavily cloaked man stepped out from beneath the tented entrance to Malmaison. A carriage waited for him, small, dark, and sleek, twin lanterns set on either side of the box casting a thin light over the gravel and the dozing post boys. From the theatre, yards away, came the distant sound of thunder, but outside all was peaceful and silent, save the crunch of the horses' hooves against the gravel.

The man wore a cloak with the collar turned up around his chin, and a wide-brimmed hat pulled down low over his forehead. Beneath one arm, he carried a roll of paper; behind him hurried a serving man carrying a small trunk with a rounded top.

"Set it up there," he said impatiently. "Yes, there—no! Carefully, you fool! Don't you know a Vuitton trunk when you see one? If it's nicked, I'll take it out of your useless hide. Hurry, damn you! What?"

A pale figure glided up behind him. Dressed all in white satin with a spangled shawl draped around her shoulders, she looked like a wraith in the torchlight.

"Georges?" she murmured. "Don't you want to see me?"

"It's not that I— Of course, my sweet." Marston juggled with the roll of paper and his temper. "You startled me."

Emma looked up at him from under her lashes. "I'm so sorry," she said. She was moving backwards, drawing him with her, step by step, so naturally, he wasn't even aware of it. "I didn't mean to. It's just that . . . I needed to see you."

Her shawl slipped on her shoulders, a slow, sensual movement, baring pale skin that seemed to shimmer in the moonlight. Skin or silk? Augustus couldn't see from where he stood, but his own mouth was dry, his hands curled in fists from the tension of remaining silent.

Marston licked his lips. "Flattered as I am, my darling, it will have to wait. As you can see . . ." He gestured at the waiting carriage, the restless horses, the coachman on the box. "The tide waits for no man."

"Five minutes only," said Emma breathlessly, fluttering her lashes up at him for all she was worth. Her shawl slipped further, revealing skin this time, quite definitely skin, and a décolletage as low as permissive fashion permitted. "I couldn't let you leave without wishing you luck . . . properly."

Or improperly.

Marston wasn't the one to say no to temptation when it offered itself to him, be it strong brandy, fast horses, or a quick lay.

"Five minutes," said Marston so condescendingly that Augustus ached to flatten him then and there. He schooled his breathing to stillness. He had agreed to this plan.

Of course, when he had agreed to it, he hadn't pictured Marston's eyes on Emma's bosom, his hands grasping for her waist.

Emma evaded him with a laugh and a wiggle, taking him by both hands. "This way," she murmured, her voice low and husky. "There's a nice, soft patch of grass just around the side. . . ."

She kept up a constant stream of patter, fluttering and promising, as she led Marston around the side of the house, out of the view of the page boys, out of the glow of the carriage lamps.

She did her job well. Marston's gaze was fixed on his prize, the blood flowing to parts of his body other than his brain.

As Emma released his hands, taking a step back, it took him just one moment too many to spot Augustus lying in wait.

"What the—"

"No need to waste time on the amenities," said Augustus. "I've been wanting to do this for some time."

His fist connected with the other man's jaw, sending Marston sprawling backwards. It was meant only to be a warning shot, but the other man's head slammed back into the side of the wall, hitting the stone with a neat smack. Marston's eyes opened wide with alarm before rolling back in his head.

Marston slumped down against the side of the house, leaving Augustus standing en garde, feeling slightly cheated.

Augustus inspected his knuckles. Barely grazed. Nice to know that all that boxing during his university days had paid off.

He glanced tentatively at Emma. Even though this had been, in the larger sense, her idea, she might still be put off by seeing her former lover laid out flat in front of her, without so much as an "en garde" for warning.

"Nicely done," said Emma, retrieving the real plans from where she had stashed them behind a potted plant. Stepping over the unconscious man, she considered the plans for the wave machine, made a little clucking sound at the back of her throat, and plucked them out of Marston's grasp, adding them to the roll of papers.

"Not exactly sporting . . ." demurred Augustus.

"He would have hit you over the back of the head and thought nothing of it," said Emma crisply. Dropping down beside the unconscious man, she plucked his hat from his head and tossed it to Augustus. "Quick. Put that on."

"Yes, ma'am," he said.

Emma ruthlessly stripped Marston of his cloak. "This, too. You'll have to pass yourself off as Georges, at least for the first stretch. Once safely away, you can resort to bribery instead."

"I'll take a long bath after," Augustus joked, muffling himself in the cloak as directed.

Emma's white silk dress shimmered in the moonlight, laughably inappropriate, her feathers and jewels at odds with her determined tone and the fierce set of her shoulders. How could he ever have thought her silly? She was a tiger, a tiger in dove's clothing, and he had never admired anyone more.

Augustus watched as she crouched down next to Marston's recumbent form, rifling through Marston's pockets with more determination than skill. Emma squinted at the writing in the dark, then thrust a crumpled handful of papers up at Augustus. He could dimly make out the official seals at the bottom.

"Here. His papers. These might be useful to you. And," she added, "he seems to have multiples of them."

She staggered to her feet, grabbing at the wall for balance. Augustus caught her before she could stumble.

"Thank you," she mumbled, not looking at him, and twitched away.

"Emma—" How in the hell did they say good-bye? He couldn't let her go, not now. But what other choice was there? Short of picking her up and flinging her into his carriage à la the pirates in their masque, and that was the sort of thing he didn't see Emma taking to terribly well.

"Here," she said quickly. She stripped the diamonds off her wrist and dropped them in his hand, closing his fingers over them. "Take it. It may be paste, but most people see the glitter first and ask questions later. It should get you past at least one checkpoint. As for the others"—she wrenched the earrings from her ears, cascading, elaborate things composed of a dozen or more small stones—"there are these."

She held them out to him. The looped chains of tiny diamonds swung back and forth, glittering in the moonlight. She looked, Augustus thought, even lovelier without them.

"Augustus?" She thrust the earrings forward. "They're only paste, really."

They might be paste, but she was the real thing, diamond to the core.

"I don't know how to thank you," Augustus said.

Emma bit down on her lower lip. "There's no need to waste time on that now, not with the carriage waiting."

Come with me, he wanted to say, but the words stuck in his throat. He was asking her to risk her life on a frenzied run to the coast, then to entrust herself to whatever band of cutthroats Marston had in his pay.

"You could never be a waste of time," he said softly.

"With imperial guards in pursuit? You might change your mind. Besides—" She mumbled something. Whatever it was, Augustus didn't quite catch it.

He leaned forward, breathing in the familiar scent of her, the tickle of her feathers against his nose, trying not to think that this would be the last time, the last time he would smell her perfume, the last time she would make him sneeze.

Come with me.

"Pardon?" he said.

Emma twisted her hands together behind her back, not quite meeting his eyes. "I said . . . I said there will be plenty of time for that later." She took a deep breath and lifted her eyes to his. "Once we get to England."

Chapter 33

The world, once old, is now made young;
Our tale, once told, is now begun;
Love knows no season, age, nor time,
But sings as well in prose as rhyme.

—Emma Delagardie and Augustus Whittlesby,

Americanus: A Masque in Three Parts

"We," Augustus repeated. "England. We?"

Augustus blinked at her, as though he, rather than Marston, had sustained a blow to the head.

That wasn't entirely the reaction Emma had been hoping for. For a man who had been urging her to come live with him and be his love, his reaction savored more of shock than joy.

"Unless you don't want me," Emma said quickly. "I quite understand. You're leaving in haste. The last thing you need is—"

She never finished the sentence. The air swooshed out of her lungs as Augustus swept her into a crushing embrace. There was a pin digging into her shoulder blade, and her right arm was caught uncomfortably somewhere between his chest and her side, but Emma didn't care, not with her nose squished into his waistcoat and his lips against her hair and Augustus holding on to her as though she were his only port in a storm.

"Want you?" Augustus laughed breathlessly. Emma could feel the shiver of it straight through his chest to hers. His arms, which she had thought as tight as they could go, somehow, impossibly, tightened around her. "I want you more than I've ever wanted anyone or anything. I want you even though I know it would be better for you to let you go."

"Just enough for breathing," croaked Emma.

"For—oh." His chin nuzzled against her hair. "I didn't mean to crush you."

Emma leaned back just far enough to look up at him. "That sort of crushing," she said softly, "I don't mind. I—oh!"

Something was grabbing at the back of her skirt. She kicked back and heard a squishy crunch, followed by a loud curse. She turned in Augustus's arms, treading on his toe as she backed up against him in an instinctive reaction of revulsion.

Georges had always had a hard head.

He had levered himself up onto his hands and knees. His nose was streaming blood, dripping rivulets of red down the folds of his cravat. His eyes slowly fixed on the plans beneath Emma's arm—and on Augustus, dressed in his cloak and prepared to travel.

"Bitch." A spatter of blood and spittle accompanied the word. Georges shook his head like a dog's. "Should have known . . ."

Emma backed away, into Augustus.

Augustus's hand tightened briefly on her waist before moving her aside. "There's nothing to worry about," he said beneath his breath. He moved purposefully towards Georges. "I'll take care of this."

A cunning glint lit in Georges's eyes. He was no match for Augustus, but there was one thing he could do.

"Thieves!" he shouted hoarsely. "Murder! Treason! Fire!"

He left out rape, but otherwise it was a fairly comprehensive cry for help.

Augustus acted with remarkable speed, dealing Marston a well-calculated kick in the jaw that sent him sprawling flat out in the bushes, but it was too late; Emma could already hear the rumblings from within the house. There was the sudden glint of candles in the windows, the sound of scurrying feet, voices raised in confusion.

"Quick!" Augustus grabbed Emma's hand and ran with her for the carriage, Marston's cape flapping around his ankles. Emma stumbled along with him, her slippers skidding and scuffing on the gravel. Augustus boosted her up into the carriage with such force that Emma bounced as she hit the squabs, hauling himself in behind her, and swinging the door shut.

"Drive!" he shouted to the coachman. "Drive like you've never driven before."

The coachman didn't have to be asked twice. With a crack of the whip, the coach lurched into motion, careening down the drive of Malmaison, sending Emma sprawling onto Augustus's lap.

He must have thought Augustus was Georges, Emma thought dimly, struggling to try to sit up. Georges's cloak, Georges's hat—that had been her plan, to be sure, but she had known it was a weak one. It was the sort of thing she had read about in novels, but she never thought it would actually work.

"We did it," she said wonderingly, squirming her way to a sitting position. She looked at the plans jammed half beneath her, and at Augustus, with Georges's hat pulled down low over his eyes. A laugh bubbled up in her, a laugh of sheer glee. "We actually did it."

Augustus's face was lit by a similar exultation. "We didn't even have to use your diamonds!"

"Diamonds construed loosely," Emma reminded him, laughing up into his glowing face. The brim of Georges's hat kept sloping down over his eyes. She pushed it back, setting it rakishly askew. "There. Now you look like an adventurer."

"And you—" He broke off as the carriage hit a particularly deep rut. "You—"

"Yes?" said Emma breathlessly. Her arms were around Augustus's neck, although she really couldn't remember putting them there. "What do I look like?"

The carriage rocked back and forth, traveling far too fast for safety, sending them swaying with the motion. It was a dizzying effect, but not nearly as dizzying as the expression in Augustus's eyes.

"Heaven," he said, and his arms closed around her, and there was no more carriage and no more rocking, just her head spinning with the delight of his arms around her and his lips on hers, dizzy and scattered and exactly where she was supposed to be.

It was some time before she could speak again, and when she did, she said, "Heaven's a place, not a person."

Augustus touched a finger to her lips. "Hush," he said. And then, with a slow smile, "You always did criticize my poetry."

"Jane thought I was trying to get your attention," said Emma ruefully. She wondered, belatedly, whether mentioning Jane was the best of ideas, but Augustus didn't even seem to notice. His eyes were all for her.

"And were you?" he asked.

"Mmm . . ." Emma pursed up her lips. "No?"

Augustus grinned. "I'll take that as a yes."

Emma ran her hands up his torso beneath Georges's cloak. "Can we compromise on maybe?"

"Keep doing that," said Augustus, "and we can compromise on anything you like."

"Good," murmured Emma, her eyes already closing as her face tilted up towards his. "I'll let you know when I think of something."

"I," said Augustus, his breath playing against her lips, "wasn't planning on doing any thinking at all." And then, "How far is it to the coast?"

"Far," said Emma.

"Good," murmured Augustus.

Not precisely good from an escape point of view, considered

Emma, but very, very good in every other way. Georges hadn't stinted on his carriage. It might have been built for speed, but it was nicely padded, with a wider than average bench. Naturally. Ordinarily, Emma might have rolled her eyes at that. But Emma was too busy rolling other things to worry about Georges and his morals. She was feeling rather delightfully immoral at the moment.

"They warned me about poets," she whispered, kissing the side of his neck. "Out for just one thing."

"Inspiration?" Augustus suggested, touching the side of her cheek in a way that made her feel like every Venus ever painted or carved.

She cradled his hand, mirroring the curve of it with hers, putting everything she felt into her touch and her lips as he eased her slowly back against Georges's extravagantly padded cushions.

"What?" Emma scooted sideways, breaking the kiss as something collapsed noisily beneath her back.

Augustus levered himself upright, his breathing labored. "Not. Again."

"Yes, again." It would have been amusing if it hadn't been quite so annoying. Emma removed the slightly squashed roll of plans from beneath her back. "These plans are alarmingly ubiquitous."

"For you," said Augustus wryly. "Others search for them. You sit on them."

Had that only been last night? It felt as though a lifetime had passed since she had last sat on these plans. Like Shakespeare's great reckoning in a little room, it took only a tiny speck of time for everything to change around one. She wondered, now, how she hadn't known before.

"What did you resolve with Mr. Fulton?" she asked. "Is he to follow?"

Augustus settled back against the seat. "Fulton will pretend to be properly indignant. Then he'll join us in London en route to New York."

Us. He said it so unself-consciously. She hadn't been part of an us for a very long time. "Are we to settle in London, then?" she asked tentatively.

He didn't answer directly. Instead, he looked at her from under the brim of Georges's hat. "Will you miss your house?"

She didn't ask which one. He had never seen Carmagnac. She knew the one he meant, the one in town, the one where they had spent hours together in her book room. It wasn't just her house he was asking about, she knew; he meant her cook, who prepared those tea cakes he liked so much, and the footmen who opened the door to him, and her own personalized sedan chair, and all the rounds of parties and friends that had been so much a part of her life in Paris. She had only, she realized, the clothes on her back, and those were now rumpled and stained. They would be even worse by the time they reached London.

She had the clothes on her back and some paste jewelry. She went to a place where she knew no one, a place where she would have to learn everything except the language, and even that had its own divergences from the one she knew.

Back in Paris, there was a town house decorated to her specifications; a wardrobe full of clothes they couldn't afford to replace; a whole world, a life. Emma looked at Augustus, and down at his hand, where it held hers. No, she thought. She regretted none of it.

With the exception of one thing.

"I never said good-bye to Hortense," she said.

Augustus's hand tightened briefly on hers, in an almost convulsive gesture. When he spoke, his voice was so low that Emma had to strain to hear him. "You can still go back."

"What?" said Emma.

"If you wanted to." Augustus's face was earnest in the shadows. He tried to draw his hand away, but Emma held on to it and wouldn't let him go. "You could tell them that I kidnapped you, that I took you along as a bargaining chip in case of capture. They'll believe you."

"You're willing to give me up?" said Emma, half laughing. "As easily as that?"

"Don't think it's easy," he said quietly.

The smile died on Emma's face. He meant it. If she asked him, he would let her out of the carriage, drop her off wherever it was that she asked, let her go back to her old life without him. Fair enough. On the face of it, what she was doing was absurd. Another elopement, this time with treason, in the middle of the night, with a man who had repeatedly lied to her.

It might be wrong, but it felt entirely right.

"You're being noble," she said. "Don't be."

"I don't want to take your choices away from you," he said. "Just because I pushed you into the carriage——"

"It was more of a pull, really," said Emma absently. "With a bit of a yank."

Augustus wasn't smiling. "I'm serious."

Emma lifted her eyes to his. "So am I. I made my choice. I made it long before you pulled me into this carriage. Well, several minutes before, at least. As soon as I heard de Lilly trying to get to the Emperor, I knew."

"What did you know?" he asked quietly.

Emma pleated the folds of her dress between her fingers. *Nervous hands*, she could hear her mother say. Smoothing the fabric down over her thighs, she raised her eyes and said, "That some things are worth the risk."

Outside, the countryside rattled past, but inside, all was still, the world reduced to Augustus's eyes on hers. "Such as?"

Emma looked away. "I've always wanted a floral kirtle, embroidered all with leaves of myrtle. I'll start a fashion for it."

"Flowers wither," Augustus reminded her. His hand found hers in the darkness, his thumb stroking up along the side of her hand towards her palm.

"Your masterful way with alliteration, then," she said. "Your knee-weakening rhymes."

"I thought they were stomach weakening," he said. His finger moved in small circles in her palm, concentrating all sensation, all thought, on that one small motion.

Emma cast around for nonsense and couldn't find it. Her arsenal of frivolity had deserted her, as surely as her jewels. She felt bare and exposed. Flowers withered; words lied.

"You make me feel like I'm special," she blurted out. It sounded very silly, but Emma couldn't think of any other way to put it. "You make me feel like I matter."

Augustus lifted her hand to his lips. It was one of Georges's favorite gestures, the kiss to the palm, but when Augustus did it, it felt different. It felt like he meant it. "You do matter. You matter to a lot of people."

It was clearly meant to be a compliment, but Emma found herself feeling oddly disappointed. Yes, it was nice to matter to a lot of people, but she wanted to matter to him.

Augustus pressed his lips to her curled fingers. "You matter to your old school friends." Another kiss. "You matter to your cousin." He paused, brooding over her fingers, before adding, "You mattered to Delagardie."

"Paul?" She felt Augustus stiffen a little at the name. If she had to get used to there having been a Jane, he would have to get used to there having been a Paul. "I never mattered as much to Paul as Carmagnac. As for Hortense and the others, they love me, but they don't need me."

She looked at him, asking a question she couldn't make herself ask.

"You matter to me," he said quietly. "Do I matter to you?"

What fools they both were, Emma thought. Here they had just written reams of extravagant poetry together, in which they had lightly tossed about such terms as "passion," "devotion," and yes, "love." But when it came to their own hearts, they were like children, robbed of all their sophisticated vocabulary and grand ideas.

"I love you," she said. "Will that do?"

His fingers twined in hers, holding her fast. "Only," he said, "if you give me leave to spend the next fifty years showing you how much I love you."

"Showing?" said Emma, a whisper away from his lips. "Not telling?"

Augustus raised his brows. "Do you really want me to write you poetry?"

Chapter 34

He's really not half bad," I said, without turning around.

I was standing on the veranda at the back of Selwick Hall, leaning against the stone balustrade that overlooked the gardens. Below, Micah Stone, looking rather dashing in knee breeches as a Regency era Benedick, was informing the camera that one woman was fair, yet he was well, and another wise and so on. He didn't pretend to an English accent he didn't have, and the overall effect was surprisingly mellifluous. He had one of those rubbery, flexible faces, nondescript in repose, expressive in role.

"Shouldn't you be working?" said Colin.

His sleeve brushed my bare arm as he leaned against the balustrade next to me. It was one of those unseasonably warm May days, one of those days when England tried to make up for the previous nine months in a blaze of sunshine and a riot of spring flowers. In short, it was very heavenly and I was definitely going to get a sunburn.

"I hit a breaking point," I said. "Did you know that Napoleon commissioned a submarine to blow up the Channel fleet? He un-commissioned it because he claimed it leaked."

There was also the small matter of Augustus Whittlesby running off with the plans and Bonaparte's stepdaughter's best friend. I'd been curious enough to look up Whittlesby in the *Dictionary of National Biography*. He had a whole two paragraphs, not bad for the *DNB*. Not one of them mentioned him as either a poet or a spy. Instead, he was known as a progressive member of Parliament—some faction of Whig, which had splintered into more factions than members—and the editor of a journal called *The New Spectator*, a direct challenge, one presumed, to the old *Spectator*.

He had a wife called Emma.

Women seldom fare well in printed history. It's only the murderesses and adventuresses who achieve recognition in their own right. Otherwise, they seem to be remembered primarily in relation to the men in their lives, and Emma was no exception. Augustus Whittlesby was married to Emma Morris Delagardie, niece to the American president James Monroe. Of the rest of it, nothing. There was nothing to indicate what her life would have been once she followed Augustus to England.

Was she happy? I wondered. Did she regret the loss of her old school friends in France? Was she lonely without them, without the world she had built up around herself?

It wasn't Emma Delagardie Whittlesby I was worried about, I realized. It was me. I wasn't asking so much whether Emma had fit in, but whether I would. It made sense, I supposed. Two New Yorkers, two Englishmen, two centuries apart. The parallels were hard to ignore, especially with the question so very much on my mind: Would I be a fool to stay in England? Or would I be an even worse fool to go?

There was a major difference between me and Emma Delagardie. France was an adopted country for her, a transitory place, changing all around her. She had already left her family and home far behind. Whereas for me . . . .

Well, maybe Cambridge was, too. Our first day of grad school, the head of the department had given us a speech, of which the most memorable—and most repeated—line was "Cambridge is a lovely place to live. It is also a lovely place to leave." Translation: They wanted us to finish our degrees and get out, not hang around forever.

Like Emma in Paris, my Cambridge was transitory. Liz, Jenny, the whole fellowship I had built up around myself, would also depart, taking jobs in far-flung history departments across the country. Would UCLA really feel closer to home than London? California was the same six hours from the East Coast and just as culturally divorced.

Colin and I hadn't discussed it, not since Jeremy had dropped his bombshell. There's nothing like the rumor of buried treasure to effectively change the topic.

Jeremy swore that the Pink Carnation had somehow run off with the missing treasure of the Rajah of Berar, lost during the third Mahratta War in 1803, and hidden it in Selwick Hall. I could have told him that the Pink Carnation had never been in India, or in Berar, at least not according to my research, but Jeremy wasn't interested in fact when legend was far more enticing. What with confronting Jeremy, herding everyone else into dinner, and apologizing to Micah Stone, there hadn't been much time to talk about our future.

And since then . . . Well, let's just say that both Colin and I are very good at avoiding things. Neither of us are what you would call "let's talk about our feelings" types, which means lots of time spent talking around things and playing with subtext. Clever, but not precisely healthy.

On the plus side, at least Serena and Colin were speaking again. She was staying in the house for the week, having been given a very small walk-on role in the film. She looked lovely in her scoop-necked Regency frock, even if a bit bony around the collarbones.

Between the film people and Serena—not to mention having to run off all the crazies who had been attracted by the rapidly spreading rumors of buried treasure—there really hadn't been time to talk, I rationalized to myself.

Excuses, excuses.

"They're lucky to have such good weather for the filming," I said, looking at my rapidly freckling arms instead of at Colin. "Isn't it great that it didn't rain?"

"Mmph," said Colin. It was a very expressive "mmph." I felt him shift uncomfortably against the balustrade. "Eloise . . ."

"And the flowers look so pretty!" I babbled.

"Eloise." Colin took me by the shoulders and very gently turned me around. There was nowhere to look but at him. Or, more accurately, the second button from the top on his button-down blue shirt. "We need to talk."

"Isn't that supposed to be my line?" I said. "Expression of emotion, state of the relationship, that sort of thing?"

I have mentioned that I'm very good at talking around things, right?

Colin let out his breath in a long exhalation that ruffled the hair on my brow. "Do you want to go back to the States?"

I tried to jam my hands into pockets that I didn't have. Blast this good weather. "It isn't so much about want," I said slowly. "My career is there. My apartment is there." Already, it was apartment, not flat. I'd gone back to Americanisms in my head. "I can't presume on your hospitality forever."

"Hospitality?" Colin's laugh had an edge to it. "Christ, Eloise. You make me sound like a bed-and-breakfast."

I licked my dry lips. "I don't want you to feel like I'm presuming anything. I don't want you to feel crowded."

There was a long moment of silence. Colin pressed two fingers to the bridge of his nose, the way he did when he was tired. I knew that gesture now, so well, just as I knew so many other things without knowing I knew them, like the way he tilted his head when he was thinking, or automatically removed the cushion before he sat down on the couch. I would miss him so much if I left. I would miss not just the conversations, but the essential Colin-ness of him, all those intangibles I got to take for granted, his laugh, his smell, the comfort of curling up against him at the end of the long day. No matter how good the phone plan, one could never get that back, not the same way.

"You're welcome to stay," Colin said, "for however long you like, in whatever capacity you like. How's that for an invitation?"

"Can I have it engraved?" I have a very bad habit of trying to make a joke out of those things about which I feel most strongly. It's a defense mechanism, I suppose, and sometimes an inconvenient one.

"There are silver platters, if you'd like one," said Colin. "Although I believe they're mostly silver plate."

"No. Thank you." I looked down at my feet, at the weather-pitted stone of the veranda, the stray tendrils of ivy creeping between the flags. "It's a very generous offer. Even without the platter."

Colin was a bright boy. He knew, even without my telling him.

"But," he said.

"But," I agreed. I balled my hands into fists, feeling my old class ring biting into my skin, like an anchor to my past. "It's not that I don't appreciate the offer. And it's not that I don't want to be with you. Because I do. Really."

Shaking back my hair, I glanced anxiously up at Colin, the breeze whipping strands of hair in front of my eyes, blurring my sight, making my eyes water. He nodded to show that he understood, although I could tell that he didn't.

"I'm taking the job," I said. My throat felt stiff and tight, reluctant to give voice to the words. "The one in the history department."

Colin's face revealed nothing. "Why?" he asked.

"It's too soon." I tried to make sense of it, as much for myself as for him. "I have a whole life in America. I can't give it up on the strength of six months—no matter how wonderful those six months might have been. Might *be*," I corrected myself hastily. "Might be." It was too soon for the past tense.

When Colin spoke, his voice was very carefully controlled. "Are you breaking up with me?"

"No!" I said, so vehemently that a bird whirled out of a nearby tree, shimmying past us in a whirr of feathers. "No. I want us to stay together. If we can. I just can't—"

How to say it? Around us, the sun was shining and the birds were chirping and the actors acting, but I was stuck in my own private Hades, sorting through my personal pile of pomegranate seeds.

I held out my hands to Colin, willing him to understand. "I can't make myself entirely dependent on you. It's not fair to you, either. I don't want you to feel burdened by me or feel like you couldn't do what you would otherwise do because I'm around."

"What if I want you around?" he said.

It was so tempting, so incredibly tempting. Long days in the library, fall drifting into winter, cold winter nights together in the den, mulled wine and chips at the Heavy Hart, occasional trips into London to see an exhibit or get dressed up and go out with his friends or mine. I could see it all playing out before me, an entire life in a snow globe, a picture of perfect domesticity.

At least, that's how it looked from there. But would it be? I didn't think Colin would let me pay rent. And even if he did, what cash did I have coming in without a teaching job? I'd be dependent on him from everything from the files I was reading to the roof over my head. And if we broke up—not a happy thought, but one that had to be considered—I would have lost a year of teaching, a year of positioning myself for the job market. I would be thought of as "that girl who stayed in England for a guy," and, even though England was where my documents were, even though I might produce a better dissertation for it, I would be taken less seriously as a scholar because of it. Such is the way of the world.

I bit down on my lower lip. "But do you want me around twenty-four seven? Twelve months a year?"

Colin's silence was all the answer I needed. I felt something ache a little inside, but there was no going back now. This was the right decision for both of us, no matter how painful it might be in the short term.

"You see?" I said. "It's too much too soon."

I watched him rub his thumb against his index finger. That was another Colin gesture, another thing I would miss when I was back in my tiny apartment in Cambridge, alone, listening to the radiator clank, wondering what I had been thinking.

He didn't argue with me. Instead, he said in a low voice, "Will you stay for the rest of the summer?"

"If you'll still have me."

He held out his arms to me and I went into them, leaning my head against my favorite spot on his chest, wrapping my arms around his waist in that dent that seemed to have been made just for them. Colin leaned his cheek against the top of my head.

"We'll work it out," he said into my hair.

"It's only for one semester," I said to the pocket of his shirt. "I could come back in the spring. If you still want me then."

Colin lifted his head. I wiggled back just enough to look at him. He was thinking, the wheels turning. Tentatively, he said, "I've never been to Cambridge—your Cambridge."

Something pinched in my chest. Or maybe it unpinched. I could feel the tears tickling the back of my eyes, threatening to fall, but they were the right kind of tears, the kind that happen when someone does something that touches you too deeply for mere thanks. I knew what it was to him to leave Selwick Hall, even for a little while. It was his project, his baby, his distraction from all those personal demons of which I was only just beginning to have an inkling. I couldn't imagine Colin away from England for too long, but . . . a visit would be nice. A visit would help bridge the gap. If he came to Cambridge in the fall and I came back to England around Christmas, between us, we might actually be able to make this work.

It was a far cry from the heady euphoria of the early days of our relationship, but, for the first time, I really believed that what we had might be real, that it might last.

I swallowed the lump at the back of my throat and smiled mistily up at him. Through the tears, I saw him wreathed in rainbows—not an image he would thank me for, my practical, down-to-earth Colin.

"I could show you around," I offered softly. "It's pretty nasty in winter, but you're used to that. And there's something nice about all that snowy brick right around Christmas."

With a crooked finger, he moved a stray strand of hair out of my eyes, very gently, as though I might break otherwise. "You can show me your microfilm readers."

"Everyone's favorite tourist destination," I agreed, and we smiled foolishly at each other, happy just to be together, with the sun beaming down on our bare heads and pots of flowers in artificial bloom all around us. In the gardens, someone was playing a harpsichord, a simple and beautiful melody.

"*Sigh no more, ladies, sigh no more,*" sang Balthazar. "*Men were deceivers ever.*"

Some men. Not my Colin.

"Will you be okay going away?" I asked. "With Jeremy treasure hunting?"

Colin made a face. "I can deal with Jeremy."

"Is there any truth to this whole treasure thing?" I asked.

"Honestly?" Colin looked out over the scene playing out below. "Probably not."

Hmm. This was Colin. If the answer was no, he would have just said no.

Emboldened by our new accord, I leaned over to get a look at his face. "You think there is, don't you?"

Colin's face twisted. "Well . . . I looked for it as a boy. I didn't find anything."

"Yes," I said, "but you're older and wiser now. And you have me."

Colin's eyes crinkled. "Yes, and we know there's just one thing for which I'd want you."

I looked at him from under my lashes, aiming for sultry and missing by a mile. "We can talk about that later."

Colin mustered a perfunctory leer, but his mind was obviously elsewhere. "Do you know . . ." he began.

I knew many things, but I didn't think he needed to hear the entirety of the Prologue to the *Canterbury Tales* right at just this moment.

"Mmm-hmm?" I said encouragingly.

He looked to me as if for approval, half excited, half sheepish. In other words, endearingly boyish. "The best way to stop Jeremy might be to try to find it first. If it exists, that is. It probably doesn't. But saying hypothetically that it did . . ."

"We might hypothetically try to find it."

"Are you in?" He held out a hand, palm up.

I settled my hand in his and felt his fingers close around mine. "Us against Jeremy? He doesn't have a chance."

"With you on my side," Colin said softly, and what I saw in his eyes made my knees feel like goo, "how can I possibly lose?"

In a few moments, I would go inside and e-mail Blackburn and tell him I was taking the head TF job. In four months, I would be back in Cambridge. But for now . . . It was only May. We had the entire summer before us.

With the two of us together, what couldn't we achieve? Right then, I would have been willing to volunteer us for moving mountains.

I grinned recklessly at Colin. "Let the games begin."

Historical Note

*T*he best part about writing historical fiction is that the strangest bits are usually true. Submarines in the Napoleonic Wars might sound like something straight out of Jules Verne, but, in fact, Robert Fulton (primarily recognizable from grade school textbooks as the inventor of the steamboat) did do his best to hawk a submarine, named the *Nautilus*, to the French government. Born in Philadelphia, Fulton spent time in both England and France in the 1790s. After moving to France in 1797, he pitched his plans for an underwater naval craft to the government in power at the time, the Directory. They weren't interested. Bonaparte, who came to power in 1799, proved more receptive.

Conquering bits of Europe might be fun, but Bonaparte had his heart set on invading England. There was a slight problem: the English navy. Bonaparte, an army man by training, had no idea how naval warfare worked. Some of his plans for the invasion of England would have been laughable if Bonaparte's admirals had the nerve to laugh in his presence. One of his favorite schemes involved launching two thousand flat-bottomed ferry boats containing 114,000 troops and 7,000 horses, all on a single tide, within six hours, from a port where there wasn't yet a port. His advisors were forced, reluctantly, to explain that flat-bottomed boats swamped; it would take several tides; and that it would take far more than six hours, within which time the English ships guarding the Channel would undoubtedly take defensive action. Impervious, Napoleon nonetheless founded new shipyards to build his fleet and designed a whole new port and set of fortifications at Boulogne, the harbor from which the invasion was to launch. For the details of Napoleon's disastrous naval plans, I recommend the relevant chapters in Alan Schom's *Napoleon Bonaparte*.

How could Bonaparte possibly resist the prospect of an easy way to undermine the English Channel fleet? With the go-ahead from the French government, models of the *Nautilus* were built and tested in the waters outside Le Havre in 1800 and 1801. The ship came complete with what Fulton euphemistically referred to as a "carcass," otherwise known as underwater mines. Fulton's carcass successfully demolished a forty-foot sloop in the trials in 1801. Although Fulton was able to sustain several crew members below water for as long as four and a half hours, the ship leaked. Fulton dismantled it, leaving him without a model when Bonaparte demanded a demonstration in September 1801. Although various officials reported favorably on the earlier trials of the *Nautilus*, Bonaparte decided it was a hoax and a swindle and refused to consider it further. Miffed, Fulton responded to British persuasion (in the form of an £800 bribe) and took himself and his plans for an undersea naval vessel off to England, where he conducted trials of *Nautilus II* in 1805.

As you can tell, I played around with the timeline a bit, moving Fulton's submarine trials up from 1801 to 1804, the height of Napoleon's invasion plans. The rest—the submarine itself and Bonaparte's reaction—are taken from the historical record. For those wishing to know more about Fulton and his submarine, you can read about it in Cynthia Philip's *Robert Fulton: A Biography* and Kirkpatrick Sale's *The Fire of his Genius: Robert Fulton and the American Dream*. During his time in France, Fulton met Robert Livingston (Emma's "cousin"), a New Yorker of some distinction, who served as the United States Minister to France between 1801 and 1804. As described in the novel, Fulton and Livingston teamed up to produce the steamboat, which they tested, not at Malmaison in 1804 but on the Seine in 1803. For more on Livingston, who also negotiated the Louisiana Purchase during his tenure as Minister to France, you can read about him in Frank Brecher's *Negotiating the Louisiana Purchase: Robert Livingston's Mission to France, 1801–1804*.

American feelings towards France, as demonstrated by Emma's cousin Kort, were decidedly equivocal. Although supposedly united by republican values, Americans found the French dissolute and eyed the increasingly regal rise of Napoleon with mixed feelings. As William Chew puts it in his article, *Life Before Fodor and Frommer: Americans in Paris from Thomas Jefferson to John Quincy Adams*, "to the American eye, evidence of Parisian immorality appeared at every turn." An American visiting France in 1795, a year after Emma's arrival, referred to it as the "seat of luxury and dissipation." They disapproved of both the Frenchwomen's scanty attire and their tendency to meddle in politics. As always, biographies and letters provide the truest sense of opinion at the time, including those of that quintessential New York Knickerbocker Washington Irving, who wrote vividly of his travels in France.

My own New York heroine, Emma Morris Delagardie, was inspired by two very different historical characters (both of whom happened to be named Eliza): Eliza Monroe and Eliza de Feuillide. Eliza Monroe came over to France with her father, James Monroe, during his tenure as American Minister to France (1794–1796). Enrolled by her parents in Mme. Campan's school for young ladies, Eliza became lifelong friends with Hortense de Beauharnais, daughter of Josephine Bonaparte by her first marriage. Portraits of Hortense and her brother Eugene still hang at the Monroe house, Ash Lawn.

If Eliza Monroe provided the beginning of Emma's story, Eliza de Feuillide gave me the next step. Jane Austen's first cousin, Eliza Hancock, married a French "nobleman" (the title was dodgy), Jean Francois de Feuillide, whose primary passion turned out to be the drainage of his estate near Nerac. Like my Emma, Eliza de Feuillide was fashionable and witty—and was left in Paris while her husband focused his attention and her dowry on the drainage of Le Marais. My information on de Feuillide comes from Deirdre Le Faye's *Jane Austen's Outlandish Cousin: The Life and Letters of Eliza de Feuillide*.

While that particular house party at Malmaison was my own invention, Josephine's country house and the tensions within the Bonaparte clan were very real. As described in the novel, Hortense, Josephine's daughter by her first marriage, had been married off to Napoleon's younger brother, Louis, in the hopes of providing an heir to the Bonaparte dynasty. The marriage was a disaster. By the summer of 1804, when Napoleon seized the imperial crown, it was becoming increasingly possible that Hortense's matrimonial sacrifice had been for nothing, as Napoleon's family urged him to set the barren Josephine aside and take a younger and better-connected wife. For more on the Bonapartes' private lives, at Malmaison and elsewhere, there are a host of books to choose from, including Theo Aronson's *Napoleon and Josephine: A Love Story*, Evangeline Bruce's *Napoleon and Josephine: The Improbable Marriage*, Andre Castelot's *Napoleon*, and Christopher Hibbert's *Napoleon: His Wives and Women*. For more on my favorite of the Bonaparte clan, Hortense de Beauharnais, you can read about Hortense in her own words in her memoirs or in Constance Wright's biography, *Daughter to Napoleon*.

While the specific masque performed in this novel may have been a fiction, amateur theatricals were very much a part of life at Malmaison. The Bonapartes were all theatre mad, so much so that Napoleon had a complete theatre erected on the grounds of Malmaison in 1802 for the family's amateur theatricals. The inaugural performance was *Barber of Seville*, with Hortense as Rosina. As Peter Hicks describes in his *Napoleon and the Theatre*, Napoleon commissioned plays for his pet theatre and brought in the famous actor Talma to direct them—although one imagines that nothing quite like Whittlesby's masque ever graced the stage.

Finally, I would like to crave my readers' pardon for introducing Cyrano de Bergerac ninety-three years before Rostand brought the wordy cavalier to life. My only excuse is that these histories are filtered through the imagination of Eloise, for whom "poet" and "Cyrano" are inextricably interwoven. While we're pointing the finger at Eloise, she also confuses "Ubu" with "Boo-boo" when misquoting the tagline from the 1980s production company. That choice was a very deliberate one on the part of the author, despite agitated notes in the margin from two copy editors. In real life, we (or at least I) misquote lines all the time. To make Eloise entirely accurate would be to make her altogether less human. To err is human; to misquote is Eloise.

Acknowledgments

This book goes out to Jenny Davis and Liz Mellyn, the other two thirds of the Triumvirate of Terror. Thank you for being my friends, as well as Eloise's, and for always giving the very best advice. Cambridge wouldn't have been Cambridge without you.

Huge hugs to Claudia Brittenham, for being my first and best reader; to Nancy Flynn, for Pony Post Wednesdays; and to Brooke, for being Brooke. To Mutt and Jeff (aka Kristen Kenney and Jen Chen) for evenings at Alice's; to Abby Vietor, for afternoons at Gotham; to Sarah Camp, for elegant outings; and to the entire Crawford family (and Catharine), for the best book tour weekend ever.

Thanks go to Tasha Alexander and Deanna Raybourn, the best book tour buddies any author could desire. (Our plan for world domination commences! Oh, wait. Did I say that out loud?) And to Sarah MacLean, my favorite book release sister—tiaras become us, my dear.

Thank you, parents, for putting up with me; Joe Veltre, for

advising me; Erika Imranyi and Danielle Perez, for editing me; Erin Galloway, Jamie McDonald, Liza Cassity, Dora Mak, and the rest of the gang at Dutton/NAL, for doing all those magical things you do; and everyone on the Web site and Facebook, for distracting me when I need it—and sometimes when I don't.

Last but not least, to James Ratcliffe. I promised you a sentence, but you deserve a paragraph.

About the Author

The author of eight previous Pink Carnation novels, Lauren Willig received a graduate degree in English history from Harvard University and a J.D. from Harvard Law School, though she now writes full-time. Willig lives in New York City.

The Garden Intrigue

LAUREN WILLIG

A CONVERSATION
WITH LAUREN WILLIG

This Q&A is brought to you by all the wonderful people on my Web site and Facebook page who, when I asked, "What do I write about??" came back to me with exactly what they wanted to know. If I missed your question, I apologize—but I promise I'll get to it in the next Readers Guide!

No Napoleonic spies were harmed in the making of this Q&A.

Q. This book seems much more pro-Bonaparte than the others. Was that intentional?

A. One of the things I love about writing a series is that I get to revisit the same people and places from different viewpoints. In the very first book of the series, my resolutely royalist heroine, Amy, visited Bonaparte's court. We got to see the whole crazy Bonaparte clan through her rather critical eyes. In *The Garden Intrigue*, my heroine, Emma, is coming at the situation from the opposite side of the fence. Unlike Amy, Emma isn't particularly political. She doesn't have a horse in the Anglo-French race. As an American, and one from a prominent political family, her loyalties would likely lean more to the French than to the English if she bothered to think about it. Emma has also lived in France for ten years and has very close ties to the Bonaparte family, or, at least, to the de Beauharnais side of it. Where Amy came at the situation from an ideological angle, Emma approaches the Bonaparte regime from an intensely personal one: She's worried about her friends and what Bonaparte's ambitions will do to their personal lives, not any abstract ideas of the benefits of monarchy versus republic versus Empire.

Q. Why do you have such an attachment to Hortense de Beauharnais?

A. I discovered Hortense when I was ten or eleven. One of those Napoleon and Josephine miniseries had aired on TV. I wanted to know more, so my former historian father gave me a pile of weighty tomes on the Bonapartes, probably hoping they would keep me quiet for a while. I immediately took to Hortense, Josephine's daughter, who sulked at her mother's marriage to Napoleon and cheered when Josephine's pug bit Napoleon on their wedding night. Hortense was pretty much my age at the time. Like me, she attended an all girls' school, where she excelled in English and music and anything humanities-esque. She immediately became my imaginary best friend and I wept for her when she was forced into marriage with Napoleon's unattractive younger brother Louis.

At the time, I desperately wanted to be Jean Plaidy or Norah Lofts when I grew up. (Remember those old fictionalized biographies of English queens?) I spent much of my senior year of high school researching and writing a novel about Hortense, *Napoleon's Daughter*, which followed her from her days at Madame Campan's academy through her stepfather's rise to power, right up to her marriage. That novel is still living in one of my desk drawers (and it's not coming out!), but it did provide me with an excellent background on Napoleon's transition from general to Consul to Emperor, as well as a lifelong affection for Hortense de Beauharnais.

When I sat down to write *The Garden Intrigue*, it felt only natural to make my New York–born heroine best friends with Hortense. Emma is based on Eliza Monroe (Emma's "cousin" in the book), who, like Emma, went to Madame Campan's school and became lifelong friends with Hortense.

Although that old manuscript about Hortense is staying in the drawer, Stephanie Barron (author of the wonderful Jane Austen mystery series) and I have joked that one of these days we're going to write a Young Adult series about "the girls of Madame Campan's Academy"—everyone who was anyone in the Napoleonic regime seems to have gone there!

Q. What was the inspiration for casting Miss Gwen as a pirate?

A. Three words: *Pirates of Penzance*. My parents made the mistake of taking me to see the revival of *Pirates* with Linda Ronstadt and Kevin Kline back when I was a wee thing. I was enthralled and developed a rather annoying habit of escaping from my room and dancing around in my petticoat at grown-up parties, warbling about "climbing o'er the rocky mountains, skipping rivulets and fountains" (all this with a rather pronounced four-year-old lisp). I eventually outgrew the petticoat, but Gilbert and Sullivan's madcap comedy, tongue in cheek humor, and huge plot holes still suited me to a T. Although I sang with the Gilbert & Sullivan Society in college (so many sisters and cousins and aunts!), I never did get to be in *Pirates*. It only seemed appropriate to place Miss Gwen in the role of Pirate Queen, for it 'tis it, 'tis a glorious thing. . . . You know the rest.

Q. What is your writing process like?

A. Process? What is this "process" of which you speak? It makes me sound way too organized. Primarily it involves lots of caffeine. And procrastination. And, occasionally, laundry.

Q. What's next for the series?

A. Emboldened by her stint as Pirate Queen, Miss Gwen metaphorically took to the high seas and hijacked the next book in the Pink series. In Pink X (now officially titled *The Passion of the Purple Plumeria*), Miss Gwen and Jane are forced to return to England when Jane's younger sister disappears from Miss Climpson's Select Seminary in Bath along with her bosom buddy, Lizzy Reid. Are the girls off on a pleasure jaunt? Or has someone discovered Jane's secret identity? Determined to get Agnes back, Gwen reluctantly teams up with Lizzy's father, Colonel William Reid.

Known throughout India as "the Laughing Colonel" for his easy sense of humor and his way with women, Colonel Reid soon discovers that Gwendolyn Meadows is proof against his patented charm. But is he proof against her?

Pink X—complete with Miss Gwen's patented sword parasol—should be making its way onto bookshelves in August 2013.

Q. What's this about a non-Pink book?

A. The rumors are all true. I've gone off series to write a book that I call my "*Downton Abbey* meets *Out of Africa*" book. Set in England around World War I, Kenya in the 1920s, and New York in 1999, it traces the tangled lives of two cousins and the fallout their actions cause for their modern descendant, who discovers that nothing about her family is as she thought it was. *The Ashford Affair* will be out in April 2013.

Although this book is technically non-Pink, I never do seem to be able to keep my characters from crossing their fictional boundaries. In this case, a descendant of Lord Vaughn (*The Seduction of the Crimson Rose*) infiltrated my 1920s book. You can imagine the sort of havoc the offspring of Lord Vaughn and Mary Alsworthy might wreak!

Q. Will you be writing more Pink books?

A. Yes, yes, and yes again! There's Miss Gwen's book coming up (see above), and after her. . . Well, let's just say it might be time for the Pink Carnation to have a book of her own.

Thanks so much for joining me on this journey! As always, if you have any questions that haven't been answered here, please do come visit me on my Web site, www.laurenwillig.com, or my Facebook author page, www.facebook.com/LaurenWillig. I'm always happy to ramble on about the books.

QUESTIONS
FOR DISCUSSION

1. What was your first impression of Emma Delagardie? How did your feelings toward her change throughout the story?

2. How are Emma and Eloise alike? How are they different? Do you think any of these differences arise from the social norms of their respective time periods, and if so, which ones?

3. Discuss the differences in social etiquette in Paris and New York. Why does Emma feel more of an affinity to Paris? Why does she feel like she can't return home?

4. How is the theme of loss addressed in *The Garden Intrigue*?

5. "He donned rhyme like armor, keeping her at bay. She could have told him he didn't need to. She flirted without thinking. That was armor, too." Discuss how various characters in *The Garden Intrigue* use spectacle and armor—and the forms their armor takes—to conceal their true selves from society.

6. Did you know much about Napoleon's court at Malmaison prior to reading *The Garden Intrigue*? What surprised you most?

7. Discuss the presence of past lovers in *The Garden Intrigue*. How did the characters behave when they encountered each other? Would exes of today behave in a similar manner?

8. Compare Augustus Whittlesby's relationships with Jane and Emma. What affected his choice in the end?

9. How might the course of history have changed if Napoleon had liked Robert Fulton's invention?

10. "Women seldom fare well in printed history." Do you feel this is true? If so (or not), who are some examples (or counterexamples)?

11. Discuss the future of Colin and Eloise's relationship. Do you think they will be able to stay together after Eloise leaves? Why or why not?

12. Is there really a treasure of Berar? Do you think Colin and Eloise will find it before Jeremy does?

Read on for an excerpt from

The Passion of the Purple Plumeria

another book in Lauren Willig's
bestselling Pink Carnation series.

Available from New American Library.

> *The building sat on a low rise, shaded by a
> stand of trees. In spring, it might have been a
> happy place, but not now. A bolt of lightning
> forked through the sky as Sir Magnifico
> clattered into the courtyard, his senses rent
> with misgiving. Where were the joyful carols
> of the cloistered ladies? The voices of the
> virgins were hushed and anxious, as muted as
> the rain that dripped down the cold, gray
> stone.*
>
> > *Was it an ancient curse that lay over the
> building? Or some more recent evil?*
>
> —from *The Convent of Orsino* by A Lady

England, 1805

England wasn't at all what Colonel William Reid had expected
it to be.

Back in the mess in Madras, his fellow officers were always nat-
tering on about the lush green of the fields, the cerulean blue of the

sky, the delicate touch of a spring breeze, as soft and sweet as a lover's kiss. They hadn't mentioned the driving rain that got beneath a man's collar, or the mud of the roads that sucked at cartwheels and caked the bottoms of a man's boots. If the wind was the touch of a lover, this was less a kiss and more a hearty slap across the face.

Shivering in his newly purchased, many-caped coat, William felt like a piece of wet washing—damp down to the skin and then some besides. Winter, yes. He'd expected winter to be cold. But this was spring, for the love of all that was holy. Birds should be on the wing and buds on the thorn, or wherever it was that buds went.

So much for April in England, of which the poets sang so sweetly and so falsely. William would have traded it in a moment for May in Madras. Faith, he'd even take July in Jaipur, sweating in his regimentals in the blazing sun, hotter than hell and ready to wilt.

Not that he had that choice. It was England for him now, will he, nill he, a classic case of blithely making one's bed only to discover, when the time came to lie on it, that it was full of lumps. He was good at that.

And didn't I warn you? He could hear his mother's outraged Highland brogue in his head, exaggerated by time and distance.

His mother would be turning in her tartan grave if she knew that he'd chosen to take up residence in England in his old age. They'd been committed adherents to the King Over the Water, his parents; fled from Inverness in '45 in the wake of the disaster at Culloden. Committed from a distance, that was. In the safety of the Carolinas, their commitment had extended mostly to derisory epithets about the English and toasting the Pretender's health, such as it was. They'd had some lovely glasses made up: crystal, with thistles, and some Jacobite motto or other scrolled about the bowl. Latin, it was, but what the words had been, he couldn't say.

Memory blurred. Or perhaps it was the drizzle driving into his eyes, that maddening, peculiarly English form of precipitation—not quite mist, not quite rain, but something in between, all but impossible to keep off. Give him a proper thunder storm any day, like the sort they'd had in his youth in the Carolinas—winds howling, thunder crashing; not like this—insidious, invidious and damnably damp. He felt like someone's wet washing hung on the line.

For choice, he would have stayed in India. He'd had nearly forty good years there, posted all around the country, from Calcutta to Bombay. He'd served in the East India Company's army. Not as lucrative, perhaps, as the royal army, apt to be sneered at by snobs, but he couldn't see himself taking the king's shilling; not then, not now. Old prejudices died hard. It had been a polyglot group with whom he'd fought in the Madras cavalry, most of them wanderers like himself, all out to make their fortune in the fabled land of jewels and spices.

He missed India, missed it with a visceral longing he'd never felt for Charleston. It was in India he'd married and buried his Maria; in India he'd raised his children, three boys and two girls, only two of them what you might call legitimate. What did it matter? He loved them all, conscientious Alex, prickly Jack, sunny-natured George, stubborn Kat, and his youngest, his sweet Lizzy—legitimate, illegitimate, British, half-caste, all alike. If the circumstances of his family life were sometimes a little . . . irregular, well, it was India, and such things were common there.

Common, yes, but not always easy. He'd learned that the hard way. Of his three sons, two were barred employment in the very regiment to which he'd given so many years' service, simply by virtue of having a native woman as their mother. William had got George settled, finding him a place in the retinue of a local ruler, the Begum Sumroo. As for Jack. . . It didn't matter that Jack's mother had been a lady of quality in her own land; he'd been barred all the same, barred as though his mother were the lowest bazaar strumpet.

The boy had taken it hard. Jack had ridden away, offering his sword to whoever would employ him against the men who had denied him his place. They hadn't spoken since. Jack's absence was a wound in William's heart that wouldn't heal.

The worst of it, though, had been sending his daughters away. It had been nearly a decade ago now, Kat eighteen, Lizzy an imp of eight, all curls and dimples. For their education, he'd bluffed, but the truth was that it wasn't safe for them, especially not for Lizzy, who was a half-caste, the child of a native mother. There were some young bucks who thought a half-caste girl fair game. He'd seen it happen— to his horror—to a friend's daughter, raped and tossed aside. She'd died of the pox—and the shame, some said. Her father had aged ten years in as many months. And William had packed his girls onto a ship bound for England, bundling them off in the face of all their protests.

Just a few years, he'd told his girls, as he had handed them onto the launch in Calcutta harbor, Kat glowering, Lizzy clinging to his neck. Then he would come to England and join them and what grand times they would have then! But then had come Tippoo Sultan's rising in the south and unrest in the north, and what with one thing and another, a few years had stretched to another and another, until here he was, ten years later, standing on the stoop of a young ladies' seminary in Bath, a bouquet of wilted flowers in one hand, prepared to surprise a daughter he wasn't sure he would recognize. When he'd last seen her, she'd had two missing teeth and a scrape on her left knee. He could picture that scab as he could picture his own hand, every moment of their parting branded on his memory.

Would she be happy to see him, his Lizzy? He hoped so. He felt like a nervous suitor, about to call on a young lady for the first time. William straightened his collar and cleared his throat.

"It's Miss Elizabeth Reid I'm here to see," he said to the woman standing at the door, a young woman with soft dark hair in a modest gray dress that matched the weather. She was a small woman, with the mushroom-like complexion of someone who had never encountered a tropical sun. She had identified herself as the French mistress, Mademoiselle de Fayette.

She also looked distinctly wary. William supposed he couldn't blame her, faced with a strange man holding a bouquet of battered flowers standing at the doorstep. One couldn't be too careful with a house full of impressionable young ladies.

"I have the fear——" she began, taking a step back. "That is, I am most desolate, but——"

"It's her father, I am," William said quickly. He swept a quick half bow, smiling to show her that he wasn't a rake, rogue or seducer, but just a parent come to call. "Colonel William Reid. Lizzy might have mentioned me?" He tipped the French mistress a wink. "Not that a mere father is much in the mind of a young girl."

If anything, Mlle. de Fayette looked even more distressed.

Was he losing his touch in his old age?

"Colonel Reid," she said, rolling out the syllables of the title in the continental fashion. She twisted her hands together, pale against the dark material of her dress. "I am of the most sorry. Miss Reid, she is—— It is of the most unfortunate!"

"What's she done now?" William asked resignedly. "In disgrace, is she?"

That sounded like his Lizzy. He could hear the lamentations of his housekeeper back in Madras, ten years past, in different accents, but with the same general tone. Lizzy had a way of wreaking havoc, but with a smile so sweet it was hard to take against her.

"Miss Reid, she——" Mlle. de Fayette bit her lip hard enough to leave a mark. "We would have sent the letter, but we did not know where——"

The hairs on William's neck prickled. This wasn't just a case of Lizzy eating the jam out of the biscuits or trying to climb the trellis on a dare.

"A letter?" he said as casually as he could. "And what would that be about, then? She's not got herself sent down, has she?"

"No, no. That is—" The woman in the doorway made a notable effort to compose herself. She pressed a hand to her lips.

"There, there. I'm sure it's not so bad as all that," said William reassuringly. "Whatever she's done, I'll see it put right. Now what's the minx done now?"

"Minx, indeed!"

William's head snapped up as a voice rang imperiously through the hall.

A woman strode forward, wafting Mlle. de Fayette out of the way. The glass prisms on the wall sconces quivered from the force of her movement. Next to the diminutive French mistress, the newcomer looked like an Amazon, although a great part of her height was the tall plumes that curled from her elaborate purple turban.

She moved with rangy grace, her skirts moving briskly against her long legs. Paris tailoring, unless William missed his guess, the material fine and cut narrow. An expensive rig for the proprietress of a young ladies' academy.

"Are you the parent of Miss Reid?" she asked in ringing tones.

It felt like an accusation.

William retaliated with the full arsenal of his charm. "I have that honor," he said easily. "But I fear I haven't yet had the pleasure of your acquaintance, Madame . . ."

The woman sniffed. It was a most effective sniff, conveying the full range of her displeasure. "Don't call it a pleasure until you've had a chance to judge." Using the point of her parasol, she neatly prodded the younger woman out of the way. "In or out? Make up your mind. You're letting in the most appalling draft."

William chose in. The door snapped shut behind him. Mlle. de Fayette stepped prudently out of the way.

William smiled determinedly at the woman in purple, whose imperious air implied that she was the preceptress of this academy. Either that or the ruler of a small but warlike kingdom. William had met rajahs with less of an air of command.

He sketched a bow. "And is it Miss Climpson I have the honor of addressing?"

The woman drew back as though struck. "What an appalling notion," she said. "Most certainly not. *I* am Miss Gwendolyn Meadows." She said it much as one might say, *I am Cleopatra.*

Was he meant to know who she was?

"A pleasure," William said again. He deliberately included both women in his smile. He had one objective: finding his Lizzy. "Now, if you'd be so kind as to enlighten me, it's my daughter I'm looking for, Miss Elizabeth—"

"Hmph," said Miss Meadows, striking the ground with her parasol hard enough to strike sparks. "You won't find her here."

William dodged out of the way, shocked into brevity. "Why not?"

Miss Meadows looked down her nose at him, a rather impressive trick given that he would have wagered on her being some few inches shorter than he. "Your Elizabeth has run off with our Agnes."

"She's— What?" Who in the blazes was Agnes?

"Run off," said Miss Meadows succinctly. "Run. Off. Do pay attention, Colonel Reid. Really, it's quite simple. Your Elizabeth has run off with our Agnes."

William was stung into retort. "How do you know your Agnes didn't run off with my Lizzy?"

Miss Meadows looked superior. "Really, Colonel Reid. Do be sensible. Agnes isn't the running kind."

Whereas his Lizzy—what did he know of his Lizzy? He'd had a letter a month for ten years, just that. Twelve letters a year times ten, with an extra on his birthday . . .

William pressed two fingers to the bridge of his nose. "Forgive me, ladies. I've just come six months by ship, five days by coach, and the rest of the way uphill by foot. My wits are not their own. Are you telling me that my daughter has gone missing?"

Mlle. de Fayette opened her mouth, but Miss Meadows got in first. "That is precisely what we have been telling you. Elizabeth and

Agnes have both gone missing. Presumably with each other. Theoretically of their own volition. Does that answer your question?"

Hardly. William's head was reeling with questions. He settled for the most pressing. "What's been done to find them?"

Miss Meadows's lips pursed. "Precious little. Come with me." She jerked her head down the hall. "You'll want to speak to Miss Climpson—for what good it will do you."

She set off down the hall, her skirts swishing around her legs, heels tapping briskly against the wood floor.

William hurried after her, his wet boots squelching. "Are you employed at the school, then?" he asked dubiously. Somehow he'd got the idea that schoolmistresses were meant to be quiet, downtrodden creatures.

Quiet and downtrodden were not terms one could apply to Miss Meadows.

"Merciful heavens, no! You couldn't pay me to be a teacher." The idea was horrifying enough to stop Miss Meadows in her tracks. Drawing herself up, she regarded him with great dignity. "I am Agnes's older sister's chaperone."

It sounded like a French exercise. "I see," said William, although he didn't see at all. "And that makes you . . ."

"The only one with any common sense in this debacle." Miss Meadows stopped in front of the open door of a drawing room decorated in shades of blue. It was adorned with an alarming array of porcelain knickknacks, mostly of the cherub variety. Porcelain cherubs simpered from the mantel, more cherubs lurked at the corners of the windows, and a truly appalling assembly of them smirked from a large oil painting in the center of the ceiling.

Of the non-cherub population William counted four. A woman in late middle age, with a cap like an overgrown cabbage, sat in a chair before a tea table, flanked on either side by a man and a woman dressed in clothes of equally outmoded vintage. The man wore a frocked coat and a slightly moth-eaten periwig, the woman a wide-skirted gown of heavy brocade. A slim girl in a blue gown stood by the windows, blending in neatly with the draperies.

"Mr. Wooliston, Mrs. Wooliston and Miss Jane Wooliston." Miss Meadows fired off the names like pistol shots. She nodded at the woman in the immense cap. "And that's Miss Climpson, the prime preceptress of this academy, such as it is." She grinned at him, rather grimly. "Let's see if *you* can get any sense out of her."

It felt like a challenge. "I'll do my best."

His companion indulged in a smile that looked alarmingly like a smirk. "Do," she said. "Do."

It was not entirely encouraging.

Advancing into the room, William approached the woman in the massive cap. "Miss Climpson? I'm William Reid. Elizabeth's father," he added when Miss Climpson looked at him rather blankly.

Miss Meadows gave him an *I told you so* look.

William turned his back on her and concentrated the force of his charm on Miss Climpson. "What's this about my Lizzy going missing?"

The ribbons on Miss Climpson's enormous cap bobbed dizzyingly. "It is most inconvenient," she said spiritedly. "How is one to teach a girl when she is not on the premises? It presents a distinct pedagogical problem."

William would have thought their problems were more than pedagogical. "How long have the girls been missing?"

" 'Missing,' " said Miss Climpson, "is such a strong word. I prefer to think of them as having misplaced themselves. Most inconsiderately."

"Are you sure she's gone? Agnes was always such a quiet child." The woman in the old-fashioned gown peered at a chair as though expecting to find her daughter lurking between the threads of the upholstery.

"Can't be trusted not to wander off. Temperamental things, ewes," said the man in the periwig expansively. "But they tend to find their way back to pasture, don't they, er?"

William dodged a genial whack on the shoulder. "Reid. Colonel Reid. It seems we're in the same boat—er, pasture. My ewe appears to have wandered from the fold as well."

The man stuck out a hand. "Bertrand Wooliston." He nodded to the woman next to him. "My wife, Prudence. And I see you've already met our Miss Meadows."

"Yes," said William guardedly. "You might say that. Now, about the girls . . ."

"Never a bit of trouble," said Mrs. Wooliston, squinting at him through a pair of pince-nez pinched far too low on her nose. "Agnes wound wool so beautifully."

"There, there, my love." Mr. Wooliston pounded her soundly on the shoulder, setting his periwig askew. "Leave them alone and they'll come home, that's how it goes."

"Wagging their tails behind them?" Miss Meadows snorted, an emission of air that rather adequately summed up William's feelings. "I sincerely doubt it."

William was beginning to experience grave doubts about Miss Climpson's academy. "Do the girls here misplace themselves frequently?"

"Fencing," said Bertrand Wooliston firmly. "That's what's needed. Good, strong fencing. None of these doors and windows." He nodded scornfully at the long sash windows that looked out on to a scrubby sort of garden.

"Be that as it may"—William had always prided himself on his ability to adapt to the local idiom—"the, er, ewes have already left the pasture. I'd suggest we put our efforts to finding them, wouldn't you? How long have they been missing?"

Miss Meadows cut into a confusion of garbled explanations and deliberations from the others. "Two weeks," she said bluntly.

William's eyebrows soared towards his hairline. "Two *weeks*?"

He'd sent Lizzy to England to keep her safe, by God. She'd lived those first few years with his wife's mother, in Bristol, but when the letter had come suggesting Lizzy be sent to a young lady's academy for a bit of polish—well, it seemed a good solution to an awkward situation. Mrs. Davies was Kat's grandmother, not Lizzy's. It was a golden opportunity for Lizzy, Kat had assured him. The school catered to the children of the upper gentry, the daughters of landed ladies and gentlemen. The reflected luster would smooth Lizzy's way in the world, wiping out the taint of her birth. It was an opportunity William could never have afforded for her and he had responded enthusiastically.

He had never imagined this. Didn't the affluent of England keep closer watch on their offspring?

Mlle. de Fayette stepped forward. "It is not entirely as it sounds," she said hesitantly. "In the beginning, you see, it was thought that Miss Reid and Miss Wooliston followed one of their schoolmates to her home. Miss Reid was of the most unhappy when Miss Fitzhugh left the school."

"You've sent to this Miss Fitzhugh?" said William brusquely. He hadn't much of a temper, as a rule, but the idea of harm to his Lizzy . . . Lizzy whom he hadn't seen in ten years. He could see her as she'd been when he put her on that ship, eight and without guile.

"We sent to Miss Fitzhugh at once!" Mlle. de Fayette hastened to assure him. Her face fell. "Miss Fitzhugh expressed the confusion entire."

William grasped at straws. "It's sure you are that she was telling the truth?"

Mlle. de Fayette lowered her eyes. "Miss Fitzhugh was of the most indignant at being, as she said, 'Left out of the fun.' Her brother, Monsieur Fitzhugh, was of the most accommodating. He searched through all the wardrobes and under the beds, and even under the vegetable beds in the gardens. The girls, they were nowhere to be found."

"All right, then," said William grimly. "Where else?"

Mlle. de Fayette and her employer exchanged a long look.

"In other words," said Miss Meadows, before William could, "you haven't the slightest idea where they are."

"We know where they aren't," provided Miss Climpson brightly, and it was only with the greatest effort that William kept his hands from closing around her shoulders and giving her a hearty shake. There were no words for the nightmare images that assaulted him. They were too terrible to be given a name. "By the process of elimination . . ."

"There are only several million places the girls might be," said Miss Meadows crisply. William looked at her with gratitude. "This is useless. We need clues." She paced across the room, drawing all eyes as she whipped back and forth, back and forth, tossing out directives as she went. "The Fitzhugh girl will need to be questioned, as will the staff. Is there a porter in this establishment? No. Then we'll need to interview someone who can tell us of their comings and goings."

"Really, Miss Meadows," protested Miss Climpson. "I don't see why that should be necessary. The girls are most strictly chaperoned. . . ."

"Then why aren't they here?" said Miss Meadows, with withering sarcasm. "Right. Let's to business."

Young Miss Wooliston untangled herself from the curtains and stepped forward, her voice pleasant and level, a soothing patch of calm in the whirlwind that was Miss Meadows. "Were there any let-ters before they left? Any"—she cast a glance over her shoulder at the older Woolistons—"billets-doux?"

"She means love letters," said Miss Meadows baldly.

Love letters? William's mouth opened indignantly. He could pic-ture his daughter, all tousled curls and sun-browned hands, a little imp of mischief. Why, his Lizzy was too young for that sort of thing, practically a baby yet. She was all of—

Seventeen.

The realization hit him like a stone. Seventeen. His Maria had been fifteen when he'd met her, sixteen when they'd married. When he remembered what they'd got up to behind her parents' backs— well, it was a distinctly sobering thought. William's mouth snapped shut again.

"They've not been"—William had trouble getting the words out— "consorting with men?"

The French mistress hastened to correct him. "Oh no. They were not the type. I have seen"—with a guilty look at the headmistress, she quickly caught herself—"that is, one comes to recognize the signs of an affair of the heart. These girls, they were still girls."

Oh, one did, did one? "You've had girls run off with men before?" William asked faintly.

"'Run off' is such a harsh term," said the headmistress. "It was really more of a precipitate departure."

"It was only the once," put in the French mistress. "The gardener who passed the notes, he was—how do you say?—let go."

William failed to find that entirely reassuring.

"I think," said Miss Meadows crisply, "that we ought to see their rooms."

"Yes," William agreed hastily. "Yes, we ought."

Miss Meadows regarded him imperiously. "Come along, then. Mademoiselle de Fayette, you'll show us the way? No, no, Prudence, no need to come with us. We'll see ourselves back, won't we, Jane? Bertrand, see your wife home; there's nothing more for you to do here."

William watched with amazement and admiration as Miss Meadows neatly sent everyone packing. The elder Woolistons departed for their lodgings. Miss Climpson, routed, made excuses about seeing to the girls. Miss Wooliston watched the proceedings with a faint smile of amusement.

"Well?" Miss Meadows turned to William with a raised eyebrow. "What are you standing around for? Are you coming to their room or going home?"

William saluted. "I am yours to command. At least so far as the second landing."

Miss Wooliston covered a smile.

Miss Meadows regarded him haughtily. "Hmph," she said. "Come along, then."

Without waiting to see whether he and Mlle. de Fayette followed, she stalked toward the stairs.